THE
SIXTH
EXTINCTION

d leonard freeston

THE SIXTH EXTINCTION

A Novel

DUNDURN
TORONTO

Editor: Cheryl Hawley
Design: Jennifer Scott
Printer: Transcontinental

Library and Archives Canada Cataloguing in Publication

Freeston, D. Leonard
      The sixth extinction / D. Leonard Freeston.

ISBN 978-1-55488-903-7

      I. Title.

PS8611.R437S59 2011   C813'.6   C2010-907298-7

1   2   3   4   5   15   14   13   12   11

Conseil des Arts   Canada Council   ONTARIO ARTS COUNCIL
du Canada   for the Arts   Canada   CONSEIL DES ARTS DE L'ONTARIO

We acknowledge the support of the **Canada Council for the Arts** and the **Ontario Arts Council** for our publishing program. We also acknowledge the financial support of the **Government of Canada** through the **Canada Book Fund** and **Livres Canada Books**, and the **Government of Ontario** through the **Ontario Book Publishing Tax Credit** and the **Ontario Media Development Corporation**.

Care has been taken to trace the ownership of copyright material used in this book. The author and the publisher welcome any information enabling them to rectify any references or credits in subsequent editions.

J. Kirk Howard, President

Printed and bound in Canada.
www.dundurn.com

MIX
Paper from
responsible sources
FSC® C011825

Dundurn   Gazelle Book Services Limited   Dundurn
3 Church Street, Suite 500   White Cross Mills   2250 Military Road
Toronto, Ontario, Canada   High Town, Lancaster, England   Tonawanda, NY
M5E 1M2   LA1 4XS   U.S.A. 14150

For my beautiful, steadfast wife Barbara

PROLOGUE

Geneva. April 2006. In the palatial, belle époque Royal Suite of Geneva's Hotel des Bergues, the tall, skeletal man met with his board at its urging. The twelve members were deeply concerned, for in the course of the organization's systematic raids on seed banks, zoos, and game preserves, innocent people were getting killed. It struck these good souls that the methods employed in securing the genetic material for their vast, clandestine facility might be at odds with their humanistic goals. The tall man, smoothing his collar-length black hair as he studied each of them with ravening, hooded eyes, listened to their concerns like a great predator listens to the wind.

"How sadly ironic it is that innocents perish even as we attempt to bank as many life forms as possible for the post-apocalyptic world," he finally said in a satiny baritone. "Rest assured that our agents will, in the future, exercise more restraint."

There wasn't a fool among them. Each was at the top of his or her profession, and had contributed immeasurable expertise in the realization of the spectral man's subterranean metropolis. Yet such was his wealth, power, and charisma that any reservations they had entertained now lay gashed, bleeding, and gasping for life.

After they'd left, he stood alone in the drizzle on his private terrace, smiling to himself as he looked out over Lake Léman. With its blue night-time illumination, Europe's tallest fountain looked like a giant icicle. It reminded him of home.

Beyond the shimmering reflections of the old town's lights in the tranquil waters, he could make out the spire of St-Pierre, the seven-hundred-year-old Catholic church that had become a Protestant cathedral in 1536, and in which John Calvin had subsequently preached for twenty-eight years. He smiled again. Gone were the days when the stewardship of planet earth could, in even the smallest part, be entrusted to God. Others would have to take His place.

Tsavo National Park, Kenya. April 2006. He was the undisputed lord of the savannah, as implacably ferocious and cunning in his ways as he was immodest in his proportions. Due in no small part to his treatment of hyenas, the Maasai who'd strayed east over the Great Rift Valley during the droughts to graze their herds had named him I-árishóni, the Destroyer of Life. Whether from boredom or simple hatred, he regularly savaged hyenas and almost always decapitated them.

On this particularly torrid day, two khaki-clad park rangers from the Akamba tribe drew their rickety Land Cruiser up to a gnarled old giant of a baobab tree, disembarked, and prepared their lunches. The I-árishóni pride was lolling about in an acacia grove barely a quarter of a mile away. To dare to be in the presence of such menace reflected well upon the spirit.

But there was more menace about than they could have imagined, and in no time at all their spirits had been mercilessly extinguished in a hail of machine-gun fire. Three trucks then charged the lion pride at high speed and felled the great beast with several darts. The two most aggressive females were similarly brought down while the rest of the pride was either shot dead or scattered like burnt leaves on the hot, desiccating wind.

Kentucky. July 2006. At seventeen hands and fourteen hundred pounds, Zarathustra was a big horse. But what really made the red stallion a giant among thoroughbreds was that he'd never lost a race. Not one. Indeed, he'd just won the Triple Crown in unprecedented style. In each leg of that prize, he'd not only set track and world records, but had executed negative splitting. That is, in the Kentucky Derby, the Preakness, and the lengthy Belmont Stakes, he'd run each quarter mile faster than the one before. The only other horse who'd ever achieved such a feat had been Secretariat in the 1973 Kentucky Derby, and Zarathustra had managed to shave a full two seconds off that champion's time of 1:59 2/5 minutes.

But when the assault team of four vehicles and ten men came out of Lexington, along Old Frankfort Pike, and laid siege to the Benedict farm, Zarathustra had nowhere to run. It was all over in five minutes. The team of hooded men cut all telephone lines, bound and gagged the lord and lady of the manor, pounded the trainer and the resident veterinarian into unconsciousness, herded the stable hands into a tool shed, and shot dead both the security guard and a groom who'd tried to call for help on his cell.

For good measure they killed one of their own as well. A young Japanese commando had gotten behind Zarathustra as their horse whisperer was leading the stallion to the trailer. Zarathustra had unleashed his rear hoofs with the force of a trebuchet and shattered every bone in the man's face. He was summarily executed on the spot and his remains were left behind.

"*Eres un hombre estúpido*," snarled the Spaniard who'd shot him. "Do you not know that animals are never to be trusted?"

CHAPTER ONE

Montreal. September 4, 2006. In the east-end suburb of Ville d'Anjou, a weary Athol Hudson staggered into homicide headquarters, slumped into his seat, and plopped his forehead on his desk.

Sergeant-Detective Irina Drach, a statuesque woman with forbidding cheekbones and predatory grey eyes, was devouring a Danish pastry to make up for having skipped breakfast. Without missing a bite, she buried Hudson's head under the *Montreal Gazette*. "Page six. A certain Miriam Burns. It seems you make global warming and habitat destruction more and more sexy every time you hit the planks. If vaginal secretions were ink, you'd also be on pages seven, eight, nine, and ten."

"Fifteen presentations in four months," murmured Hudson from under the newspaper. "It's killing me, Irina. Now I know how wrung out Mick Jagger must feel after a concert."

"Perhaps you should cut back on it before it starts cutting into your day job. Let lesser mortals take on some of the engagements."

Hudson sat bolt upright, as if he'd just been violated by a cattle prod. "What? And abandon my *public*? And the cause? The sixth extinction, Irina! It's I who can best tell them that mankind is the root of all environmental evils. People have to know that the current extinction rate is between five and ten thousand times the normal background extinction rate, established after the great fifth extinction which closed the Cretaceous Period and sealed the fate of the dinosaurs —"

Irina held up her hands, begging for mercy. Having faithfully attended every one of his appearances, she'd heard it all before.

"Oh, and Irina?"

Irina knew that creaky sound and braced herself. It was the one he always produced when leaping from one hobby horse to another. "Yes, Hudson?"

"Don't you think it's about time you got back to eating healthy food instead of that junk? You're going to blimp out."

Irina raised her hand to brush the greying auburn hair from her face, but suddenly remembered that it was pulled tightly off her face and gathered up in a schoolmarmish bun at the back of her head, as it had been every day of the eighteen months since her husband, Walter, had been gunned down during an RCMP operation. She chastised herself for the robotic gesture and resolved to get a henna treatment — one of these days. She then withdrew another pastry from a grease-stained bag and munched away at it like a starving rodent.

Sizzling in disgust, Hudson bent over and scooped up the *Gazette*. He was soon staring, bug-eyed, at the unopened paper.

"I said page six, Hudson. You're not quite ready for the front page. Give it a few more outings."

Hudson jabbed frantically at the lower right corner of the page with his finely manicured forefinger. "Did you see this? The world's largest seed bank, at Ardingly, in England, was hit last night by a quasi-military force. Some sixty men with twenty trucks and enough firepower to overthrow an African government stormed the place just after closing."

"Who on Earth, eh? One would sooner expect a blitz by a flock of hungry finches."

Hudson rattled the newspaper in a snit. "They locked up all the staff, including the scientists, then locked down the whole place and made off with a good share of the seed collection. We're talking about the better part of a billion seeds."

"Was anybody hurt?"

Hudson was reading so voraciously that his lips were moving. "No, I don't think so ... yes, yes, a security guard was shot dead."

"None of the staff's family or friends noticed they were late or missing? And all those trucks just disappeared into thin air?"

"Hold on a sec, I'm just getting to it ... no, because all the people were night staff, or known to keep long hours, and yes, the trucks can't be traced."

"So the vehicles didn't caravan on their way in or out of that place. Good logistics."

"I can't believe you didn't see this story. What'd you do? Go straight to the one about me?"

"I won't be asking for your autograph anytime soon, if that's what you're thinking. But what you do reflects on the force."

Hudson turned to page three, read for a bit, then pulled out his calculator. "They still don't know how much of the collection was taken, but if the seeds came in batches of twenty thousand, that would mean about —"

"Fifty thousand containers at the most," declared Irina, without missing a beat. "More, if they had smaller batches."

"And they did. Rare and incredibly precious seeds. Fifty thousand containers, twenty trucks." Hudson tapped away at his calculator. "That works out to about —"

"Twenty-five-hundred jars per truck."

"Yes, exactly." Hudson's aristocratic brow was creased. "Is that possible?"

"Indeed. If the seeds, and therefore the jars, were small."

Hudson read on. "And now I'm wondering how fifty men could lug all those ... ah, organized buggers. They had conveyor belts with them. Several to get the stock up from the underground vaults and one to load it onto the trucks."

Lieutenant-Detective Stanley Robertson suddenly loomed in the doorway of his office. "Officer down," he announced in a strained voice. "Jerome Perron of the K-9 squad. Fifteen minutes ago, in front of his house, just as he was getting ready to drive off."

A cop who came to harm while off-duty was always open to suspicions of corruption. The twenty officers looked at each other, but none said a word. They held their breaths and waited for the stringy, greying lieutenant to tell them just how much more serious things could be.

"Sergeant Perron died of three gunshot wounds. He did not suffer. Death came instantly, the staff at the Lakeshore General report."

A collective moan rolled through the room like a dank fog. Two of the detectives wept quietly.

In a level voice, Irina Drach said, "Tell us about the dog."

"You want to know about a dog at a time like this?"

"I want to know everything."

"Not a trace of him," scowled the lieutenant.

"Any witnesses?"

"Come into my office, Sergeant."

Irina closed the door behind her and settled into a flimsy chair that groaned with her every movement.

"No witnesses. A quiet, secluded neighbourhood in Dorval. His wife found him when she left the house for work. A silencer must have been used. Now, I want you over there right away. Take all the officers you want with you. You've got the best solve rate in the force, Irina, so keep it going and close the deal quickly, eh? A cop killed off-duty always excites those pricks over at Internal Affairs." He handed her a computer printout. "Here's the address."

"The dog was Bismarck, of course."

"Yes, so?"

"He's swept the Canadian Police Canine Championships for three years running, hasn't he? Obedience, obstacle, criminal apprehension — the works. In a class by himself, from everything I hear."

"You're insinuating somebody killed a cop just to get his hands on a German shepherd? That dog would be useless to anybody but Jerome Perron. Too bonded."

"Exactly. Too bonded. He would have stood guard over Perron's body, if permitted. Or his carcass would have been next to his handler's."

From her jacket pocket, Irina withdrew a small handful of mints and began picking at them.

"Jesus, Irina. You were a really good-looking woman, always so well turned out, until … not that you aren't good-looking now, of course, but I could almost swear that you've put on a few pounds. You should get a grip. It's time."

Her tone would have freeze-dried the Mediterranean Sea. "Has my work suffered, Lieutenant?"

"Not at all. If anything, you're more diligent than ever. But still —"

"Then I thank you for your concern, Stanley, but I believe *we* — meaning the police — were concerned about how Bismarck would be useless to anyone but Sergeant Perron."

Robertson shrugged helplessly.

"Now, I'm thinking of a few episodes that have taken place in the last year or so. Zarathustra, for one. That horse would be useless, too. Stealing him would be something like stealing the Mona Lisa. You couldn't show him anywhere because he'd be as distinctive to horse people as Brad Pitt would be to us. And you certainly couldn't race him, even if you tried to disguise him. Only thoroughbreds with a clear lineage and DNA conformity from the American Jockey Club are allowed to do that. And on top of everything, even if someone tried to use him as a sire, his foals would get caught out by that same process.

"And then there's the case of this brood mare, Divine Right, who's descended from Secretariat and has produced more than her fair share of winners. Or this Charolais bull in France who just disappeared. The biggest and the best. A European champion worth millions. Also, there's the case of the pair of breeding pandas that went missing from the Chiang Mai Zoo in Thailand. Should I go on? There are many more. It's a wonder you haven't been abducted, too."

Lieutenant Stan Robertson rose from his chair and began pacing, all the while chewing furiously on his pen. Irina concluded that this was Robertson's secret to keeping trim. That eschewing such delights as Danishes and doughnuts might have anything to do with it was not something she cared to consider. She popped another mint into her mouth.

"Ah … there's one little matter I want to raise with you."

"Hudson?"

"Just so. I've been hearing things, reading things. I'm not sure it's what the force needs."

"With all due respect, Sir, I don't think this is the time to discuss

Hudson's extracurricular activities. We've got a dead officer to think about, and I really should be going. I don't care to leave everything to the uniforms and the scene-of-crime types. They'll just foul the site."

Robertson stopped in his tracks and leaned over his desk. The veins of his forehead bulged and his neck muscles were drawn in clear relief. "Should I point out that it was you who, just moments ago, was taking me on a tour through the animal kingdom?"

"My primary concern, Lieutenant, lies in preserving the good, reputation of a fallen comrade. Not subjecting that of another to critical scrutiny."

Irina knew that the affectation of obdurate sanctimony was not only infuriating but also an excellent conversation-stopper. Within moments, Robertson was holding the door open, with all his ganglia knotted as tightly as a Persian rug.

"You should do something about that bloody blinking. It's getting worse and I can't concentrate when I look at you."

"I've found that not even the worst thugs have trouble concentrating around my blinking, Stanley. Maybe you should consider a life of crime. Might be best for everybody concerned."

Within a few minutes, Irina and Hudson were in their car and Hudson had it darting and slashing westward through the morning traffic of the elevated Metropolitan like a piranha through a school of minnows. The other three cruisers tried in vain to keep up.

The suburb of Dorval lies on the southwest shore of Montreal, which itself squats like an overweight bather in the shallow murk of the St. Lawrence River. As they sped past Trudeau International Airport, then squirted through the Dorval traffic circle, Hudson broke the silence that had engulfed them. "This is going to be my worst experience in fourteen months as a detective, Irina. My first dead cop. I feel sick just thinking of his car's blood-spattered interior."

"Oh, the interior won't be blood-spattered. He'll have been shot before he got into his car."

"But Robertson said he was just getting ready to drive off."

"Unless his dog was able to open the door and let himself into the car, Perron would have been lying on the street."

"I don't follow."

Irina repeated what she'd said to the lieutenant.

"Ah, I get it," murmured Hudson, running his fingers through his strawberry-blond hair. "They'd have preferred to bring the dog down while he was out in the open rather than having to face him and his bared fangs as they opened a car door. So if Bismarck was still outside the car then so, too, must have been Perron."

"Correct. Perron would naturally get the dog into the car before he himself got in."

And then Irina let Hudson in on her theory about the animal abductions. She did not fail to mention the seed raid at Ardingly.

"Wow!"

"Wow indeed, and you need a haircut, Hudson. You're pandering to your 'public.' You're convinced they expect you to look like a rock star or something. Maybe all that fan mail is going to your head and morphing into hair, I don't know. But I do know you're a cop and a grown man, and you should never forget that."

It should be mentioned at this point that Irina Drach's precious Walter had loved her with a passion that was humbling, while Hudson — however prepossessing he might have been — had thus far been unlucky in love, due in no small part to excessive fussiness of dress and housekeeping, and a silky charm that could uncharitably be described as effeminate. It was Irina's mission to make Hudson over and thus assure his happiness and success.

Irina being Irina, however, her endeavors in this area were not in the least subtle. She was as inelegant in her interpersonal relations as she was ratiocinative in her professional life. But Hudson didn't take the slightest bit of offence at Irina's efforts, for those very efforts represented the sum total of warmth and fellow feeling in the life of a lonely man.

"I'll see about getting it trimmed on the weekend, Irina. Whoops, we're here."

Sergeant Jerome Perron's home was a modest bungalow on a corner lot in western Dorval, just a block up from the river. Its most prominent feature was the ten-foot chain-link fence bordering the backyard. As they approached the home from Lakeshore Boulevard, the two detectives could make out Bismarck's doggie McMansion abutting the rear deck. His name was emblazoned over the arched doorway in bold brass letters.

Irina and Hudson disembarked from their cruiser and stepped over the yellow police tape. From among the forest of uniformed policemen a sergeant strode forward to greet them in a thick French accent. "We are doing the door-to-door, Madame, but so far there is nothing. *Rien.* Nobody saw anything, nobody heard anything. His wife was transported to the hospital shortly after he for reason of deep shock. *Tabernacle,* I knew him well, eh? A good man, an honourable *officier de police.*"

Irina gesticulated in the direction of the late model Chevrolet in the driveway. Three latex-clad SOC technicians were going over it and the asphalt on which it sat with magnifying glasses, black powder, sticky rollers, a small vacuum cleaner, and all the other tools of their trade. "The doors were all closed?"

"*Mais oui!* The car is as we found it."

"And Perron's body was lying beside it?"

"By the left rear passenger door. Exactly where is the technician who is on his knees. We did the chalk outline, of course."

"Anything of interest for me?"

"These," said Sergeant Plante. He hoisted up a transparent plastic bag with three long cartridge casings in it.

"Where'd you find them?"

"But all here, Inspector. Where are, at present, our feet."

They were standing on the curb at the foot of the driveway.

Hudson took the bag and held it at eye level. "5.56 mm Nato shells. Could've been fired by anything from an AK-102 and a Spanish Ameli to an AR-15 or M-16. In any event, the gun was used in the semi-automatic mode, or Perron would've had way more than three holes in him. The AR can get off eight-hundred rounds per minute, the AK six hundred."

"If they had time to load up a dog, then they had time to pick up these shells," said Irina bitterly. "Cocky so-and-so's, aren't they?"

Hudson filled out a chain-of-evidence chit, handed it to the uniformed officer, and pocketed the bag of shells. "And why not? They kill one of their own in Kentucky and leave his body behind, and what happens? Nothing. Sure, the Japanese authorities get an artist's reconstruction sketch of that guy on TV, and they locate his family and childhood friends in a fishing village on the Sea of Japan, but nobody has a clue as to where he's been or what he's been up to for the last five years. He'd just disappeared."

At that point the three other unmarked cruisers arrived with their six occupants. Irina immediately dispatched all three pairs of detectives to take over the door-to-door questioning from the uniforms. Because the uniformed constables had begun with the houses closest to Perron's and fanned outward, the detectives would have to begin their questioning at some distance from the crime scene. Irina answered their grumbling by pointing out that the farther one got from Perron's house, the more subtle and experienced the interrogators had to be.

Once the three teams of detectives had trudged off, Irina breathed a sigh of relief. She had the crime scene to herself. *"Pardonnez moi,"* she said to one of the SOC technicians. "That skid mark over there?"

The mark, at the foot of the driveway, was no more than four inches long, and would have been laid down by little more than the chirp of a tire. A sample would reveal exactly what make of tire was responsible for it.

"The acceleration mark? I have already taken *l'échantillon, Madame le Sergent."*

Irina favoured the technician with a radiant smile that immediately had him humming happily to himself. She turned to the uniformed sergeant, who was still at her shoulder. "Jerome's gun was in his holster, I suppose?"

"Clasped shut, Madame."

Irina crooked her finger at Hudson. "Let's have a look in the house."

"But they obviously didn't go in there. The wife didn't know anything was amiss until she came outside."

Sighing heavily, Irina dismissed the uniformed cop and guided Hudson up the path to the front door with one arm slung over his shoulder. She whispered, "It's our duty to confirm that nothing was amiss before this morning, understand?"

As they stepped through the front door and into the hallway, it was immediately evident that if Sergeant Jerome Perron were in any way the beneficiary of some nefarious income supplement plan, then he'd cut a poor deal. The furnishings were middle-period Ikea, and any value the lamps and knickknacks might have possessed had to have been purely sentimental.

Like a wolf to a fresh side of elk, Irina Drach went straight to the financial nerve centre of the home — a messy computer and gaming room that contained more canine chew toys than it did financial folders. Having briefly been an investment banker before he became a cop, Hudson sat at the plain veneered desk and got to work. It wasn't long before he'd determined that household income was running only slightly ahead of expenditures due to a crushing mortgage and monthly car payments. Taken together, Perron's investment portfolio and bank account wouldn't have enticed a panhandler into crossing the street.

Irina was enormously pleased until she walked to the end of the main hallway and discovered a freshly painted nursery stuffed with new, unused baby linen and enough toys to stock a daycare centre.

"Perron's wife," she shouted. "Is she pregnant?"

"Couldn't tell you," replied Hudson from three rooms away. "All I know is that for the last few months they've been pouring all their spare cash into a place called Winken, Blinken and Nod."

Irina went to the master bedroom and threw open the closet door. The only maternity dresses she saw still had the price tags on them.

The doorbell rang.

"Irina? It's Marcel Sevigny and he's got somebody of interest with him. Someone from up the street."

With fists clenched so tightly that her palms threatened to bleed, Irina stalked down the hall to greet Sergeant Sevigny and a wiry, white-haired little man of about eighty. The old man had an uncommonly ugly little animal on a leash. It looked like a cross between a chihuahua and a wolverine. Irina assumed it was a dog.

The strapping, mustachioed Sergeant Sevigny said, "This gentleman, Mr. Elmore Quigley, informs me that he and his ... uh, pet ... were only forty minutes ago almost run down by a speeding late-model Chrysler sedan."

Irina wasn't so sure that the Chrysler had not, in fact, run over the hideous little beast, but his owner was identifiably human, and that was good enough for her.

"I live in the second last house before Carson," said the old man. "Apollo and I were crossing the street for our morning constitutional when this brand new Chrysler 300C comes roaring up the street and slams its brakes on just inches from us."

"Did you get a look at the passengers?"

"Yep."

"Well?"

"Two were black, one was a Chinese guy, and one was white."

"Would you recognize them if you saw them again?"

"Hell, no. Well … maybe the white guy. He was kind of fat, had bushy silver hair, and a really pink face. But I only saw them through the windshield as they bore down on me. The side windows were heavily tinted. Couldn't hardly see the black guys in the back as they pulled away from the stop sign. Dark as night, they were."

"Did you get a look at the licence plate?"

"Yep."

"Would you mind telling me what it was, just as soon as you get your pet off my leg?"

Quigley, quite accustomed to Apollo's lewd tendencies, simply gave the leash a quick jerk without even looking down. "A Quebec plate. ME34251."

As he jotted down the number, Hudson said to Irina, "It makes sense they'd use a sedan rather than a van. Two side windows for clear, simultaneous shots, and then toss the dog into the trunk. It would also make sense that the plate is stolen, but I got it anyway. Are you sure *you* got it right, Mr. Quigley?"

"I used to be an accountant. I can recall numbers the way most people recall pornographic images."

"You must have enjoyed your work very much." Sevigny laughed. But his merriment was short-lived, for Apollo was now at his own leg. Shaking it proved futile and Sevigny appealed to the little man.

This time, Elmore Quigley did not tug at the leash. "Heh-heh. Stepping on his tail usually works."

Sevigny needed no convincing. He trod on the crooked, mangy tail and Apollo detached himself immediately.

Hudson was utterly scandalized at such treatment of one of God's creatures and he made it known. His reward for such concern was having Apollo's passionate exertions at his own shinbone.

"Oh, dear," observed Irina drily. "It appears that Appalling has a masochistic streak in him."

"Uh … that would be Apollo, Officer," said Mr. Quigley. "But yes, a little bit of pain does turn him into a regular Casanova."

When Sergeant-Detective Sevigny closed the door of Jerome Perron's house behind him, Irina was shedding tears of laughter and Hudson the Conservationist was reconciling himself to the terrible beauty of nature.

CHAPTER TWO

Vienna. September 4, 2006. Jason Conrad had a passion for chocolate. This may go a long way toward explaining why, of all the great hotels in Vienna, he consistently chose the Hotel Sacher. In his opinion the Sachertorte — first created in 1832 by Franz Sacher for Prince Metternich, and later becoming the sweet, beating heart of the Hotel Sacher — was the *non plus ultra* of baked goods. The light chocolate cake, with its layer of apricot jam lurking seductively under a dark and silky chocolate icing like a harlot in the shadows, never failed to transport him. Even its appearance was a delight. The exterior of the flat, round cake was so smooth, so free of imperfection that it might have been burnished by the hand of Michelangelo. Normally an aggressively individualistic personality with a particular penchant for the rigidly exclusive, he didn't mind at all that the Sachertorte was among the most celebrated chocolate confections in the world.

In fact, as each of the twelve members of his doomsday board filed into the five-room Madame Butterfly Presidential Suite, which was a study in Hapsburg opulence, he had his aide leading them directly to the conference room where, at each place setting, sat a double portion of Sachertorte with a large dollop of unsweetened whipped cream at its side.

He wanted each of them to savour the indulgence and subsequently con-
tribute to its fame.

He also wanted to soften them up a bit, for he rather suspected that
some of them — the BBC doyenne and the Norwegian climatologist
in particular — might be quite agitated about the carnage surrounding
Zarathustra's abduction. To that end, he'd seen to it that everyone had a
glass or two of Romane Conti 1997 to wash it down.

Facing the Hotel Sacher was the Vienna State Opera house, upon
which Jason Conrad was gazing as he stood on the balcony and sucked on
his Cohiba cigar. He'd already had his fill of Sachertorte, and was merely
waiting for the right moment to confront the restless natives.

A heavily perspiring Chinua Amadi came up behind Conrad. His aide
was a short, portly, and prematurely balding Nigerian. "Sir," Chinua whispered tentatively, "they're all gobbling their cake, many are on their third
piece, and they've gone through five bottles of wine. It might be time."

"Has anyone mentioned the stallion?"

"No, Sir. They are enjoying themselves immensely and are quite
overwhelmed by their surroundings. You must remember, Sir, that even
though each are highly respected specialists, not one of them could afford
such luxury as this. Not even the executive suites on the seventh floor."

"We'll give them a few more minutes. Keep the wine flowing, Chinua."

"Should I let it slip, Sir, that the Romane Conti is fifteen hundred
dollars a bottle?"

"No. A good glass beats a debit entry any day. Just keep pouring."

Conrad wondered whether he really needed his board anymore. As
technical consultants, they'd been invaluable while he'd set up his grand
project, but things were now in hand. The facility was nearing completion
and the species card was filling out quite nicely. Did he really need a nag-
ging conscience?

He reflected for a few moments, then decided he didn't. He was
beyond that. But … they could still serve as a barometer of public opinion,
so he'd keep them. For now. He took a final pull on his Cohiba, downed
the last of his forty-year-old Highland Park and swept through his suite to
its conference room.

"Good day, ladies and gentlemen. I hope you aren't feeling too cramped, since this table's really designed for ten." He sighed. "But we must make do, eh?"

"*Au contraire,*" chirped the BBC lady. "It's rather cozy, the dessert and wine are to die for, and this room is exquisite. Hapsburg yellow, is it?

"It is. Now, my dear friends, you'll have noticed this item." He gestured toward the artist's easel in the corner, which was draped in a white linen cloth. "I have something special to announce, today —"

The Norwegian climatologist, Tore Harstad, had raised his hand and was waving it. Conrad thought this rather gauche and stared the man down into embarrassed silence. When Harstad had squirmed long enough, Conrad acknowledged him in a frigid voice, "Yes, Mr. Harstad. Something is troubling you?"

"Only this, Sir. It is now since April — four months — that you intended a reduction of violence to accompany our collecting activities. Yet what do I see? The violence continues. In the case of that race horse, for example, two innocents were shot dead. Also, one of our own. With the lion, two more. And there are many such examples. The walruses. The San Diego tiger. The Moscow sables. The seed banks at KwaZulu-Natal University and Ardingly. Always with the guns and the killing! How can this be when you said you would halt it?"

"Really, Mr. Harstad. It takes time for things to filter down through the system. And it takes even more time to seek out and remove the bad apples in any barrel. Am I right, Mr. Liadov?"

The bearded young Russian said yes, but with about as much conviction as the parent of a teenager affirms the existence of the tooth fairy. Conrad was not pleased. His dark eyes became flame throwers. When Liadov had been reduced to a cinder, he studied each of the other eleven in turn. Harstad was intimidated, but undeterred. "I do not understand," he said in a quavering voice. "You are so powerful. You command the largest financial empire in the world. You have only to snap your fingers and someone, or some great enterprise, is either raised up or ruined. How can it be that your orders are not immediately followed in this matter?"

Conrad left his post at the head of the table and walked around to where Harstad was seated. He laid his hand on the climatologist's shoulder and squeezed hard. "Are you implying that I misled you?"

Harstad was trembling, and on the verge of tears. "No, Sir, but I do not know what to think!"

Conrad signalled to Chinua that his whisky glass needed a refill and returned to his spot. He took a sip of his drink, then stared with slitted eyes at some invisible speck on the far wall, looking like a general surveying the lay of some distant battlefield. "Let me explain something to you, Mr. Harstad, something which should have occurred to you when you signed on with us. Our agents cannot simply walk into a zoo or onto a reserve and say to those in charge, 'Do you mind terribly if we borrow your very finest specimens for, say, ever?' These animals, Mr. Harstad, and the seeds too, are precious assets and are jealously guarded. People will naturally fight to retain them. Thus, we must fight back. Our project, I'm sure you'll agree, is far more important than theirs. We are guaranteeing the perpetuation of plant and animal species in the event of global catastrophe. The great cataclysm. On our shoulders rests the future of our planet. Now, if some trigger-happy guard threatens our agents and our work, then we have no option but to indispose him."

"*Dispose* of him, you mean," muttered an increasingly dismayed Harstad.

"In certain extreme cases, yes. But take heart. They are inevitably of a lower order than the specimens they would deny us. We're talking, for the most part, about guards, zookeepers, park rangers, test-tube scrubbers, and the like. Hardly people like a foremost scientist such as yourself."

"They are human beings. They have life. They have lives. They have love!"

"Come, now. A human being is more than a biped who knows how to put on a condom, flush a toilet, and turn on the television. A human being is defined by the depth of his soul, the breadth of his mind, and the scope of his dreams."

Tore Harstad leapt out of his seat in a torment. "I can conscience this no longer! I depart! And the world will know about this, mark my words!"

He stormed out of the room.

Complete silence. The sweetness of the cake and wine was but a bitter memory.

"Does anybody agree with him?" asked Conrad imperturbably. "Would any of you like to follow suit?" He bent over the marine biologist, Ted Seacrest, who was seated close to where he stood. "You, Mr. Seacrest?"

The feckless Ted Seacrest, whom Conrad had designated as the group's spokesman at the Geneva meeting, almost fainted from fright. His pale, stubby fingers danced about the tabletop like maggots on a hot plate. "Oh dear, no. No, no, no. Nothing dramatic for me ... I'm, uh ... quite content to save life on Earth from utter extinction."

Conrad next turned his sights on the BBC doyenne. "And you, Miss Livingston. Is there anything you'd like to add to what Mr. Harstad said?"

Penelope Livingston was extremely flustered. As far as she was concerned, the only thing more painful than guilt was guilt by association. "Mr. Conrad! I am most discomfited that you should question my integrity and my loyalty to the cause! Rest assured that I am as committed to this enterprise as I was on the day I was conscripted. We have work to do!"

The other ten, and Chinua as well, thumped the table with their fists and bellowed "Hear, hear!"

Conrad withdrew his cellphone. "Then I trust none will be shocked by a certain necessity." He dialed, then spoke into the mouthpiece. "Hello, this is JC Alpha, JC Omega, singular. I want a package removed. Call Chinua for details."

Chinua's phone rang less than thirty seconds later. While Conrad sipped at his Scotch and the board members listened as if to a launch countdown, Chinua gave the name, a physical description, and the home address and present location of one Dr. Tore Harstad, M.Sc., Ph.D.

There was a long, breathless silence. Everyone but Chinua shifted uncomfortably in their seats. At last, someone spoke. It was Arnold Blum, the American geneticist. "Uh ... Mr. Conrad? What just happened? Was that what I thought happened?"

"And just what do you think you thought happened, Mr. Blum?"

"He was slated for extinction?"

"Ah, I like that. Someone who can stay on topic. Yes, Mr. Blum, he has been slated for extinction. Gives one food for thought, doesn't it?" Conrad gave them a few moments to digest things, then abruptly clapped his hands together a few times. "Okay, everybody. Chop-chop! I have an agenda and I'd like to keep to it."

Without benefit of notes, he launched into a dissertation on cryogenic preservation, not only of animal sperm and ova, but of the seeds of many vital tropical plant species such as citrus, cacao, coffee, and rubber — those very plants that would be especially viable in the event of global warming. The seeds of these plants, so-called "recalcitrant" seeds, cannot be preserved by slow drying and then kept at temperatures of minus-twenty-degrees Centigrade, as could be those of the other eighty percent of the world's plants, because of their excessive moisture content. The water in them would crystallize, he explained, and therefore rupture the cell walls.

"Dreadful," sputtered the BBC doyenne. "Who'd want to live in a world without chocolate?"

Conrad slung Penny Livingston a look that would have shattered granite. Once she'd been reminded of her place, he went on to recount how researchers had found that these particular seeds could only be preserved in a two-stage process. First, by separating the growing parts of the seeds from their moisture nutrient reserves and flash-drying them in a laminar air flow, and then drenching the dry shoot-root continuums in a cryoprotectant and cooling them rapidly by liquid nitrogen to a temperature of minus-one-ninety-six Centigrade, or minus-three-twenty-one Fahrenheit. At those temperatures, metabolic activity would cease, thus forestalling harmful changes that could occur in the plant cell genome. Also, due to the cryoprotectant, such as glycerol, the water would have undergone vitrification, the process wherby it goes from a liquid to a glassy state without the intervening steps of ice nucleation: ergo, no damage to the cell walls.

Conrad then elaborated upon how the process is reversed, and cryogenically preserved tropical seeds could best be pressed into service as needed. He talked of synseeds and alginate encapsulation.

"And we haven't even mentioned the many plants that are propagated vegetatively. For these plants, seed banks are not an option. Their survival would be dependent upon in vitro storage, where their cuttings are kept under strictly monitored conditions in glass tubes and vessels."

Then came the nub of it all. Energy. Energy for the maintenance of the cryopreservation systems to store sperm, ova, and recalcitrant seeds. Energy for in vitro storage. Energy for the controlled thawing of recalcitrant seeds, such as by centrifugal removal of cryoprotectants and convection warming.

Conrad closed his eyes and pinched the bridge of his aquiline nose for a few moments as if entertaining painful thoughts. The twelve devotees had an inkling of where the great man's comments were leading, but none of them moved a muscle, much less opened his or her mouth. Instead, each watched, rapt, as the long, pale fingers flitted like agitated cave fish toward the prominent chin and began stroking it. Chinua Amadi scurried to the head of the table and topped up Conrad's glass. There was not even the slightest acknowledgment of Amadi's solicitude, and the heavily perspiring black man had to take his reward from the fact that Conrad deigned to raise the glass to his lips and drain its contents in one long, silent sip.

"So. In the event of a cataclysm — be it man-made or interplanetary — and the subsequent total collapse of infrastructure, where would this energy come from? Generators? Couldn't stockpile enough fuel to last anywhere near a century. Solar panels? One need only contemplate the possibility of a nuclear winter or dust from an asteroid impact. Thermal energy? We have, as you know, drilled some three miles into the substrata at our site. On the plus side, we haven't hit any magma, but on the negative side, it doesn't look as if there's any highly compressed, superheated water down there. Windmills? Erected beforehand, they'd most likely give away our location. Plus, they could easily be destroyed during the Apocalypse. As for after the event, where could we have stored these giant structures and the equipment needed to erect them?

"Now, I'm pleased with the work that's being done at our installation, which some of you so glibly refer to as 'The Doomsday Complex.' All these years and almost four billion dollars in construction costs, not to mention millions upon millions in bribes to customs officials, airport and dockworkers, and such, have resulted in what, when completed, will be something the likes of which the world has never seen. *If* the world were to be made aware of its existence, of course. But there is still one missing ingredient. Something that will make our facility different from all the other seed banks and frozen zoos on this planet. Would anyone care to venture what that is?"

The spectral man looked at each of the twelve in turn, but they'd riveted their eyes to the table. He took a few steps backward and hovered above the covered artist's easel. When all were focused on the object, he smiled broadly and nodded at Chinua Amadi. His assistant, sweating profusely, rushed to the tripod; he knew how much his master hated manual labour. He whisked away the cloth, hoping he'd done it with the right degree of élan.

The eleven were staring at a large colour photograph of a mushroom cloud. With the exception of Chinua Amadi, who'd set up the display, they gasped as one.

Chinua Amadi was relieved. Jason Conrad had gotten precisely the reaction he'd sought. "I'm kidding, of course," Conrad cackled with glee. "But only partly. Apart from my considerable number of commercial enterprises, I hold nearly fifty billion dollars in personal funds. If I have to, I'll spend a sizable chunk of it in order to secure total energy independence. Ladies and gentlemen, we *will* have nuclear power."

While everyone was huddling together like witches at a seance, Conrad slipped out of the room and down to the street. For six blocks, he walked purposefully along Kärntner Strasse, that glittering and golden row of exclusive shops. All the way, he pondered the unhappy fate of Tore Harstad, and that of the hundreds upon hundreds of harmless souls who'd fallen victim to his storm troopers. How idealistic he'd been when he'd launched his grand project, he thought, swallowing hard. He'd believed every last, lofty word he'd spouted while recruiting his board members. When three-thousand square feet of red velvet had parted, revealing the sloping entrance to the most colossal man-made cavern in history, he'd been able to tell them, with utter conviction, "Ladies and gentlemen, I give you the tunnel that is the light at the end of the tunnel."

Upon ushering those twelve quixotic spirits down into the facility for the first time, he'd been awestruck, as they had been, by the magnitude, complexity, and promise of his underground Atlantis.

The great visionary, the great humanitarian he'd been, who could no more conscience the death of a single man than the extermination of an entire species.

What had changed? Nothing, he shuddered to himself. He'd always known, and seen for himself, how preconceptions form mankind's understanding of the universe. He'd always known, and observed, how those very ideas refashioned the world. In fact, he'd watched how his own dreams of a commercial empire had refashioned the reality of competitors and smaller operators, inevitably for the worst.

He'd merely lost sight of all that in an efflorescence of altruism.

After all, had the world not been turned into a shambles by mankind's design? The very disaster he was working to counter had been brought about by man's striving to refine things. Reality for people and animals alike had been degraded by grandiose ideas of progress and enrichment.

In fact, was not the rescue of that reality the very thing for which his facility had been conceived? But because of it, legions of people were dying.

The irony pierced him like a tempered blade, but as he stalked into the epicentre of the Old Town, the Stephansplatz, he withdrew it and slammed it down onto the cobblestones. What was done was done, and here was his destination anyway.

It was the square upon which resides St. Stephen's Cathedral, a towering twelfth-century fusion of Gothic and Romanesque architecture.

The church is most famous for its green, gold, and grey roof, composed of 230,000 glazed tiles. However, Jason Conrad had not come to see them. He'd come to gaze upon the bell towers. It was from one of these structures that birds flew frantically one day while Ludwig Van Beethoven watched. At that moment in 1801, since he could only deduce that the bells were ringing, he finally realized the extent of his deafness. His reaction? "I will seize Fate by the throat."

So, too, would Jason Conrad. No, he would go farther. He would throttle Fate until it sank, lifeless, to his feet.

CHAPTER THREE

Montreal. September 4, 2006. Not unexpectedly, the licence number that Elmore Quigley had given Irina and Hudson turned out to be fake. Or, rather, it was a real number but the plate was fake. The number was registered to a certain Gaston Gélinas of the village of Percé, some six hundred miles up the river on the Gulf of St. Lawrence. Within an hour of Sergeant Jerome Perron's murder, the Quebec Provincial Police in Percé had ascertained that Monsieur Gélinas was in possession of his car, which was incontestably in possession of its licence plate. Given that the fastest jet could not have transported the plate from Montreal back to Percé in the time since the murder, it at first seemed that the nervous little undertaker was the victim of coincidence.

"And what kind of car does he drive?" Irina barked into the phone.

"A black late-model Chrysler 300C," responded the QPP desk.

"Smart," said Hudson as he slid behind the wheel of the cruiser. "And no coincidence. Any patrol car doing a routine plate check wouldn't flag them. No discrepancy. So where do we go from here, Irina?"

"Headquarters."

"That's not quite what I meant, Irina."

"Well, no Chrysler 300C has been reported stolen, so I've got the team calling up every car rental agency in the city. And since Marcel Sevigny and the SOC team are all over the neighbourhood and crime scene like fleas over that unfortunate little Apollo creature, we should go back to headquarters. We need to get on the Internet and start fishing about for more reports of animal abductions. We need to know the scope of this thing."

"Just from the little we know, I'd say it's a global operation."

Irina did not respond. She never responded to the obvious.

"I wonder if anyone else has connected those captures?"

"Let's hope so, Hudson. I wouldn't want to live in a world where we're the best cops."

Galvanized by Drach's use of "we," Hudson tromped heavily on the accelerator pedal and soon had them steaming east along the Met at speeds that could only have been justified by a mass slaying. Irina, who was seldom oblivious to the consequences of her pronouncements, took it with fairly good grace and slapped the police flasher onto the dash. It was almost time for the midmorning coffee break anyway, and she had a cinnamon bun waiting impatiently for her.

Once there, Hudson went directly to his desk and began Googling missing animals. His fingers danced lightly over the keys, entering varying combinations of such words as "prize-winning," "champion," "abducted," "stolen," and "kidnapped." The first few sites he opened and read, but soon the balletic movements of his fingers gave way to a salsa-like frenzy and he merely bookmarked the hits. Dozens and dozens of them.

Irina stood over Hudson's shoulder, gnawing at her cinnamon bun like a rat gnaws at a cheese crate. "My fingers are sticky from the sugar glaze," she declared between bites. "Not much point in me gumming up my keyboard."

"There's a better way to keep from gumming up your keyboard," he hissed.

"I'll trust you, Sergeant Hudson, to keep your nose out of my private affairs."

"Geez, Irina! Who was just telling me I should get a haircut? And what's more, we're partners. I trust you with my life, you trust me with yours. What could be more personal than that?"

"I am recently widowed, Hudson. I am still in mourning. Witness this nervous tic I have with my eyes. End of conversation. Now, open that one up, Partner. Third down. There, the one about the Indian elephants and the Calcutta Zoo."

"You know, I could swear your hands are looking a bit chubbier."

Irina Drach backed away, horrified. "They are not!"

"It sure looks like it to me. How can be so sure they aren't?"

"Because I weigh them regularly!"

Hudson sighed heavily and turned back to his computer. They both gawked at the screen. A male and a female elephant had been taken in a nighttime paramilitary raid that resulted in two fatalities. The police chase had been foiled by a series of strategic roadblocks.

"I don't get it," said Hudson. "Why take elephants from a zoo when they could get them from the wild with only a fraction of the risk?"

"I'm no tree hugger, but I'm a fast learner. You mentioned in one of your lectures that Indian elephants are disappearing rapidly from the jungles. Also, transferring an elephant from a cage to a trailer would be a great deal easier than trapping one in the wild. Finally, I don't doubt that zoo animals are healthier than their free-range cousins. Does all that make sense?"

Hudson swivelled in his chair and looked up at Irina. He also looked at her long and censoriously enough to let her know that the previous conversation was not forgotten. "Another thought: If it's the same people behind all these kidnappings, and if the theft of Zarathustra in Kentucky and of El Capitán the silverback in Tenerife are any indication, then they don't mind taking casualties or sacrificing their own. We're up against an army of zealots."

Irina's phone rang. "Hold one moment, please," she said into the mouthpiece, then gestured toward the computer screen. "Stop with the bookmarking, Hudson. Open up what you've got so far and give me a body count, theirs as well as the good guys.'"

Lieutenant Stan Robertson's door swung open just as Irina put her ear to the receiver.

"Sergeant Drach," said Robertson. "Can I see you in my office…?"

Irina raised her arm in Robertson's direction. The gesture was meant to silence Robertson. It did, but its very insouciance infuriated him. He slammed his door shut.

It was the telephone detail on the line. Officer Jean Dupuis informed her that they'd located a small, independent car-rental agency in Montreal West that had let a new, black Chrysler 300C to a man who fit the description they'd been given. A heavy white man with bushy silver hair and a face the colour of bubble gum.

Irina handed Hudson a slip of paper with the man's name and driver's licence number on it. "Oliver Harvey of Botany Bay in Sydney, Australia. Check the Interpol database, then get on the blower with the New South Wales Police and get some input on this man. If they say 'are you suggesting we try to track him down,' tell them a policeman has fallen. If they're still less than co-operative, tell them you're calling for Detective Irina Drach, who helped their present commissioner track down a wife killer by the name of Gerald Stinson just a few years back. They'll remember that name. And if they *still* won't play ball, tell them I would love to fill Commissioner Newell's ears because I'm a vindictive bitch. In the meantime, I'm going to bring Lieutenant Robertson up-to-date."

"What about the body count you asked for?"

"Put a hold on that. They aren't going anywhere. The living are far quicker than the dead."

Irina knocked politely on Robertson's door. In Hudson's presence, she always made a point of being deferential toward the lieutenant.

"Come in!"

Irina plopped into the chair with a thud that startled Robertson and made him pace back and forth even more frenetically.

"What's up, Sergeant? Why didn't you come see me first thing? Am I supposed to get the update from CNN?"

"You're venting, Stan. That's counterproductive."

"I am not venting! A cop has been killed! I need something to tell the commander, so he can tell something to the chief, so *he* can tell something to the bloody media!"

"If you'll stop that bloody pacing, I'll try not to blink. Deal?"

Robertson flung himself into his chair. If it were possible to pace nervously while seated, then Robertson was accomplishing it.

Irina launched into a detailed account of the morning's activities. In the end, she couldn't refrain from blinking but by then Robertson was back on his feet, anyway. "And we've found someone who talked face to face with one of the perps. A car-rental guy — Anthony O'Leary. As soon as we're done here, I'm going over there to talk to him."

"I've been doing some thinking while you were gone, Irina. It occurs to me that we're onto a global operation of some kind. What do you think of that?"

"I think it's a bloody brilliant idea, Stan. There's a reason you're the lieutenant and I'm just some poor sod of a sergeant."

"Good. Now get the hell out of here and do me proud. And remember, the whole world will be watching us. The whole world!"

Hudson was looking quite pleased with himself as Irina leaned over his shoulder. "Nothing on Oliver Harvey at Interpol, but the Aussie police were splendid and volunteered to dig up his last known address. I didn't have to cash in your chips. And that gave me time to dig into some of these bookmarked sites. Twenty sites, sixteen innocents killed. The bad guys lost six, and in each case their commando took a couple of insurance bullets from his own people. As for the animals, we've got everything from a pair of Amur tigers in the Tokyo Zoo and prize llamas in a Peruvian market to a gargantuan Nile crocodile in the Cairo Zoo. If it's the best genetic specimen, it's a target."

"Come on, Hudson. We're off to Montreal West."

But Hudson wouldn't budge. He sat drinking his coffee, glued to the screen. "You know, Irina, I don't see how we can be the only people who've cottoned to all this activity. It doesn't make sense."

"Someone has to be first, Hudson."

"Yes, but we — I should say *you* — were alerted to it because of something that happened in our own backyard. What about all those other backyards?"

"Most backyards have fences around them, and some are pretty high."

"I just had a thought. The animals we're aware of are either domesticated or zoo animals. I wonder if anything's been going on in the wild? It wouldn't make sense if it isn't."

"You're the expert on ecosystems and such. Who do we go to for information on that?"

"The World Wildlife Fund, headquartered in Gland, Switzerland. They've got a global network."

"Then you'll contact them as soon as we get back. Are you ready to leave?"

Hudson was on his feet, as impatient as a thoroughbred at the starting gate. "I wonder if the World Wildlife Fund has something on Percé. It's no accident that the undertaker's licence plate was slapped on a car just like his, is it? Our unsubs must have been to Percé, where they saw his Chrysler — and it's doubtful they were there for the sights."

"A change of plans, Hudson. I'll drive, and you can call your wildlife people from the car."

As Irina — unlike her partner — tended not to regard other cars as mere irritants or obstacles, Hudson had time enough to establish contact with the WWF's senior press officer in Switzerland. His probing aroused considerable consternation and confirmed the official's worst fears. Olivier Van Kleek assured Hudson that by the time he and Irina got back to their desks, a lengthy email — complete with links — would be awaiting them. Hudson requested that he include, if possible, a reference to Percé and the Gulf of St. Lawrence.

"Ah yes, the Gulf of St. Lawrence," Van Kleek had lamented. "The world's largest estuary. Very worrisome. There has been a seventy percent drop in the krill population there during the last ten years. It is most likely due to global warming. Colder water enters the gulf due to the melting of arctic ice, you see, and that compromises the living and reproductive cycles of those tiny creatures. And krill, as you are no doubt aware, are the primary food of blue, humpback, fin, and sei whales. So, less krill, fewer whales, as has been definitively observed."

"Well," exclaimed Hudson as they turned into the lot of Indulgence Car Rentals. "Half their fleet is made up of brand new Caddies, Lincolns, and Jags, and the rest are Chrysler 300Cs. And not one has a company plaque or bumper sticker. Our man didn't just pick these guys at random."

"Listen, Athol, isn't it possible, as some people say, that global warming's an entirely natural phenomenon? The tail end of the thaw from the last ice age, for instance?"

"Haven't you been listening when I do my speeches, Irina? It's all been happening in the last fifty years. Habitat destruction, species extinction, global warming, the lot. The events of the last fifty years should be taking hundreds of thousands, if not millions, of years."

"Well … that still doesn't mean it's not natural. The warming of the Earth could have just reached a tipping point, that's all."

"The tipping point is biotic, Irina. It's us!"

Hudson slammed the car door behind him and stormed into a rental office that looked like a poorly conceived wedding cake. When Irina caught up to him, the young policeman's badge was on the counter and he was addressing one of the attendants in a tone usually reserved for serial rapists. Irina was gratified that she'd finally get to play the good cop to Hudson's bad one, but irate that Hudson was conducting himself in an unprofessional manner.

"So," said Irina in the low rasp that Hudson had come to associate with acute disapproval, "this is our Mr. Anthony O'Leary?"

Cowed by Irina's demeanour, Hudson let the pale, pimply redheaded youth speak for himself. Even the youth's voice was pimply. "That's me, and I rented a car to the guy you're looking for. Or someone who looks like the one you're looking for."

"Describe him to me."

"Thick silver hair, short and stocky, and a really pink face."

"Colour of eyes?"

"Kind of a shocking colour. Blue-grey. Don't see that too often. What really got me, though, was the way he used those eyes. He looked at me, but not really, y'know? Like I wasn't there. As if I was just standing in his way. Creepy."

"He paid by credit card?"

"The only method of payment we accept." Anthony O'Leary laid a rental agreement on the burled walnut counter. "Here. I kept this out for you. Visa."

Irina scanned the document quickly. "Yesterday afternoon. Was there anyone with him?"

"He had an Asian guy in here with him. Small and twitchy-like. Outside, two big black buggers with bean shaves waited with their hands in their pockets. Opposite of the Asian. Didn't budge. Like they were ebony carvings."

"I'll take that," murmured Hudson, reaching for the rental agreement. "Having a sample of his writing — in particular, his signature — will be nice, but better yet, his Visa data should tell us where in the world he's been."

"But what about when he brings the car back?" whined the youth. "I'll need it to close the account!"

This was just the comic relief Irina and Hudson needed, but neither of them laughed out loud, for the young man already looked as if a violin sonata could be played on his nerves.

"Oh, he won't be bringing the car back," smiled Hudson. "It will be dumped somewhere, and when we find it, we'll impound it for a thorough going-over."

Irina's cellphone rang. As one hand plundered the silver serving tray of complimentary Peek Frean biscuits, the other raised the device to her ear. "Sergeant-Detective Drach here," she mumbled through a mouthful of crumbs.

Hudson presumed the call was of some import because her fingers waved a sad farewell to the biscuits and began stroking her sharply etched jaw. He knew it was of great import when the blinking ceased and she stared, with widened eyes, at O'Leary. With her mouth pulled down at the corners she looked something like a reptile baking on a rock, in full contemplation of a succulent bug.

"What? What did I do?"

"I'm trying to decide whether or not you can be a first-class witness, Mr. O'Leary."

"I've done all right, so far. Try me!"

"Could you describe what this Oliver Harvey was wearing?"

One would suppose, as Hudson had during the early days of his partnership with Irina, that her minatory stance would completely discompose a witness. Yet the opposite was invariably true. It provoked a retreat from sensory input and had the subject stealing around the ideas and images in his brain like a shut-in prowls around reassuringly familiar furniture.

"He was wearing a khaki shirt with those strap thingies on the shoulders."

"Epaulettes," prompted Hudson.

"Epaulettes ... yeah, and black shorts and brown Doc Martens. Oh, and he had a Rolex watch and a diamond-encrusted crucifix hanging from his neck."

"As deserving as he may be, this young man most certainly won't be seeing his vehicle for a while," Irina said to Hudson as she pocketed her phone. "Oliver Harvey has been found dead and slumped over the automobile's steering wheel near Rue St-Denis and the Met. He has two puncture wounds at the base of his skull."

CHAPTER FOUR

The Wilderness. September 4, 2006. The chief of security had just finished his morning tour of the facility in his electric runabout. As was his custom, Julio Menendez had driven up and down every single street of the densely developed area. He'd cruised past every living quarter, emporium, cafeteria, bar, administration office, maintenance shop, laboratory, and security post. He'd passed the sports complex and stopped to chat with a few players on the soccer field. And, of course, he'd threaded his way through the storage buildings — hundreds of them, many the size of hockey arenas — sometimes having to pull over to the side of the narrow roads to make way for the heavily laden cargo trucks that seemed to stream endlessly toward them. Satisfied that all was well, he headed toward the main entrance. At the foot of the ramp he checked in at the principal security bunker, then sped his vehicle up the gentle incline for a quarter mile.

Daylight and warm, fresh air at last.

He pulled into the parking lot of the zinc processing plant, which was being refurbished and reactivated. He smiled and lit a cigarette. The man up there sure had his wits about him. In the event that someone from the nearest outpost of civilization should ever venture as far as this Godforsaken tract of land, few questions would be asked. The heavy excavation and earth-moving machinery had already accomplished its task of carving out a cave that was a full three-storeys high by one square mile without arousing the slightest bit of attention, much less suspicion. For ten square miles around the facility the soil level had been evenly raised by three feet then planted with scrub and the occasional windblown coniferous tree. There were no giveaway mountains of earth anywhere except for the slag heaps from the zinc mine, which neatly camouflaged the facility's primary entrance. The whole thing was as inconspicuous as a gopher's hole, and when those monstrous and impregnable clamshell doors, with their roughcast exterior finish, slammed shut, not even the most alert busybody would detect anything more mysterious than a working zinc mine.

As he watched the delivery trucks rumble back and forth in clouds of dirt, he considered how the sheer number and size of the excavation and earth-moving equipment, not to mention the endless stream of supply vehicles through those distant towns on the inbound highway, must have raised more than a few eyebrows, even if the last few hundred miles were strictly private road.

Government people had to have been bought, he figured. In his two years on the site he'd never seen so much as a single safety or environmental inspector. They should have wondered, at the very least, about the vast quantities of hydroelectric power that the site was consuming, for it would be out of all proportion to the energy requirements of even the largest mining operation.

He spat out a mouthful of dust. Fuck it. He was just a security officer, not a poobah. It was not his place to contemplate matters of such magnitude and complexity. Like every other employee at the site, past and present, he merely had to do his job perfectly and keep his mouth shut. For that, he was paid a king's ransom and given a guarantee that his family would come to no grief.

He flicked his cigarette butt a good ten feet then clambered back into his buggy. Back to the shadowy world. He started down the paved ramp, grateful as always that a waist-high steel barrier separated him from the hurtling truck traffic. Without it, he'd be roadkill.

At the bottom of the hill, as he wended his way past the vast and crowded shipping area, he thought he might take a look at the animals. They were two very special animals, housed in the most opulent of compounds. He sped along Boulevard of the Americas, took a right at Trafalgar Square, and within ten minutes was parked in the driveway of Block H12, a three-storey affair of glass and granite that, like every other building in the complex, doubled as a support beam. Unlike at Cheyenne Mountain, the buildings here were not isolated from their surroundings, nor were each perched on a set of one-ton coil springs. But then, the complex wasn't designed to take a direct nuclear hit like the high-profile Norad installation. It was supposed to be a secret.

Menendez passed through the heavily guarded doors. Even though he was head of security, in this building he was subject to the same scrutiny as was everyone else. After a full three minutes, he finally stood outside the horse's corral, watching a handler ride the animal at a trot around the small oval track.

Julio Menendez had last observed Zarathustra ten days earlier, and he was certain that he could see still more signs of the animal's decline. In his opinion, this simply was not the same fire-breathing stallion who'd arrived only two months earlier. Zarathustra was born to gallop at the head of a thundering herd under open skies, not to barely keep pace with the flies in the world's largest burrow. His heart ached for the great horse.

"Hullo, Mr. Menendez. Keeping well?"

It was Jósef Krasicki, the stooped and balding little Pole who tended and fed the animals.

"Yes. Yes, thank you. And how is the stallion?"

"Truthfully? He eats, but barely. His eyes grow dimmer by the day. He is like a child without his toys."

"And the cat?"

"Ah, that one! His rage grows daily. He paces endlessly, very often making threatening passes by me. He roars and lunges and claws at the Plexiglas barrier. And he constantly pisses against it. Oh, and he has stopped eating butchered meat."

"Then he is starving himself?"

"Oh, not at all. Last week, after he had not eaten for five days, I introduced a live caribou into his enclosure. It was a horrible spectacle, and very messy, but he feasted. So that is what I give him now. Luckily there are many caribou up there, eh? He is voracious."

"But he will not have many more meals. Nor the stallion. The great man will be here at the end of the week to view them, and then —"

"And then *what?*"

"Well, Jósef, they must be put down, mustn't they? This is no place for live animals, even a select few. It's a question of provisions and space. It's a matter of policy. Their sperm are all that is required, especially now that our scientists have perfected in vitro egg maturation."

"But he cares enough about these animals to wish to see them!"

"He will inspect them as exemplars of particular bloodlines."

"Ah, yes ... of course. Not as individuals, but as exemplars."

Menendez cleared his throat as if a burr were stuck in it. "You know, I have often wondered why, of all the animals we have processed, it should be this stallion and this lion that he wishes to witness in the flesh. Have you?"

"But it is obvious. In I-árishóni we have the king of beasts. The king of the king of beasts. And in Zarathustra, we have the king of the sport of kings. One can only suppose that the great man wishes to see himself reflected in other species. He wants to feel a part of nature, but only of that part which is exceptional."

"But of course," said Menendez, stroking his voluminous mustache. "Nothing less would be appropriate." He studied the agitated little man. Menendez hadn't liked the intonation that had been lent to "the great man."

"You will miss them, eh?"

Jósef Krasicki turned away from Menendez and watched Zarathustra do his last lap. In order to keep the stallion from breaking out into a canter, his rider strained mightily on the reins.

"It is not right," whispered the old man.

Menendez loomed over Krasicki. "I beg your pardon?"

"It is not right!"

The security chief's voice hardened. "To criticize even one small aspect of this enterprise is to criticize the enterprise as a whole. I would be careful what I say, if I were you. Especially to me."

The little old man was dwarfed by the burly Menendez, but undaunted. "And what could you do to me? I am an old man. I have not much left but my admiration for these animals."

"Your family!"

"My family? Hah! My wife died ten years ago of cancer, and my son was killed six months ago in his automobile. I have nobody."

Julio Menendez turned on his heels and stormed out of Block H12. He would have to reconsider Jósef Krasicki's situation. A man without love was a danger to more than just himself.

CHAPTER FIVE

Montreal. September 4, 2006. By the time Irina Drach and Athol Hudson had returned to their squad room, the email from the World Wildlife Fund was awaiting them. It was, however, far shorter than they'd anticipated. Somewhat apologetically, Olivier Van Kleek explained that the national offices scattered across the globe were inundating him with accounts of mysterious disappearances. Some of the disappearances were not even all that mysterious: in several instances, park rangers or wardens were held at gunpoint while animals — inevitably the finest specimens — were carted off. And the incidents in which preserve or park staff had been killed were being re-evaluated. Perhaps they amounted to considerably more than incidents involving quotidian poachers. In any event, said Van Kleek, it would take some time to get a clearer picture of things.

"Still, he's done a whale of a job," said Irina. "There must be a hundred episodes here. Where to begin, eh?"

"Speaking of whales, let's start with Percé and environs," said Hudson, eagerly scrolling through Van Kleek's list. "I'm sure our bad asses weren't there for the beach and Percé Rock. Aha, listen to this: Percé Rock and

Bonaventure Island, which is within spitting distance of Percé Village, together form a provincial park and conservation area. Bonaventure Island is home to three-hundred-thousand sea birds, including razorbills, cormorants, gulls, murres, puffins, and the largest concentration of northern gannets on the continent. There are two hundred and twenty-three species of birds on that tiny island. And get this: two months ago, four men clambered around the island for close to a week. They didn't take any of the guided tours, but none of the park employees thought anything of it because they had naturalists' credentials. Then, one day, a warden spied them with cages and what looked like thermal containers. She called the Quebec Provincial Police, but by the time they got out there our nature lovers had scooted away in a high-powered boat."

"Did the police give chase?"

"Are you kidding? The Quebec Provincial Police? They didn't think it was worth it for the sake of a few sea birds. Putting a helicopter in the air would have cost them too much, they said." Hudson jabbed at the computer screen. "Oh … look at this. Apparently, there are just over two thousand bird species listed for all of North and Central America. That makes Bonaventure Island a happy hunting ground, harbouring about ten percent of the entire continent's species and, I suppose, a much, much higher percentage of its sea bird species. Wow. These guys are nothing if not thorough."

"If there were wings on the kitchen sink, it would no doubt go missing too." Irina glanced at her Bulova watch, the last gift Walter had given her. She suddenly felt hungry. "Mr. Elmore Quigley should be at the morgue by now, identifying our dead animal lover. I wonder if he took that dog of his with him? That creature could scare a confession out of a corpse. And it's almost lunchtime. Before we go, though, call up the police in Percé and get that park warden's description of the four bird poachers. Let's see if the local constabulary considered it worthwhile taking down a witness statement."

"But we know it has to be the four guys who killed Sergeant Perron. The licence plate, the car —"

"But we don't know it for sure, do we? And how are we going to get anywhere if we're not sure of our facts?"

Hudson got on the phone and within minutes he had what Irina wanted. "Two black guys, an Asian, and a white guy with big, silver hair."

"I've been thinking, Hudson," whispered Irina.

In Hudson's opinion there wasn't a time when Irina wasn't thinking, but he'd noticed that when this glorious woman actually announced the fact, it would be as deep and penetrating as a torpedo.

Hudson sat at attention. "I'm listening, Irina."

"What have we in the way of missing animals? Thousands of them at least, just from these preliminary Internet checks and the abbreviated list that wildlife gentleman sent us. We can extrapolate to thousands upon thousands. Everything from elephants and rhinos and lions to dogs and pandas and sea birds. If they're to be kept healthy, these animals need space, and lots of it. In fact, something like a puffin needs a cage as big as that of an elephant. So what we have are the makings of the world's largest zoo, especially as each species needs its own particular climate. A polar bear, after all, is not going to be happy taking a sauna with a crocodile. And where, I ask you, is anyone going to put such a zoo and remain undetected?"

"Maybe on a remote island?"

"We live in a world of satellite imagery, Hudson. Any school kid can go to Google Maps and see how many cars are parked in his uncle's driveway halfway around the world."

"But how often is Google Maps updated? And even then, you have to know where to look."

"Exactly. Something of this scale and gravity warrants the utilization of real-time satellite observation. My guess is the military would be only too happy to co-operate with law enforcement agencies in a matter of this consequence. And whoever has organized this plunder of our animals will be fully aware of that fact."

"*Our* animals. Has a nice ring to it. The greening of Irina Drach. So are you suggesting they've gone … underground?"

Irina's phone rang. It was the coroner's office. Elmore Quigley had identified the dead man with the pink face as the same person he'd seen a block from Sergeant Jerome Perron's home. She relayed the news to Hudson, then stared thoughtfully at him for a few moments.

And she stared thoughtfully at the ceiling.

And she scrutinized her outstretched hands for a few moments.

And then she quickly stared at Hudson again, for the hands did seem a little fatter. "So what we have under consideration is a huge zoo, maybe one of the world's largest, being underground. One sheltering creatures that have to live their lives in fresh air under open skies."

"Looks like."

"Is that a smirk I see on your face?"

"I'm sorry, but I think it might be."

"Okay. I will humour you, not just amuse you. For the moment we'll assume that somewhere on the *surface* of this planet — maybe a remote island, like you said — someone is building an enormous zoo. And we shall proceed accordingly. We'll notify our armed forces and see if they have satellites that can provide detailed images of the Earth's surface. And whether or not they do, we'll get them to ask other military services, namely the Americans, if they can help us out. Next, we'll contact our National Central Bureau of Interpol so they can relay our alert and request for information to Interpol headquarters in Lyon, so that they can relay our alert and request for information to each blessed one of the seventy-eight National Central Interpol Bureaus around the world, so that each of them can, in turn, relay our alert and request for information to every national, state, provincial, and municipal police agency. Therefore, after we go downstairs for a bite to eat, you will compose an email that details what we've uncovered so far and asks for co-operation in the investigation. You will ask, in particular, for information about any suspicious trafficking of animals across international borders, new zoo projects, unusual construction sites, and the suspicious movement of heavy construction machinery."

"And this email will be read around the world?"

"It will."

Hudson lovingly stroked the keyboard of his computer as would a sniper stroke his rifle as he set up for a shot. "And it will go out under my name?"

"If you like."

"I think I'll skip lunch, Irina. I'm going to get started on this thing right away. It could take me hours."

"If it's going to take you hours, then you'll need to eat. Smoked meat?"

"Can you bring me back something?"

Irina reluctantly nodded her assent. "In that case I'll take a few minutes to bring Stan up-to-date."

As much as Irina enjoyed eating, she did not like to eat alone. In particular, she enjoyed lunches with her young partner. Along with her sister Latinka's, it was Hudson's company she most relished. Listening to him discuss his hopes and dreams, even the minutiae of his life, was a link with normalcy — or something approaching it. The Irina Drach brain, a hermetically sealed contraption whose workings defied common understanding, needed to be ventilated on a regular basis. Otherwise, its gears tended to become gummed up with the condensed vapours of death and destruction. Especially during the last eighteen months.

"Come in!"

Irina plopped into the chair with a heavy thud. She knew how much Lieutenant Robertson fretted about that rickety piece of furniture. It was a stripped French Canadian kitchen chair that he'd found at a flea market, and he was convinced it was a valuable antique. In Irina's considered opinion, it was junk. "Stan, why don't you take this thing home where it won't cause you pain? Every time I sit in it, you look as if I'd just tugged at your wattles."

"I'm trying to add a bit of class to this place. Look," he said, pointing to an expensively framed print on the wall behind his desk. "Did you notice? It's a Van Gogh."

"Yes, Stanley. *Starry Night*. Very nice. A window onto the soul of the world. Now your office looks like the room of every second college student."

"You'd know what a college student's room looks like, wouldn't you? Well, not me. *I* came up the hard way."

"My years at university were not a picnic, Stanley. I've told you hundreds of times before and I'll tell you again: I worked hard for my degree, and I had to hold down two jobs while I was doing so."

"Philosophy!" Robertson shook his head dismissively and began to pace like a nervous colt. "So? What have you got for me?"

Irina told him. While doing so, she made every effort to increase the frequency of her blinking. This nervous tick, which had presented itself upon her beloved Walter's death, mortified her to no end. But she was willing to make a sacrifice for the benefit of Stan Robertson.

At one point during Irina's dissertation, Robertson stopped and leaned across his desk toward her. "You hate me, don't you?"

"Aren't you interested in the rest of my report?"

"First of all, what makes you think I wouldn't know about the death of Oliver Harvey?"

"But did you connect him to Jerome's murder?"

"Of course I did. You think I can't put two and two together? So, answer the question."

"Hate's a very strong word, Stan."

"All right, then. You resent me. You resent me for being made lieutenant instead of you."

"That was four years ago, Stan."

"But nothing's changed since then. You were a better cop than me then, and you're a better cop than me now. How could you not resent me?"

"Because while I may be a better cop, you might still be a better lieutenant than I could ever be."

"There's your university degree for you! You offer a perfectly seaworthy statement, then with your tone of voice you make it walk the plank!"

Irina's cellphone rang. It was Sergeant Laurent Levine from ballistics. The AR-15 that had been found in the car with Oliver Harvey's body bore his fingerprints. And preliminary indications were that the three bullets retrieved from Jerome Perron's body had been fired from that very weapon.

"Well," said Robertson after Irina had given him a digest of the call, "it's pretty much a wrap, then."

"Excuse me?"

"It looks like we've got Sergeant Perron's killer. We can think about shutting down this case."

"No we can't. There are still three more of them out there. Accessories to Jerome's murder, not to mention the fact that at least one of them is Oliver Harvey's murderer. That qualifies as a crime on my turf."

"You'll never find them. They're part of a very regimented international organization. Very powerful, very sophisticated."

"And the print and ballistics reports are just preliminary. They're probably no more than just educated guesswork. Levine was only giving me a heads-up, that's all. How can you say the case is closed?"

"I want you to get back to the Leblanc murder. Lefarge was in here while you were gone, and it's clear he's in way over his head."

"And what about all that business with the animals? You want me to drop that, too?"

"This department has a budget. We tend our own garden. We can't go pulling up weeds all over hell's half acre."

"We should if it'll clear Jerome completely. And unless we prove that Jerome was killed solely for his dog, we won't have done that."

"Unless those preliminary ballistic reports are mistaken, we have his killer. That should satisfy everyone, including his widow."

"Well *this* widow wants to know who've you been talking to! The commander? The chief? You *know* Beauregard. If it weren't for cops like us, he'd be content to run a force where they rely on anonymous tips just to find their squad cars."

Robertson held the door open. "Our discussion is over. Please leave."

"Or what? You'll call the police? Oh, wait! You don't want to be around policemen, do you? It's bureaucrats you want. Quick! Call out the *fonctionnaires!*"

Robertson slammed the door behind Irina, clipping the tendon of her heel. She didn't feel a thing.

"Sure was noisy in there," said Hudson, looking up from his computer.

"Grab your laptop and come with me. We're going to have lunch and bang out that email together."

There were times when saying no to Irina was guaranteed to incur her wrath, and then there were times when she merely needed a friend. Hudson knew the difference, so he gathered up his effects. "Smoked meat sounds good. I'll have the platter."

Wordlessly, they tromped down the stairs and through the mall to the little deli kiosk. While they were standing in line, Hudson said, "The New South Wales guys called. They found Oliver Harvey's last known address. His sister's house. But he hasn't been there in over a year. Periodically he sends her a wad of cash through the mail and she pays the bills from it, including those for his Visa card. They asked to see his Visa bills for the last year, and she not only produced them but actually turned them over."

Hudson pulled a hastily scribbled list from his pocket.

"They faxed copies of the bills to us. Here's a small sampling of the places Mr. Oliver Harvey has visited in the last year: Argentina, China, England, France, Germany, Japan, Kenya, New Zealand, Sri Lanka, Thailand ... should I go on? There are dozens and dozens of them."

"I'll look at the bills when we get back to the squad room. I suspect we'll be able to match his movements with a fair number of those animal incidents ... yes, Miss ... give me the jumbo smoked meat platter, will you?"

They took their trays to a secluded corner of the cordoned eating area and immediately began work on the email. Hudson was distressed to note that Irina's clash with Robertson had not diminished her appetite. In fact, it seemed to have sharpened it. Irina took a few moments to visit a dessert kiosk and came back with a lemon tart the size of a Frisbee. She was thoughtful enough to bring back a little something for him, as well.

The two officers worked together for a quarter of an hour, until Hudson's hand began to tire from the frenetic pace that Irina was setting. He turned his attention to his fruit cup. "So, Irina. What are we doing here if the powers that be want us to close the file on Jerome Perron?"

"So you overheard?"

"No, but I know you, Irina. When you stepped out of the lieutenant's office you looked like someone who'd had her fist held to the fire. Now you're using that hand to fan the flames."

Irina swallowed a wedge of tart the size of a doorstop and stared straight ahead, unblinking. Unblinking because she was not staring into space but into time, and she knew that was how the future would have to be faced.

CHAPTER SIX

The Doomsday Complex. September 4, 2006. Armed with the thoroughly plausible excuse that the stallion's waning condition warranted extra attention, Jósef Krasicki announced he would stay late that night. Perhaps even overnight.

When Mustafa Arman and Han Xinwu completed their shifts at 10:00 p.m., only two sentries were left to manage.

Apart from being lame and far from robust, Jósef Krasicki was nonviolent by nature. How best to handle Ronald Jones and Bjorn Enquist, both of whom were big and burly enough to crush him like an origami figurine? As he prepared Zarathustra's bedding by heaping fresh straw into a large mound, he considered the matter. Should he knock them unconscious? Not feasible, because he was a full eight inches shorter and at least fifty pounds lighter than either of them. Should he lure the men into the empty pen adjacent to the stallion's and lock them up? A stupid idea, unless he could think of a way to separate them from their AK-47s. A decoy, then? Hardly, since he had no accomplice.

It came to him while he was stroking the reclining stallion's powerful neck. Utter simplicity!

He urged the horse to his feet and first put on his bridle, then his saddle. Next, he went to the guard station and announced that he was on his way to check up on the lion. The guards, who were playing cards in their office, paid the old man little heed.

Jósef limped down the short corridor to I-árishóni's lair. The beast was dozing, so Jósef tapped on the Plexiglas and awakened him.

The great lion rose to his feet and stretched and rippled every muscle in his massive body. He yawned, revealing a cavernous mouth and fangs that could puncture a tractor tire. Then he ambled over to the Plexiglas barrier and returned Krasicki's gaze. When the cat cocked his head sideways, Jósef knew he was requesting an explanation for these unorthodox proceedings. He gave it to him soon enough. With the tranquilizer gun in hand, he unlocked the door to the lion's cage and wedged himself in the triangle formed by the intersections of the door, the pen, and the wall. I-árishóni hesitated for only a few moments, then advanced into the anteroom without so much as a sideways glance at the old man.

Jósef gingerly swung the door to the cat's cage closed, thus exposing himself. I-árishóni swung his great head in Jósef's direction, issued a low rumble, then went back to assessing the short corridor that lay before him. Excellent, thought the little man. Finally, my unappetizing physique is of some value. He threw the tranquilizer gun into a distant corner of the lion's cage where it would not be seen, locked the door, then pushed the key into a heating vent.

Reminding himself that being mauled by a lion was, in the end, not much worse than the summary execution that awaited him for his present actions, Jósef squeezed past the beast and limped as quickly as he could down the corridor, turned the corner by the guard station, and headed for Zarathustra's stall. Once there, he took hold of the stallion's reins and led him down the hallway. By the time he and the horse had arrived at the guards' station, I-árishóni was lunging menacingly at the Plexiglas window of the office while Ronald Jones and Bjorn Enquist cowered behind their desks. When the lion knocked the window out of its frame, it occurred to them that they might want to get on the phone and sound the alarm. As he held the front door of the building open for the lion, Jósef Krasicki said, "Don't forget, you two. You and everyone else harm these animals upon pain of death."

The lion, sensing freedom, bolted through the door. Jósef Krasicki led Zarathustra through it and struggled into the saddle. Once on the pavement of the Champs Élysées, the bizarre little band did not tarry. Krasicki pointed Zarathustra in the direction of the facility's main entrance and the stallion exploded beneath him in a surge of awesome speed. This was the most exhilarating moment Jósef Krasicki had ever known. "If this is what they call reaping the whirlwind," the old man cackled maniacally, "then tallyho!"

I-árishóni hardly needed to be shown the way. He not only could sense from which direction the tendrils of fresh night air emanated, but he was all too aware of the frightful, bone rattling racket produced by the tungsten-carbide discs of the colossal TBM, which was at work boring a back entrance to the facility. Without hesitation, the lion struck out after Jósef and his mount. That the cat could not keep up with Zarathustra did not bother the old man; I-árishóni couldn't outstrip the wind, but he had the power to turn it back.

I-árishóni didn't even run full out. He was a beast who knew freedom, but not fear. Those few souls who happened to be out on the street along which he loped did know fear, however. Most dove for the nearest doorways in a state of complete panic. Those who were taken by surprise collapsed on the pavement, palpitating with fright. A young man who'd been making a delivery of computer equipment fainted. But the lion ignored them all. He bore down on the front entrance, which lay a quarter of a mile away.

"The two animals have escaped!" Ronald Jones shrieked into the emergency phone.

"Ahhh?"

"The two animals have escaped! Close the front entrance!"

Julio Menendez shrieked right back at him, "That thing takes half an hour to close, you stupid fuck! And how in hell did they get loose?"

"The old Pole. He did it! He's riding the horse!"

Suddenly, hundreds of thousands of overhead spotlights were flashing and the entire facility was filled with the screeching of sirens. I-árishóni's ears stung, but he neither slackened nor quickened his pace. Nor did Bjorn Enquist, who was following him from a safe distance in an electric car. Enquist was in radio contact with Julio Menendez's second-in-command. "Just give the word, and I shall bring him down with one shot."

"Where's the tranquilizer gun, for Christ's sake!"

"I could not find it. The old man disposed of it."

Julio Menendez blared into the radio, "Do not hurt that animal, or we will all be disciplined. Just follow him and report his progress to us. We'll try a blockade. Now … where are the old man and the horse?"

"They're too far ahead! I don't know!"

Menendez handed the radio back to his assistant and ran to the shipping dock. He ordered all the truckers to form a barrier across the ramp with their vehicles. The immediate result was mayhem. Men were screaming, and their trucks bashed and scraped each other as they jockeyed into position.

Suddenly there appeared Jósef and Zarathustra, thundering toward the ramp. Julio Menendez aimed his rifle, muttered a quick prayer, and pulled the trigger. But the stallion did not slow. In twenty-two seconds he'd covered the entire distance up the ramp and was galloping under the stars.

When they'd penetrated the night by a quarter of a mile, Jósef reined in the horse and dismounted. He slipped off the bridle and saddle, and slapped Zarathustra's hindquarters.

"God speed, and go south."

He then collapsed to the ground with a hole the size of a nickel between his shoulder blades and one the size of a fist in his chest.

The stallion shook his blood-spattered mane and nuzzled at the old man's lifeless face for a few moments. He reared on hind legs as if in tribute to Jósef Krasicki and stormed off into the blackness, going south.

They were ready for the lion. At the bottom of the ramp, eighteen panel trucks with low road clearance were jammed side by each across its full width, and tightly enough that there were acres of scraped and crumpled metal. Their cabs were pointed toward the ramp so that the cat would approach their high, sheer backsides. The uneasy drivers huddled in their trucks with the doors locked and the windows shut tight.

Julio Menendez and his aide-de-camp were in the security booth. Francois Rousse crossed himself and made promises to the Almighty that would have embarrassed the Pope. Menendez fingered an assault rifle and offered his prayers to the Kalashnikov Corporation.

"Okay, here he comes," radioed Bjorn Enquist. "Just about to turn the corner."

Menendez silenced the sirens and turned up the overhead lights to full strength. He waited. All was still and quiet but for the rhythmic grinding and thumping noises of the tunnel boring machine. They sounded like a drum roll, and only added to the sense of crisis and anticipation.

Suddenly, I-árishóni was poised at the edge of the shipping dock, only fifty feet from the security booth. Julio Menendez sucked in his breath. He'd seen the beast often enough in its cage, behind Plexiglas two inches thick, and had felt omnipotent. But at this moment the animal's wild, brutish power made a mockery of this magnificent construct, and a shambles of their organization. And as if that were not enough, it was now he, Julio Menendez, who was in a cage.

Without thinking, Menendez tapped the Plexiglas window to reassure himself that he was safe. This attracted the lion's attention, and it approached the booth. Francois Rousse bit his knuckles until they bled. Menendez's trigger finger was oily with sweat.

"You have to kill him," whined Rousse. "You have to!"

"Shut up! I can't or we're dead men for sure. Just let me think —"

It was over in seconds. The great cat flung his six hundred potent pounds against the door of the booth and tore it from its hinges. It fell inward, landing on Francois Rousse and covering him. He was the lucky one. Julio Menendez was completely exposed. Before he could raise his Kalashnikov to a firing position, an immense paw with four inch claws had torn away half his neck and a good part of his upper chest.

I-árishóni did not stop to savour the sight of a man in his death throes. He exploded through the back door of the security booth and charged up the ramp.

"Well I'll be fucked," said one of the truckers to his co-driver. "The bugger just went around us!"

The man seated next to him asked, "Should we go after him, or something?"

"Not on your life. What do we do when we catch up to him? Swing open our back doors and offer him our crates of milk? Besides, we don't move until Julio Menendez says so."

At the top of the ramp, I-árishóni paused to lick his blood-soaked paw. Having done that, he let out a fearsome roar in the direction of the humans. Satisfied that they'd been sufficiently intimidated, he dove due south.

CHAPTER SEVEN

Montreal. September 5, 2006. After lunch of the previous day, Irina Drach had spent the afternoon helping Sergeant-Detective Normand Lefarge with the Christine Leblanc murder, in accordance with Lieutenant Robertson's wishes. She'd reviewed all the evidence and mapped out the direction Lefarge would be taking. Given that it was not an overly complex case, Irina had been bored to tears. So much so that she'd scripted Lefarge's lines of questioning right down to the primary suspect's tastes in reading material.

Robertson had witnessed Irina's ostentatious interactions with Sergeant Lefarge, and had been gratified.

What Robertson had not witnessed were the efforts of Athol Hudson with respect to the activities of Oliver Harvey and his coconspirators. Hudson had, of course, alerted Robertson to the fact that ballistics' final report confirmed that the AR-15 semi-automatic with Harvey's fingerprints all over it was the weapon that had been used in the slaying of Sergeant Perron, and that pathology had reported Harvey had been killed within an hour of Sergeant Perron's death by two one-and-one-half-inch puncture wounds to the spinal cord — one above C1 and the other between C1 and C2.

But at the same time, Hudson was furiously matching Oliver Harvey's Visa charges with animal disappearances, compiling incidents as they poured in from the World Wildlife Fund, and polishing up the email and firing it off to both the Canadian Armed Forces and the Canadian National Central Bureau of Interpol.

Robertson had witnessed Hudson's overwrought interactions with his computer, assumed he was helping out Irina and Sergeant Lefarge, and had been gruntled.

It was early. Hudson and Irina were the first to arrive at the squad room.

"Any treats?" Irina asked as Hudson handed her a coffee.

"Here, have a piece of carrot cake ... uh, where are you going, Irina?"

"Never mind. Just have all the data ready for when I get back."

By the time Irina returned, chewing on a chocolate-dipped doughnut, Hudson had everything laid out. He eyed her as she finished off the doughnut and dug into the bag for another.

"Geez. You're not even ashamed."

"Everything has a cost. Even acts of benevolence."

"Benevolence?"

"My mental well-being will benefit the force far more than my shedding a few pounds."

"Ah! So you admit you're putting on weight!"

Irina's wedding ring felt as if it had shrunk several sizes. Before her very eyes, her hands seemed to swell up and turn pink until they looked like baked hams. "I admit no such thing."

"You know, you're really quite the babe, for your age. I don't know why you do these things." With ill-concealed melancholy, Hudson directed her attention to reams of printouts. "All of Oliver Harvey's Visa transactions match up with some kind of animal abduction."

"Stupid. No wonder they killed him."

"Which is not to say that all the animal abductions match up with his Visa transactions. There are tons of episodes where he couldn't possibly have been involved, Irina. This organization is huge and humming."

Irina shuffled through the thick pile of papers. "There isn't a single continent not mentioned here, except for Antarctica. I notice they got their king and emperor penguins from Australian and Danish zoos. You've done a splendid job collating all this information, Hudson. Everything at my chubby little fingertips."

"You joke about it," Hudson scowled, "but it's a downward spiral, Irina. Jokes mean recognition and acceptance. Next comes abandon. However, I won't say a word. Not a word. There are topics more important than your swollen thighs. For instance, I built a database. Everything cross-references. But Irina, there's more here than you realize. If I can direct your attention to here ... and here ... and here —"

"Seed banks?"

"Including the Millennium Seed Bank at Ardingly, England. The people at the WWF are pretty chummy with the folks over at the International Society for Horticultural Science. One of the big-shot botanists had mentioned to Van Kleek that there've been a number of puzzling seed bank raids in the last few years, so what with the Millennium Seed Bank job and our inquiry, Van Kleek got to thinking. He then had Monsieur De Gentilly of the ISHS send us a list of all known seed bank raids. What do you think?"

Irina stared at Hudson for the longest time.

Hudson stared back at Irina.

And everything fell into place for the woman cop.

Irina studied Hudson's lists again, this time in more detail. "Do you know what's missing?"

Hudson was crestfallen. "What?"

"Marine life."

"Well, it would be a logistical nightmare to raid aquariums and SeaWorlds. I guess they get those animals from the wild."

"And where would they put them?"

"I beg your pardon?"

"Assuming that we're dealing with some kind of Noah's ark, and that what they're after is a breeding pair of every kind of plant and animal, where do they put some of the bigger items? Blue whales and great white sharks, for instance?"

"Well ... if they have a tropical island, I guess they have some kind of sea pen, or something."

"Does that make any sense?"

"No. Not really."

"I'm thinking about that seed bank in England, Hudson. And all these other seed banks you've listed here. Seeds, not live plants. Catch my drift?"

"The seeds of animals?"

"Exactly."

Hudson had been standing. He now sank to his seat slowly, the whole time tapping away at his keyboard. "Actually, the incidence of marine kidnappings is virtually nil, now that you mention it. Sea birds, for the most part. Some sea lions and seals, and such. Not fish though, and especially not sharks kept behind two inch Plexiglas. Certainly no whales ... oh, wait, a pair of bottlenose dolphins from the Mallorca Marineland ... and that's about it."

Hudson swivelled in his chair to face Irina. She was avidly inhaling the bouquet of her doughnut. He quickly averted his eyes. "Maybe they figure that the oceans, rivers, and lakes will survive a global catastrophe, so they feel no need to collect aquatic life?"

"Rivers and lakes are drying up at an astonishing rate, or so you say in those talks of yours. Didn't you tell everybody just the other day that the River Jordan's been reduced to a trickle in places? And then there's the pollution and the ocean's acidification. So how safe is marine life?"

Hudson leapt from his seat, aflame with indignation. "If it's not feasible to keep whales and other marine animals, then they must be harvesting eggs and sperm. And that means they're cutting them open and killing them. And if they're killing aquatic life, they could be killing everything else they get their hands on, too!"

"It would simplify the transport of animals across international borders, wouldn't it? Easier to smuggle a vial of elephant sperm than the creature itself."

"You know what this means, eh?"

Irina was already there, but she wasn't going to deprive Hudson of his tiny triumph. In fact, she took it as a matter of personal pride that Hudson was on his way to becoming the second-best detective in the squad. "Do tell."

"It means that your idea about an underground zoo isn't such a half-baked idea, after all."

"Why, thank you, Hudson. I'll try not to let that go to my head."

Hudson was back at his computer. Beaming, he brought up a letter from the office of the chief of Defence. "From General Rick Hillier's very office. It was waiting for me this morning. Read it."

Irina grabbed the nearest chair and positioned it next to Hudson's. She sat and squinted at the screen. "From a Colonel Roger Demers. Not a matter of national defence ... blah, blah, blah ... but he pursued some of the links you gave him and says 'it's clearly a matter of national interest' ... he suggests we contact the Minister of the Environment ... dum, dee dum, dee dum ... yes, here we go! 'Please know that we are taking this matter very seriously. Our satellite data analysts will be alerted to the kinds of activities and projects which you have described. We will also give due consideration to alerting our allies in Nato and Norad concerning this matter.'"

Irina threw her long arms around Hudson and gave him a good shake. "That must have been a heck of a letter you sent them!"

"I don't doubt that it was." The voice was high and strained. Irina spun around to confront Lieutenant Stan Robertson, who was hovering over them like an angry bee.

"I thought I told you, Sergeant Drach, that this case was closed!"

"This is not the kind of case that gets dropped, Stan. It's not some little rubber ball, but something the size of our planet. Oh, wait. It *is* our planet."

"You will refer to me as *Lieutenant*, Sergeant, and you will join me in my office. Now."

Robertson scurried into his office, leaving the door wide open. Irina whispered into Hudson's ear, "Start putting out feelers to the Minister of the Environment's office. I'm going to see a man about a dead horse. Oh, and give me a printout of the letter you sent to the military."

"Right away?"

"Right away."

Irina slammed Robertson's door behind her with the usual gusto, then dropped into the creaky chair as if her legs had been chopped off at the knees. Robertson stopped his pacing long enough to claw at his desk. "Insubordination, Drach! Insubordination, not to mention attempted sabotage of a valuable antique!"

Imperturbably, Irina began to read Hudson's letter aloud. Robertson tried to interject several times but she kept reading as if Robertson were little more than a rude heckler.

"So, *Lieutenant*," said Irina, putting away the printouts, "what do you think?"

"I'll grant you that there's some convincing evidence there, and maybe something should be done about it, but I can't spare you for something like this, and we don't have the budget for something of this scope. Christ, you'll be wanting to galumph all over the bloody world chasing leads. No, this is a matter for the RCMP. The Royal Canadian Mounted Police, our *national* force, in case you've forgotten —"

Oh God. The RCMP. Irina's husband. Dead. "Christ, Irina ... I'm sorry." Robertson grabbed a heavy reference book from the corner of his desk and thumped his head with it.

Irina had been badly stung by the remark, but she recovered quickly. "Careful, Stanley, you might dent it — the book, I mean."

Robertson studied Irina. There was something in her eyes. Not the twinkle of a star in the night sky, but that of a star reflected in a brackish sea. Nonetheless, it was a twinkle. "Christ, what a trooper you are, Irina. Now, if only you could curb your appetite for junk foo —"

"Come now, Lieutenant. Don't push your luck. And I should point out that this letter got a positive response from General Hillier's office. General Rick Hillier!"

"All I wanted to say is that you're a handsome woman, Irina. Extremely handsome. I would hate to see you —"

The tone was sharp. "Where *were* we, Lieutenant?"

"Right," said Robertson. "I was ranting about the RCMP, wasn't I? Well, this is the kind of thing that's right up their alley, Irina. So we're going to turn the file over to them. Might as well, since as soon as they get wind of it they'll relieve us of it anyway. Understood?"

"It's nice of you to say 'us,' Stan. Makes me feel toasty all over. Almost as if you've been with me every inch of the way."

"I beg your pardon, but did I not, yesterday afternoon, suggest that this was a global operation? And did you not say, in response, that my idea was brilliant?"

"What's your point, Stan?"

Robertson stared in disbelief at Irina, shook his head a few times, then bolted for the door. "Sergeant Hudson? Would you please step into my office?"

Hudson closed the door behind him and stood beside Irina. He looked as if he was balancing on a yoga ball. This made Robertson even more irritable. "Oh for God's sake, Hudson. Sit down!"

Hudson sat, crossing one leg over the other. He knew how much Robertson hated that, seeing his men cross their legs. "A flatfoot should keep his feet flat on the floor," the lieutenant was fond of saying. "The furthest he should go is resting an ankle on the knee. If he's got balls, he shouldn't be afraid to show them."

For good measure, Hudson wrapped his foot around the back of his ankle.

"Jeez … don't do that in front of civilians, Hudson. They're liable to think you're a cross-dresser. You're already pretty enough as it is."

Affecting an air of boyish innocence, Hudson unfurled his long legs. "You were saying, Lieutenant?"

"As I've been telling your colleague here, this case is too big for us to handle. So kindly round up any material you have pertaining to it, and all information about your communications with other agencies, and put it all on my desk."

"But Lieutenant, Oliver Harvey was murdered in our jurisdiction. It's our duty to pursue the case."

"Given the wider implications of that event, we can safely say that the RCMP should take over the investigation."

"Oh, by the way, Irina," whispered Hudson to Irina, "they've started to trickle in; emails from forces around the world. And I just got one from our Interpol bureau, too. They say they're being inundated with reports from all over the globe. Murders connected to animal abductions, that sort of thing."

"And Interpol doesn't even have a presence in most of the Third World," Irina replied out of the side of her mouth. "God only knows what's really going on out there."

Robertson slammed his fist on the desk. "Hello? Hello, you two? Do you mind if I break up this little meeting of yours to remind you that I'm your lieutenant, and not one of the cleaning staff?"

"But you're not interested, Stanley," hissed Irina. "This is something you want to fob off onto another agency."

"Whether I'm interested or not is beside the point! And Hudson, I would remind you that Irina Drach is not your commanding officer but merely another sergeant-detective, just like you. You don't report to her, but to me."

"With all due respect, Lieutenant, Irina Drach is not just another sergeant-detective like me. It's safe to say that she is the most astute detective in the Montreal Police Force. Quite probably in the country."

Robertson slumped into his chair and rubbed his eyes with the palms of his hands. "Anything else, Sergeant Hudson?"

"About Sergeant Drach? I could go on for hours —"

"About this case, I mean! Any other messages I should know about?"

"Well, I got a response from the Canadian High Command. And then there's this observation from Interpol Ottawa. Strictly off the record, of course. A lot of the communications they received are from RCMP jurisdictions. You know, outside the big cities, in all provinces but Quebec and Ontario, where they're the only law. Apparently, not a single Mountie twigged to what's going on out there. Not like our own lowly Sergeant-Detective Irina Drach."

"Show me."

"Yes, Sir!" And Hudson bounded out of the office.

Irina purred, "Ah, the optimism of youth, eh?"

"Neither you nor Hudson know what I have in mind, Irina, so keep your observations on human nature to yourself."

"Whatever you say, Stanley."

During Hudson's absence, Robertson paced impatiently while Irina helped herself to the jelly beans in a bowl on the corner of Robertson's desk. Periodically, Robertson would stop in his tracks and fix her with an injured look, as if the latter were robbing him of his virtue. Irina would blink at him vacantly, like a cow contemplating the horizon, and Robertson, exasperated, would resume his pacing with redoubled vigor.

"Here it is," said Hudson as he slid into his chair and deposited the printout on Robertson's desk.

Robertson flung himself into his chair and read avidly. "Hmm. A married couple with a petting zoo near Prince Rupert were bound and gagged and relieved of a breeding pair of grizzlies." Robertson ripped off his reading glasses. "Can anyone tell me what the fuck a grizzly bear is doing in a petting zoo?"

"I'm not sure, Stan," said Irina, "but it certainly speaks well of Canadian children, doesn't it? Tough little nuts."

Robertson replaced his glasses. "To continue: a tagged male moose, nearly eight feet at the shoulders and with an antler spread of seventy-five inches — the biggest such animal in existence, they claim — went missing from a private preserve near Miramichi, New Brunswick. The gatekeeper was bludgeoned nearly to death and they made off with the beast in a horse trailer." Robertson removed his glasses again. "Now, I ask you, how in hell do you get a wild animal that weighs fifteen hundred pounds into a horse box?"

"They're a large, well-organized, and multifaceted group, Lieutenant. They probably have a moose whisperer."

Robertson scowled. "You better be careful, Hudson, or you'll grow up to be another Irina Drach."

"I've got my fingers crossed, Sir."

Robertson read on, then sighed. "And so on, and so on. Plenty of incidents in RCMP country, and the clueless bastards didn't connect the dots. Now show me the letter from Hillier's office." He read, then took off his glasses and studied the two officers seated before him. Finally, he said, "I'll give you a week — one week — to make some headway in the murder of this Oliver Harvey. But no travelling. Use your brains, not your feet. In the meantime, I'll run interference for you, starting with Commander Belanger."

CHAPTER EIGHT

The Doomsday Complex. September 4–5, 2006. Fortunately for its human denizens, not all of the animals at the facility were in test tubes or petrie dishes. There were the tracking and guard dogs — or what remained of them after I-árishóni had slashed his way through their ranks.

Unfortunately, it had taken hours to get the trackers on the trail. The loss of the facility's chief of security had left something of a gap in the organization. And his second-in-command, having been within inches of the carnage wrought by the lion, had been traumatized to the point of complete inertia. Then there was the matter of tranquilizer guns. Given the nature of the complex, there weren't any, apart from the one that Jósef Krasicki had tossed into the cage. They'd had to dispatch their fastest float plane to fly out to the nearest airstrip for a rendezvous with a private jet that had flown in a supply of the devices from the nearest city.

By the time the bloodhounds, bassets, and German shepherds had their snouts to the ground and the two helicopters had left it, the horse and the lion were miles away. I-árishóni had travelled a good forty miles and Zarathustra had gone one hundred. Both had plunged into the boreal forest.

"Jesus H. Christ," grumbled Antanas Sruoga as he adjusted his infrared binoculars and peered into the bush below. "What good is thermal imaging if you can't tell the buggers from deer and bears?"

"But you must use your head, my friend," intoned Vikram Ghosh as he swooped the chopper to within fifty feet of the treetops. "The lion is big and the horse moves fast. And what else will be roving around at this time of night?"

"The wolves, you idiot, and I'm watching a pack of eight even as we speak. They're headed southeast."

"Ah, yes. The wolves. Pray they don't get the stallion. The big man will be visiting the complex soon, and if anything happens to either of those animals —"

They both shuddered.

"Have you heard from the dog teams?"

"Five minutes ago," said Ghosh. "They're still heading due south, so we must be searching the right general area."

In fact, both animals had altered their courses. Independently of each other, they were now moving in a southeasterly direction, putting them at a remove of several miles from the helicopters' target areas. It was a chilly night, and even if the horse and lion weren't set upon putting as much distance as possible between themselves and the facility, the falling temperature would have encouraged them to stay on the move. This was neither Kentucky nor Kenya. The gap between the two fugitives and the helicopters kept widening.

But the tracker dogs, followed by their handlers in all-terrain vehicles, were holding to a relentless pace. Within three hours of leaving the facility, they too were being swallowed up by the forest. The ATVs had to slow up a bit, but the drivers rightly calculated that they were moving along at least as briskly as their prey. And they guessed that the swifter of the escapees would soon be slowed considerably as the bush became denser.

They guessed correctly. In his fourth hour of freedom, Zarathustra was finding it increasingly difficult to negotiate his way through the deepening woodland. As well, the quick gait to which he'd been keeping was taking its toll. He was tired, and the breath he expelled into the raw night swirled and billowed like steam from a locomotive. When he happened upon a deer path that had been carved out of the wilderness by fleet, dancing hooves since time immemorial, he followed it at a slow trot.

It was not long before the stallion came upon a herd of six white-tailed deer huddled together for the night in a small meadow. In accordance with the laws of peaceful coexistence among ungulates, they were completely unperturbed by his presence. For ninety minutes he rested in their company and cropped contentedly at the long, tough grass. Eventually, the stag raised his head high, shook his antlers, and pawed at the ground with great agitation. There was something ominous on the northwest wind. Zarathustra sensed the fear, but he could not begin to fathom its cause. There was a vaguely canine scent, but in his experience dogs were no threat at all.

Nevertheless, fear is as contagious as any virus. When the deer noiselessly bounded off in a southeasterly direction, leaving him alone in the clearing, he edged in the direction of their flight. As the canine scent grew stronger, he became yet more alarmed, for it now had a component that he could not comprehend.

He followed the deer trail, breaking into a trot. The faster he went, the more fearful he became. He was now moving along at a canter, but that was as fast as he dared go. The trail was narrow, winding, and bumpy, and although it was only days away from a full moon, the tall trees cast deep shadows. Like all horses, he had acute night vision, but at times the gloom beyond the silvered leaves was nearly impenetrable.

From those shadows there suddenly emerged three spectral forms with yellow eyes. They were directly in his path. Predators of any kind, let alone wolves, aren't a notable feature of Kentucky's Bluegrass Region, but Zarathustra immediately recognized these thigh-high creatures as a mortal threat. He stopped in his tracks. He knew that the beasts could not be outrun on this path, and that running would only expose his flanks to them, anyway. He pawed the ground. He reared and churned the air with his forelegs. And while he was doing so, he became aware that three more of the creatures were closing in behind him.

He was trapped. The woods to either side of the trail were too dense to be negotiated at anything more than a crawl.

From those woods, two wolves came at him without warning, as if launched from a catapult. One lunged for his underbelly, the other went for his throat. Zarathustra shook off the forward wolf, but the one at his gut clung to him like a leech. He stepped forward, he backed up, he turned in circles. He even managed to tread on the wolf's hindquarters, but it hung on. In the meantime, the wolf he'd shaken from his throat had vaulted onto his back and had the scruff of his neck in a viselike grip. Both wolves had drawn blood, and now the other six were moving in for the kill. In rapid sequence, the stallion kicked two of the wolves at his rear, sending their broken bodies spiralling off into the forest, but he was vulnerable at his front. One launched himself at his throat and the other two clamped their powerful jaws shut on his forelegs. Now Zarathustra couldn't move, and the remaining wolf to his rear slithered between his hind legs and joined his pack mate in attempting to disembowel him. Zarathustra was in a complete fury, but the more he thrashed about, the more tightly the wolves clung to him.

If the wolves had not been in such a murderous frenzy, and their nostrils so charged with the strong odor of the stallion, they might have sensed his coming. But they did not, and almost instantaneously three of them paid for that with their lives. An enraged I-árishóni was upon them. The two wolves at Zarathustra's gut were mauled almost beyond recognition, and one of the pair at his foreleg had his head mangled and incised from his body. The alpha male at Zarathustra's throat relinquished his grip and turned to flee, but a vicious and powerful downward thrust of the lion's forepaw tore one of his haunches from his torso. While I-árishóni turned his attention to the two remaining hunters, the alpha dragged himself into the dense bush to die a slow and painful death.

The wolf at the stallion's left foreleg escaped. He bolted through a small opening in the underbrush. However, the alpha female at Zarathustra's mane was not so lucky. As she leapt from his back, the horse's hind legs bucked with the force of a jackhammer and caught her in the ribs. She was easy pickings for I-árishóni. As she lay writhing on the path some fifteen feet behind Zarathustra, a maelstrom of fangs and claws descended upon her. Once the lion was done with her, she was completely eviscerated and her head lay at a distance of five feet from her body.

I-árishóni lifted his bloodied snout and looked in Zarathustra's direction. He then moved a few feet in the stallion's direction. The horse, his body covered in lacerations, stood frozen. The lion halted, and Zarathustra then whirled around and set off down the deer trail. Whether I-árishóni had just saved him out of a sense of familiarity and kinship or because he hated anything that in the least resembled hyenas must remain a matter of conjecture, but the thoroughbred definitely sensed that he was no longer in mortal danger. His pace was slow and steady.

I-árishóni spent a few minutes grooming himself, then struck off down the deer path as well.

"This sucks," said Antanas Sruoga. "We keep going in wider and wider circles, but still nothing. Why don't we just set Reg, Victor, and their dogs down in that little clearing. Maybe they can pick up the scent there."

"Not on your life," protested Reg McDuff as he stroked the head of his basset hound. "This is the direction the wolves were headed in. Unless you can equip me with a rocket launcher, you set me down when I say so and not a minute sooner."

"I believe we have strayed a little too far southeast," said Vikram Ghosh, the pilot. "And in my opinion, Bird-Dog Two is too far south. Perhaps we should both backtrack a little bit."

Reg McDuff was a seasoned tracker. He knew full well that Zarathustra and I-árishóni were somewhere below them. The direction the wolves had taken, and the speed at which they'd been travelling, was highly suggestive. But he said nothing. Better to face the wrath of the big man as one of hundreds than to face I-árishóni and a pack of wolves alone.

Vikram Ghosh got on the radio to Bird-Dog Two, and together he and the other pilot determined that they should adjust their trajectory. Just five-hundred yards northwest of I-árishóni's killing ground, Bird-Dog One did an abrupt about face and headed north.

However, the ground crews with their bloodhounds and ATVs had not slackened their pace. They'd gained nearly two hours on the desperadoes.

CHAPTER NINE

Montreal. September 5, 2006. After a lunch of modest proportions — during which she forsook dessert in favour of a salad smothered in ranch dressing — Irina was ready to work. So, too, was Hudson, but the enormity of the task at hand had him bowed, if unbloodied.

"Geez, Irina, where do we start?"

"At the beginning."

"Where's the beginning?"

"Where we came in, of course. Sergeant Jerome Perron's murder, and the murder of his murderer."

"All right. The forensic guys are busy lifting prints and gathering hairs and fibres and such from the insides of that Chrysler 300C, but so what? Where in the world are we going to find a match for them?"

"The boy at the car rental place said that two of the men were not just black, but *really* black. Just as Mr. Elmore Quigley stated, right? And he also overheard Oliver Harvey speaking to the Asian man in a language that had lots of 'ching' and 'yaw' sounds. Now, I'm no linguist, but that sounds like Chinese to me. So, what we probably have are not locals, or even nationals, but internationals. Much as we'd expect of such a far-reaching outfit. Now, what do internationals do?"

"I dunno. Practice inscrutable ways?"

"Is that what your MBA did for you, Sergeant Hudson? Make the world a complete mystery?"

Hudson was not going to be dragged into a discussion about the merits of his education. It was his particular conceit that he read from the thick and heavy book of knowledge. He shrugged.

"Okay, Hudson. Wake up, and let's concentrate on those ways that *are* scrutable."

Hudson leafed through the book of knowledge and drew a blank sheet. He shrugged again.

"Here's a hint. By definition, internationals travel."

"Surely you're not suggesting that we check the airlines to see if two very black men and a Chinese guy booked passage?"

"And why shouldn't we?"

"Because it's ... it's —"

"It's what? A lot of legwork? A long shot? Impossible?"

Hudson sighed. He loved airports. He loved being in them. They always made him feel like a citizen of the world. But the thought of tromping from one wicket to another for hours on end made him queasy. A lot less Sherlock, a lot more gumshoe.

"Relax, Hudson," said Irina, grinning knowingly. "We do it by examining passenger manifests, which I've already lined up."

"Uh ... what if the two black guys aren't internationals. What if they're Americans, with names like Jones or Smith?"

"We'll have to hope they aren't, right?"

"Uh ... what if the two black guys are Somalis or Ethiopians or something, and they have Muslim names? Then somebody could say we're guilty of racial profiling."

"Let me worry about that, okay?"

"Really?"

"No, not really! Don't be such an ass. So far as I know, there's no penalty for nailing a guilty Muslim. At least not yet."

Hudson still looked uneasy.

"Tell you what, though," said Irina. "It's doubtful our unsubs will be

Muslim. Saving the world, being custodians of God's creatures — that's more of a Judeo-Christian thing, isn't it? Protestant, in particular. Look at the Brits. They build underpasses specifically for toads and the like."

Hudson passed his hand through his fair hair and arched his fine eyebrows. He looked at Irina quizzically. He didn't look like a cop. More like a pale, bruised young poet, Irina thought. It was at moments like this that she wished she could clasp that beautiful head to her breast and perhaps even suckle him.

"So you're beginning to have an idea of what kind of person could be behind all this, Irina?"

It took Irina a few moments to respond because she'd suddenly become aware that her nipples were engorged. "You might say. Christian, for the reason I just mentioned. Richer than Midas, for obvious reasons. Middle-aged because young people don't have guilty consciences and go looking for redemption and old people are just too tired. Male, because women's ideas of nurturing don't usually entail killing in the process. Oh, and probably American, for the simple reason that Americans tend to dream about bright, shiny new worlds more than most other people."

"American, as in North American? Does that include Canadians?"

"Possibly, but not likely. Americans dream of reinvention and rebirth. Canadians dream of adapting. That's what makes us so exciting."

"So what if we go through airline passenger lists and find some likelies? How do we corroborate?"

"We'll need the co-operation of police forces around the world. Cops willing to do what we're just about to do. Then we'll look for intersects, and perhaps narrow things down to one locale. It'd be nice if we knew where their head office was, or at least one of their branch offices."

Hudson exhaled heavily.

"Yes, I know, Hudson. Seems hopeless, doesn't it? But that's why they pay us, and why we should get cracking. Besides, it's already been an hour since Stan gave us the green light. We've only got one hundred and sixty-seven left."

"You know, Irina. It's a pretty big assumption that our boys hopped on an international flight. They might still be here, or have taken a domestic flight."

"So we check the domestic flights as well," she replied somewhat defensively. "Can you think of any other way we should be going about this?"

"I'll ... uh ... get in touch with Interpol and see if I can't kick start something. Should we assume that these three guys — and before Oliver Harvey's death, the four of them — travelled together?"

"We have to assume they sat in adjacent seats, or we'll never get anywhere."

At his computer, Hudson began composing yet another lengthy email. Irina went to hers and worked her way through Trudeau International's passenger manifests from the preceding twenty-four hours. While doing so, she munched away at the bag of baby carrots Hudson had given her. She felt quite pious, and even convinced herself that eating them would cleanse her of all the transfats she'd consumed in the previous eighteen months.

For the next half hour, Hudson typed away and Irina scrutinized lists until she was half blind. Then, chewing ferociously, she said, "I think I have something. Last night at 9:35, some people by the names of Mafika Banoobhai, Mazisi Gwala, and Liang Xueqin flew in adjacent seats by British Airways to London, England. They touched down at Heathrow at 9:05 a.m. That's 4:05 a.m. our time."

"Sure sounds like our friends."

"Google those names, Hudson. Make sure they're all males."

"But don't the manifests give their sexes, as well as all other passport info?"

"You will pursue an independent line of inquiry, Hudson. I'll give you nothing but their names."

"What makes you think their names are legit?"

"A hunch. Oliver Harvey used his own name.

"So. Mafika, Mazisi, and Liang?"

"Mafika, Mazisi, and Xueqin. The Chinese put their family names first. As far as I know, Africans don't."

Hudson Googled. "Males. So they touched down at 4:05 a.m. our time, eh? Well ... so much for organizing a greeting party."

Irina drummed her fingers in frustration. "Damn. I wish we'd thought of this sooner."

"Hey, Stan only gave us the go-ahead on this a couple of hours ago. We'd have been exceeding our authority."

"We already were, Hudson."

"But not on all fronts, Irina. And what you've just done with the passenger lists couldn't have been considered until we'd grasped the enormity of the situation, which is what we spent all yesterday afternoon and this morning doing. We don't go running to the airport every time we have a homicide, and you know that. Besides, on what evidence could the London Police even presume to detain and question those suspects? Stop beating yourself up, and look on the positive side. Now we have some names — or probably do, we can't be sure — and we have a destination. And my email is almost ready. I'll be incorporating what you've just learned and, God willing, we might come up with some vectors."

Irina growled like a cat who'd been expecting a trout and had instead been handed a bowl of kibble.

"One more thing, Irina. Given that all we know about them has blossomed from the report given by an old man with a ghastly little pooch, they've no idea we're onto them. They won't feel compelled to assume new identities. Better for us in the long run."

"If they don't know we're onto them, then why did they bolt last night?"

"If they'd known we were onto them, do you really believe they would have gone through customs and security and taken a plane? I'd think they would have lain low in Canada for quite some time. It's a vast country, Irina. Genghis Khan's Mongol hordes could disappear in it without a trace. What's more, if they'd been the bolting kind, they wouldn't have waited until 9:35 last night. They'd have been long gone by then."

Irina laughed. "And to think we started out by my trying to bolster *your* spirits."

"That's what partners are for, Irina. If you hadn't tried and succeeded, I'd have had nothing to give you in return. Oh, and Irina?"

"Hmm?"

"You don't have to eat all those carrots, eh? They're not doughnuts, you know."

A few hours later, Irina had Elmore Quigley and the pimply youth from Indulgence Car Rentals brought in to view the security checkpoint CCTV tapes from the previous night's 9:35 p.m. British Airways flight to London. Elmore Quigley was of no real assistance, since the only face he'd seen clearly through the black Chrysler's windshield had been Oliver Harvey's. The youth, however, made a positive identification of the three men in question, although it did take countless viewings before he made up his mind about the alleged Liang Xueqin. "I can't help it," he'd said somewhat obstreperously. "Orientals all look the same, don't they?"

CHAPTER TEN

Beijing. September 5, 2006. "Master? Mr. Conrad? It is nine o'clock."

Jason Conrad opened his eyes, stared at the Bohemian crystal chandelier set into the glossy coffered ceiling, and did a few backstrokes under the Irish linen sheets. "Did I not tell you 8:30?"

Chinua Amadi began to perspire profusely. "But no, Mr. Conrad! No, Sir!" His clammy hand dove into his jacket pocket and produced an appointment book. "Behold, Sir! Not only did I write it down, but I also wrote down where and when I wrote it down! It was at 10:30 last night, after dinner at the Aria!"

"Are you contradicting me, Chinua?"

"But never, Mr. Conrad! I am merely reminding you that you would never be so foolish as to hire anyone but the most efficient aide!"

Conrad laughed. It might as well have been the wind whistling through a charred tree. "Relax, Chinua. I was only teasing you."

Chinua Amadi conjured up an appreciative laugh. "Oh, Master. Ever the prankster. If only the rest of the world could see you as I do."

Conrad struggled out of bed and slogged, naked but for a towel, to the window. Chinua Amadi gazed upon the emaciated form with the hollow chest and skin the colour of pancake batter, and wondered how a body with so little life in it could hold so much of it in its hands.

"I will go now to my room, Sir, to prepare for the day. If there is anything you require of me, there is the intercom at your bedside."

He closed the heavy door behind him.

Conrad went to the ensuite bathroom. It was slathered in Italian marble and had a sunken whirlpool. A bath? No, rather, a swim. He'd been impressed by the pool. Its raked white columns and suspended egg-crate ceiling with dramatic blue backlighting had brought to mind the Starship *Enterprise*. He jabbed at the intercom on the night table. "Chinua, I feel like a dip. Have them clear the pool. I shouldn't need more than twenty minutes."

"Immediately, Sir!"

Chinua Amadi stood guard while Conrad mostly floated about the pool on his back. It always amazed Amadi that his boss, with so little flesh on his bones, didn't sink as would one of Giacometti's tortured metal sculptures.

After his swim, Conrad dressed himself in casual grey slacks, a navy blazer, and his most comfortable shoes, then prowled around the presidential suite while he waited for Chinua to ascertain that the hotel management would have everything ready at the allotted time. They were in the Beijing Suite, twenty-six-hundred square feet of European neoclassical opulence. He was pleased as he went from bedroom to bedroom, from living room and dining room to the rosewood study, noting that the materials and workmanship were of the highest quality.

"I'm ready, Master," said Chinua Amadi, patting down his jacket pocket. In that pocket was a spanking new Chinese pistol, the 5.8 mm QSZ-92. Notwithstanding that his employer had friends in high places here, Chinua had thought it imprudent to enter China carrying his trusty Beretta.

Anyone who believed Chinua to be nothing more than a fretful flunky didn't know what Jason Conrad knew: that with just a sidearm, Chinua could plug a penny at a hundred feet.

They descended the curvilinear glass tower by elevator, prowled the spacious, splashy, and emphatically Chinese lobby, dominated by massive red-lacquered pillars, while Conrad had a cigarette, then quit the China

World Hotel. On their way to the street, Conrad insisted on both seeing the lobby of the World Trade Center and strolling through the gleaming, thoroughly Western mall that featured outposts of every high-end couturier from Prada, Burberry, and Vuitton to Cartier and Givenchy. At Alfred Dunhill, Conrad bought a kid leather jacket for himself, the same one that Jude Law was pictured modelling in the window, and had it sent up to his suite. And in a fit of largesse, he bought Chinua a red V-neck lamb's wool and angora sweater that the latter had been slavering over. Dripping perspiration the way an ice-cold beer bottle drips condensation, Amadi immediately slipped it on under his jacket, all the while maintaining that there was no ensemble too warm for an African.

They exited the complex on Jianguomenwai Avenue. They were in the Choayang District, Beijing's financial and diplomatic centre, and Jianguomenwai Avenue is the main thoroughfare. It's a divided, ten-lane boulevard that runs from embassy row to the Forbidden City, the notorious Tian'anmen Square, and the Gate of Heavenly Peace in the DongCheng district. This three mile stretch was what Jason Conrad aimed to cover by foot.

"But, Master," Amadi shouted above the roar of the heavy traffic, most of it comprised of European and Korean cars, "the pollution! Is it wise for you to walk such a distance? The sun is shining yet we cannot see more than one thousand feet down the street!"

Conrad did not slacken his pace. "Did you know the International Energy Agency says that if China continues on its present course, it will produce more carbon dioxide within the next twenty-five years than all the world's twenty-six most affluent countries combined? And that, Chinua, includes the U.S., Japan, and all of Europe."

"A fascinating thought, Sir. And sobering. All the more reason to take a taxi. There are over a million cars in this city. Can we not avail ourselves of at least one? Or I could call the chauffeur and he can catch up to us in about two minutes."

"We will walk, Chinua. I will not give in. Furthermore, there are things to be observed on foot that are missed when one is being chauffeured about. For example, have you noticed the dogs that people are walking?"

"Ugly little creatures with squashed faces."

"They're Pekingese, Chinua. The predominant breed in Peking is actually the Pekingese. Isn't that the best? And speaking of squashed faces, have you noticed their heraldic lions?"

"Flat faces, also. Grotesque!"

"That, my dear Chinua, is because people anthropomorphize animals. The Chinese people themselves have flat faces."

Chinua thought of the terracotta horses they'd seen in Xi'an. They'd had elongated snouts, just like the real animals. But he didn't mention it. First, because contradicting his master was the last thing he'd dare do. Conrad would better tolerate a fatal stabbing than a dissenting view. And second, Amadi knew in his heart of hearts that the sophistication of his master's thought processes was such that there would be a perfectly plausible explanation for the exception he'd just noted. Perhaps horses were considered by the Chinese to be of a lower order than lions and dogs, and were therefore thus less subject to anthropomorphizing.

The standards of dress of the majority of pedestrians, and the fact that practically every one of them was not only flaunting a cellphone but jabbering exuberantly into it, caught Chinua a little off guard. Of course he knew that China's economy was booming. Nevertheless, the level of affluence and Westernization had far exceeded his expectations. There was still a poor China in the rural areas, the old communist projects, and in the narrow, winding hutongs left over from imperial China, Mr. Conrad had said, but it was rapidly being replaced by a burgeoning middle class.

"When," Chinua wondered aloud, "will the upward pressure on the old ruling party cause another Tian'anmen Square?"

"Not too far in the future," replied Conrad. "The Chinese leaders talk of progress as if it can be divorced from Westernization, but it can't. Technological progress *is* Westernization. The only people who seem to have grasped that fact are Islamists."

Chinua did his best to sound like a dull but eager student. "What about the Russians? There seems to be a growing anti-Western sentiment among them."

"Ah, the Russians. Good question, Chinua. Good question. They would seem to be the exception, eh? But think about it. Through a series of grievous missteps, progress and prosperity has largely bypassed them. It's no wonder that the proto-fascist Putin is able to consolidate his power. Next thing you know, he'll be actively promoting anti-Western sentiment and getting away with it. He's positioning himself at the centre of a vicious circle."

They were at the intersection of Dongsi Dajie Street and Jianguomenwai Avenue, a third of the way toward their destination. Jason Conrad was tiring. And Amadi, who'd at all times been careful to keep on the street side of Conrad, was tired of glancing sideways and fingering his QSZ-92 every time a car slowed in their vicinity.

"You're right," said Conrad. "The heat and fumes are starting to get to me. Why don't we cut through the Oriental Plaza? It spans an entire block, and it will get us to the next street in air-conditioned comfort. Wangfujing is where I want to turn north, anyway. Big pedestrian shopping street, Wangfujing. The Italians, by the way, have set up camp there for a few days. There'll be plenty of Italian cars to gawk at."

On the steps of Oriental Plaza, at the corner of Jianguomenwai Avenue and Wangfujing Dajie, Conrad pointed to the Beijing Hotel across the street. "I see that Australian steakhouse, Outback, still exists. Maybe on our return we'll stop there for lunch. And over there, on Xiagongfu Street, is — or was, anyway — a massage parlour that gives the best foot massages in town. You up for that?"

Amadi nodded emphatically to both plans. His feet were killing him and the previous night's meal in the China World Hotel — although it had upheld Aria's reputation as the best European restaurant in Beijing — had left his palate in need of a good cleansing. He was a simple man: a green salad and twenty ounces of charred beef were infinitely preferable to coquilles St. Jacques and magret of duck with walnut and garlic sauce.

They sliced through the milling crowds of Wangfujing and were soon winding their way through the Xila, Shaojiu, and Dengshikou hutongs. This was Chinua's first exposure to the underclass of Beijing and the narrow, winding, walled streets in which they lived. He enjoyed it thoroughly. It was nice to get away from the rich and the powerful and the courtiers who attended them. When he remembered that he himself was trailing one of the most powerful men on Earth like a faithful puppy, he stopped in his tracks and laughed out loud. A toothless old woman wrapped in a grimy shawl stared at him as if he were mad and took flight on her dilapidated bicycle. Her own faithful puppy, an equally dilapidated Pekingese, growled ineffectually at him and then it, too, disappeared.

Conrad, who was twenty feet ahead, stared back at him incredulously. As he rushed to catch up, Chinua said, "Sorry, Master, Sir, Mr. Conrad —"

"Christ, Chinua. You're sweating like a pig again. Don't you ever get tired of it?"

"No, Sir. It is an adaptive feature of we black Africans."

"You're shitting me. I know plenty of Africans, and I've never noticed any of them sweating as you do."

"They are perhaps not as well adapted as I am."

"If you're so adaptive, why don't you take that sweater off?"

"This sweater, Sir, was a gift from you to me. To remove it would be extremely maladaptive."

"Ah, I see. Well, how about if I insist you take it off?"

"I would refuse. It is also the first gift you have ever given me."

Conrad laid his hand on his assistant's shoulder. It was the first time he'd ever actually touched him. He'd never even shaken the man's hand. "You don't have to prove your devotion to me, Chinua."

"Yes I do, Sir. In every way and every minute of the day. Otherwise, you would have nobody."

Conrad thought about that for a second. Then he squeezed Chinua's shoulder.

They resumed their trek in lockstep.

"There was a young man back there," whispered Chinua, "better dressed than the rest of the people here. On a new bicycle. He watched me with unseemly interest. Was he a —"

"A policeman? Probably. They're pretty thick on the ground in this city. On my last visit here, I witnessed a drunk and disorderly. He staggered and fell, but he never hit the pavement. Immediately, there were about ten cops to catch him and whisk him away feet first. They just came out of the woodwork."

One hour and five miles from their hotel, they arrived at their destination: Beihai Park, site of the monumental White Pagoda. The temple sits on a hill, which sits on Jade Island, which sits in Beihai Lake, which itself was part of a three-lake system that is near the centre of Beijing, and had been the city's water source in the days of Imperial China.

Conrad paid the admission fee of fifteen Yuan (just under two American dollars) for each of them, and they were inside the park. The one-hundred-and-sixty-five-foot Buddhist pagoda, brilliant under the midday sun, loomed ahead of them, rising out of the lush forest of the island, with its gold-covered copper tip from which bells that jingled in the wind were hung. To Chinua it looked like a pale breast adorned with a pasty, and protruding from a swath of boa feathers. It occurred to him that he was perhaps not having as many sexual encounters as was normal for a man of his age.

"Ah, I remember these," exclaimed Conrad as they approached an ice-cream wagon stationed just before the bridge that led to Jade Island. He rushed the last ten feet to the wagon and bought two confections. He'd already unwrapped one of them and was nibbling away at its chocolate shell by the time Chinua caught up to him. "Here," he said, handing the other over. "Their version of the Nutty Buddy. Iced milk with pistachios and caramel. Delicious. Now let's move. I've got ten minutes."

Conrad led Chinua over the stone pedestrian bridge to Jade Island. To his right, the tranquil waters of Lake Beihai were choked with the largest lily pads he'd ever seen. To his left was the open part of the lake, upon which various rental boats bobbed. By the time they'd reached the islet, Conrad was all business. "For your information, Beihai Park covers one-hundred-sixty-eight acres, more than ninety acres of which is lake. Ten centuries ago, during the Jin Dynasty, Jade Island and two others — which are now joined to the mainland — were created using the earth dug up to create the lake. In the thirteenth century the Mongols conquered the Jin and established the Yuan Dynasty. The first Yuan emperor, Kublai Khan, expanded the site of Beihai Park and made it the centre of Beijing. He lived in what is now the Round City of Beihai Park, which is back near where we came in. We'll look at it on our way out. During the Ming Dynasty, the imperial palace was moved from here to the newly built Forbidden City. In 1651, during the Qing Dynasty, they erected the White Pagoda, which is a Buddhist tower in the Tibetan style. As a political sop, so to speak. Any questions?"

"Uh … perhaps the last Chinese sop to the Tibetans?"

"Could very well be. Now, I want you to stay right here, on this spot, and contemplate what I've just told you and enjoy the sights." Conrad pointed to the brilliant red and gold building one-hundred feet away from them, directly in the path to the White Pagoda. It conformed to Chinua's idea of what a Chinese Pagoda ought to look like, right down to the flying eaves and tubular ceramic tiles. "This here is the Yong An Temple. I'll be seated on that bench just to its west side, over there. Now, he'll know you're here with me, of course, given that he's watching us even as we speak. But he won't be alarmed so long as you don't approach us. Got that?"

"Yes, Sir."

Conrad spun on his heels and started to walk away.

"Uh … Master?"

Conrad stopped in his tracks and retreated toward his assistant. He had an uncommonly acute ear for the sound of distress. It had accounted, in large part, for his success. "Yes, Chinua?"

"I don't understand why it should be you, personally, who makes this transaction. You are putting yourself at risk. Why do you not send an underling?"

"In matters of great importance, Chinua, the Chinese don't like to deal with lieutenants. Or mere aides, if you don't mind my saying so. Also, he knows exactly what I look like from the newspapers and magazines. There can be no mistake or duplicity. Anything else?"

Chinua Amadi shrugged and nibbled at the remains of his iced treat.

Conrad went to the bench and seated himself. Within minutes he was joined by a small, middle-aged Chinese man in a drab business suit and gargantuan glasses that kept sliding down his nose. He kept pushing them back up with his middle finger. If Conrad was annoyed by this overt display of bad nerves, he did not show it. Instead, he began leafing through his park brochure and inquiring about various features of interest. By and by, the little man settled down and responded to Conrad's overtures. Chinua smiled to himself. Just another dumb tourist badgering the natives.

When the Chinese man got up and departed, he left behind a thick folder. Conrad waited a few minutes, then put it into his attaché case along with all the other claptrap he'd removed from it while searching for his Beihai Park leaflet. He rejoined Chinua and they marched back across Yong An Bridge to the Circular City, which had at one time been one of the three islands in Beihai Lake.

"Our friend will be out of the country in two hours. He'll be shunted from cell to cell all over the world until only one person — I know not who — will know his final destination."

At the gates of Beihai Park, they hailed a taxi and, for the grand sum of fourteen Yuan, or just under two American dollars, were soon deposited two miles away at the Beijing Hotel on Wangfujing Street. The taxi driver had recognized Conrad from the newspaper and television coverage.

"You more rich than Bill Gates, yes?"

Conrad had not deigned to answer. He was busy leafing through the folder. To Chinua, he pronounced himself satisfied with his acquisition. So satisfied, in fact, that after lunch at the Outback, when they presented themselves at the reception of the massage parlour, he elected to have a full body massage. He encouraged Chinua to follow suit.

"Happy endings, Sirs?" the tall, saronged beauty asked them without blinking.

Conrad shook his head then turned to Chinua with a whimsical smile. "What about you, Chinua. A happy ending?"

"I'm not sure what that means, Sir."

"Use your imagination, Chinua."

Chinua Amadi did, and he was soon sputtering in indignation. "Sir! What kind of place have you brought me to?"

"Relax," Conrad cackled at his sweating, squirming assistant. "First off, this place is about as wholesome as it gets. Secondly, there are thousands of massage parlours in Beijing, and in each of them it's considered nothing out of the ordinary."

Chinua was emboldened by his virtuous pique. "Then why, Sir, are you yourself not indulging?"

"Because I, Chinua, am not nothing out of the ordinary."

"Well, in certain matters, neither am I. In fact, I've changed my mind. I will have only the foot massage."

As he was led away by a prim young woman in a gold satin uniform, Conrad said, "Fine, suit yourself. But you'll have about forty-five minutes to kill. I suggest you go out to Wangfujing Street when you're done and soak up the atmosphere, maybe go to the Starbucks in the Sun Dong An Plaza. Just be sure you're back here by 1:30."

Alas, there were more outrages in store for the puritanical Chinua Amadi. He'd no sooner endured a foot massage that was sinfully pleasurable — it was almost like having his feet plunged into a vat of warm Vaseline — when he was accosted in the plaza by three attractive young Chinese girls in thoroughly Western garb.

"You American, no?"

"Nigerian."

"Ah. You come to Hotel Beijing? See our paintings? Very nice. Special for you, good price."

Amadi fled along the tiles of the nine-hundred yard Wangfujing Street to the sanctuary of the Starbucks in the Sun Dong An Plaza and had himself a good, stiff triple-shot latté. He gave himself about twenty minutes to take a quick tour of the grandiose and self-conscious seven-level monument to capitalism and was taking in the twin atriums, the glass elevators, and the chrome escalators when a teenage Chinese girl with platinum blond hair and a backpack intercepted him as he paused by the Ralph Lauren shop.

"You American, yes?"

"Nigerian."

"Ah, yes. We China big friends of Africa. Great benefactors. You come Hotel Beijing, see my drawings? Special for you, good price."

Chinua Amadi was not an athletic man. Given his pudgy physique, one would have ventured that he was a particularly unfit academic, especially as any exertion more strenuous than a yawn generally provoked tsunamis of perspiration. On this occasion, however, he sprang like a startled turtle, hopped down the escalators two steps at a time, and flung himself out the doors of the shopping centre. He briskly barged his way across the square in the direction of the massage parlour, all the while informing Conrad by phone that he would not be late.

Suddenly, a big, officious Chinese man was obstructing his path. Another was grabbing hold of his shoulders from behind. His cellphone flew to the ground and broke into several pieces.

"You big hurry?"

Chinua Amadi sputtered and blubbered in protest as the man behind him applied a hammer lock, but nothing vaguely coherent emanated from his mouth. His worst nightmare seemed to be coming true. And the fact that he had a gun in his jacket pocket only added to his distress.

"Why big hurry?"

Chinua babbled on about having to meet his boss, and about the girls who'd try to solicit him, but his clarity of expression was as straitened as his interrogator's comprehension of English.

"Nice sweater," said the big man. "Very nice. You pay?"

Chinua now understood what was going on. In a torrent of words, he tried to explain where he'd gotten the sweater, but the man didn't understand any of it. He began to shout at Chinua in Chinese. And the less it appeared that Chinua understood him, the louder he got and the tighter grew the hold on Chinua's arms.

A sizable crowd of shoppers had now gathered around Chinua and his tormenters. Two more agents materialized and set about dispersing them. Obediently the mob began to recede, even though Chinua's plight was taking on the gruesome glamour of a car crash. The majority of bystanders began to ebb away in the direction of Jianguomenwai Avenue.

Suddenly, they flowed once more in Chinua's direction. The two agents whose job it was to control the hundreds of people were now apoplectic, and began shouting that the full and fearsome weight of the state would be brought down upon their heads if they didn't co-operate. Instead, the crowd parted as if by the hands of God and Jason Conrad strolled through the gap as if he were one of His greatest creations.

His presence was immediately felt by the policemen. Even if one of them had not recognized Conrad, they would have been cowed, such was the force of his personality when he felt like turning it on. They unhanded Chinua and one of them bent over to retrieve the remains of his cellphone for him. Chinua ran to Conrad and babbled out an account of his misadventures. With Chinua bobbing at his side, Conrad strode right up to the agents and stared them down. He looked, Chinua thought, like a field marshall reviewing the troops.

Given what was in the attaché case dangling at Conrad's side, Amadi had to concede that this was an act of breathtaking brass.

Conrad produced the sales slip for the sweater and held it out for the officials' inspection. They bowed, but declined to look at it. The word of such an estimable man was enough for them.

Conrad told them in a thoroughly respectable Mandarin why his assistant had been bustling through the plaza with such agitation. The four policemen listened as if Conrad were divulging state secrets. Then Conrad allowed a slight smile. The men smiled. Conrad began to cackle, and the four men cackled. Finally, Conrad could no longer contain himself, and he began to laugh uproariously. The policemen now laughed uncontrollably, and slapped their thighs as they traded quips. Chinua was quite displeased to note that two of them were wiping tears from their eyes. He was even more displeased to note that many of the bystanders were in on the joke.

"What's so funny, Master?"

"You're in China, where the lower orders all practice the hard sell," wheezed Conrad. "Those girls weren't hookers. They really were art students, and there really is an exhibition of their work at the Hotel Beijing."

Chinua Amadi didn't know whether to laugh or to cry, so he settled for a sheepish grin and some copious perspiration. Things got so bad that he removed his jacket.

"For God's sake, man," gasped Conrad. "It's ninety degrees out! Why not remove the sweater, too?"

"It would be a sign of surpassing ingratitude, Sir," Chinua replied somewhat sanctimoniously. "I shall endure."

And then he bowed to the policemen, and then to the crowd, and everybody decided that the joke was over. Conrad was conspicuously studying his watch.

"Taxi?" said the dominant agent. "You want taxi?"

Immediately, one of the plainclothesmen ran to the corner by the Hotel Beijing, commandeered an Audi A6 with deeply-tinted windows, and, waving aside the crowd of bystanders, had it cross the pedestrian plaza and drive right up to within two feet of Conrad. "This taxi nice one," said the cop as he held open the door. "Air conditioning. Very clean."

Conrad and Chinua Amadi climbed in, the cop barked out the *laowais'* destination — along with a somber warning to drive safely — and the two men were at the China World complex within minutes. For a full half hour they faxed the document that Conrad had secured in Beihai Park, then showered and changed, and were down on Level One of the hotel by 1:45.

Conrad had rented the conference hall for the meeting. It covered a third of an acre, had a thirty-foot ceiling, and could seat two thousand. He'd ordered the hall entirely cleared but for one table and five chairs at dead centre.

"Check the furniture for bugs, Chinua."

Chinua got down on his hands and knees and gave everything a thorough going-over. "Sir, is that why you've rented this hall? So nobody can listen in?"

"Not just, Chinua. When conducting business with the Chinese, the preliminaries and preparation count as much as the deal itself. They will be flattered that I've taken the trouble to rent the most expensive space in town. It will be seen as a sign of immense respect."

"Not to mention prosperity."

"That, too, is of signal importance. Men like these don't want to deal with smallfry. It would reflect poorly on them."

At precisely two o'clock, the large doors swung open and what were obviously three high-ranking government officials were ushered in. They were clearly pleased with the venue, and after the ritual greetings and obligatory refreshments, were ready to do business.

The three men looked identical. Each had wire-rimmed glasses, closely cropped hair, and a blue suit, but the one seated directly opposite Conrad, in the middle chair, Zhang Kaige, was the ranking official. His suit was the bluest. Quite correctly, Conrad acted as if the other two did not exist.

"I have a proposition for you, Mr. Zhang."

"An exciting prospect, Mr. Conrad. You already have extensive interests in our great country, but there can never be enough co-operation with a man as esteemed as yourself."

"I appreciate the compliment, Mr. Zhang. I can only hope that your esteem does not diminish too much as a result of our next transaction."

Zhang was puzzled, but his face gave nothing away. "Oh, Mr. Conrad, I do not believe that building more factories in our country will do anything but increase our esteem for you."

"That's not what I had in mind, Mr. Zhang."

"So then you wish to buy something from us? That, too, is good. Our manufacturing sector grows by leaps and bounds and, as you know only too well, we the government have a fifty percent share of all businesses. Therefore, what you propose can only benefit the Chinese people."

Conrad smiled enigmatically. "Chinua. The documents, please."

Chinua laid the attaché case on the table, withdrew the folder, and pushed it toward Zhang Kaige. Zhang inspected it slowly, page by page. At first he was perplexed, but by the time he was handing the sheets off to his subordinates, he was plainly horrified. "Mr. Conrad, this is highly irregular. These are top-secret documents. May I ask where —"

Conrad leaned forward and looked Zhang straight in the eye. "Of course not. And by the time you have used your considerable resources to answer that very question, that person will have disappeared off the face of the Earth. So, to our transaction?"

"But there can be no transaction. It is preposterous."

"Oh, come now, Mr. Zhang. Surely you don't believe that the file in your hands is the only copy I possess? Or that a copy is not already out of the country? Or, especially, that I would not turn possession of it to my advantage?"

"There is nothing that you, even with all your vast riches, could offer in return for this."

"There is one little thing, Mr. Zhang. My silence. You Chinese are a secretive but proud people. Nothing matters more to you, and especially this regime, than appearances. You want to drive the flashiest car in town, but you don't want anyone to know what's going on under the hood. Now, how would it look to the world if it became known that a security leak of the highest order has plopped the final plans for your pebble-bed reactor into my hands? That the results of your great push to secure three hundred gigawatts of nuclear power by 2020 — three hundred gigawatts, Mr. Zhang, when the *world's* entire output is currently three hundred and fifty gigawatts — are in foreign hands?"

"The world would never tolerate a nuclear reactor in private hands, Mr. Conrad."

"It will be our little secret. You save face, and I use the reactor for a project that is both covert and noble."

"How would you get it into your country?"

"It helps immeasurably that your device is no bigger than a one-car garage and can be shipped in unrecognizable bits and pieces. Heck, given that they can be daisy-chained onto a turbine, I might even take more than one. But to answer your question, we will work together on its transport. You will use your usual bullying tactics, and I will probably play the job-creation card. For all the authorities of my country will know, you'll be exporting mining equipment, and I'll be importing it. It's amazing the accommodations they'll make in order to suck up to China. We're clever people. We'll figure something out."

Zhang and his associates traded telling looks, then applied themselves to sipping at their tea. Only Zhang was able to maintain his composure. He stared hard at Conrad in calculated disbelief. He even condescended to glance at Conrad's secretary. Chinua Amadi squirmed, for rarely had he been in the company of such a cold-eyed autocrat. The only autocrat who surpassed this man sat next to him, and he now spoke again, in the same tone a lesser mortal might use to make an offer on a car. "This would mean a great deal to me, you know. Your 200 megawatt HTR-30 is perfect for my purposes. It's miniscule by current standards, it can't meltdown, and the fuel is sealed inside layers of graphite and impermeable silicon carbide that's good for a million years. And those twenty-seven-thousand uranium-flecked graphite pebbles — they're actually about the size of golf balls, eh? — can just be tucked away into lead-lined coffers once they're depleted. No cauldrons for spent fuel rods, no reinforced concrete fortresses to contain superheated water. Oh, and as if that weren't enough, the thing produces gobs of hydrogen as a byproduct. That could prove very useful."

"You need fuel. Would you expect us to supply that, as well?"

"Among my holdings is a uranium mine. I also have first-class scientists and the facilities to manufacture the pebbles. We'll have no trouble coming up with enriched uranium."

"You have the plans. Why do you want us to supply you with the reactor? Why do you not build it yourself?"

"Risk-taking is what made my fortune, Mr. Zhang. It's also what gets me out of bed in the morning. Besides, it would take me months to tool up. Why should I do that when you have the things ready to go?"

"How can I be sure these plans are what you claim them to be?"

"Well, to begin with, they're on the letterhead of Tsinghua University."

"Still, I must take them and have them authenticated."

"Of course you must. And at the same time, my subtle friend, you'll be convinced that I hold duplicates offshore. So go ahead, take them. And by the way, when your agents track down the destination of my fax from the hotel's machine, they'll find nothing but a dummy telephone account and an empty flat in Manila. A dead end. So tell them not to waste their time."

Zhang rose, gripping the folder. His lackeys followed suit. "You will be in Beijing for a while longer?"

"In this very hotel, Mr. Zhang. As if you didn't know."

Conrad rose from his own seat and offered Zhang his hand. Chinua was astonished that Zhang not only accepted it, but shook it vigorously. "We will contact you. First we verify these documents, then I take your proposal to my superiors."

"Your superior, singular. This will no doubt to go all the way to the top."

"Just so."

Zhang turned and departed with his two assistants in tow. Chinua collapsed face-forward onto the table. "Please tell me that went well, Sir."

"It went exactly as planned," said Conrad as he lit a cigarette. "There's little guesswork involved when you're dealing with a doctrinaire regime."

CHAPTER ELEVEN

Montreal. September 5, 2006. "Geez, Irina," said Hudson in something of a whiny voice as he brought up his emails, "I thought you were on the wagon. You're killing yourself! Do you know there are almost four hundred calories in that bloody doughnut, half of them from trans and saturated fats? Now I'm wishing I'd brought more carrots."

"I'll have you know that this item is smothered in fair-trade chocolate."

Hudson scowled and turned his attention to the screen. "Huh. Not too much. Just a few, mostly from small places. Rotorua in New Zealand, Bandundu in the Democratic Republic of the Congo, Viborg in Denmark, that sort of thing."

"Stands to reason. Cops in large metropolitan areas are going to be far busier and therefore slower — if they're inclined to co-operate with us at all, that is."

"The interesting thing about these emails is that they've been sent directly to us by these foreign forces. Oh, look. Stanley, in the Falkland Islands. Another direct communication. Their superintendent, Auberon Hart, says our three characters boarded a plane for London at Mount Pleasant Airport three months ago, along with a fourth named Oliver

Harvey, not too long after it was evident someone had been trapping culpeos. Wow. Oliver Harvey. That kind of clinches our ID of the other three, doesn't it?"

"What, pray tell, is a culpeo? Sounds like something from a blame game. *Mea Culpeo.*"

Hudson knew Latin, so he was comfortable ignoring her inanity. "A fox, it says here. The Patagonian fox, native to South America and the Falklands."

"Your email mentioned the connection between these three and harvested animals?"

Hudson was indignant. "Of course. And between those four, not just the remaining three."

"Hm. Good police work."

Hudson was mollified, but not completely. Watching Irina eat her doughnut was about as gratifying as watching a snake swallow a frog. "It was a bit of a no-brainer, given that Harvey died only yesterday. Still, it's nice to hear such words from a woman who could die of a stroke at any moment. They have a certain *gravitas.*"

Irina smiled impatiently. "You're getting off-topic, Hudson."

Hudson had scored his point and he didn't want to press his luck. "All right then, let's have a look at the others. A-ha. The Bandundu passenger database in the Democratic Republic of Congo says the fab four flew from that airport to N'Djili International on June 3. I guess we better contact the constabulary in Kinshasa right away, eh? What's next? Oh, five months ago, the quartet went from Rotorua Regional Airport in New Zealand to Auckland. And, *politibetjent* Henning Larsen says our boys, all four of them, flew from Karup International in Viborg direct to Heathrow, back in February of this year."

"Get hold of Kinshasa and Auckland right away. Put some pressure on. Let's see if they flew to London from those places, as well."

"There's beginning to be a bit of a pattern, eh?"

"Sure seems like it."

"Also, it's beginning to look more and more like we're the go-to guys in this case, eh?"

"Insofar as I'm 'one of the guys,' I suppose so Hudson."

"Does it make you just a little bit nervous, all this?"

"The fact that the eyes of every policeman and eco-weenie in the world will be on us?"

"Ouch. I wish you hadn't put it like that."

"You're a cop, Hudson. There is no truth so hard that it can't or shouldn't be put into words."

"You didn't answer my question. Are you nervous?"

Irina brushed at her hair, even though it was pulled back into a ponytail. "The long answer is that we are consummately professional police officers, that we take one case at a time and that the notoriety of a case should have no bearing on our personal sentiments as we doggedly pursue justice." She popped the last morsel of doughnut into her mouth. "The short answer is that if this thing didn't taste so damned good, I'd bring it right back up."

Lieutenant Robertson was standing in his doorway. "Sergeant-Detective Drach! You've not recently condescended to pay your superior a visit. Are you holding something back?"

Robertson disappeared into his office but left the door open.

"Call Kinshasa and Auckland," Irina said to Hudson. "Tell them conclusive evidence links Harvey to a cop's murder and that there's probable cause where the other three are concerned. Get those passenger manifests. Then go to the British Telecom site and look up all four of them in London. Call me as soon as you've got something."

"But you'll be in a meeting."

"That's what he thinks."

The chair had four legs. Why it didn't run when it saw Irina coming must remain one of life's imponderables. "Good afternoon, Stanley."

"Don't good afternoon me. What's up?"

Irina told him. All the while, she strove mightily to neither blink excessively nor torture the chair. "I might need a ticket to London."

"I was wondering why you were going so easy on me. But it won't do you any good. You'll just have to get warrants and the Brits can extradite them."

Irina's phone rang. "Sergeant Drach here."

She listened for a few moments. Her forehead was furrowed like a freshly plowed cornfield as she signed off. "That was Hudson. Who would've thought it, a city like London? You'd expect at least one of every kind of name possible, but there are no Banoobhais and Gwalas listed at all, let alone a Mafika Banoobhai or a Mazisi Gwala. And no Oliver M. Harvey, either. There are about a dozen Liangs, but no Xueqins."

"And that surprises you?"

"Assuming they call London home base, there was a chance there might be. Oliver Harvey used his real name when he rented that car, after all. If he was capable of such a howler —"

"And look what happened to him!"

"Listen, Stanley. Do you have any bright ideas?"

Lieutenant Robertson put his hands in his pockets and intensified his pacing. Irina grew tired of watching after awhile. It was like following the action in an endless pinball game. She leapt from her seat and opened the door. "Hudson! Run Boonabhai, Gwala, and Liang through the Interpol database, pronto!"

"I'm surprised you hadn't already thought of that," said Robertson without slowing a step.

"I had, but there's only so much Hudson can do at once."

Robertson stopped in his tracks. "I'm surprised Hudson hadn't already thought of it."

"I'm sure he had, but he's been busy. I'm surprised you haven't already thought of that."

Wearing a triumphant smile, Robertson slowly and methodically rolled up his sleeves. He then leaned across the desk, his insubstantial torso resting on stringy arms. "Here's what I *have* thought of. If you're so sure Hudson had thought of it, why did you feel it necessary to tell him?"

"Well, Stan, I guess you're not the only one who likes the sound of his own voice. But I do wish you wouldn't second-guess me. It's very unbecoming."

"It's my job, for Christ's sake! I'm your commanding officer —"

Irina's phone rang. She held up her hand as if she were silencing an obnoxious child. Robertson turned purple and resumed pacing with such purposefulness that he might have been trying to stamp out an army of ants.

Irina listened for a few moments then cupped her receiver. "Xueqin Liang, 2002. Robbery and assault in London." She spoke once more into the receiver. "Listen, Hudson —"

"Oh, for Christ's sake!" blustered Robertson. "You're like two teenagers, with your phones. Tell him to get his ass in here!"

Irina signed off. Her smile was a model of forbearance. "No need. He heard you."

The two cops stared at each other expectantly for some time. Then, with a sigh, Robertson began straightening the pictures on his walls. Irina desultorily picked away at Robertson's jelly beans.

"What's keeping him?"

"Probably police work, as opposed to what we're doing. We might as well be a pair of old women."

"Given that stealing someone's jelly beans is normally considered a juvenile transgression, I can only assume you really mean *I'm* acting like an old woman."

"Well, really, Stan. You've straightened those things so much that they're cockeyed again. *Starry Night* looks like Van Gogh himself hung it."

"Listen, you. I know we have something of an awkward relationship, but keep in mind that I've gone to bat for you over this case. I spoke to Commander Belanger and he agreed you could have a week. So please don't give me a hard time."

They lapsed once more into an uncomfortable silence. Silent, but for the chair upon which Irina sat. She managed to get it creaking like a storm-tossed sailing ship. Robertson grew tired of pacing and fiddling, and flopped into his seat. He was already too worn out to comment on Irina Drach's provocations.

Suddenly, Irina ceased her squirming and the office became eerily quiet.

The lieutenant was convinced that this was merely some new chicanery. No doubt she was lulling him, all the while plotting to shock him out of his wits either by some physical or psychological manifestation. Irina was like that. She was larger than life. Not only did she overwhelm the senses, but her very being seeped into and then clogged every cell of one's consciousness. Why he, rather than Irina, had been made lieutenant was beyond him. How could the brass have fallen for his pretense of efficiency and dedication, his jumped-up rendition of spit and polish, when the woman seated before him was clearly not only a superior police officer but the very incarnation of God's wrath? Perhaps the only individual powerful enough to bring down the creeps behind Sergeant Jerome Perron's murder?

Suddenly, Irina brought her hands down hard onto her ballet-dancer's thighs, producing a loud smacking sound. It startled Robertson and he looked up warily, expecting to see a malevolent grin. Robertson's fatigue floated away like a silk scarf on a high wind, for Irina was smiling. A smile full of warmth and fellow-feeling.

"Thanks, Stan," murmured Irina.

"For what?"

"For going to bat for us. That took courage."

Robertson had no time to savour the moment, for there were two perfunctory knocks on his door. Hudson bustled in. "Sorry I took so long, but I just got replies from Kinshasa and Auckland. In both instances, our four nasties flew to London."

Irina said, "Which doesn't necessarily mean they live there, but we can safely say London is a hub of some kind."

"Let's hope it's their head office," said Robertson.

"So what's next, Irina?"

Irina turned apocalyptically to her partner. "What do you think?"

"Well, I guess I'll Google Banoobhai and Gwala. Given that there isn't a single Banoobhai or Gwala in London — with *any* initial — they must come from some very particular region of the globe. South Africa, I'd guess ... from when I was verifying their sex last night."

"I'm confused," said Robertson. "Don't the airline manifests show where they're from?"

"It's a long story," replied Hudson. "Independent lines of inquiry."

"Ah, yes. The recondite ways of Sergeant Drach." Robertson sighed. "So you Google Banooby and Gala. What then, Hudson?"

"See if I can't persuade the London Police to track down Mr. Liang?"

"That's asking a lot of them unless you've done everything else possible," retorted Robertson. "See if your Mr. Liang isn't someone's relative. You have my dispensation to be underhanded about it. Pose as a debtor or something. That usually makes people forthcoming. Oh, one more thing. Check that gang's flights *out* of Heathrow."

Hudson hurriedly left the office. That left Irina and Robertson staring at each other for a few moments.

"Well," said Robertson, clearing his throat, "I suppose I should thank you for letting me get a word in edgewise."

"You and I were partners for years, Stanley. I happen to know that what comes out of your mouth isn't always drivel."

Knowing Irina as well as anyone could, Robertson rightly took that as a compliment. He relaxed, and the two officers then embarked upon a sentimental journey through the past. Their reminiscences about their years together served to remind them that they were not completely unalike, notwithstanding Robertson's position. For a good half hour they laughed, they became contemplative, they almost cried together over the heartbreak to which policemen are exposed almost daily. But it was only when they recalled a case in which a ten-year-old child had witnessed the cold-blooded execution of her parents that they'd had enough.

"So, Irina," mumbled Robertson as he wiped his eyes, "what's behind all these killings and animal-nappings? A government or an individual?"

"I've been giving it a fair bit of thought. An operation of this magnitude and expense would indicate a government. Except for one thing."

"Bureaucracy?"

"Exactly. No matter how like-minded people in a government might be, they're fundamentally wage earners. Employees. People might join government for patriotic reasons, but every civil servant I've ever known is in for selfish reasons as well. Security, pensions, vacations, personal goals, prestige, that sort of thing. But there's something about this case that smacks of cultish behaviour. Surely the people involved — and there must be hundreds and hundreds of them — are aware they'll be called upon to sacrifice everything, even their lives, for the cause?"

"What about cops and the military? They are, too."

"But executed by their own, like that fellow in Kentucky or the woman in France, rather than rescued?"

"We could be talking about fanatical regimes like Iran, or North Korea, or even China or Russia."

"Which brings me to my other point. Our globe-trotting foursome seem to always return to London. Not Tehran, or Pyongyang, or Beijing, or Moscow. And I don't know about you, but I can't see the UK being behind something like this."

"You're right," said Robertson, as he got up to pace. "All the signs point to a cult.

"And cults aren't democratic, or run by committee. There's always a leader. A charismatic leader who commands unquestioned loyalty, obedience, and sacrifice."

"Our leader would be richer than Croesus. He'd have to hold the equivalent of a small country's GNP."

Hudson burst into the office without knocking. "Banoobhai and Gwala are indeed South African names."

"That squares with the Montreal manifests?" Robertson asked Irina.

"It certainly does."

"And, I talked to a Heather Liang on Leighton Gardens in Kensal Rise," Hudson triumphantly announced.

"That's London?" asked Robertson.

"Sure is. Northwest London. And Heather Liang is, guess what?"

"I'll bite," drawled Irina. "His one-year-old daughter?"

"Now how could I speak to a one-year — ah, Irina, you're in one of your good moods, eh? You two must be getting along, for a change. No, Heather Liang is his wife. Or, rather, his estranged wife. She hasn't seen or heard from him in three years, since just about the time he began acting funny. Secretive and mysterious, she says. Talking about a higher power. She thought it pretty weird that he should be interested in doing 'good works.'"

Lieutenant Robertson levitated himself out of his seat and paced back and forth with his hands behind his back, doing his best to look nonchalant. "She'll consent to an in-depth interview?"

"She sure will. She'll even consent to a guided tour of his old haunts. Nothing would please her more than to see him back behind bars."

"And did you check to see if any of them took flights out of Heathrow?"

"Ah ... no. I guess I was kind of swept away by my discovery of Heather Liang."

Robertson looked at Hudson as if he'd just confessed to being a cross-dresser. "Oh, jeez. You were swept away? You actually said that you were *swept away*?"

"I did, Sir."

Robertson slid into his chair and proceeded to tap his pen frenetically on his desk, all the while staring hard at Hudson.

"I, uh ... I guess I meant to say excited, in a tizzy —"

Robertson moaned. "Why don't you quit while you're ahead, Hudson?"

"And forget about those Heathrow calls for now," declared Irina. "We have to discuss our trip to London."

"Our trip? Me too? With you?"

"Someone has to watch my back, not to mention ensure that I'm not swept away by English desserts."

CHAPTER TWELVE

The boreal forest. September 5, 2006. Billy Light Wing was far in advance of the other trackers. The young Ojibway man had grown up in the bush far to the north of Thunder Bay and could guide an all-terrain vehicle through the dense forest like a seamstress guides her fingers through a tangle of thread. Still, he was having some difficulty keeping up with the dogs. The deer path was narrow, bumpy, and so twisty that his headlamp never threw its light more than ten feet ahead of him. Worse still, heavy clouds had rolled in and extinguished the moon and stars. He had a compass, but he much preferred the guidance of the heavens.

Billy had just thumped over the exposed root of a giant old cedar with bone-jarring force when five pairs of eyes lit up at the next bend. He slowed and shouldered his M16. Breathing a sigh of relief, he closed the gap between himself and the illuminated orbs. It was the dogs.

"Come on, you stupid fucks. What're you doing here? Mush!"

Notwithstanding the encouraging words, they did not mush. Instead, they crowded around Billy Light Wing and his ATV with their snouts lowered to the ground and their tails between their legs.

"What is it? Is the lion up ahead? That it?" He laid the barrel of his weapon across the handlebars and scowled at the dogs. "Chickenshits! Just follow me, why don't you?"

As he started up again, the dogs did just that.

They didn't need to exert themselves, however, for Billy was proceeding slowly and cautiously. He'd crept three hundred yards along the path when he stopped, aghast. Never in his twenty-six years, or in his thousands of miles trekked through the wild country, had he witnessed such carnage. He dismounted the ATV and approached the wolves slowly, with his M16 at the ready.

Ugh. There were four of them lying dead on the path, all of them dismembered. Two of them were actually beheaded. He stood in their midst for a few moments, watching the steam rise from the mangled corpses, until a whimpering sound came from the left. Pushing his way through the dense underbrush, Billy came upon a *Ma'iingan* with hindquarters that looked as if they'd been caught in a snow blower. Two bullets to the head ended the wolf's misery. Once back out on the path, he stood stock-still and listened carefully. The faint rustling of leaves coming from the vicinity of his ATV immediately caught his attention. He backtracked those five feet, then veered off into the woods. At a distance of six paces he discovered two more *Ma'iingan*. It was a scene as bizarre as it was grotesque. One, clearly dead, was spread-eagled across the thick lower branches of a maple tree. The other, still alive but struggling to breathe, was lying on the ground. When it lunged for his leg, he put a bullet through its brain.

As he spun in the direction of his ATV, it occurred to him that he was turning his back on something quite extraordinary. With powerful flashlight blazing, he returned to the wolves and carefully examined each of them. The one in the tree had a broken jaw and crushed ribs. The other also had a collapsed ribcage, as well as a broken front leg. The conclusion was inescapable: neither had been savaged by tooth or by claw.

He plowed through the underbrush like a drowning man freeing himself from the roiling surf and ran to the four dead animals strewn about the deer path. Bending to one knee he studied the ground carefully, and found what he was looking for. A horse's hoof prints.

Billy Light Wing let out a tortured scream that scattered the dogs, who'd been skittishly milling about his ATV. He almost ran one over as he gunned the vehicle in the direction he'd come from. There was nothing that could persuade him to continue the chase. A horse and a lion allied in the slaughter of wolves? This was a dark and powerful magic that no mere mortal could hope to combat.

In his frenzy to quit the cursed ground, Billy Light Wing forgot to radio his position and his findings.

The fact that both lions and horses have keen night vision worked in I-árishóni and Zarathustra's favour. A steady pace, in conjunction with Billy Light Wing's disinclination to pursue them, allowed Zarathustra to open up a gap of three hours as the ATV flies, notwithstanding his wounds. I-árishóni managed to maintain a lead of two hours.

Every once in a while, Zarathustra would come upon a small meadow and graze for a few minutes, or would stumble upon a small stream and slake his thirst. The lion, however, had not eaten for days, and required something considerably more substantial than grass shoots. Thus, when he sensed a large body of water, he made straight for it. Gazelles, zebras, giraffes, wild boar ... he would feast.

He abruptly veered off the deer trail, which was redolent with Zarathustra's scent, and plunged into the thicket. The clouds had dispersed, leaving the moon and the Milky Way to cast just enough cold, white light to permit him to dodge those strange and intensely annoying trees and bushes with needles for foliage. Within minutes he was standing on a grassy bluff overlooking a small shimmering lake.

Wading in the shallows and periodically dunking his head to pull up water plants was a beast some six feet tall and weighing about eleven hundred pounds. He was a fright — mouse-coloured and gangly, with an outsized head, a long droopy snout, knobby knees, and large antlers that looked like tattered angels' wings. As if that weren't bad enough, he also had a pouch dangling from his throat. But to I-árishóni he looked enough like a wildebeest to represent dinner.

The lion was downwind from the animal, so he took his time and stealthily worked his way down the slope into a thicket near the lake's edge. He crouched, waiting for the animal to emerge from the water. The average lion can run as fast as fifty miles an hour in short bursts, and leap nearly forty feet. I-árishóni could do much better than that. And he was more than half his prey's weight, making the outcome as certain as if he were setting up for a young antelope.

Half an hour passed before the moose gave any indication that he was interested in anything but eating. When he lifted his head to test the wind, I-árishóni knew that the moment was near, but still he did not move a muscle. The moose could have remained in the water for hours more and the great cat would have remained as inert as granite. But the moose tested the wind again with a sense of smell comparable to a bloodhound's, then began swivelling his large, receptive ears in an effort to triangulate any ominous sound. Satisfied that there was no threat, he waded ashore.

I-árishóni knew precisely when he was going to launch himself at the moose. There was a grassy patch just ten feet inland and twenty feet from his position. If he waited any longer, the moose would be downwind of him and an unnecessary battle would have to be waged.

Unfortunately, another great predator had been stationed in the bushes on the far side of the moose, and had picked a strike zone that was closer to the water's edge. I-árishóni could only watch as a brawny golden creature charged the moose, reared up on its hind legs to a height of eight feet, and delivered a crushing blow with its forepaw. The moose collapsed immediately, and the prodigious brute quickly finished it off with an annihilating bite just behind the skull.

I-árishóni had just had his first exposure to the animal that sits atop an entire continent's food chain — a twelve-hundred-pound grizzly bear.

Like I-árishóni, the bear was far from his native habitat. Two decades earlier, a group of naturalists had determined that it might be exciting to populate these remote forests with an animal whose ancestral home was one thousand miles to the northwest. What they had not taken into account was the fact that the bear's natural prey — mostly muskox and salmon — were entirely absent from this region. Deprived of rich, easily harvested quarry, the trial population had dwindled. Those few that remained were casehardened and ferocious in the extreme, even by grizzly standards.

At any other time the lion would have discreetly retired, for great predators tend not to engage each other in battle unless they're of the same species and are establishing their credentials as prime breeding partners. But I-árishóni was hungry, and this beast had taken his prize. Just as the bear hunched over the moose's swollen belly and began tearing at it, I-árishóni bounded twice and leapt onto the bear's back. The startled brute immediately curled up into a ball to protect his throat, all the while batting at the lion as if he were a bothersome mosquito. That ended when I-árishóni's razor sharp claws razed the bear's face. Immediately, the grizzly reared up on his hind legs and began rubbing at his now useless eyes. This gave the lion all the opening he needed. He dismounted the bear and leapt for the throat. I-árishóni applied twelve-hundred pounds of pressure on the jugular vein and windpipe, then hung on for dear life. His gargantuan adversary's thick, coarse fur damped some of the pressure, but the three-and-three-quarter-inch fangs found their mark. The bear was losing blood and oxygen at a critical rate. He thrashed wildly, pummelling and tearing the lion's torso, but still I-árishóni clung to him like a barnacle to a battleship.

It was over in ninety seconds.

Although the grizzly had been twice I-árishóni's weight, he and the lion were comparable in brute strength. The deciding factor was experience. Bears tend to bluff each other more than they actually fight, and to the largest bear goes the jackpot, be it a female or a fish. Male lions spend much of their time locked in mortal combat with each other. As fearsome as the grizzly had been, he'd never really had a chance against the wily veteran.

With a deep gash in his side and another in his hind leg, I-árishóni limped over to where the moose lay and began to feed. It was not, however, a leisurely meal. I-árishóni felt the pull from the south and the push from the north. Within half an hour, the fugitive was hobbling along the deer path, once more following the horse's scent.

CHAPTER THIRTEEN

Beijing. September 5, 2006. Only hours after his first meeting with Zhang, Jason Conrad was lounging in front of the largest of the flat screen televisions in the Beijing Suite. It was recessed in an eight-foot baroque hutch of some dark, exotic wood. To his immediate left was a marble fireplace flanked by white marble columns. On the mantelpiece of that fireplace sat a baroque mahogany clock and above it was a gold baroque mirror. On the far side of the fireplace, which doubled as a divider, was the elegant little baroque sitting room.

The Chinese, he'd observed, had a weakness for things baroque. Even many of their buildings, whether old or new, commercial or residential, were in the European baroque style. Conrad found that immensely amusing.

If he leaned leftward on the sofa, he could make out Chinua at work in the study. Probably on the schedules. He himself was not working, but relaxing. The television was tuned into CCTV-9, the English language news station. Being an organ of the government, it featured an endless parade of Chinese politicians greeting foreign dignitaries, close-ups of Chinese politicians signing treaties with their foreign counterparts, and soul-stirring vignettes of life and progress in China. The news stories themselves were interesting insofar as they revealed how heavily the Chinese population was still propagandized. CNN it was not. What did interest him in particular, though, were the financial commentators and analysts. They had that same intense, hungry look as their counterparts in the West. Perhaps even more so, given the rapid expansion of the Chinese economy. One almost got the feeling they were calling a race at Le Mans.

When a feature about his visit to China came up on the screen he watched it — but with only marginal interest. He was preoccupied with his collection of golden oldies. Chinua had downloaded twenty-four-hundred tunes from LimeWire and iTunes for him. That collection — unrivalled, he was sure — represented the vast majority of the top-forty songs recorded between 1957 and 1964. Doo wop, rock'n'roll, early soul, surf and car music, the girl groups, it was all there. That was his music, the stuff he'd listened to as an adolescent. And his adolescence was the time when his testosterone had coursed like the Colorado River, when he'd lost his virginity, when he'd gotten his first car, when he'd first fallen in love ... when he'd made his first million.

To be sure, he was a connoisseur of classical music and opera, and generously supported symphony orchestras and opera companies in more than a dozen cities, but given a choice between Bobby Freeman's "Do You Wanna Dance?" and Shubert's "Der Hirt auf dem Felsen," he would not have been hard-pressed for a decision.

He reached for his iPod.

"Master? Sir? Mr. Conrad?"

"Huh?" he muttered, as he concentrated on disentangling the wires.

Chinua Amadi held out the telephone. "It's Mr. Zhang. He wants a meeting within the hour."

"Tell him ninety minutes, and no sooner."

Chinua relayed the message while Conrad jammed the tiny speakers into his ears and tuned in Randy and the Rainbows' "Denise," a celebratory song soggy with the juice of youth.

"He says that will be fine."

"What? Speak louder!"

"He says that will be fine!"

Conrad's head was bobbing up and down. "Where!" he shouted.

"The south wing of the Great Hall of the People!"

"What?"

"The south wing of the Great Hall of the People!! An army detail will meet us at the main entrance, under the big red star!!!"

"We'll be there! Tell him!!"

Chinua relayed Conrad's words to Zhang Kaige, then bustled off to lay out his boss's clothes. Conrad listened to a few more tracks then removed the headphones and smiled to himself. The Great Hall of the People. Zhang was trying to top his renting of the China World Hotel's conference hall. Well, the bugger had done it. Even though it was a glorious example of typically characterless Soviet architecture, the building had forty-two acres of floor space.

He leaned back and did a little mental arithmetic. Then he laughed out loud. Bugger, indeed! The Great Hall of the People was the area of thirty-two football fields, not including the end zones!

"You called, Sir?"

"Yes, I suppose I did. I've got what I want from them!"

Chinua was unused to seeing Conrad in the least bit effusive about some triumph or other. On the other hand, it was not every day that Conrad pitted himself against a superpower. Not so blatantly, at any rate. "Congratulations, Master. Now, I've laid out the Dege & Skinner suit with the coral Timothy Everest tie and the white Rayner & Sturges shirt —"

"The one with the mother-of-pearl buttons?"

"Yes, Master. Now, either the Pradas, the Ferragamos, or the John Lobbs will go nicely with that outfit. Which pair would you prefer?"

"Let's do Savile Row all the way, Chinua. The Lobbs. In my Lobbs, I shall go forth to meet the yobs."

"Very good, Sir."

Conrad listened to a few more tracks, including "Walkin' the Dog." It may not exactly have been a metaphysical reflection on man's place in the universe, but it was funky, and he danced all the way to the shower.

An hour later, Conrad and Amadi were in their chauffeured limousine on Chang'an Avenue, with Tian'anmen Square immediately south and Tian'anmen Gate — a massive red edifice with flying eaves that leads to the Forbidden City — immediately to their north. "Ah, I recognize that building," said Chinua, pointing to Tian'anmen Gate. "Chairman Mao used to wave to the people from that balcony there and review endless processions of troops and missiles. Look. There's a huge portrait of him hanging over the entrance."

"The Tian'anmen, Chinua, means Gate of Heavenly Peace. Ironic in view of what you've just said. We'll get out here, Henry," Conrad said to the chauffeur.

The big black Bentley slid to a halt. Conrad and Chinua disembarked, then took the pedestrian subway under the ten lanes of Chang'an Avenue before emerging onto Tian'anmen Square. "Behold, Chinua," said Conrad with a sweep of his arm, "the world's largest public square. One-hundred-and-eight acres. Don't you just love China? In any other country, this would be considered a waste of prime real estate."

The sun was beating down on the grey stone tiles of the square and sweat was streaming into Chinua's eyes. Between that and the handkerchief with which he was mopping his brow, he could actually see very little.

"That massive obelisk in the centre of the plaza?" exclaimed Conrad, walking briskly through the crowd of tourists, holidaying Chinese, and vendors selling everything from kites and postcards to ice cream and magnetic toys. "That's the Monument to the People's Heroes. One-hundred twenty-five feet high. More than ten thousand tons of stone. Notice that the military doesn't let anyone near it. Not since the Falun Gong protests."

Chinua struggled to keep up with Conrad, who comported himself as if he had an air-conditioning unit integrated into his suit. When he could focus, Chinua was amused by the appearance of the many military personnel patrolling the square. They were skinny young kids, every last one of them, and in their ill-fitting khaki uniforms they looked as if they were dressed up in their fathers' regalia.

They were now halfway across the square. Conrad pointed southward to a large, boxy building with a two-tiered roof and columns ringing it. A line of at least two-thousand people waited to enter the building. "That's Mao Zedong's mausoleum. He's pickled in a crystal sarcophagus. Every time I've been here, there have been that many people lining up to get in there and see him. Sobering, eh? Notice the large composite monument in front of it. See the guy holding the book? I imagine that's young Mao himself leading his soldiers and people forward into a bright and shining future."

Chinua pointed to a plain and monolithic building on the western edge of the square. "Is that where we're going, Sir?"

"It is, Chinua."

Amadi was overcome with relief, for the Great Hall of the People couldn't have been more than a fifth of a mile away. He took little comfort from the fact that a light breeze had arisen and was fluttering the myriad red flags that dotted the square. Chinua dreamed only of sitting down in a cool spot, and from the looks of this building it would likely be no warmer than the Carlsbad Caverns.

Within fifteen minutes they'd come to the edge of the square, crossed the street, climbed innumerable stairs, and were standing under the gigantic Chinese emblem that was suspended one-hundred-twenty-five feet above them. Nobody emerged from the great bronze doors. There was no one there to meet them.

Chinua was leaning against one of the hundred-foot columns that graced the entire facade of the immense building. "Are they snubbing us, Sir?"

Conrad was unperturbed. "Look on the positive side of things, Chinua. The rest of you may be boiling hot, but at least you're cooling your heels."

"How long do you give them, Sir?"

"It depends what they have on us. And if they have what I think they have, then five minutes, not more. I have an option, and they know that."

Chinua was about to ask what Conrad meant when the door suddenly flew open and a detail of seven soldiers emerged. The one at the rear stepped forward and stuck his face within inches of Conrad's.

"Mr. Conrad?"

Conrad glared at the rangy sergeant. The soldier backed off about two feet and repeated his question in a much more civil tone.

"I'm Conrad. Lead on."

"There has been a change of venue, Sir. The People's Congress is not in session. Therefore, your meeting will take place in the main auditorium."

Conrad smiled. "Not in session, eh? Gee whiz, that must have come as a shock. Let's go, then."

The mammoth doors swung open, as if by magic, and Conrad and Chinua were trooped directly to the main auditorium. There, on the stage of an opulent hall that could easily seat ten thousand people, were Zhang and two men Conrad had never before seen. Clearly, these men were not flunkies. The fact that they were mere dots on a dais that could accommodate four hundred did not diminish their glowering presence at all.

As Conrad and Chinua took their seats at a vast table, Chinua looked up at the dusky, remote ceiling and gawked. Imbedded in it were hundreds of lights, giving the appearance of a starry heaven. At its centre, in a scallop with wavy edges that glowed with diffuse white light, an enormous red star was mounted on a circular gold background. The whole thing was galactic in proportions and effect.

"Is impressive in its symbolism, yes?" said one of the strangers to Chinua. "Every individual is a shining star in the firmament of the people's democracy."

Conrad said, "If you're going to use the word democracy, you should at least attach a modifier to it. Centralized, for example."

The man, somewhat porcine in aspect, laughed and thumped the table. "Of course! That is the great strength of the People's Republic! But enough small talk, Mr. Conrad. My colleague Mr. Zhang has something to show you."

Without making any attempt to explain who the two men were, Zhang withdrew a photograph from a folder and pushed it across the table. It pictured Conrad and a small, nervous man with large glasses sitting together in Beihai Park. On the bench between them lay the schematics of the pebble-bed reactor. "So, you see, Mr. Conrad. It is not only the London Police of the UK who avail themselves of closed circuit cameras. Unfortunately, the film was properly interpreted only upon review, and you had departed by then to perform your nefarious task with the documents. However, I can tell you that Professor Song never completed his journey to the airport. He is currently under arrest for high treason."

Conrad did not blink. "And?"

"For obvious reasons we cannot put him on trial, but let me tell you that he will be detained for a long, long time. In fact, he will have disappeared off the face of the Earth."

"Yes?"

Zhang's smooth veneer was beginning to crack around the edges. His superiors were but a curse removed from scowling. "Things will not be easy for him. He might suffer from more than neglect."

"And?"

"Where is your compassion, Mr. Conrad? Your Western preoccupation with the rights of every individual to life, liberty, and the pursuit of happiness?"

"Gentlemen. You're dealing with someone in pursuit of a higher good. There are bound to be martyrs. Surely the honourable representatives of a country that's produced millions upon millions of joyful martyrs can understand that?"

There was a great, long silence. For much of that time, Chinua became the unhappy focus of attention, for he was sweating profusely.

Finally, Zhang looked to the fat man on his left. Barely perceptibly, the fat man nodded. Zhang then looked right to the diminutive man with the white toupee. He, too, nodded.

"Very well," said Zhang. "You shall have what you want. But you are not to share this technology with anyone."

Conrad laughed. "First of all, Mr. Zhang, my project is top secret. Secondly, if it were to become public, then I'd be a dead man, wouldn't I?"

The meeting adjourned abruptly and with few niceties. "The Chinese are generally very formal people, Sir," said Chinua as they were being escorted to their car. "Why did Mr. Zhang not introduce his colleagues?"

"Because if anything goes wrong, they will need to be quite invisible."

"And Mr. Zhang?"

"He will become more visible than he can imagine."

"What do you suppose is going to happen to Professor Song?"

"After some rigorous exercise, he will die a gloriously anonymous death. A pity about that, really, but he knew the risks when he signed on. Now, how would you like to have a peek at the Forbidden City? They have a Starbucks in there, you know."

CHAPTER FOURTEEN

Montreal. September 5, 2006. Lieutenant-Detective Stanley Robertson promised Irina and Hudson that he'd bring up the matter of their London jaunt that very evening, during his regularly scheduled supper meeting with Commander Belanger. Although he knew that Irina's primary intent was to bring the killers of Sergeant Jerome Perron to justice, Robertson also knew that Belanger was less sensitive to the siren song of glory than most. Therefore, Robertson would play the international card.

He didn't foresee much in the way of resistance now that Irina had what appeared to be some solid leads.

It was therefore two rather cheerful detectives who trundled off to supper. Being a Tuesday, the mall's food court was closed, but on this particular occasion the fare there would not have sufficed, anyway, so they jumped into their cruiser and motored to a mid-range Italian restaurant in nearby St-Léonard. Hudson manifested his good spirits by endlessly crissing and crossing the menu, deriving as much delight from the exercise of discrimination as from the actual prospect of consumption. Not having been in a decent restaurant since Walter was killed, Irina thought she might commemorate him by ordering what he would have wanted.

While Hudson was savouring his roast rack of lamb with sautéed zucchini, black olives, garlic jus, and salsa rossa, and Irina was excavating her way through a double dollop of spaghetti and meatballs, they discussed their earlier efforts to get a fix on Mafika Banoobhai and Mazisi Gwala. They most likely had the right country insofar as Telkom South Africa, which controlled all land lines in that country, had given them several Mafika Banoobhais and Mazisi Gwalas. The cellular companies — Vodacom, MTN, and Cell C — also pitched in their lists. So far none of their phone calls had turned up *their* particular Mafika and Mazisi. The task was made a little easier by the fact that if a particular Mafika or Mazisi was home, then he couldn't be their boy, given that he was likely still in London — if the airline manifests were a reliable indicator, that is. But it had nevertheless been a fair bit of drudgery, made much worse by the fruitlessness of it all. Not even their fishing for relatives, using the same subterfuge that Hudson had used for Liang Xueqin, had yielded anything.

"So. What's next, Irina?"

"More of the same, of course."

"Bloody hell. We might as well be telemarketers."

Irina popped a meatball the size of a small apple into her mouth and chewed on it. It was a good twenty seconds before she replied. "Don't be so negative, Hudson. You'll spoil my appetite."

The young couple at the next table snickered.

Irina looked up and set her fork aside. Both outfitted in the latest designer fashions and immaculately groomed, they were feasting by candlelight on the house's most elaborate dishes and sipping a 2001 Nuits St-Georges pinot noir.

Hudson feared the worst.

"You're right to laugh," Irina said to them in an injured tone. "What a spectacle I must make. But you should understand that I am just a poor policewoman who's been on duty for the last twenty-four hours and has not in that time had so much as a stick of gum to chew on. Why, you ask? I have no rational answer. I can only say that I feel compelled — no, driven! — to combat evil and make the world safe for good, law-abiding people such as yourselves in order that you might do something as simple as enjoy a dinner without fear of some thug bursting through the door of this very establishment and spraying its interior with an automatic weapon."

The couple were speechless. Hudson was taken aback, for he'd expected a decidedly more acid riposte. He had no idea where Irina was headed, but he knew one thing: it was the spaghetti talking.

"So I offer you my apologies," oozed Irina as she buttered a roll. "I have not been at all ladylike."

"No, No, No," said the contrite young woman. "It is we who owe you an apology. We had no idea —"

Her paramour spoke in a firm voice. "Officer, let us make it up to you in at least some small way. Please allow us to pay for your and your colleague's lunch."

"No, no, I cannot accept," replied Irina as she swallowed a hunk of bread the size of a small rodent. "It is we who must serve you!"

"I insist!"

Despite Irina's increasingly feeble protests, the young man called over the waiter and offered clear directives as to the arrangement of payment.

"I am overwhelmed," said Irina, seemingly on the brink of tears, "to think that the public — no, not the public, but *you* good people — care enough about your humble servants to visit some small consideration upon them. Thank you, Sir. I thank you. We both thank you. We both thank you both! There is only one small thing —"

"Name it, Officer!"

"Since it's been so long since I last ate, I find I have a headache. From the lack of sugar, experience tells me. In order to rectify that, I'd been planning desert and a cappuccino —"

"Then you shall have it, Officer," declared the young woman grandly. "And your partner too. Might we recommend the chocolate mousse? It is among the best in the city."

"I humbly accept your advice. Consider it done."

With burgeoning enthusiasm and largesse, the young man said, "And your partner looks like a fruit man. He should try the Mediterranean Fruit Salad."

"You should be ashamed," Hudson fumed as he guided the cruiser south-bound on Langelier toward Sherbrooke East.

"Why, fruit man? It made their night, it saved us each sixty dollars, and they now have a new sensitivity toward Montreal's finest."

Back at headquarters, Irina and Hudson spent much of the evening making more phone calls to South Africa. Still no Mafika Banoobhai or Mazisi Gwala of any interest. Airport manifests showed the felons making one round trip together from London to Johannesburg a year earlier, but the trail ended there. They'd taken no connecting flights from Johannesburg to any other part of South Africa.

Irina and Hudson took considerable consolation from the fact that they would rather visit London than Durban or Johannesburg, anyway. Or Donkerpoort or Mosselbaai, for that matter. As they manned the phones, Lieutenant Robertson's meeting with Commander Belanger was never far from their thoughts.

"Time to think about filthy rich people," announced Irina as she munched on one of the dry oatmeal biscuits a desperate Hudson had supplied her.

"I'd rather not until I get my raise. At this point, it would be too much like leafing through *Architectural Digest* or *Forbes* magazine."

"Bingo. *Forbes.* They'll have a list of the world's richest people. Go to their site."

Hudson did a quick check of his mailbox before he did so. There was an email from Interpol Canada, one from Whalewatch, another from the International Society for Horticultural Science, and dozens more from police forces, seed banks, nature preserves, and zoos around the world. "Yikes. This is really picking up steam, eh? Shouldn't we open some of these emails?"

"At this particular moment, Hudson, we don't need to be told that a long-tailed tit has gone missing. We want the names of the richest people around."

"But those are some of the most powerful and respected people on the planet, Irina. Bill Gates, for example. The Bill and Melinda Gates

Foundation actually matches the contribution of the United Nations World Health Organization toward global health. That's equal to the combined effort of one hundred and ninety-two countries! And now that Warren Buffet is in on the act and matching their contribution —"

"Just go to the site, Hudson."

Hudson Googled and within seconds they were staring at *Forbes*'s list of the world's known billionaires and multibillionaires. Eight hundred names. "What now, Irina?"

"Well ... it's time to wave our little Canadian flags. I see we have two entries in the top ten. Jason Conrad ties Gates for first with fifty billion, and Ken Thomson comes in at ninth with nineteen billion."

"What *else*, Irina?"

"Click on a name. See if they give bios and thumbnail sketches of their holdings."

Hudson clicked on William Gates III. There was, indeed, a photograph, a short biography, an account of how he made his fortune, and his current holdings.

"Now click on Conrad."

Hudson clicked on Conrad.

"There," said Irina. "See a difference?"

"Well ... Gates looks like a well-fed chipmunk, whereas Conrad looks like the raven that quoth 'nevermore.' Geez, you'd think with his money he could afford a square meal now and then."

"I read that he's ill. But I'm not talking about their pictures, Hudson. Read about his holdings and how he made his money."

Hudson read. "Hmm. He's got his fingers in more pies than a baker. Mining, manufacturing, steel, telecommunications, pharmaceuticals, shipping, an airline, newspapers, construction, computers, travel, et cetera, et cetera, et cetera."

"See the difference between him and Gates?"

"Well, yes. Gates is Microsoft all the way. A one-trick pony, while Conrad grabs at everything going."

"Exactly. If I were asked to pick which one is a megalomaniac, which one would I go with?"

The reply was swift. "That's a no-brainer. Conrad."

"Yes, Conrad. Now, we know that whoever's behind these animal-nappings has to be fabulously wealthy, right? And we have to assume, for the sake of having some hypothesis, that a person with holdings and interests as diverse as Conrad is the one more likely to be a megalomaniac, right?"

Hudson hesitated again. "Well —"

"And that the person behind the animal business has to be a megalomaniac, right?"

"I guess so."

"So get busy."

"Profiling multibillionaires?"

"Only the top hundred or so. It seems to me that our man would need at least seven billion to maintain an organization of this type."

"How do you arrive at seven billion?"

"Because one hundred is a round number, because seven is a lucky number, because I had to arrive at *something*. Who knows? All I can say is that it's not just a question of hiring hundreds, maybe thousands, of highly specialized people and getting them back and forth across the globe, or of capturing and transshipping animals. There's also the matter of the facility in which his prizes are kept. Even if it's only seeds and sperm and eggs, there's got to be umpteen millions of dollars invested in secure land, storage equipment, and the scientists to make it all work. The felon has to have bottomless pockets."

A crumb from Irina's biscuit landed on Hudson's keyboard. Hudson immediately tried using his spray duster to rectify the problem, but to no avail. The crumb disappeared under the X key. "That's it. This computer is fucked!"

"Relax, Hudson. My keyboard has enough junk in it to feed a family of field mice and it works just fine. Now hold still while I get rid of those crumbs on your shoulder."

Hudson leapt to his feet and brushed at his suit as if it were on fire. "Goddamn, Irina! This is a brand new Hugo Boss!"

"It's a health cookie, Hudson. No grease."

Hudson was not placated. White with rage, he stood inches from Irina and glared at her.

Irina brushed away at his shoulder. "I've changed my mind," she said with infuriating equanimity. "You're obviously in no mood to deal with people who can afford to throw away designer suits like used Kleenexes. I'll do the billionaires while you check the emails."

Fuming, Hudson sank to his seat and began pounding away at his keyboard. "And just what do you propose to do once you have a list of possibles? They must each have armies of lawyers and accountants running interference for them."

"The rule of law applies as much to these people as it does to the shmoe down on the corner. I can march right up to them with my questions and they can't do a damn thing about it."

"Provided they're in our jurisdiction."

"Oh, I don't think I'll have a problem conscripting their local constabulary. Everyone, be they priest, proctologist, or policeman wants to see for themselves whether there's anything ordinary about them."

Irina and Hudson both got busy at their computers. Every once in a while Hudson would remark upon some new animal abduction, or read aloud a communication from some scandalized peace officer. He did it as much to hear himself snarl as to keep his partner informed. For her part, Irina blithely remarked that a pattern was beginning to emerge: while all the top billionaires had diversified their interests to some extent, the vast majority had stuck with the enterprises by which they'd made their fortune.

"Here are the people, in order, after Gates and Conrad. Warren Buffet, forty billion, investments. Carlos Slim Helú of Mexico, thirty billion, communications. Ingvar Kamprad, twenty-eight billion, Ikea. Lakshmi Mittal of India, twenty-four billion, steel. Paul Allen, twenty-two billion, Microsoft cofounder, although he's getting into oil and gas. Bernard Arnault, twenty-two billion, luxury goods like Vuitton, Fendi, and Dior. Prince Alwaleed Bin Talal Alsaud, twenty billion, investments — notably in Citigroup and Fairmont Hotels. Our very own Ken Thomson, nineteen-point-six billion, media and entertainment. It's not until we get to our number ten position, Li Ka-shing of Hong Kong, at nineteen billion, that we get a truly diversified empire. Real estate, communications, retail, hydroelectric power, container terminals, et cetera, et cetera.

"How far have you gotten?"

"That far."

"Well, I'm sure someone as fastidious as you will find more guys like Conrad and Li Ka-shing above your cutoff point."

"Do I detect a sardonic note, Hudson?"

"You knowingly dumped cookie crumbs onto my suit. I am an embittered man."

Irina rolled her chair to within feet of Hudson's. She was blinking uncontrollably. "I am astonished at that statement, Hudson. And very hurt."

"Well ... so maybe it wasn't on purpose."

"You owe me an apology."

"You soil my suit and I should apologize?"

"I did not soil your suit."

"Oh, no?" Hudson took off his jacket and examined it closely. Not even the tiniest of stains. Grunting with dissatisfaction, he put it back on and reseated himself.

"Just for the record, I apologize for being so heedless. Now then, something else is bothering you. What is it?"

"It's your assumption that whomever among these guys has diversified is a megalomaniac. I'm not sure I buy it. More often than not, such practices are based on sound business principles and nothing more."

"Well," said Irina, riding her chair back to her desk and bending over her computer. "Now that you've gotten that off your chest, I hope you feel better. So let's get back to work."

And they did, each unclear as to why their nerves should be raw to the point of oozing. It didn't occur to either of them that Irina's tight little dress, black with yellow piping, might have something to do with it.

During the next hour, Irina bore down and ran through the list of the one hundred richest people, determining that twenty-three of them were worthy of scrutiny. Hudson managed to open the majority of his emails. One entry, a joint letter from Whalewatch and the Chilean chapter of Greenpeace, was especially compelling.

"Fucking asshole! Fucking, fucking asshole!"

Irina raised an eyebrow. It was uncommon for Hudson to swear. "Come now, Hudson. Bury the hatchet."

Hudson let that assumption stand for a few seconds longer than was necessary, then said, "Not you ... one of the people on your list. A female blue whale washed ashore in the Gulf of Corcovado. She'd been killed with a grenade harpoon to the brain and then — get this — her reproductive organs had been surgically removed. Nothing else. No blubber, no meat, just her reproductive organs. With a chainsaw."

"So you're warming to my idea about the billionaires?"

"Well ... maybe. We're talking about a whaling ship, here. And a whaling crew. Major bucks —"

Lieutenant Robertson blew into the squad room. He went right past Irina and Hudson without saying a word, nor even looking at them. His office door slammed shut.

"Odd for him to be here so late. But it still doesn't look good for our trip," whispered Hudson.

Irina had been looking forward to London. She'd never been there. In fact, the only overseas trip she'd ever taken had been to Budapest forty years earlier, to visit her grandparents. But she was not going to let her disappointment show. Instead, she settled for some tuneless humming.

"Do you think maybe we should go ask the lieutenant what happened?"

"That's exactly what he wants us to do."

"What's wrong with doing what he wants? He's our commanding officer!"

Irina hunched over her computer. Damned if she was going to go grovelling to Robertson about her trip. She would sooner go through every single one of the eight hundred names on the billionaire's list.

For the next fifteen minutes, the two detectives worked in a tense silence that was punctuated only by an occasional eruption of outrage from Hudson. Irina uncovered another twenty people who fit her profile.

During that time Robertson's door remained closed, and there was not a peep from within.

Finally, as Irina and Hudson were packing things up for the night, the door flew open. Robertson stood in his doorway, snapping at his suspenders. Irina and Hudson were as still as two gophers studying an eagle overhead.

"C'mon in, you two. Close the door behind you."

They took their seats. Robertson remained standing. For a change, Irina's chair was not creaking and Robertson was not pacing. The two sergeant-detectives stared at him expectantly.

"You're wondering why I've called you in here, no doubt."

"As a matter of fact, no," said Irina.

"You liar."

"I'm offended by that, Stanley! A man like you could want a million different things from us. So what can we do for you?"

Never in a thousand years would Robertson have expected sycophantic behaviour from Irina, but this degree of bloody-mindedness irked him. "All right, then. I have some good news and some bad news. Which would you rather have first?"

"If you want to play games, the bad," said Irina.

Robertson looked at Irina. "You're going to England tomorrow."

Hudson could barely contain himself. "And the good?"

Robertson continued to look at Irina. "You're going to England tomorrow."

Hudson was confused. He looked to his partner for an explanation.

"What he means to say is I'm going and you're not. That right, Stan?"

"I'm afraid so."

While Robertson went on at length about budgetary considerations, Hudson went from disappointment to complete distraction. He looked like someone who'd just been cut from his little league team.

"Well, I too have some good news and some bad news," said Irina in an uncommonly husky voice. "Which would you rather have first?"

"The bad," said Robertson.

"I'm not going to England."

Robertson sighed. "All right, I'll bite. What's the good?"

"I'll go if Hudson is allowed to go."

"It's the commander's decision, Irina. I can't change it."

"Yes, you can. Pick up the phone and call him."

"At this hour? I'll have to frigging call him at his home! And I have no bargaining power!"

"Yes you do. Tell him that before I let him send me on a dangerous mission alone or rob this young officer of a prime learning opportunity, I'll resign."

There was the long, resonant silence of a stone plummeting down a deep well.

And then came the splash.

"Oh, come on, Irina," implored Hudson. "Don't do that. Not on *my* account."

Robertson was now pacing furiously. "Are you serious?"

"I'm close enough to retirement."

"You could be discharged for insubordination. What then of your retirement?"

"I'm willing to take that chance. Call him."

Robertson reluctantly picked up the phone and dialed. After mumbling his apologies to Commander Belanger, he repeated his conversation with Irina. He then scrutinized Irina's impassive face. "Is she serious? I believe so, Sir. Why? Because she's Irina Drach, Sir."

Robertson hung up.

"So?"

"He's busy at the moment."

"Indeed."

"He'll call back in five."

The next few minutes were excruciating for Hudson and Robertson. Hudson crossed and uncrossed his legs dozens of times, and chewed at his nails until his fingertips looked as if they'd been dipped into a Cuisinart. Robertson had ceased pacing. He stood behind his desk, shifting his weight from one outstretched arm to the other while watching the telephone as if it were a ticking time bomb.

Irina, by contrast, displayed all the animus of a marble statue.

"It's hard to believe we got involved with all this only yesterday morning," Hudson chattered. "Seems like a lifetime."

With as much authority as he could muster, Robertson said, "Sergeant Perron's funeral is tomorrow. Even if the commander okays your trip, I trust you'll stick around for it."

"No, Stan," Irina intoned blandly "We're going to England to avenge his death just so we can avoid going to his funeral."

The phone sounded and Robertson grabbed it on the first ring. Despite his best attempt at solemnity, his haggard face bloated with pleasure. "You're on Hudson," he said, cupping the receiver. "Uh, Irina? The commander wants a word with you."

"Good evening, Sir. A shrewd decision. Pardon? What would I have done if you'd refused? Why, I'd have resigned, of course. And then I'd have gone to England at my own expense. No, I would not have been a woman alone. Sergeant-Detective Athol Hudson would have been with me. Do you really think I'm the only one who wants justice for a fellow officer?"

Hudson was at a loss as to how Irina had fathomed thoughts that only seconds before had been hidden from even him. Did she know him better than he knew himself? In any event, it was the proudest moment in his brief career as a detective. He rambunctiously kissed Irina on the cheek, perilously close to her mouth.

Lieutenant Robertson could not help but notice that Irina unconsciously leaned toward Hudson, with her lips parted ever so slightly.

CHAPTER FIFTEEN

Manali, India. September 6, 2006. Although some may think that one yak is pretty much the same as another, nothing could be farther from the truth. As much as they all look like tents with horns and feet, there are considerable differences between wild yaks inhabiting the highlands of western China, Tibet, and northern India, and the domesticated ones that have for centuries been crossed with cattle. First, the wild yaks are blackish in colour while their domesticated cousins can be brown, red, or even white. Second, a wild male yak may be as much as six feet tall and weigh more than a metric ton, while a domesticated yak is barely two thirds that size. Finally, wild yaks are among the hardiest creatures on Earth. These horned, hairy beasts live at higher elevations than any other mammal — often as much as four miles above sea level — and can survive temperatures as low as minus-sixty-degrees Fahrenheit. They subsist on a scrimpy inventory of weeds, scrub grass, and lichen. Domesticated yaks are pampered by comparison and can look forward to a meal more substantial than whatever can be peeled from a rock.

Pony nuts, for instance.

To the uninitiated, pony nuts may sound like what tumbles from the hindquarters of hoofed animals, or an indelicate allusion to the testes of a small horse. In fact, pony nuts are a highly nutritious feed for ponies and horses engaged in light work. They're about eight millimetres in diameter, light brown in colour, and composed of wheat, oats, grass, sunflower meal, molasses, limestone flour, salt, and a host of vitamins and trace elements.

Which brings us to the subject of yak skiing and Manali, India.

Manali, a small town of just over one square mile, is located in the foothills of the western Himalayas, in the northern Indian state of Himachal Pradesh. To roughly ten-thousand people, many of whom are Tibetan, it is a permanent residence. To more than half-a-million tourists annually, it is an idyllic setting offering a temperate summer and a sporting winter climate, breathtaking mountain scenery, and the best hashish in all of India. Manali sits at seven-thousand feet above sea level, but that still isn't high enough for the young backpackers who fill up its hundreds of hotels and guesthouses year round.

Little wonder, then, that Manali should generate something as esoteric as Yak skiing, for which the world owes its gratitude to an enterprising Tibetan named Peter Dorje. He decided there was a crying need for a sport in which a skier is pulled uphill at breakneck speed by a yak steaming in the opposite direction. Although this sport sounds complex, given the two-thousand-pound yak, it is actually simple. Dorje leaves the skier at the bottom of the hill with one end of a rope and a pail of pony nuts. He climbs the hill with his yaks, secures the rope to a tree with a pulley, and ties it around the yak's neck. Here's where the pony nuts come in: the skier ties the rope around his waist, shakes a bucket of the treats, then braces himself for the ride of his life. Oh, and he leaves the pony nuts at the base of the hill. If he can remember to, that is.

In short, the spiritual oasis of Manali has a little something for everybody. And it had a lot for Derek Hull and Jonathan Diamond.

The two burly, ponytailed men, both in their early thirties, brought their cargo truck to a full stop in front of a café on the Mall, downtown Manali's cramped and tumbledown shopping drag. They were tired, having driven the three-hundred-fifty miles from Delhi all the day and night before. And they were cranky, for the truck was old and badly sprung. National Highway Twenty-One had been congested and bumpy, and the rarified air left them feeling less than fit. Not even their sojourn at the Holiday Inn had done much for their moods.

"So tell me again why we couldn't fly from Delhi to Bhuntar?" said Hull in his thick Yorkshire accent as he slammed the door behind him. "That would've given us just thirty fucking miles by road."

"I didn't feel we could take a chance on the truck. What if there'd been none in Bhuntar?"

"Mate! You should've phoned ahead!"

"We're in India, for God's sake! Some guy could have put an outboard motor on a wheelbarrow and called it a truck!"

The two men approached the café window and stared at the boldly lettered notice taped to the glass. "Well," said Hull, "I can see why there's so much static between the Jew-boy tourists and the locals in this town. You all think they're either backward or crooks."

"For your information, whatever friction exists between the Israeli kids and the natives is strictly a function of the Israelis' numbers. Just about every young Israeli who's between military service and his first big job is given a packet of money by his parents and told to get out of the country and blow off some steam. So — to their credit — they come here seeking enlightenment."

Derek Hull laughed maliciously. "Enlightenment, my arse." He turned to the mob streaming along the Mall. "Look at them! They're all pie-eyed, and they stink of *charas* and incense!"

"And you of course know they're all Jewish," replied Diamond irritably.

"You can tell. They're swarthy, and at nine o'clock in the morning they already have five o'clock shadows."

"Maybe they just haven't shaved yet," sniffed Diamond.

"Which proves my point that they've got enough hash up their wazoos to tranquilize a bull elephant. Even the operation of electric razors is beyond them."

Diamond turned in exasperation to the sign. YAK SKIING. INQUIRE WITHIN, it said.

They entered the café, which advertised cappuccinos, lattés, sandwiches, and French pastries on the door, and approached a short, slender Indian man who was in the process of depositing a bill on a customer's table.

"We want to know about the yak skiing," said Diamond.

The little man's tinkling laughter reminded Diamond of wind chimes. "But it is out of season! Our hills are having snow between December and May only. Not now! Only then, the yak skiing!"

"Then why is the sign still up?"

"Ah. Bhagwati Prasad believes in advertising. Don't forget, Peter Dorje was first to present yak skiing to an eager public. My cousin must be trying harder. Market pressures, you must understand. And my name, gentlemen, is Munshi Prasad."

"Well, we're Diamond and Hull and we want to see him anyway. We've come a long way."

"But no one comes a long way to see Bhagwati … ah … *Dhamaki!* You want to see Dhamaki! Every person does. He is well named, eh? Menace and intimidation, that is the English meaning of his name. His fame has spread through all the valleys of Himachal Pradesh. Born wild, you know. Bhagwati raised him as his own child, but still he is a great, evil beast, and there is no yak who descends the mountain faster than Dhamaki. We are even thinking sometimes it is not merely for the treats, but to terrify the skier. To pull, even, the skier's arms from his sockets. But Bhagwati had no choice but to offer a water skiing handle to clasp instead of requesting the customer to tie the rope around him. Much more safety that way. One unfortunate was dragged all the way up the mountain with his face in the snow and never did Dhamaki slacken his pace. Never for one moment, even —"

"Hey, Chingachgook, you're freakin' me out, man." It was the muscular white youth with the frizzy Bob Dylan hair to whom Munshi had been handing a bill when Diamond and Hull had entered the café. In one hand he held an open copy of the Bhagavad Gita in translation. In the other was his bill. He was shaking it violently, as if it were a can of paint. "You charged me for four cappuccinos. I only had two!"

"But no, Sir. You have had four. I have kept a careful record. And how else to explain that you have been here since opening. Two hours plus, even?"

"You're a crook and a rip-off artist!"

The little man was shaking with indignation, but Diamond and Hull could see that he did not want to cause offence. "I assure you, Sir, that this is a reputable establishment —"

The young man rose from his seat and loomed over Munshi Prasad. "And one that depends upon my compatriots for survival. You think I don't know? How would you like it if I organized an Israeli boycott of this dump?"

The little man wilted under the scorching gaze of the youth. "One moment, please," he said as he backed away. "I will even again check my receivables."

"You do that," smirked the youth.

This was more than Derek Hull could stomach. A complete inventory of prejudices had, in his mind, just been validated. He thrust his scarred, weather-beaten face to within inches of the youth's. "You're pretty hard-assed when you're dealing with some little wog, eh? Well, how about someone like me?"

This caught the youth off guard. He took a few steps backward. "This is none of your affair. And I should warn you that I have had military training in hand-to-hand combat."

"Yeah? Well let me tell you about my military training. I haven't had any. And why? Not because they didn't think I wouldn't be a danger to the enemy, but because they were convinced I'd be a danger to my comrades-in-arms. So? You wanna try something?"

Jonathan Diamond stepped between the two men and simultaneously straight-armed them both. The youth was knocked off his feet and Hull was staggered.

"And one more thing," spat out Hull, standing over the youth. "My friend here was in the Golani Brigade for six years. Where were you? Standing sentry in a Jerusalem market?"

"Shut up, Derek, shut up! And *you* —" said Diamond, as he helped the young man to his feet, "are a complete disgrace to our people. So why don't you just pay up and leave with some dignity."

Munshi Prasad, who'd been watching the proceedings with mounting dismay, suddenly burst forth from behind his counter and set about brushing down the clothing of the young man. "I am so sorry, Sir. So sorry. And I have good news. Good news, indeed. I have checked my notes and I have discovered that you were right. Only two coffees, you had. Only two! In addition, I will forgive you them, as you have been so inconvenienced. So, my friend. You are well?"

The young man stared at the cringing little fellow for a few moments, scowled in the direction of Diamond and Hull, then sank his hand into his pocket. "There," he said with withering condescension. "That should cover the two cappuccinos."

And he scooped up his Bhagavad Gita and strode out into the hot morning sun without looking back.

"Well," said Munshi, rubbing his hands together, "well, well, well. Would you two gentlemen like something to eat or drink? My cappuccinos are unrivalled in this town."

"We only want to know where to find your cousin."

Hull stared at the little man through slitted eyes. "That blighter really did have four coffees, didn't he?"

With head bowed, Munshi Pradesh shrugged. "Like you, like any man, I must protect my interests."

"But he'll be back expecting the same deal. And then his friends will come, and *they'll* be expecting the same deal. What then?"

Munshi shrugged again, and persuaded the two men to accept cappuccinos. As they drank, he drew a rough map of Naggar Road just outside the city limits, in the vicinity of the Mountaineering Institute. There, he explained, they would find cousin Bhagwati and his animals. "His abode is not palatial, I even warn you, but who in Manali can afford the lodgings that tourists can?"

"Just one last question," said Diamond. "Does Dhamaki have a preferred treat?"

"He of course craves pony nuts, but he is especially fond of my chocolate eclairs. And why not? They are the best in town."

The two men bought up every chocolate eclair that Munshi Prasad had on hand, along with a few mille-feuilles for insurance, then slowly ground their way through the heavy traffic on the Mall. It was only after they crossed over the churning Beas River by Nehru Park and alighted in East Manali, where the Tibetans and Nepalese live in utter squalor, that it changed from chaotic to merely distressing. From there they chugged south on Naggar Road and finally arrived at what Munshi had called a "suburb" of Manali. It was, in fact, a shanty town. The houses, mostly of wood scraps and rusty corrugated metal, looked as if they'd been erected in a typhoon. At Bhagwati Prasad's property they were hard-pressed to determine which was the house and which was the barn. They looked at each other and shrugged. This was India.

Bhagwati Prasad, having been apprised of their imminent arrival by Munshi, pounced from his front door almost the instant they drove onto his property. Unlike his cousin, he was a large, surly man with a handlebar mustache. His first order of business was to flaunt his new flip-top cellphone. His second was to say he had no tea to offer them, which they would have politely declined, anyway. His third was to lead them to his stable.

"There is a fee to see Dhamaki," he said, as he heedlessly waded through a rivulet of sewage. "He is famous. He has been in the newspapers. Therefore, five hundred rupees for each pair of eyes."

Hull and Diamond readily agreed. But not as readily as Bhagwati turned to face them and extend his hand. With his fourth order of business having been concluded, Bhagwati resumed sloshing through the muck toward the stable. For their parts, Hull and Diamond gingerly tiptoed their way along circuitous routes.

"You Westerners," Bhagwati Prasad said scornfully as he waited for them at the stable door. "You have forgotten that even the most beautiful garden is composed of shit and piss and pus and blood and decayed flesh and plant matter. You stand on the decomposed entrails of your forefathers!"

Once in the stable, Prasad paused before each stall to introduce them to his six other yaks. Neither Hull nor Diamond was particularly keen on prolonging the visit, given that their eyes were watering from the stench, but they made appreciative noises and even inquired whether Bhagwati was married.

"So, you want to know if I live alone here," he said with a fair degree of suspicion. "Well, I am never alone." He withdrew a .357 Smith & Wesson semi-automatic from within the depths of his grimy, baggy trousers. "My friend here is the best kind of friend," he said, waving it about. "He talks only when I want him to."

The two men were not unduly concerned. They were in cramped quarters. As well, each man was quite capable of carving up a pheasant on the wing.

"So here he is, Dhamaki the Great," said Bhagwati, returning his pistol to his pocket.

Although they're bovines, yaks do not moo. They grunt. And this enormous black brute grunted a great deal when he saw the strangers.

"Is he bad-tempered?" Jonathan Diamond asked nervously, jiggling his bag of chocolate pastries.

"At all times, except when he is eating. You may now give him some of Munshi's creations, but not all. I do not want him fat. In but a few months he will be running up and down the hill."

Diamond approached the stall and peered at the yak. Dhamaki was an intimidating beast. He was jet black, stood taller than six feet at his humped, muscular shoulders, and had lethal, upswept horns that were at least twenty inches in length. When the animal suddenly lunged in his direction and thrust his massive head over the stable door, Diamond quickly retreated.

"He smells the chocolate," laughed Bhagwati. "Give it to him now, or he will break down the door."

Diamond did as he was instructed. He offered the pastries slowly, one at a time — for he wanted to keep some in reserve — and was relieved to see that Dhamaki became as compliant as a drooling lapdog. He was just at the point of offering the creature a third eclair when Hull took hold of Bhagwati's long, unkempt hair and slit his throat with the ten-inch blade he'd withdrawn from his boot. "Sorry about this, mate. For the inconvenience, I'll let you keep the thousand rupees."

Prasad's life blood exploded from his body with violent force. It showered Diamond, who was standing three feet in front of him. Bhagwati Prasad's head wobbled about, as if he were a bobble doll, but he did not fall. Hull had severed the strap muscles, the jugular vein, the carotid artery, and the windpipe, but he'd not sliced deeply enough through Bhagwati's thick neck to affect the nervous system. With his chin on his chest, and emitting gasping and gurgling sounds ghastly enough to curdle even the blood of professionals such as Hull and Diamond, he reached into his pocket, pulled out his weapon, and got off a shot before he collapsed to the ground.

Diamond fell almost immediately after him, with a bullet wound to the head.

Hull felt a momentary pang of regret for his ally, but he had work to do. He checked Bhagwati Prasad for a pulse. There was none. Then he stood over the motionless Diamond, wondering whether it was necessary to slit his throat, too. No, he decided. Diamond was done for. He couldn't see an exit wound, which surely meant that the bullet had ricocheted around the inside of his skull, turning his brain into mushroom soup.

Hull scooped the bag from the ground and held out an eclair as he unlatched the stable door. Then, as the yak slobbered happily away at the treat, he backed his way out of the stable and toward the truck. This time, he couldn't avoid fouling his boots with yak and hog excrement, but as long as the yak kept docilely following him, he was on his way toward a successfully completed mission. It was a little tricky keeping the beast occupied while he flung open the doors of the cargo box and pulled out the ramp, but his years of circus work paid off and his yaksmanship was equal to the task. Once the ramp was in place, he flung the last eclair into the back of the truck. The beast obligingly chased after it. Hull secured him in place with a wall-to-wall harness and he was done.

He felt like a yak whisperer.

By the time Bhagwati's young nephew arrived that evening to milk the yaks and feed the pigs, Derek Hull was back in New Delhi. What the nephew found was one dead uncle and a stranger who was seriously wounded.

Wounded, not dead.

CHAPTER SIXTEEN

The boreal forest. September 5, 2006. Billy Light Wing had his ATV roaring like a chainsaw as he plunged back along the deer path in the direction of the facility. He was close to full speed and was paying a heavy price for it. Tree branches whipped and snagged his sweat-stained face and clothing. Rocks and roots rose up to meet him with punishing regularity. By the time he reached the main search party, a full hour after he'd fled the killing ground, he was covered with cuts and bruises and his frame felt as if it had been dismantled then reassembled by a blind man.

"You look like shit and you smell worse," barked Commandant Franz Hauptmann as he stepped forward from the hunting party of thirty dogs and five men. "And your dogs are scared shitless. What in hell is going on?"

Billy Light Wing collapsed to his knees as he disembarked the ATV. Quickly, he scrambled to his feet and saluted the blond, blue-eyed commandant with the lantern jaw. He gave a gasping account of his misadventures.

The commandant was not impressed. "You mean to tell me that you thought magic was at work? You're as much a superstitious savage as your shitting ancestors! So why, at least, did you not radio your findings and your position?"

"It was not in my mind! Besides, you were already travelling as fast as you could. What good would it do?"

"The helicopters, you hopeless turd. The helicopters!"

Commandant Franz Hauptmann was not a tall man. In fact, he was exceedingly short. It would not have been easy for him to get off a head shot at such close range. The heart would be easier. And that is precisely what he did. He withdrew his Walther 9 mm P-1 from his shoulder holster and shot Billy Light Wing twice in the heart. Only when Billy's body was spread out on the ground did he administer the *coup de grâce*.

Franz Hauptmann holstered his smoking pistol and addressed the remaining five men. "A similar fate awaits any one of you pricks who fucks up. Do you understand?"

The five men nodded obligingly.

Having no less an appreciation of Franz Hauptmann's proclivities than did their handlers, the dogs wagged their tails.

"Right," he said to the big black man with his hair in cornrows. "You. Lumumba-dumba, or whatever the fuck your name is. Get on the radio and get those helicopters down here right away. They should fly over us and continue in a southeasterly direction, following the deer path if the stupid shits can find it. Tell them that fuck ups will not be tolerated. We are an efficient, motivated, and highly unified team!"

Meanwhile, some three hours down the trail, I-árishóni was struggling. Though intense, the pain was not the problem. It was the fact that his hind leg was stiffening and slowing him down. As the rising sun cast rapidly shortening shadows, the great cat was making barely ten miles an hour.

Worse still, he was becoming increasingly distracted by thirst. Although he cleaved to the trail and Zarathustra's scent, he would easily be drawn aside by the first intimation of water.

Phillip Heward III and George Bjorn of Minneapolis stood on the pontoon of the DHC-3 Otter as it bobbed on a cold, spring-fed lake ringed by dense forest. As the pilot tied the bush plane to the roughhewn dock and the guides began unloading their hunting gear, Heward and Bjorn took a moment to breathe deeply the crisp morning air and absorb the untamed wonders that surrounded them.

"Shee-it. If this is a dream, don't wake me."

"Gotcha."

"Probably not another soul for four-hundred miles."

"The plane does one-hundred-and-fifty miles an hour. I reckon four hundred and fifty."

"Hey, John," said the balding and heavyset Heward to the pilot, "what do you reckon is the nearest decent-sized town to here?"

"That'll be Dryden, Sir. About three hundred miles due south."

A tall, fit, and taciturn man, George Bjorn took upon himself the task of expressing their immense satisfaction. "Damn."

As one, they seated themselves on the upturned red kevlar canoe lashed to the pontoon rigging. They listened in reverent silence to the call of a loon, the light splash of a feeding fish, and they watched the sun burn the morning mist off the crystal waters.

"George," said Heward, "you see that? The trout that just surfaced was about sixteen inches long."

"Damn."

The two men were here to hunt bears and moose. But at this particular moment, neither would have been vexed if they didn't move again for the rest of their lives. The waters of the lake reflected the tranquility of their minds and spirits.

"Uh, Gentlemen," whispered Willie Gleason, the wiry, weather-beaten chief guide, "mind if I ask you to step onto the dock? I've gotta get this canoe into the water."

Both men obliged him and stood in companionable silence while the three guides swiftly and methodically finished unloading their four-hundred pounds of hunting and camping gear. After a few minutes, Heward removed the binoculars from the case slung around his neck and lifted them to his eyes. He studied the far shoreline. "Willie, something I've always wanted to know: do bears have tails?"

"They do, Mr. Heward," smiled Willie through his gapped teeth. "About four inches long. Just a little flap of skin that dangles over their assholes."

"Why is that, do you know?"

"Well, most animals use their tails for communication. Wagging tails, stiff tails, arched tails, drooping tails, they all mean something special. Wolves, for instance. Bears are different. All their communication is done head on. When they rear up on their hind legs to maybe make a threatening gesture, the other bear can't even see their asses. A tail would be useless. So over millions of years, the tail shrivelled to nothing — or so the theory goes. Makes sense to me because anybody who's ever come across a grizzly knows just how seldom you'll get to see their backsides. Which is another way of telling you just how dangerous bear hunting can be, so don't make a move unless I tell you to."

George Bjorn said, "One would think that such large, powerful animals don't need sharp senses. Am I right?"

"With all due respect, Mr. Bjorn, you couldn't be more wrong. Their vision, in living colour, is as good as humans'. They can hear ultrasonic sounds, and their sense of smell is five or six times sharper than a bloodhound's. Like I said, bear hunting can be extremely dangerous."

"What do you know about lions, Mr. Gleason?" As Heward spoke, his binoculars acquired a distinct wobble, and his voice became exceedingly reedy.

"Oh, not a helluva lot. Biggest cats we have around here are lynxes. For lions, you have to go west."

"I'm looking at one right now, Mr. Gleason."

"That's impossible. Cougars are found in the Rockies and the southwest U.S."

With hands twitching in excitement and awe, Heward handed the binoculars to his friend. "There! On the far side of the lake at the water's edge. Immediately to the left of that pile of big grey boulders!"

"Holy Christ. Phillip's not talking about some mountain lion, Willie. He's talking — quite rightly — about a ... a lion! Capital *l*, capital *i*, capital *o*, capital *n*. Simba ... the freaking king of beasts!"

Willie Gleason was beside himself with joy. At last he had a pair of jokers, and not some grim-faced backpackers who were all set to fight World War III. "Can I have a peek, Mr. Bjorn?"

Bjorn was mesmerized. He would not budge. He would not lower the binoculars. "No. Get your own."

Cackling merrily, Willie peered across the lake with squinted eyes. Well ... what these two were going on about was at least tawny in colour. A lynx. It had to be a lynx. Or maybe even one of those relocated grizzlies. With the dexterity of a monkey, he climbed into the Otter and brought out his own binoculars. He then jumped down from the door of the airplane onto the dock, lifted the binoculars to his eyes and sought out that pile of big grey boulders. "Well, I'll be fucked ... it *is* the Lion King."

"What now, Mr. Gleason?" asked Phillip Heward III with particular relish.

Willie Gleason was silent for a good minute. His bronzed, deeply creased face seemed to shrivel even more from deep concentration. Then, quite abruptly, he began shouting at the pilot. "John! Get the plane started! We're crossing the lake!"

George Bjorn lowered the binoculars. "To what purpose, Mr. Gleason?"

"To bag him, of course. Guys who've hunted everything say a male lion is the most dangerous of all the big game, and I'm not going to miss my chance at one. John! Start the bloody plane."

"Never mind, Captain," Heward yelled up to the pilot. "We aren't going anywhere."

"Sorry, Mr. Heward," said the pilot, "but I answer only to Willie. He's in charge here."

Willie clambered up the ladder to the door. "C'mon, you two. We'll come back for your gear later. But bring your rifles!"

The two Americans unsleeved their weapons. Heward's gun was a lever-action Marlin 1895G, with 45/70 ammunition. Bjorn packed a Browning BLR with .300 Winchester Magnum cartridges. Both men quickly and efficiently loaded their guns.

"What in hell are you doing?" barked Willie from the doorway. "You can do that while we cross the lake. Get in!"

Bjorn levelled his rifle at Willie. "You're not crossing that lake, and you're not harming that cat."

"Don't point that thing at me, for Christ's sake! John, let's get this machine moving!"

Willie's two assistants freed the airplane from the dock while the pilot started up the supercharged engine. As the craft began to inch away from the dock, the two assistant guides slithered up the ladder and into the cabin, past Willie, who was still in the doorway. "You've got enough food to last you a long while," Willie shouted with hands cupped to his mouth. "But we'll be back before day's end, anyway, so don't go anywhere! Stay close to the dock!"

Phillip Heward III lifted his powerful weapon to his shoulder, then aimed it at the Otter's engine compartment and squeezed off several shots. The highly destructive 45/70 Win Mags did their duty. There was a horrendous whine, followed by unearthly clattering, followed by dead silence.

"Smart," said Willie as the craft drifted away from the dock. "Absolutely fucking smart! And look, the goddamn lion is gone!"

"Good for him," replied George Bjorn. "Now do us a favour and radio Thunder Bay. Arrange for a pickup in exactly one week."

Bjorn's patronizing tone was more than Willie Gleason could bear. "Fuck you," he frothed as he disappeared into the cabin. "Fuck you, fuck you, fuck you." When he reappeared moments later, he had his hunting rifle at his shoulder and proceeded to point it at the men on the dock. "I could shoot off both your dicks before you can say 'Minnesota Fatheads.'"

And he squeezed the trigger.

Just as he did so, however, the airplane coughed and lurched forward. Pilot John was trying to restart the motor. And what Willie Gleason had intended as an intimidating and humbling gesture — ideally causing the two Minnesotans to soil themselves — ended up putting a hole through Phillip Heward's thigh.

If Willie'd known that Phillip Heward III and George Bjorn had seen action together as Green Berets in Vietnam, he might have thought twice before taking such a precipitous initiative. To be sure, the two men had demonstrated a sound knowledge of their weapons for him during the trip up to the bush, but like many Vietnam vets, they'd been silent about their past.

And now Willie Gleason paid the price. The instant George Bjorn realized his comrade had taken a bullet, he reacted swiftly and without mediation. As a consequence, Willie Gleason was dead on his feet, with a big hole right between the eyes and his brains, blood, and bone tissue decorating the hull behind him.

"Shee-it," murmured Bjorn as Willie collapsed backward into the airplane.

"Damn straight," said Heward as Pilot John and the two remaining guides raised their hands and pleaded for their lives.

"Bullet missed your femoral artery and vein," said Bjorn as he bandaged his friend's leg. "For all its size, a flesh wound, basically."

"Sounds like the least of our problems, eh?"

Bjorn was bent over Heward. Heward shouted over his shoulder. "What kinds of laws you got in this country? Do they respect the principle of self-defence?"

Severely traumatized, and certainly not wishing to disappoint, Pilot John and the two young guides chanted as one. "The true north, strong and free —"

"Good," said Bjorn as he straightened up. "Now, there's just one thing. When the authorities get around to questioning us about this incident, nobody mentions the lion. Got that? Your friend Willie became deranged and trigger-happy and he paid the price, and that's all there was to it. No mention of the lion. He's on a long, lonely journey, and there's a lot of shit in his future, but we're not going to add to it. Understood?"

"Understood!" said Pilot John and the two guides in unison.

What Pilot John dared not add was that when he'd radioed Thunder Bay about the condition of his bush plane, he had not neglected to mention the lion and the contribution it had made toward the Otter's engine failure.

Having drunk nearly two gallons of cool, sweet water before a gunshot told him it was time to move along, I-árishóni was feeling much better. The hind leg was still throbbing, but to a much lesser degree now. A wade in the lake had reduced the inflammation.

He clambered up the steep bank, took a last look at the noisy goings-on across the lake, then set off once more along the deer path. It was redolent with the reassuring scent of Zarathustra. Even the horse's droppings were a welcome discovery.

From the lake, the deer path took a sharp turn east. I-árishóni was cognizant of the change in direction, but it did not bother him in the least. As long as he was on the trail of that horse, things felt right. Freedom in the abstract may have been beyond his comprehension, but freedom in the abstract is a doubled-edged sword, anyway; it can as much stab at the heart as it can cut the cords of bondage. I-árishóni, on the other hand, experienced an awakening sense of freedom with every fibre of his being, much as he experienced the very air that he breathed.

The change in direction of the deer path would turn out to be fortuitous.

As the lion padded along it, the two helicopters from the Doomsday Complex were on their way. Within half an hour, they'd flown over Commandant Franz Hauptmann's radioed position and another ten minutes of flight on a southeastern trajectory had them gazing down at the wolves' mutilated carcasses. They couldn't put down at either site because the forest was too thick, but they considered this to be a blessing in disguise: whatever came out of Hauptmann's mouth would surely be less loathsome than close scrutiny of the wolves' remains.

From the site of I-árishóni's bloodletting they skimmed the treetops, occasionally glimpsing the deer path, always keeping to a southeastern bearing. Some ten miles beyond the savaged wolf pack, they found a small meadow. There they set down and disgorged Reg McDuff, Victor Tarasenko, and their dogs, then resumed their southeastern flight.

On the banks of a lake they spotted a dead grizzly and a gutted moose. They landed on the beach and concluded that only the lion could have been capable of such butchery. Paw prints in the sand merely confirmed the obvious. Regretting that they'd put Reg, Victor, and the dogs down so soon, but concluding that by now McDuff and Tarasenko were equidistant from the small meadow and the dead grizzly, they took off and continued southeast. They spotted the deer path infrequently, but it was often enough to convince them they were headed in the right direction.

"There's another lake over there," pilot Vikram Ghosh said over his shoulder to Antanas Sruoga. "Perhaps we will be seeing more evidence of the cat."

Sruoga set aside his infrared binoculars, partly out of frustration. "Saying there's another lake down there is like saying you've found another cootie on a whore. Relax, Ghosh."

As Vikram Ghosh approached the small lake, he spotted something quite unexpected at its far end. A single-engine Otter. Immediately, he radioed Bird-Dog Two, which was a half-mile to the northwest, to hang back. He then hovered for a few moments and watched several people jumping up and down on the dock, trying to flag him down.

"Probably their plane is out of commission," said Sruoga. "Well, fuck them. Let's get out of here before they get a make on us."

"I am not seeing the deer path. Should I continue southeast?"

"Obviously," snarled Antanas Sruoga. "That's the direction he's been heading in for the last eight hours. Why would he change now?"

To the immense anger and perplexity of the people on the dock, the helicopter picked up speed and flew off into the rising sun. And every mile they flew in that direction widened the gap between them and I-árishóni.

CHAPTER SEVENTEEN

Montreal. September 6, 2006. Place Ville Marie is a forty-five-storey cruciform building sitting at the very core of downtown Montreal.

In fact, given that Place Ville Marie's basement shopping mall represents the epicentre of an underground city that comprises miles of tunnels and indoor access to over sixteen-hundred shops, restaurants, and businesses (not to mention several subway stops, a bus terminal, and a train station) it could easily be said that Place Ville Marie *is* the very core of downtown Montreal.

Built in the International Style, Place Ville Marie was, from the moment of its completion in 1962, the premiere business address in the city. Its slip to fourth place in height among Montreal's skyscrapers neither diminished its prestige nor its rental rates. Occupying the top five floors of this gleaming glass and aluminum cathedral of capitalism was a testament to the immense power and prosperity of Conrad Inc. Jason Conrad did not wholly occupy or bother to own the building only because he possessed a ninety-floor, black granite building on King Street in Toronto.

Having attended Sergeant Jerome Perron's sadly muted funeral in the morning, Irina Mary Drach and Athol Curzon Hudson had an hour to kill before their early afternoon appointment with Conrad. They were hungry, so they parked in the garage under the tower and struck off in search of hamburger platters at Mister Steer.

Perhaps in anticipation of meeting the celebrated Jason Conrad, Hudson found the shoppers, hustlers, and bustlers that jammed the sidewalks of Montreal's main thoroughfare to be an electrifying kick. The sidewalks thrummed, the storefronts hummed. Even the midday traffic that huffed along like an arthritic millipede galvanized him to such a degree that he was soon sliding and gliding along on a dense, Byzantine network of high-tension wires that allowed for maximum volts and jolts.

Irina saw only blackness. The eight of September was fast approaching, and it was on the eight of the month that Walter Drach had been cut down by a youth who should never have been released from the Pinel Institute for the Criminally Insane.

She fortified herself with two slices of cherry pie.

Once back at Place Ville Marie, Irina and Hudson disembarked from an elevator and trudged, somewhat awed, through a reception area the size of an airport lounge to a mahogany desk that had the surface area of a small runway.

"Holy geez," whispered Hudson. "A fair-sized rain forest and the entire herd from the back forty must have been sacrificed to gussy up this place. Look at the wall coverings. Suede — every last square inch."

"We're here to see Mr. Conrad," Irina announced to the aggressively alert, smartly attired, and severely coifed young woman behind the big desk. "We have an appointment for two o'clock. I'm Sergeant-Detective Drach, and this is Sergeant-Detective Hudson."

The receptionist picked up the phone and briskly announced their arrival.

Between her thumb and index finger, Irina was absently rubbing a petal of the opalescent orchid that graced the desk. "Please don't do that, honey," said the young woman curtly. "Mr. Conrad is very particular about his flowers. Now, please have a seat. It will not be long."

"I should hope not," Irina sniped as she and Hudson took the nearest chairs. "It's already 2:05."

The young woman did not deign to reply. She instead applied herself to righting whatever wrongs Irina had inflicted upon the bloom with a mist sprayer.

"That thing there," whispered Hudson to Irina, pointing to the logo on the wall behind the young woman. "Stunning in concept and execution. Dynamic tension. It pits the restful exoticism and allure of teak against the high-tech energy of stainless steel. I'll bet it cost a pretty penny."

"High teak?"

Hudson was not amused. Pricey fitments were no laughing matter.

"The mahogany there is a nice touch," Irina said idly of the vertical slats that adorned the mocha suede walls.

"Like the trim on these chairs. Geez, this is kid leather. Soft and sensual, isn't it?"

Irina perfunctorily stroked the arm of her chair then glanced at her watch. "It is now 2:10 ... *Honey*."

The receptionist looked up from her desk with a start, only to be confronted by a look that would have withered a mummy. She picked up the phone and again announced Irina's and Hudson's presence, this time with a little more urgency.

On each side of the reception desk was a double set of heavy mahogany doors with lustrous stainless steel hardware. Without benefit of human exertion, one set suddenly swung open and disgorged Chinua Amadi.

"Follow me, Officers," he said, with barely a glance at either of them.

As he led Irina and Hudson toward the great mahogany doors, they swished open to reveal a short, wide, brightly lit corridor. Down this corridor they went, past several employees in their bays and into a corner office that presented a spectacular knee-to-ceiling view of the densest and most colourful part of downtown Montreal, of the McGill University campus, the southern face of Mount Royal in its early autumn colours, and a good part of the city's west end.

As for the office itself, it so far surpassed any preconception or expectation that the policemen were speechless. The least notable features were its immense size, the snow-white walls, and the deep pile wall-to-wall white carpeting. Much more notable was that every item of furniture — from desk to credenza and tables to molded chairs and sofa — and

d leonard freeston

every accessory, from lamps to phones to desk set to vases and Apple Cube computer, was of either clear glass, crystal, or Plexiglas. It all caused a most unusual sensation in Irina and Hudson, for files, the contents of Conrad's desk, ergonomic cushions for the seating, the potted plant, even such mundane objects as pens and coffee-table books, all seemed to float in midair. Irina and Hudson felt as if they were in a zero-gravity chamber.

"It's perhaps a bit dated in concept," smiled Jason Conrad as he simultaneously rose from his chair and dismissed Chinua, "but the execution and materials are of such high quality that I cannot bear to part with any of it. Besides, it sends a rather strong message about the transparency of Conrad Inc.'s practices, don't you think?"

Apart from Jason Conrad himself, it was the art that most interested Hudson. It was comprised of clear glass sculptures on spiralling crystal pedestals. The art on the wall was similarly of glass or crystal, in clear frames, and accented at most by etching or touches of white.

"It's all Murano glass," Conrad volunteered as he smoothly helped Irina into a seat. "I have a soft spot for Venice. It's a pearl of a city."

"Why wouldn't it be when the world is your oyster?"

Conrad fixed Irina with his dark, deep-set eyes and smiled indulgently. Irina brushed imaginary hair from her face.

"Good one. Nobody's dared take a shot at me since I was in diapers." Still standing, he pointed to a translucent coffee service. "May I offer you coffee?"

Irina nodded self-consciously as Hudson slid into the chair next to her. As he indicated his own interest in the coffee, Hudson couldn't help but notice that Irina was now exerting considerable energy in tucking her skirt tightly about her knees. Fearing that she was succumbing to Conrad's spectral grace and commanding presence, his heart sank.

Conrad pushed a button at the corner of his desk and a young male attendant, suitably attired in light grey slacks and a white linen jacket, entered the office from a side door. He poured the coffee then offered the two detectives biscuits and muffins from a crystal tray. When Irina declined the offer, Hudson's heart drowned.

With a flick of Conrad's head, the young man departed as quickly as he'd appeared, shutting the door behind him in the way a shaman seals his lips on a stygian secret.

150

"So," said Conrad as he sipped at his coffee, "Sergeant-Detectives Irina Drach and Athol Hudson. You're lucky to have caught me here, given that I flew in from Beijing just six hours ago and I'm off to Toronto this afternoon. Or perhaps there was more than luck involved?"

"Just dumb luck, Mr. Conrad," confessed Hudson. "I was listening to a CBC business report early this morning and they mentioned your whereabouts in connection with your acquisition of that French-language media chain, so here we are."

"And just what can I do for you? Some charity, I presume?"

"Don't be disingenuous, Mr. Conrad," said Irina. "You know perfectly well that we know which channels to go through for something like that. Besides, we stipulated that we were here on official business. Police business."

Hudson was heartened by Irina's sharp, accusatory tone. Conrad seemed not to be.

"Oh," he said as he sank into his chair. "That sounds onerous. Is it something to do with our accounting practices? If so, you've come to the wrong place. I suggest you go to Deloitte and Touche for that."

"Before I continue, Mr. Conrad," said Irina, "I would remind you that we are from homicide, not the fraud squad. I must also state we have no probable cause and that you are therefore under no obligation to answer our questions, although it would be in your interest to do so. You are merely the first on a long list of people we wish to interview."

"Ah. A fishing expedition."

"Not quite. There are worms, but we have no hooks."

Conrad smiled a broad, incongruously charming smile, then levitated from his chair in order to top-up Irina's cup. He didn't notice that Hudson's cup was also empty, even though it, like the other two, was of clear tempered glass. What he did seem to notice, however, was Irina's cleavage. "Go on, Detective Drach. I'm intrigued."

I'll bet, Hudson grumbled to himself.

In less than one-hundred words, Irina told of the animal abductions and of how she and Hudson came to be sitting in his office. Conrad listened attentively without interruption. When she was done, he sat back in his chair, frowning. It was a good half minute before he spoke, and when he did, the tone was grave. "I suppose I should be outraged, but I understand perfectly why you've come to see me. Now, is there anything I can do to further your investigation? I am, after all, a friend of Mother Earth, and all my enterprises are engaged in reducing their carbon footprints. In fact, Conrad Inc. is a Goliath in size-two shoes. Perhaps I could defray the expense of visiting other rich and powerful sons of bitches?"

Irina could not help but be amused by Conrad's cheek. "And that wouldn't add up to a conflict of interest on our part, and bribery on yours, Mr. Conrad?"

Conrad could not help but be amused by Irina's sardonic tone. "I would do anything to get one or more of my rivals in trouble, Sergeant Drach. Even on pain of dirtying all our hands."

Hudson, on the other hand, was not amused at all. "Mr. Conrad," he grumped, "are you prepared to open your personal and company books to us, and to hand over your complete itinerary for the last year or so?"

"But of course." Conrad pushed the button on his desk. Suddenly Chinua Amadi was in their midst, as if he'd been conjured from thin air. "Chinua, these officers have expressed an interest in my movements during the last year. Please give them everything they need. And have Peter from Deloitte and Touche call me right away."

Perspiring profusely, Chinua bowed low then disappeared into the ethers.

"Your assistant looked a little perturbed by our request," Hudson remarked suspiciously.

"Chinua is Nigerian, Sergeant Hudson. They sweat a great deal. Think nothing of it."

Unsure as to whether or not he'd just been exposed to racial stereotyping, Hudson looked to Irina for guidance. If she was offended, she did not show it. However, she was quite ready to take over the questioning. "Mr. Conrad, are you the person we're looking for? Are you the one behind all those deaths and animal abductions?"

Conrad was taken aback by her bluntness. He reached for his coffee and took a few sips. "Is that a trick question?"

"No, Sir, it is not."

As Conrad stared long and hard at Irina Drach, his hooded eyes were no longer hearths for mirthful fires so much as coffers for dulled flint, and the autocratically arched eyebrows flatlined to such an extent that they almost joined at the bridge of his aquiline nose. "Then it is an absurd question, and you know it's an absurd question. Look at you. Your eyelids are flapping like blinds in a bordello."

"I've had this nervous tick ever since the death of my husband some time ago, Mr. Conrad. Don't take it personally. And you never answered my question."

Conrad threw his hands up in the air. "Isn't it obvious what my answer is?"

"It is not. Tell me to my face."

Conrad did just that. With his pale, slender hands clasped together in the form of a cathedral, he leaned across his desk, looked her straight in the eye, and said in a hoarse and barely audible voice, "No. Emphatically, no."

Irina gathered up her purse and rose abruptly from her seat. "Thank you, Mr. Conrad. That's all for now. Our people will be in touch with your people about those matters that Sergeant Hudson raised, et cetera, et cetera. Come, Hudson."

Conrad was nonplussed. "That's it?"

"Of course, Mr. Conrad."

"Wait, wait!" Conrad leapt from his chair and rounded his desk to where Irina was standing. "Perhaps my assistant has already prepared an account of my comings and goings during the last year. Let's just see."

He leaned backward over his desk and pushed the Chinua button. Chinua Amadi swept into the office. In his hands were a stack of photocopies.

"My itinerary, Chinua. Is it done?"

"Yes, Sir. All done." Chinua handed the ream to Hudson.

"I'll walk you to the elevator," said Conrad as he lightly touched Irina's elbow. "Sergeant Hudson, would you mind going on ahead? I'd like a word with your colleague."

Hudson stuffed his free hand into his jacket pocket and stomped out of the office.

The telephone rang and Chinua Amadi answered it. "Sir? Peter of Deloitte and Touche."

"Tell him to hold the line. I'll only be about five minutes."

Irina raised her eyebrows. "Five minutes? The last time we did that trip it took all of twenty seconds."

Conrad brushed the thick black hair off his forehead and stared at her. Irina felt as if she were a prison escapee broiling under brilliant searchlights. "In truth, Detective Drach, I find you to be a fascinating woman. That you risk physical and psychological trauma daily sets you apart from all other women I've ever known. That you're so attractive is icing on the cake. Perhaps we could see each other socially? Dinner sometime soon? I'll be back in Montreal next week."

"Did I not mention that I am recently widowed, Mr. Conrad? And have I not demonstrated that I am alert to conflicts of interest?"

Conrad affected a boyish plaintiveness. "Indeed you have, Sergeant Drach, but I can't be blamed for trying. May I ask when you'll be grilling me again? I'm looking forward to it."

As Irina and Conrad neared the elevator, Hudson eyed them stonily. Noticing this, Irina's tone turned from airy to arctic as she simultaneously grabbed hold of Hudson's elbow and stabbed at the elevator call button. "That was not a grilling. That was merely the marinating. Good day, Mr. Conrad."

She pushed Hudson into the elevator and the doors swished shut in Conrad's face. Hudson stared straight ahead and whistled innocuously for a few seconds. As they neared ground floor, however, he could no longer contain himself. "What a bloody lecher."

"So, anyone who shows the slightest interest in me must be a lecher? An indiscriminate whorehound?"

"Ah … nothing could be farther from the truth, Irina, but that prompts a further observation. You seemed rather ambivalent about his attentions. You fussed with your skirt, for instance, but you ended up showing more leg than before you started."

"Did I?"

"Come now, Irina. Nothing you do is accidental."

The doors parted and into the elevator stepped a greying, middle-aged businessman and an attractive girl barely in her twenties. They went directly to the back of the elevator and proceeded to lock lips and nearly every other available appendage. Together, they resembled an octopus in its death throes. Irina, discomfited by the spectacle, moved to the front of the cubicle. "If nothing I do is accidental," she replied acidly, "then does it not follow that everything I do is in the service of our investigation?"

Hudson knew from experience that should he be foolish enough to challenge Irina's sophistry, then he would be subjected to either an emotional drubbing or a logical hammer lock. He concluded it might be expedient to change the subject. "So," he said, rifling through the stack of printouts that Chinua Amadi had given him. "Conrad was certainly forthcoming. Does that make him more or less suspect?"

Irina trotted purposefully out of the elevator. Hudson had to stretch his long legs to keep up with her. "Tell me what you think," she said, without looking back.

"Well, he's certainly not trying to hide anything. And his reaction to your rather forthright question was a mixture of shock and bemusement — which I'd suppose is not abnormal. So, much as it pains me, I'd have to give him the benefit of the doubt and say he's probably innocent."

"And I would say you shouldn't have an opinion at this stage of the game. Until we've interviewed others of his ilk, we shouldn't presume to know what's normal."

"But you asked!"

"Canada has forty-six billionaires. Before we go to England, I'd like to have a chat with at least Ken Thomson, Galen Weston, the Irvings, Ted Rogers, Paul Desmarais, and Jimmy Pattison. Each of them has more than four billion. So get busy on that, Hudson. Then we can discuss what's normal and what isn't."

"All of them? You want to interview all of them?"

"You heard me. If they're available, they can't refuse me. And you should be able to line them up on such short notice. You are, after all, a master of minor miracles."

Irina was not in the habit of dishing out propitiating remarks. There was now a bounce in his step. "Paul Desmarais is in Montreal, but the Irvings are in New Brunswick and the rest are most likely in Toronto. We'll run up a travel tab that equals our trip to England."

"You leave Robertson to me."

Hudson had just guided the cruiser up the ramp from the underground parking when Chinua Amadi suddenly flung himself in front of the car. He was holding a large bouquet of red carnations. "For you, Sergeant," he said as he thrust the flowers through the window. "And Mr. Conrad is confident that you are adept at floriography."

"So," said Hudson, as he turned down University Street toward the Ville-Marie Express. "Are you?"

"Am I what?"

"Adept at floriography."

Irina brushed away a tear. "Quite."

"What does half a bushel of red carnations mean, then?"

"Fascination. I pine for you."

"Why the tears, then?"

"You're a man. You wouldn't understand."

After due consideration, Hudson did understand. But not completely. Insofar as he didn't know when to leave well enough alone, Irina had been right about him. In short, Hudson acquitted himself about as well as the husband who volunteers that a particular dress makes his wife look fat. "I get it. For eighteen months you've denied your femininity in lieu of mourning. Now you're torn between your loyalty to Walter and the need to be the beautiful, vibrant woman he loved. You're conflicted, and Conrad's attentions have only aggravated the situation."

There was a long, sententious silence before Irina answered through gritted teeth, "Bravo, Hudson. Now, why don't you just skip the psychobabble and drive. Drive!"

Hudson drove. At the first red light they encountered, Irina pushed the bouquet on an elderly woman.

CHAPTER EIGHTEEN

Manali, India. September 6, 2006. Having dismissed Bhagwati Prasad's young nephew, Inspector Raja Chadwani of the Kullu District Police stood over Bhagwati's corpse, staring at Munshi Prasad. As he so often did in such circumstances, he stroked his bushy mustache, thereby calling attention to the most adult feature of his round, boyish face.

Inspector Chadwani had summoned the dead man's restaurateur cousin simply to identify him. That the diminutive Munshi had a great deal to tell about the severely wounded man, his cohort, and their consuming interest in Dhamaki the yak, exceeded his wildest dreams. "And you are sure they were not just trekkers here to enjoy those trance parties in the woods, or to light up a chillum and find Western enlightenment?"

Munshi was adamant. "They did not smell of either charas or incense, Inspector. They were interested only in seeing the yak."

In order to confirm his suspicions, Raja Chadwani had unceremoniously unzipped the fly of the severely wounded white man before he'd been carted away. "But the wounded man was an Israeli."

"Yes, but of a different kind. He was honourable. Did I not tell you of his intercession on my behalf against the tribal Jew?"

Inspector Chadwani stroked his mustache. "Be that as it may, it appears as if he had a hand in your cousin's death."

"Ah, Bhagwati was a bad man, foul and evil-tempered. That he should have been born here, in the Valley of the Gods, was an aberration which could be righted in only one way."

"You must be careful what you say, Munshi. That you have an alibi does not preclude your being part of a conspiracy. You are, after all, his sole beneficiary, are you not?"

"I will give his household goods to the Tibetans. They need them more than I. As for this property, my daughter shall have it as part of her dowry. Perhaps there is arable land under all this ruin and swill. Eh … you are not betrothed, Inspector Chadwani?"

Having often frequented Munshi Prasad's café, Raja Chadwani was an aficionado of the little man's cappuccinos and pastries. However, he was no aficionado of Munshi's daughter. He was grateful when the head constable of Manali interrupted this treacherous train of thought by poking his head through the stable door. Wincing at the stench, the constable informed Chadwani that the yak had been removed by truck and horse box, and that casts of the footprints and tire treads had duly been made, notwithstanding the execrable muck they'd had to work with.

"And you did not see this vehicle and its trailer, Mr. Prasad?"

"Regretfully not, Inspector. Perhaps I would have gone to the door upon their departure to examine their means of conveyance had they acted toward me in a contemptible manner, but they did not, and therefore it would have been inappropriate to pry into their affairs."

Inspector Chadwani concluded that the little restaurateur had nothing further to offer, so he dismissed him. Standing alone in the barn, studying the unprepossessing remains of Bhagwati Prasad, he considered the affair while chewing on his mustache.

He had one perpetrator in hospital, unlikely to recover from his coma. The burly Brit was most likely in Delhi by now, since the officers at the roadblocks of NH 21 at Mandi and Bilaspur not only reported no sightings but had hastened to add that the traffic leading out of the Kullu Valley was moving relatively smoothly.

And he had a missing yak. People had killed for yaks before, and they would again, but it was highly irregular for two foreigners to specifically target such a beast — even if he were the most splendid specimen in all of Himachal Pradesh, perhaps even in all of the Himalayas.

Inspector Raja Chadwani left the stable to the crime scene technicians and stepped out into the sunlight. As he tiptoed his way over and around yak and swine droppings, an idea forced itself upon him. He resisted it, for it seemed too obvious, too easy. But as he got into his car, he thought of his days at the University of Melbourne. His math classes, in particular, and of how often he'd scratched his head in wonder at the elegance and simplicity of solutions to seemingly intractable problems.

He started up the Hyundai Sonata, bade farewell to the constables, and promptly discovered that his drive wheels were slithering abortively. There was little about Bhagwati Prasad's barnyard to suggest that it was ever more than a few fetid droppings short of being a cesspool, but the Kullu Valley rainy season of July and August had dragged on into September this year, turning it into a filthy bog. Several officers attempted to push him free, but their sole reward was a thorough drenching in ooze from the spinning wheels. They certainly got no accolades from a fuming Raja Chadwani.

"Use a yak to pull him out," volunteered Munshi Prasad, who'd been prowling the property and sizing up his windfall.

A yak was harnessed to the car and baited with pony nuts, but the car was now sitting in six inch ruts and wouldn't budge.

"Use two yaks," Munshi chortled magnanimously from the sidelines. "I give you leave to use two of my yaks."

Another yak was put into harness and after much flaunting of pony nuts the yaks managed, only just barely, to extricate the car.

"If Dhamaki were here, he would have freed your car in half that time, all by himself, and just for the sheer pleasure of demonstrating his prowess," said Munshi

"Is Dhamaki so very much different from these yaks?" asked Chadwani.

Munshi laughed riotously. The constables, including those who'd been slimed, also laughed riotously. Even the crime-scene technicians who'd come out to savour the inspector's difficulties laughed riotously. "Dhamaki is unlike any other yak, either wild or domesticated," tittered one of the constables. "He is the premier yak in Himachal Pradesh, perhaps even the world! He is Wonder Yak!"

Munshi Prasad, suddenly realizing that his greatest inheritance from Bhagwati had been purloined from him, waded through the slop toward Raja Chadwani's car and began supplicating piteously. "I beg of you, Inspector, you must do all you can to find the beast. My daughter's happiness depends upon it. Eh … did you mention before that you were unmarried? That you are childless? That you will leave no legacy? That your family name expires with you?"

Inspector Chadwani grunted noncommittally and sped off. How wise he'd been to use the Sonata rather than a jeep this fine day. Otherwise, his hunch wouldn't have been so resoundingly substantiated.

As soon as he got back to Shimla he would again read that curious email that had been forwarded to him from the Interpol bureau in Delhi. And then, almost certainly, he would get in touch with those two Canadian detectives. They'd be most interested to hear that he had a slightly damaged material witness in custody.

The prospect of being a key player in a case of global import buoyed him immensely, and almost made him forget that his new Bally shoes had been ruined in that Godforsaken dunghill.

CHAPTER NINETEEN

The boreal forest. September 5, 2006. Given that Phillip Heward III had shot out the engine of the Otter, the question of whether or not Willie Gleason's body should be immediately removed from the scene of the incident was moot. The Ontario Provincial Police were summoned, and two officers and a doctor arrived by bush plane just before noon, four hours after Willie had met his maker and only thirty minutes later than the mechanics. Like the mechanics, they'd come north from the grain port of Thunder Bay, which lies on the northwest shore of Lake Superior, the world's largest freshwater lake by area.

Detective-Sergeants Bill Sturgess and Arthur Laidlaw of Regional Headquarters were no strangers to hunting accidents and general mayhem, but the condition of Willie's head still appalled them. The doctor's pronouncement on his status was entirely superfluous. "You must've come here to shoot elephants," grunted Laidlaw.

"Three hundred Winchester Magnum, two-hundred-and-twenty grains," George Bjorn grunted right back. "Nothing special, but not quite right for deer. Or jerks."

The policemen had George Bjorn, the pilot, and the two assistant guides act out the sequence of events that had led to Willie's demise. When they were done, Detective-Sergeant Sturgess said to Bjorn, "We're going to have to take you into custody. You know that, eh?"

"Well that sucks, don't it, Phil?"

Save for his underwear, Heward was stripped and seated on a boulder while the doctor attended to his wound, all the while complaining bitterly about the delay in getting the patient to a hospital. "Sure does. You spend years prepping to serve your country and your president and then some little asshole with a big gun in some foreign country goes and shoots me, and you have to eat shit for it."

"This is not some foreign country," hissed officer Sturgess. "This is the democratic dominion of Canada. And besides, our actions are strictly a formality. You'll be brought up before a provincial court judge within twenty-four hours and you'll be able to explain yourselves to your hearts' content. You'll even be able to hold your hands over them, if you so desire."

"Huh. Sarcasm, Phil?"

"Now I know we're in Canada, George."

Sergeant Laidlaw thought it might be the right moment to change the subject. "So, we've seen what you all did, but what got the ball rolling? What made you use the plane for target practice, Mr. Heward? Something about an African lion, according to Pilot John's first radio report."

"That's just bushwah," scoffed Bjorn as he glowered at Pilot John and the two guides. "Wee Willie was hallucinating."

Laidlaw turned his attention to Pilot John and the young guides. "Was Willie in the habit of hallucinating?"

Pilot John and the guides weighed their options and decided that giving false statements to the OPP was riskier than invoking the wrath of two Americans up to their ears in lion excrement.

"Not at all," blurted Pilot John. "His mind was as clear as the air we're breathing."

"Nope," vouched the guides.

"If Willie was hallucinating," said Detective-Sergeant Sturgess, "then why did you feel strongly enough to shoot out the Otter's motor?"

"We were afraid he was abandoning us."

"And rendering your means of transport back to civilization was the solution?"

"At least they'd be close. We could take over the plane and radio for help."

"Uh-huh."

"What's that mean? Uh-huh?"

Sturgess peered out across the water. "If I look real hard, I can see clear across to the other side of the lake. I can't make out details, of course, but I suppose I could see the outline of something as big as a grizzly. Or a lion. What about you three? Could you make out something?"

Pilot John and the two guides told him they'd seen something big and mobile. Something tan or golden in colour.

"There," said George Bjorn. "That confirms what we told you. We saw a grizzly. A golden grizzly. And we should know because only us and Wee Willie Wonky had binoculars."

"And Willie isn't here to reiterate his hallucination. Uh-huh."

"Why do you keep saying uh-huh? Back in the U S of A, 'uh-huh' denotes skepticism."

"You're wrong there, Mr. Bjorn. This whole episode is so crazy I'd be quite prepared to believe anything right now. Even in the possibility of Simba wandering around the forest five-hundred miles north of Thunder Bay."

"But you won't repeat that opinion outside of this cozy little circle," drawled Heward, wincing as the doctor threaded the last of the stitches. "Otherwise, they'll think *you're* crazy."

Both Detectives Sturgess and Laidlaw had to admit to themselves that Heward had a point. Not even Pilot John's belated recollection of the mysteriously unhelpful chopper did much to alter those admissions.

The boreal forest. September 6, 2006. In the twenty-four hours since the humans and their machines assaulted his senses from across that lake, I-árishóni had kept to a brisk, unflagging pace and covered one-hundred-twenty miles. It was early morning, and with ever-increasing adroitness he sluiced through the dense, damp foliage like an eel through seaweed. As do the athletes of every species, he had impressive recuperative powers.

That he was a cat and could therefore wash then dress his wounds with antiseptic saliva effectively reduced his risk of infection.

Nevertheless, he was tired. And frigid, for an autumn night in the Canadian north was something completely beyond his experience. He slowed his gait and began seeking a small, sunny clearing where he could rest and wallow in the sunshine. That he would thereby be exposed would not be a factor, for African lions only hide when stalking their prey.

The sun had just cleared the treetops and the temperature had soared to forty-five degrees Fahrenheit when he found what he was looking for. The meadow, though barely large enough to accommodate a pack of baboons, was ideal for his purposes. The light, sandy soil was already heating up enough to provide a warm bed, and the soft breeze that gently bent the patches of tall scrub grass was just strong enough to keep the air clear of the mosquitoes that had plagued him all evening and much of the night.

The one problem with this little field was that it was occupied by a wolverine feasting on his prey, a large animal that had caught its foreleg in a gopher hole as it had hurtled across the meadow. Ever the opportunist, the forty-pound wolverine had made short work of a beast that could not even raise itself up off its knees.

As I-árishóni stepped into the clearing, the wolverine bristled. Like all other members of the weasel family, the wolverine had an audacious, vicious temperament and was not about to be separated from his meal by this strange intruder. In his time, the wolverine had inflicted serious injuries upon wolves and even bears, and gotten away with his life.

As it happened, the lion was not in the least bit hungry, for a deer-sized animal once a week was enough to satisfy his needs. But the wolverine didn't know that, and lunged at I-árishóni with the intention of startling him. However, the six-hundred-pound lion was not easily startled, any more than he was enamoured of a malodorous creature bearing an uncanny resemblance to a hyena. The wolverine might as well have sprung into the blades of a fully functioning blender. Within seconds he was cut to ribbons by tooth and claw, and had a crushed skull for good measure.

As I-árishóni settled into a sandy bank and stretched himself out to his full eleven feet, he gazed upon the remains of the wolverine's victim. He felt disquieted. He even felt a sense of loss.

When he awoke in a few hours and journeyed due south, correcting for the easterly diversion he'd just taken, he'd be alone. Zarathustra had run his last race, and lost.

After having slept a scant four hours, Reg McDuff, Victor Tarasenko, and their dogs were on the move again. It was morning now, and their expectations rose with the sun. "I figure we aren't more than four hours behind them," gloated McDuff, "seeing as how that grizzly we found yesterday was still warm."

"Shouldn't we radio the choppers and let them know where we are?"

"Y'know Victor, those assholes couldn't track the animals until we'd put them dead in their sights, so let's not waste our time or theirs. If they wake up and radio us for information, we won't hold anything back. But think for a second. Don't you want to be the one to bring the beasties down?"

Victor Tarasenko furrowed his heavy brow and cogitated a bit. "Hm. I'm thinking about yesterday as we flew over the wolf pack. You didn't seem so keen to be put down, then."

McDuff swatted at Tarasenko's head with his baseball cap. "First off, I didn't want to face that lion *and* a wolf pack. Second, we're that much farther along, and the situation is getting desperate. I won't have to piss around with some faggoty tranquilizer gun, because the powers that be will be grateful for any old way we can stop those animals. And I've got just the thing for it." Reg McDuff patted his Mark V rifle. "This. The strongest bolt action money can buy. And loaded with .460 Weatherby Magnums. Good enough to stop a charging bull elephant."

Victor Tarasenko's eyebrows were wriggling in consternation. They looked like caterpillars on baking asphalt.

"So whaddya say, Victor?"

Tarasenko nodded dubiously.

"Great! And when we bag those critters, we can send out for a pizza. Domino's."

Victor Tarasenko nodded enthusiastically.

CHAPTER TWENTY

Toronto. September 6, 2006. While studying for a Harvard MBA in the mid-sixties, Jason Conrad had made numerous pilgrimages to New York. The concentration of wealth and power in that city — even as manifested in its sounds, smells, and sights — had partially facilitated his sexual awakening. And of all the sights in New York, it was the stepped skyscraper at the corner of Wall Street and Broadway, One Wall Street, that had most aroused him. The fifty-storey Irving Trust Building, later to become the home of the Bank of New York, had thoroughly seduced him with its blend of Art Deco sleekness and Gothic monumentality, and as his young eyes caressed the limestone siren until his neck ached, he resolved that he would one day either own her or at least something very nearly like her.

Thus, when in the mid-eighties the time had come for Conrad Inc. to erect its own head office in Toronto, Jason Conrad secured the architectural plans for the Irving Trust Building and commissioned his architects to put up a scale model of his stone mistress. Being Jason Conrad, however, he did not mean a reduced scale model. He meant something that retained the sumptuous details and transcendent proportions, but that was actually bigger. Much bigger. His wishes were duly granted, and Canada's tallest building was suddenly a svelte ninety-storey, black granite tribute to the ascending might of Conrad Inc.

On this particular late afternoon, only two hours after he'd left Montreal and only eight since his arrival from Beijing, Jason Conrad stood staring down at First Canadian Place and Scotia Plaza, with his back to his monolithic black granite desk. In order to keep himself from chewing his fingernails down to the knuckles, a sweat-stained Chinua Amadi was swiping at the life-sized white marble statuary of Canada's more aggressive creatures with a feather duster. "I am worried, Master. Why, from among all the world's rich and powerful people, should that Sergeant Irina Drach choose first to interview you?"

"An accident of geography, Chinua. I've already told you."

"I worry. There is more to this woman than meets the eye."

"I couldn't agree with you more. Beauty, brains, and a certain *je ne sais quoi*. A lethal combination."

Chinua fumbled his duster. "Do you mean to tell me that the bouquet was not just a Machiavellian gesture?"

Conrad put his hands behind his head and chuckled. Chinua gave the bear a good whack then went to a door at the side of the office and pushed it slightly ajar. "I've turned down your bed, Sir," he said in as cool a voice as he dared. "You should get some sleep before our journey to the Doomsday Complex. Have, at the very least, a relaxing shower."

"Doomsday Complex … I wish you wouldn't call it that, Chinua. Such negative connotations. Ours is the noblest enterprise in the history of mankind. Now, stop fretting and get going. Mr. Tian isn't the type to stop somewhere for the sake of the scenery."

"I worry. True, there is no possible reason for a judge to sanction a wiretap, but there is nothing to stop the police from observing our movements. From following us!"

"*Contra felicem vix, deus vires habet.*"

"Ah, Latin. I am of course befuddled."

"Against a lucky man, a god has little power."

With his clothes now sticking to him, Chinua left the office. It took him a good minute to wend his way to the elevator through the cavernous executive floor, another two minutes to reach ground floor of

the busy tower, and five to snag a taxi on King Street. The cab got him
to his destination in twenty minutes, and although he felt more secure
for its having squirted through the heavy rush hour traffic, he was still a
bit disquieted as he marched toward the box office of the Rogers Centre.
And while in line, waiting to buy tickets for a baseball game neither he
nor Conrad would ever bother seeing, he almost fainted when a voice
suddenly snorted loudly over his shoulder, "The Blue Jays suck. The
Yankees will kill them."

Chinua's heart eventually resumed its regular beat and he slowly
turned around to confront a tall Chinese man and recite his end of the
prearranged exchange. "You, Sir, are an ignoramus. I'll have you know the
Jays are leading the bottom third of the division."

The two men proceeded to bicker about the relative merits of the two
teams while each bought their tickets. Having done that, they walked away
from the kiosk together, secure in the knowledge that they appeared to be
no more than two rabid fans engaged in the age-old practice of insulting
each others' mothers.

"Five billion dollars, American," said Mr. Tian as they tromped up Blue
Jays Way toward Front Street.

Chinua Amadi stopped in his tracks, swung around, and craned his
neck in order to take in the rakish gigantism of the CN Tower, which was
only half a block away. "They say that by this time next year, that thing will
no longer be the world's tallest freestanding structure. The honour will go
to the Burj Dubai, which will come in at one-hundred-sixty-four floors.
Its total budget is nearly five billion dollars. An absurd price for vanity."

"One man's vanity is another's *sine qua non*."

"Is that what passes for Eastern wisdom these days? You should know
that my master is beyond vanity, Mr. Tian. You should also know that he
is well beyond budgets. No mention was ever made of even five cents, let
alone five billion dollars. You are too late with your demand, my friend."

Tian studied an unblinking Amadi for a few seconds. "You are
authorized to speak for your boss?"

"I am."

"So I am to tell my superiors that their request has been denied?"

"You are."

"Very well. But they will not be happy."

Tian disappeared into the stream of young broker types who inhabited that stretch of Front Street. Quaking, Chinua took a taxi back to the Conrad Building.

"You what?" said Conrad as his curvilinear black eyebrows arched almost to his hairline.

"I let them know you wouldn't submit to their bullying tactics."

"You, who has never so much as picked out a shirt for me without first getting my opinion, presumed to speak for me on a matter of such import?"

"I know your mind, Mr. Conrad. I have just never spoken it before."

"Then why bother to consult with me about such trivial matters as shirts and shoes and so on?"

"If a man does not feel he has control over the trivial things, then how is he to feel omnipotent? And if he does not feel omnipotent, then how is he to *be* omnipotent?"

Conrad approached Chinua Amadi and stood so close that his breath fogged Chinua's glasses. Chinua became nervous to the point of severe stomach cramps, but he did not flinch. The two men stood in vivid contemplation of each other for so long that Chinua's world receded from him. He could not even feel the resistance of the floor upon which he stood.

Conrad's mouth eventually formed itself into the devilish grin that Chinua lived for. Then, convulsed with laughter, Conrad went to the bar where he poured two stiff Laphroaig whiskies. "You did well, Chinua," he said as he bade his retainer step forward for his drink. "Extortion is among the basest of offences. That the rebuff should come from my messenger will let those Chinese know how little I fear them, how I spit on them. But Chinua?"

"Yes, Master?"

"Next time you speak my mind, check with me first? Otherwise, yours will be contemplating the hereafter."

Even as his legs trembled, Chinua gulped his whisky with some satisfaction. He'd seen that coming. He was on his game.

"Oh, and Chinua?"

"Yes, Sir?"

"Don't congratulate yourself too much on your prescience. It seems to me a person can be so busy articulating another's thoughts that he doesn't have time for any of his own. And then he can't properly look out for himself."

CHAPTER TWENTY-ONE

Montreal. September 6, 2006. Hudson looked up from his computer. "Whoa. Here's a keener. An Inspector Raja Chadwani from Shimla, India. It's 3:30 here, so there it must be ... what?"

"One in the morning, September 7, if it's near New Delhi," replied Irina without lifting her eyes from the tourist guide to London. "What does he say?"

"There was a murder involving some prodigy of a yak. Dhamaki, his name is. Allegedly two perps. One escaped with the animal, the other is in a coma, having been shot by the yak's owner."

"What's so funny, Hudson?"

"A yak, Irina. A wonder yak! That doesn't strike you as slightly absurd?"

"Not at all. If we can have a Mighty Mouse, or even — God forbid — a Superman, then why not a Wonder Yak? Does he mention what put our suspect into that condition?"

"A bullet to the head."

"Yikes. Or should I say yaks. Tell this officer we want to know the instant that man snaps out of his coma, assuming he ever does. I'll flog the furniture in Lieutenant Robertson's office, including his *Starry Night* and that flimsy bloody chair if I have to, to get over there. Now, is there anything else?"

"He's a Jew."

"Who? Chadwani?"

"The perp. They, uh … performed a visual inspection."

"Hm. Thorough. But an iffy conclusion. Plenty of non-Jewish men are circumcised. For reasons of hygiene. Aesthetics, too."

"Aesthetics?"

"Yes, Hudson. Aesthetics. I had my son circumcised for that very reason."

"My God. Did you tell that to the pediatrician?"

"I did."

"And what did he say to that?"

"He didn't say anything. He just blushed. Like you are right now. Now, is there any corroborating evidence about Mr. Coma's religion?"

Hudson went back to his computer screen, then mumbled, "Yes. From the victim's cousin. The vic is Israeli, actually."

"Have you been keeping track of how many nationalities are represented in this organization, so far?"

"I'm up to thirty-seven. But witnesses could have been mistaken about their nationalities, so that's only a ballpark figure."

"If those witnesses were anything like you, we could take that figure to the bank."

Flattered, and thus emboldened, Hudson put forth an idea he'd been entertaining all day. "Irina. I have one of my speeches tonight —"

"I haven't forgotten, and I'll be there. What makes you think I'd miss it?"

"Actually, I was wondering if I should do something a little different tonight. Scare mongering of a whole different order."

Irina removed her reading glasses and dropped them onto the map.

As if he were a general, unveiling plans for a major offensive, Hudson gravely said, "Up to now, knowledge of this outfit has been confined to police circles."

"And wildlife organizations. And the military. And the minister of the environment."

"Right. But it hasn't really leaked out to the general public."

"It was just the day before yesterday that Sergeant Perron was murdered and Bismarck was dognapped, Hudson."

"I don't believe the public should have to wait a minute longer before they're told."

"And you'll be the one to tell them. Tonight, I'm guessing."

"What do you think? I'm at McGill University. There'll be good press coverage. Before you know it, the whole civilized world will be in on it. That can only be a good thing, right?"

Without taking her eyes off Hudson, Irina picked up her glasses and twirled them by one of the arms. "It's nearly four o'clock. We should go. Billionaire number two won't be happy if we're late."

"But what about my idea?"

"I'll have to think it through."

Perhaps because of his impatience and apprehension, Hudson was able to get them downtown, through the rush-hour traffic, in less than forty minutes. Their destination was 751 Victoria Square, near the westernmost edge of Montreal's financial district. The unobtrusive seven-storey Georgian building, sandwiched between the World Trade Center and the Canada Steamship Lines building, faced the lightly forested Victoria Square and the forty-seven-floor Stock Exchange tower. There were about two-dozen placard-bearing people, mostly of Asian origin, standing on the sidewalk directly in front of the building. They were representatives of the "Canada-Tibet Committee," there to protest Power Corporation's complicity with Bombardier Inc. and Nortel Networks in building a rail line from the heartland of China to Lhasa, Tibet. As they stepped through the small but animated crowd, Irina and Hudson gleaned that the major concerns were potential damage to Tibet's high-altitude ecosystem and, more urgently, the enhanced influx of both Chinese settlers and troops into that troubled land.

The guard, who'd been nervously watching the crowd from behind the heavy doors, almost fainted when Irina and Hudson charged past him and went directly through the white marble lobby to the elevators. *"Excusez-moi, mais c'est un bâtiment privé!* So sorry, *Madame*, but this is a private building!"

"I can tell that," snapped Irina as she showed her badge. "Not a single identifying mark on the building. But we are public servants, as you can see, so we can go anywhere we like. Furthermore, we have an appointment with your Mr. Paul Desmarais."

Much relieved, if not a little piqued, the guard scurried to his giant marble slab of a console and consulted his calendar. "Ah, yes," he jabbered, turning red with embarrassment. "The sixth floor, if you please."

The guard called the elevator and waited until it arrived. Then, holding the door open for them, he bade Irina and Hudson enter with a flourish. Within one minute they were in the company of the greying, bespectacled Paul Desmarais, whose financial services company did twenty-one-billion dollars in annual sales, and whose net worth of four-billion dollars made him Canada's sixth-richest man.

At first, Desmarais was a trifle cool. The chairman of Power Corporation was a private man, and he was rather taken aback by this intrusion into his affairs. The fact that he was a personal friend of four of Canada's last five prime ministers initially made it difficult for him to accept a cross-examination from two lowly sergeant-detectives. Nevertheless, he quickly grasped the nature and magnitude of the problem, and once he'd perceived that Irina was completely unbowed by his wealth and influence, he became positively affable.

The meeting ended on a high note, with Desmarais offering assistance and contacts. Irina and Hudson left lumbered down by his itinerary for the entire year, along with a comprehensive list of the financial services companies with whom Power Corporation dealt.

"This is insane," exclaimed Hudson as they dumped the material onto the back seat of the cruiser. "Where do we start with all this stuff? I feel like a field mouse wandering through a labyrinth built for elephants."

"The financial stuff, we dump in the laps of the fraud squad. They should be able to pick up on a billion or two dollars that have gone astray. As for the itineraries, we work through them ourselves. You're a smart young man, Hudson. Pattern recognition shouldn't be too far beyond you."

Hudson started up the car and headed toward the Ville-Marie Expressway. "So what do you think?"

"About what?"

"About Paul Desmarais and Jason Conrad?"

"Two gentlemen, one considerably more forward than the other. Beyond that, nothing. We'll be in Toronto tomorrow morning to interview Ted Rogers and Ken Thomson. After that, I'll let you know if I have any thoughts."

"And then England," Hudson beamed.

"Yes, England. Off in search of what is most likely an expendable foot soldier who has no idea of whom he's ultimately working for."

"Oh, look who's being pessimistic now."

"Not pessimistic. Realistic. But we can't afford not to go. Xueqin Liang and that Israeli might be just foot soldiers, but they may lead us to middle management. The lieutenants. The ones who'll connect the foot soldiers to the supreme commander."

"My money's on the Israeli," said Hudson.

"Is there something you know that I don't?"

"Raja Chadwani emailed that the victim's cousin, Munshi Prasad, had found the Israeli to be a relatively honourable sort. It seems he intervened on Munshi's behalf at the latter's café. And my experience tells me that honourable people are more aware of the world around them, and that they don't do things unquestioningly. Ergo, there's a good chance the Israeli knows something that most ordinary minions don't."

There was a heavy silence. Hudson glanced sideways at Irina and saw that she was glaring at the inside of the windshield and blinking furiously. "What? Is it something I said?"

"It's what you didn't say. I distinctly remember asking you at one point if there was anything else pertinent in that email and you instead launched into a discussion about the Israeli's penis."

"That was significant!"

"Discussions of penises are never quite as significant as men imagine them to be."

Hudson's hands torqued the steering wheel so energetically that they produced squeaking sounds.

"I suppose that's my neck you're twisting?" Irina watched him indulgently until his hands relaxed at the wheel. "There. Feel better? Am I blue?"

Hudson laughed ruefully. There was no winning with Irina.

"I've been thinking over the suggestion about your speech tonight," she said, as if they'd just been discussing the weather in some remote locale. "I, of course, have an opinion on the matter, but I believe we should discuss it with Lieutenant Robertson. Don't you?"

"Robertson's office is the place good ideas go to die."

"Now, now, Hudson. Don't presuppose that it's a good idea. The three of us will in concert determine its merit."

"Since when do you put any store in what Stan Robertson thinks?"

"He and I were partners for years. Granted, it takes far longer to discover someone's virtues than their flaws, but he has many virtues and discover them I did. Why else would I consider bringing up your idea with him?"

"Because you have no choice? Because he's our commanding officer?"

"There. You've just partially answered the question. And objectively, too, so it doesn't really matter what you think of him, does it? So there."

Hudson had the distinct feeling he'd just been beaten over the head with a blunt, fuzzy instrument, but he couldn't be sure. He shrugged. What difference did it make? Irina's saying "so there" always signified that she'd thrown off the shackles of mere logic and ascended into the realm of sheer bloody-mindedness. And in that monochromatic realm, she was the crimson sovereign.

They completed the journey back to headquarters in absolute silence. At one point, Hudson snuck a sideways glance at Irina with the intention of guessing whether or not she would support his idea of going public with the case, but he instead became hopelessly aware of her physical presence. This occurred periodically, for he found Irina to be an incontestably attractive woman. On this particular occasion, however, she completely overpowered his senses. His glance became a captive gaze, and carnal thoughts danced through his mind like naked nymphs through a heavily perfumed midnight garden. As she shifted her long, shapely legs and returned his look, he panicked and became convinced that she could read his randy ruminations. Perspiring profusely, he tried desperately to alter his train of thought by performing mental arithmetic, but the numbers soon took on a life of their own and began assuming positions that wouldn't have been out of place in the Kama Sutra.

By the time he'd roared into the parking lot and buckled the pavement with his brakes, it was not digits but digitalis he desperately needed.

"You know, Hudson, I sometimes think you get a sexual thrill from driving so fast."

Hudson smiled. What a bitch. She had read his mind, after all.

"And wipe that silly grin from your face. You've got a selling job to do, and it will further your cause to no end if you look and act like an adult."

Robertson had his coat on and was just closing his office door behind him when she and Hudson stormed into the squad room. "Ah, there you are," he drawled. "I was hoping to say my goodbyes before you took off for Toronto and London. Goodbye."

Robertson put on his hat, an old-fashioned fedora, and headed for the exit. Irina blocked his path. "We need to talk."

"We all need to talk, Irina. Keeps us from being besieged by weird thoughts. Why don't we have a nice long one when you get back?"

"Now, Stanley."

"But today's my wedding anniversary. I have plans. Or, rather, Beth has plans."

Irina removed Robertson's hat and pushed him into his office. She hung it up, stripped off his coat, then forced him into his chair. "Hudson needs your opinion about something," she said as she loomed over him.

Robertson sighed heavily. "Okay, but please sit down, both of you. And you, Hudson, be so kind as to take the antique chair."

Too late. Irina slid into the chair with such determination and dispatch that Hudson almost ended up in her lap. Still tingling from his idiopathic adventures in the car, Hudson was tempted to let momentum run its course, but he caught himself. He'd suffered enough for one day.

"Irina. You're neither tormenting my chair nor raiding my jelly bean bowl. But you *are* blinking, so this must be big."

"Go on, Hudson. Tell him."

It was then that Hudson knew Irina would support his idea. And as he was immensely proud that she'd left its unveiling to him, he disclosed it to Robertson with a gravity and assurance that would have been beyond him only hours earlier. He even shed his cynicism about Robertson.

Robertson listened without interruption as Hudson briefed him on the latest developments. He listened in dead silence as Hudson put forth his proposal. He got up from his chair and paced for a minute or two while Hudson and Irina exchanged anxious glances. Finally, he stopped abruptly in his tracks and peered at Irina over his reading glasses. "You don't worry that Mr. or Mrs. Big will be alerted to your investigation?"

"You should address your concern to Hudson, Lieutenant."

"All right, Hudson. You don't worry that Mr. or Mrs. Big will be alerted to your investigation?"

"No, Sir. Mr. or Mrs. Big has such a large and powerful organization that he or she cannot fail to know already that flags are going up all over the place."

"You don't think that as a result, he or she will pull in his or her horns for a while?"

"Oh, for God's sake," sniped Irina. "Enough of this his or her business. It's clumsy. I won't be offended if you assume the monster is a man for the sake of this conversation. Promise."

"Well, then," said Hudson, suppressing a smile. "Even if *she* ceased all activity as of this moment —"

Robertson's antique chair let out a fearsome groan. Robertson grinned. Hudson continued as if nothing had happened, "— we'd still have a wealth of material to go through. But I suspect this organization is so vast that that's impossible. The QE II needs a couple of miles to stop, Lieutenant."

"You'd be revealing yourselves as the central investigators in this case, thereby exposing yourselves to extraordinary risk."

"I beg to differ. The eyes of the world will be upon us. If anything happens to us, then everything we've said will have been substantiated. Besides, we could use the eyes of the world. They wouldn't miss much."

Robertson sat and removed his glasses. He tossed them so far across his desk that Irina had to stop them from flying over the edge. "Now, Irina, what do you think of all this?"

Irina examined Robertson's glasses and decided they needed a cleaning. She took her time in withdrawing a tissue from her purse, she took her time in wiping the glasses and handing them back to the lieutenant, and she took even more time in speaking. "Well, Mr. Extemporaneous, how prepared are you to give such a speech?"

"Very."

"What I mean is, do you have something prepared, or do you plan on just winging it?"

Hudson blushed. "Actually, I worked on it all last night."

"Documentation?"

"I'll be referring to notes a lot of the time."

"Let's hear it."

Hudson rose from his chair and began to declaim. Irina tugged at his sleeve. "Spare us the theatrics, Hudson. I want to save my swooning for tonight. Sit, and just give us the words, please."

Hudson sat, although he made it very plain that it was possible to strut while seated. Forty-five minutes later, when he was done, Irina turned to Stan Robertson. "What do you think?"

"My first thought is that there's a lot of shit you haven't told me about. My second thought is that this is going to dominate the headlines around the world for a solid week. My third is how are you going to conduct an investigation if everyone on the planet knows who you are?"

"I've mulled that over, Sir," Hudson replied. "The important thing is not who solves the case, but that it gets solved, period. If I give this speech, there'll be thousands upon thousands of cops and citizens to take our place, if need be."

"I'm thinking specifically about your trip to England. This Xueqin Liang character. Your trip is costing the department a pretty penny. How's he going to react when he sees a pair of Al Gores coming at him?"

"We'll just have to dispense with the skywriting, the brass band, and the dancing clowns, and instead appear on his doorstep unannounced. Just like policemen," Irina replied.

"But when you're questioning people about his whereabouts, you'll no doubt be recognized — or at least Hudson will be — and it'll get back to him."

"Anybody who's asking about his whereabouts is obviously a cop. And cops are cops, whether they're famous or not. In either case, he'd know exactly why they're after him and he'd bolt."

Robertson flattened his palms on the desk and exhaled heavily. "I dunno. There's a kernel of truth in what you say, but there's also a hard shell of happenstance surrounding it."

"There's a solution," exclaimed Irina as she leapt from her chair and tousled Hudson's hair. "Our pretty boy will finally get these fair locks shorn."

"No —" whimpered Hudson.

"Oh, yes. And we'll darken it by about a dozen shades. Plus, you won't shave for the next while, so by the time we get to London you'll be quite grizzled. Unrecognizable."

"But I want my fifteen minutes of fame!"

Irina sat — without torturing the chair — and stared expectantly at Robertson. Reconciled to his fate, though not above smoothing out his collar-length hair, Hudson did likewise. Robertson put on his glasses and scanned an imaginary script. Eventually, he ran out of reading material. "All right. You have my backing on this. But I have to sell it to the commander, eh?"

"Given that Hudson hits the boards in about three hours, I suppose you'll be doing that right away?"

Robertson lifted the telephone receiver and dialed. He picked at the numbers like a man defusing a bomb. Commander Belanger had left for the day. "Fuck. I'll have to call his cell. And he absolutely hates being disturbed after hours."

He dialed again. Belanger was in the middle of an early supper as he had an important civic function later that evening. Gripping the receiver until his hand turned white, the lieutenant looked to Irina like a shivering, half-naked man standing at the edge of an ice floe. But he took the plunge, and then dove deep. During the course of a somewhat tumultuous fifteen minutes, he marshalled every argument Irina and Hudson had given him, and some of his own for good measure. When he finally surfaced he was gasping for air, but he had prevailed.

"The commander is cancelling his evening appointment. He wants to be there when you do your thing. Where's it happening?"

Hudson told him, and Robertson told the commander. The commander then informed Robertson that he would do his best to get Chief Beauregard and the other division commanders to attend as well. In full uniform. Given the degree to which Commander Belanger propped up Beauregard, there was little doubt that Hudson would be playing to enough brass to mint a few eight-gauge cannons.

Irina was overjoyed for Hudson. Hudson gulped.

"The commander is going to get the chief to round up as much of the media as possible," beamed Robertson. "Should be quite a spectacle. I myself will be in attendance even though it's my wedding anniversary. I'll take my wife out for a nice dinner, then we'll catch your act. I'm sure even she would rather hear what you have to say than see *La Traviata*. History will be made! And Hudson?"

"Yes, Sir?"

"Thanks a million, eh? I hate fucking opera."

CHAPTER TWENTY-TWO

Montreal. September 6, 2006. On the northwest corner of McGill University's leafy downtown campus sits the ten-storey Leacock Building, a cheerless bunker of an edifice. This exemplar of sixties Brutalist architecture was named after Stephen Leacock, one of Canadian letters' most celebrated authors and humourists. Leacock, who died in 1944, would not have been amused.

Nevertheless, it is a highly serviceable building, not the least because it is home to Leacock 132, McGill's largest auditorium. With commendable lighting and comfortable, stepped seating for six hundred, Leacock 132 is one of the busiest theatres in town.

And it had never been busier than on this night. By 8:30, it was filled to capacity. By quarter to nine, Leacock 232 had swallowed up as much of the overflow as it could digest. Montreal's newest media darling and biodiversity guru, Sergeant-Detective Athol Curzon Hudson, would grace the semicircular stage at nine sharp. Lightning would spring from his fingertips.

The fact that eight of Montreal's finest were parked in the front row and in full regalia heightened the sense of anticipation and intrigue. That representatives of Montreal's major English *and* French daily newspapers, television outlets, and radio stations were in attendance lent the proceedings a definite air of occasion. The fact that reporters and cameramen from CNN and the BBC World Service were extremely conspicuous lent that occasion a perfervid quality that one only finds at the scene of a mass slaying, a natural disaster, or an appearance by Paris Hilton.

"Hold still, Hudson," Irina barked as she straightened out his tie. "Television has a way of magnifying flaws that would pass unnoticed in real life."

Hudson lowered the notes he'd been studying at arm's length. "I do a good Windsor knot, Irina. I don't see how it can be improved upon."

"I've got news for you, Hudson. This is a four in hand, not a Windsor."

"Oh."

"But at least you passed the wide end twice around, so you don't look like a high school junior at his first dance. Tell me, are you nervous?"

"Apparently. But nothing like when I was running through it for Chief Beauregard."

Irina didn't need to ask how that preview had gone. If it had been anything less than resoundingly convincing, there would be no police brass present. Nor any media, for that matter. In fact, there would be no speech at all, and even less of Hudson.

The curvaceous Miss Lillian Bowles, who was inevitably the moderator at many of Hudson's talks, poked her head backstage. "Two minutes Athol ... uh, Sergeant Hudson."

"Thanks, Miss Bowles."

Irina raised her eyebrows. "Miss Bowles? I'd have thought you'd progressed beyond that months ago, *Athol*."

"I'm waiting for the right moment," Hudson whispered.

Irina was now brushing invisible lint from his jacket. "The right moment was six months ago."

"I didn't want to take advantage."

"I've got news for you, Hudson. When a woman wants you to ravish her, a dinner invitation isn't taking advantage. What's the matter? Are you that timid?"

Hudson blushed and then said hotly, "You can't talk to me like that. You've crossed the line, Sergeant Drach!"

Good, thought Irina. Indignation was the best armour against penetrating scrutiny. He was ready to go out there and kill his audience.

And kill them he did.

Which is not to say that he bolted onto the stage and immediately assailed them. Quite the contrary. He slowly made his way to the edge of the stage, stopped dead, and stood in perfect silence for two minutes. The members of his audience at first became restive and fidgeted. They then became impatient and began to mutter or cough under their breaths. Next, they began looking at each other in confusion. Finally, acute discomfort set in. They empathized with his apparent plight. The more sensitive among them even experienced that cold, clammy feeling one gets at the back of the neck when either enduring or witnessing utter and complete humiliation.

Nobody could breathe anymore. The silence had become a vise, and it squeezed the air from every set of lungs in the house, Irina's included.

Finally, he opened his mouth and spoke, but ever so softly. As he did, he became a magician delivering the goods, the payoff, the resolution, the catharsis — what they call the Prestige. "An uncomfortable silence, Ladies and Gentlemen. It kind of makes you want to scream, doesn't it?"

More than a few mumbled in agreement.

"Well, I'm sorry you were subjected to that, but I wanted you to experience what law enforcement agencies and wildlife organizations worldwide have been going though for the last few days. What I'm about to say is a scream of release. Lest you think I'm being merely self-indulgent, however, I would also point out that it's a call for vigilance, not only from you few souls here tonight but from citizens around the planet."

Hudson paused long enough for his words to sink in. This was an audience well accustomed to alarmist harangues, but his slow and deliberate reference to global officialdom had even the most jaded among them perched at the edges of their seats.

"Ladies and Gentlemen, there is a vast and sinister organization that has, for the last eighteen months, been systematically plundering our seed banks and skimming the finest specimens from every animal species around the globe. Some megalomaniac and his myrmidons are then exterminating these creatures and storing their DNA — along with the seeds — at some unauthorized and undisclosed location which, for lack of a better name, we'll call 'the Doomsday Compound.' Now, some might see this as a useful hedge against cataclysmic changes in the Earth's climatological, environmental, or societal matrices, but I would point out that not only have hundreds of innocent people died at the hands of this consortium, but that it's wreaking havoc with the work of scientists and conservationists the world over. It's not engaged in this activity for your benefit or mine: its clandestine nature suggests that it is for the benefit of a select few."

Hudson had the audience's undivided attention. The only sound to be heard was the clicking and whirring of cameras.

"Which is to say that none of you here, or any of the animals you cherish, are worthy of preservation or succession."

Hudson gave the audience a few moments to huff and puff amongst themselves. He thought he was doing rather well, notwithstanding that he lacked Irina's luminous ability to be right even when she was wrong.

When the audience had finished exchanging looks and comments of mortal fury with each other and were once against leaning in his direction like flowers to the sun, he went to the lectern and began to lay out his case. Periodically referring to his notes, he quietly but artfully shed light upon nearly fifty cases of seed bank raids and animal abductions. Places, dates, pedigrees of the animals spirited away, and, of course, the names of the human victims, were meticulously recounted. Naturally, the world-renowned racehorse Zarathustra and the African lion known as I-árishóni were prominently noted. By the time he'd finished, some forty-five minutes later, the audience sat in stunned silence. Even the phalanx of media representatives momentarily set aside the tools of their trade to turn their collars against the dank gloom.

Then, as is so often the case with people who have been given devastating news, the crowd looked to him for metaphysical solace. Hudson was ready. "I should point out, Ladies and Gentlemen, that we've begun to piece together the puzzle only in the last few days, prompted by the abduction of this police department's own superdog, Bismarck."

The eight uniformed officers in the front row rattled their brass buttons in ecstasy. There, in full view of the world, Hudson had just assigned all credit for this investigation to the Montreal Urban Community Police Force. Chief Beauregard furtively perused his notes in preparation for the impromptu remarks he'd be making when Hudson was done.

"Already, law enforcement agencies around the world, including Interpol, are busy collating material and actively seeking witnesses. But I've not come before you tonight simply to give you an update on these disasters and the subsequent police activity. We need your help. And by you, I mean *you*, uniquely you, whether you live in the city or the country, whether you live in Montreal, New York, Paris, Mecca, Sydney, Moscow, Phnom Penh, or in the steppes of Russia, the Arctic, the jungles of South America, or the Gobi desert. You must be vigilant. You must look upon our fellow creatures not merely as resources but as friends and neighbours, and you must do what you would do for any good neighbour. You must be aware of them, and respect them, and look out for them, for as go your neighbours, so go you. Thank you, Ladies and Gentlemen. And thank you on behalf of the police forces around the world who eagerly await any information or insight you might have for them. And thank you, most of all, on behalf of our friends and neighbours who have the perfect right to run and jump, and burrow and bask, and climb and crawl, and swim and soar in glorious freedom."

Stooping from modesty, Hudson took his seat next to Lillian Bowles while the crowd went wild with approbation. Overcome with fellow-feeling, Miss Bowles quickly embraced him and planted a big wet one on his cheek. Hudson blushed, and the audience redoubled its stomping, whistling, and cheering.

It was rather anticlimactic when Chief Beauregard took the stage to field questions, especially since the majority of the reporters had already fled the hall to file their stories, but he took it with good grace. All in all, it had been a very good night for the force, and his political bosses would think kindly of him. Perhaps they would even let him buy the limo he'd been pining for.

"Bravo," said Irina, backstage. "A little over the top in places, especially toward the end there, when you managed to sound like Saint Francis of Assisi, or at least Doctor Dolittle, but you hit them where they live. Now, what about Lillian Bowles? Are you going to ask her for a date?"

"I, uh —"

Irina tightened his tie so much that it almost strangled him. "Listen, Hudson, it's time you lusted after someone your own age. Now, the poor girl is in the wings, panting for you. Unless you march over there and set up a cozy little dinner with her, I'll be going to Toronto and London all by myself."

CHAPTER TWENTY-THREE

Toronto. September 6, 2006. The Challenger 604, a Canadian business jet with intercontinental capabilities, lifted off from Toronto's Pearson International Airport at ten sharp. With a cruising speed of more than five-hundred-miles per hour, it would complete the eight–hundred-mile trip to Dryden, at the province of Ontario's western border, well before midnight.

Though designed to accommodate nineteen people, this particular airplane had been refitted to provide seating for just five. The lift gained by eliminating those fourteen potential passengers had been gobbled up by acres of burled walnut trim, a sizable cherry conference table with matching chairs, and kid-leather seats that converted into commodious beds at the push of a button. The predominantly grey and beige interior also housed a well-stocked bar, a pool table, and a mammoth plasma television, not to mention such essentials as a shower and a small sauna.

As Jason Conrad sipped his seventeen-year Old Pulteney whisky and puffed away on a Montecristo Edmundo, he leafed through a glossy book on Gothic cathedrals. Across the cabin from him, Chinua Amadi popped open a can of 7-Up, turned on the television, and leaned back into his armchair, hoping that the programming was boring enough to put him to sleep.

The television was tuned to CNN. He was just about to go in search of something on the order of a home-decorating show when a face caught his attention. Chinua was used to seeing people he'd met on the television, for he'd met just about everybody that mattered — including Queen Elizabeth, the American president, and the Pope — but this was someone he'd met very, very recently. And he'd been locked up in either this plane or two of Conrad's four Canadian offices all day.

Chinua turned up the sound. But of course! Sergeant Irina Drach's young sidekick! He listened for a few moments. Then, sweating profusely despite the moderate temperature in the cabin, he turned up the volume yet again.

"For God's sake, Chinua. Are you becoming deaf?"

"I think you should listen to this, Sir."

Conrad looked up from his book and recognized the face on the screen immediately. He watched and listened through a cloud of cigar smoke for a couple of minutes. "Go to the Beeb."

It was the same thing on the BBC. Clips of Hudson making his larger points followed by a tumbling, excited summation by the reporter.

Chinua almost gagged on his soda. "I didn't know he had it in him. He barely said a peep this afternoon."

"I'm not surprised. He knows body language. He bent to Irina Drach's the way a rush bends to the wind. Let's have the CBC. *The National* will be on."

After forty-five seconds of Hudson's videotaped performance, Peter Mansbridge, *The National*'s anchor, conducted an on-air interview with Hudson.

When Chinua flipped over to CTV, Canada's other national broadcaster, they found that regular programming had been interrupted in order to present Hudson's revelations. Their esteemed anchorman, Lloyd Robertson, was handling the story in tones usually reserved for the wreck of a space shuttle. A highly agitated Chinua first spilled his drink, apologized profusely to Conrad, then began pacing back and forth while the attendant mopped things up. "This is awful! Next, he'll be on Larry King and Oprah! What then?"

"Sit down, take a deep breath, and listen to what I have to tell you. There are more than seven billion people on this planet, Chinua. This was bound to happen sooner or later. The only glitches are that the blasted police dog happened to be a Montreal dog, and that Irina was able to nab me for questioning. But even then, I doubt any damage was done. My charm offensive can hardly have been a waste of time."

"You called her 'Irina'!"

"What should I have called her?"

"That evil bitch! That dangerous snoop! Even simply Sergeant Drach!"

"Ah. Point taken. Well, never mind, Chinua. You're forgetting I can read people the way a medium reads tarot cards."

"But she's a woman."

"Yes, she certainly is. And need I remind you that I've had dozens upon dozens of women in my time?"

"Yes, you've *had* them! Women who've prostrated themselves at your feet, and then on your bed. But this one is different."

"I know. That's why I called her Irina rather than 'evil bitch' or 'dangerous snoop.'"

Chinua hissed in frustration. He snatched his half-empty soda can from the attendant and bade him leave the compartment immediately. Falling to his knees at Conrad's side, he said, "One day you will meet your match, Master, and if that person is a woman, then you will be overmatched. It is the way of the world. Why do you think so many African men take more than one wife? So that no one woman will entertain delusions of equivalency! For once a woman begins to think those thoughts, then the man is lost."

"The years I was married to Linda were the happiest of my life."

"A wonderful woman, Sir, and a tragic loss, but it was only with her passing that you rose from among the ranks of quotidian megalomaniacs to become a titan."

Conrad stubbed out his cigar with more vigor than was necessary. "You can read my mind, right? Or so you say?"

"Yes, Sir."

"Then picture this," said Conrad, as he closed his eyes.

Chinua visualized a series of mortally disturbing scenarios, many of them featuring pointy objects. With great dispatch, he withdrew to his spot in front of the television and resumed his scrutiny of Hudson. Conrad's eyes were still closed as the telephone rang. He picked up the receiver without opening them. "Conrad here."

He listened for a few moments, then his eyelids flew open as if someone had just poured cold water down his shirt. "Chinua, turn that thing down."

Chinua Amadi did as instructed while Conrad switched over to the speaker phone. "It's Raphael Sparata," he said to Chinua. "Go ahead, Sparata. Repeat what you just told me."

Raphael Sparata was the governor of the facility. A big, sanguine man with a normally booming voice, he sounded as if live electrodes had been taped to each of his extremities. "Well … uh … as you will be here in a very short while, Mr. Conrad, I thought it incumbent upon me to mention that the horse and lion have gone missing. Escaped, with the help of the old man charged with their care —"

"You thought it incumbent upon you to *mention* that they've gone? Listen, Sparata, 'mention' is something you do when the waiter's forgotten to bring more butter. This is something of a completely different order. When did those animals go missing?"

"Uh … almost two days ago. But I assure you, Sir, that everything possible is being done to recapture them. We have helicopters, dog teams, expert trackers —"

"And yet it's been two days!"

"But they are singular beasts, Mr. Conrad. Indeed, that is the very reason you expressed interest in them."

"Nice try, Sparata, but that won't wash. You find those animals — alive if possible, and by the time I get there — or the Zulu Squad will flatten you in the dirt and insert a spear where the sun don't shine."

The Zulu Squad was Conrad's highly mobile, extremely brutal enforcement team. All four men were indeed Zulus, and although they all had cellphones and affected urban Western dress, they cherished the old ways. Impaling was especially dear to their hearts. At a gut level, Conrad found the practice distasteful, but the idealist in him could not help but be charmed by such a potent image. "I assume, Mr. Sparata, that you've been doing the dumb thing and are merely tracking them. Might I suggest you calculate their speed and trajectory and set up your personnel to intercept them? There's nothing quite like a trap. What works in business no doubt works on the ground, as well."

Sparata sputtered out his thanks and signed off when it was apparent the great man had nothing else to say on the matter. He'd no sooner hung up the phone when a note crossed his desk: Zarathustra was dead. After issuing orders that hewed to Conrad's suggestion, he vomited up two days' worth of Alka Seltzer.

Meanwhile, Chinua Amadi took what comfort he could from having guessed correctly about the sharp objects. But then he was suddenly gripped by a disturbing thought. What if his master was even the least bit predictable to people other than himself? For the rest of the flight to Dryden, he was haunted by the specter of Irina Drach, and especially of her pitiless grey eyes. They would miss nothing. Not deviant behaviour, nor adherence to the most arcane of motifs. Nothing.

CHAPTER TWENTY-FOUR

The boreal forest. Early September 7, 2006. "Well, this is some kind of bitch slap," exclaimed Charmaine Washington as she hopped down from the helicopter along with the four rambunctious dogs. "We're just going to sit here on our behinds and hope that lion comes our way?"

Vincent de Groot was unloading their equipment. "No. We're going to sit on our behinds and hope he *doesn't* come our way. I don't know about you, but I kind of like my behind. Of course, I like yours better —"

Charmaine withdrew her sidearm and cracked the barrel across the back of a hand that was groping its way toward her buttocks.

De Groot groaned. "Geez, that smarts! I was only kidding. But you know, if you'd wear fatigues like everybody else instead of getups like that all the time, it sure would go easier on the rest of us. *Fatigues*, get it? It means tired. But you always look so damn perky. In particular, that apple bottom of yours —"

"If I was some bony-assed white girl, you wouldn't be talking to me like that, so don't you go disrespecting me. Now hurry up with the unloading."

Charmaine led the dogs some ten yards from the chopper and tied them to a tree, leaving de Groot to shout over his shoulder. "That's it? You're going to sit there like Cleopatra while I do all the work?"

"The downdraft from the rotors was wrecking my hair and getting sand in my face. I have to be looking my best for Richard when we get back to base."

De Groot pulled their armaments from the helicopter then sent it on its way. "I must confess that being stuck in a forest hundreds of miles from nowhere at two in the morning with you is going to be bloody torture. So, Charmaine … why Richard rather than me?"

"Simple. He treats me like a lady. Now, let's change the subject, Mr. de Groot."

"Last report has the animal headed southeast. If he were to get by us and keep going in that direction for another seven-hundred miles, he'd end up in Toronto."

"Maybe we should just let him go on through. He'd probably get arrested for jaywalking, there."

De Groot resumed lighting the kerosene lamps and shutting down those powered by battery, all the while becoming increasingly intoxicated by Charmaine's presence. Reclining in the flickering light, dressed in knee-high boots, tight jeans, and a parka that did little to conceal her bosom, she was a dark and seductive empress of the night. He searched every nook and cranny of his fevered mind for something to say, for the silence breathed heavily in his ear and whispered occultly erotic thoughts. When at last he opened his mouth, he found himself offering words that were seldom said aloud at the facility. "I've heard some things at the base. Bad things."

"Oh?"

"You won't tell anyone?"

"Promise."

He forged ahead. The intimacy implicit in her murmur emboldened him. "Remember Jósef Krasicki?"

"Be serious. He's the reason we're here. And you make it sound like he died two years ago, not the night before last."

"Killed, Charmaine. Not 'died.'"

"Well, he had it coming, didn't he?"

"Why do words sound so much crueller on the lips of someone so lovely?"

"Because you know I don't have to lie."

He watched Charmaine stroke her ebony hair and moisten her lips, and he nodded dumbly. Her great cat's eyes glowed in the dim light, and he was drawn to them like a freezing man to a warm hearth.

She snapped her long, slender fingers. "Hey, lover boy. You were saying?"

"Yes ... anyway ... for a while I drew guard duty at the animal compound, and I was quite friendly with Jósef." De Groot's voice choked with grief. "He would often let me feed Zarathustra. And now they're both gone."

Charmaine gave him a few moments to compose himself, then inquired softly, "So, Vincent? I presume it was the old man who told you that thing you were going to tell me."

De Groot rubbed his eyes. "Yes, and it was this: no one ever leaves the organization alive. Nobody ever has."

"Oh? And how did he know that?"

"Because of the animals. It was some middle-management types who brought them in, and Jósef overheard them whispering together. One said some John Doe wanted out and died in a rather ugly and untimely fashion. The other one said that John Doe should have learned from other peoples' mistakes."

"What does your contract say, Vincent?"

"In return for more money than I thought I'd ever see in a lifetime, I'm bound for five years. During that time, I'm not to attempt communication with family or friends ... not that I'd have the opportunity, anyway."

"Hm. None of us, actually. You in your third year?"

De Groot nodded.

"So am I," said Charmaine. "Just like a lot of the staff up here. Right from the start. Now excuse me if I sound a little dubious, but I'm wondering what's supposed to happen when all our contracts are up. Are hundreds, or thousands, also going to die ugly and untimely deaths?"

"Doesn't seem plausible, does it? Maybe most will be offered contract extensions."

As Charmaine slowly sat upright, her voice dropped an octave. "Although … there is that bit about risking the well-being of our families if we try to decamp before our contracts are up. I've always thought that was pretty weird, but I guess I let it slide because of the small fortune I'm making."

De Groot noticed the dogs were becoming restive, but he thought nothing of it. His hungry eyes were once again feasting on Charmaine. "I don't have much in the way of friends and family on the outside. No one, actually."

"Me neither. Maybe that's one of their keys to recruiting. All the friends in the world I have are at the facility. Richard, for example —"

"And me?"

Charmaine lit up the night with her smile. "Provided you don't try to grope me again." She began to sing in a light, lilting voice. "In the forest, the mighty forest, the lion sleeps tonight —"

De Groot joined her for a chorus of "wimowehs" but then stopped abruptly and shushed Charmaine into silence. The dogs were beginning to mill about so deliriously that their leashes were becoming hopelessly tangled. "Something's out there."

De Groot got to his feet and freed the dogs from the tree. He then withdrew some wood shavings from a pouch on his belt — wood shavings from the lion's cage — and allowed each dog to nose them. All four were straining at their leashes so mightily that de Groot could barely hold onto them. "Uh, they're not by any chance pointing north, are they?"

Charmaine consulted her compass as she stood up from her sleeping bag. "Northwest, to be precise. Here, let me hang onto Sneezy and Grumpy."

De Groot handed over the two leashes. "I didn't want to mention it before, but lions don't sleep at night."

"Oh. That's bad news, isn't it? Well, how do we handle this? Do we unleash the dogs or keep them with us?"

"I don't know. What do you think?"

"Unleash them. I'd just as soon be a quarter of a mile behind them when they run into that thing."

"Here," said De Groot as he picked up an AK-47 and handed it to Charmaine. "I'm not so sure our comfort zone is as much as a quarter of a mile."

"The air's moving in from the north. Chances are he's completely unaware of us."

"I'm not so sure about that, either. A lion has a really keen sense of smell."

"Is there anything you *are* sure of?"

De Groot looked longingly at Charmaine. After reading him from bold headlines to fine print, she quickly looked away and released her dogs. They lunged, howling, into the darkness. De Groot released his hounds, and they, too, set off in full hue and cry. "Anyway, who needs a sense of smell," he said dolefully as he picked up his own semi-automatic weapon. "Those mutts are making enough racket to wake up the dead."

Charmaine moved so close to de Groot that their shoulders touched. "I'd rather you didn't speak of the dead, just now."

He put his arm around her. It was a reflexively protective gesture that almost immediately became charged with sexual energy. "We're kind of between a rock and a hard place," he croaked distractedly. "If we follow those dogs, we risk our lives in a big way. If we survive that lion, there's still the danger that comes with being part of the organization."

"Should we make a run for it? Head south?"

"So you believe what old Jósef said?"

"I believe what you said."

De Groot could hardly believe his ears. "And what about Richard?"

"He treats me like a lady, but he doesn't treat me like a woman. There's more passion in your eyes than there is in his touch."

From beyond the shadows, they heard the dogs' cries of distress. De Groot tightened his grip on Charmaine's shoulder. Then, over the course of the next minute, they heard four distinct death shrieks. Charmaine urgently slipped her arm around his waist. "Poor creatures," she whispered. "They've just run headlong through the gates of hell."

De Groot was exactly where he'd yearned to be for twelve long months, yet he reckoned that if they didn't move on, these precious moments would be his last. He disengaged himself from Charmaine and slung one of the heavy knapsacks over his back. "There's certainly nothing to be gained by taking a stand and trying to kill him. As long as he's alive, the trackers coming up behind him won't spare us much thought. And I doubt he's interested in chasing us down, so if we head due east we should be okay."

Charmaine shouldered the other knapsack, then shyly kissed him on the lips. "I'm not worried. I feel safe with you."

The four dogs had been taken completely by surprise. They'd drawn up to within ten yards of I-árishóni and begun baying loudly and triumphantly. Their experience with wolves and bears had conditioned them to regard this as a safe distance, but in a fraction of a second and in a single leap the lion had halved the dimensions of their buffer zone. From then on, they'd had as much chance of survival as a cow dozing in the path of a hurtling freight train. I-árishóni's power, speed, and agility left three of them battered and torn to pieces just as they were whirling about for a fast retreat. The fourth, a wily old Doberman named Doc, had hung back a few paces from the others in recognition of the lion's immensity, and was able to make a run for it. However, I-árishóni had overtaken him within one hundred yards and broken his back with a single swipe of his paw. For good measure, the lion had then separated Doc's head from his writhing body.

I-árishóni knew he had to continue his journey without delay. The night breeze carried with it the scent of his hunters. But he was reluctant to go in the direction whence had come the dogs, for where there were dogs, there were men.

I-árishóni set off in an easterly direction.

CHAPTER TWENTY-FIVE

London, England. September 8, 2006. Irina and Hudson had been busy in the extreme during the previous twelve hours. After Hudson had concluded his speech at 10:00 p.m. the previous evening, he'd spent an hour doing interviews with a multitude of media reporters and dignitaries, then another half hour stammering his way through dinner plans with the resplendent Miss Lillian Bowles before Irina had whisked him away to her modest cottage in Montreal West. By 2:00 a.m., his strawberry blond tresses were lying on the floor of her kitchen and Irina was holding up a mirror to a head full of spiky orange hair.

"You aren't doing much to advance my relationship with Lillian," Hudson mumbled rancorously. "She'll freak when she sees me."

"I decided that brown just wouldn't do the trick. Now, have a few more belts of vodka. It'll dull the pain."

When Irina produced a pair of zero-power horn-rimmed glasses and perched them on his nose, Hudson drained his glass then poured himself a double. "I look like a bloody busboy from the Hard Rock Café."

"Come now, there's more to you than just a pretty face. And for your information, I'm going more for the hairdresser look." She removed the glasses and produced a pair of tweezers. "Now look at me and hold perfectly still."

She began plucking his eyebrows to within a hair's breadth of tyranny. If she hadn't inadvertently caressed his cheek while steadying his head, or approached him so closely that he could feel her breath on his face and gaze deeply into those cabalistic grey eyes, he would have squawked like a baby. As it was, he fell completely under her spell, and felt not unlike a youth undergoing some primitive sexual initiation. Irina was not insensitive to this fact, and made every effort to avoid touching his knees with her own.

By 3:00 a.m., Hudson's transformation was complete and Irina bustled as she'd never bustled before. She awoke him from his trance with a hearty slap on the shoulder, thrust her bulging suitcase into his unsuspecting arms, and quick-marched him out the door and into the waiting cab. Within thirty minutes they were at Trudeau International Airport, where they consumed gallons of coffee before boarding Air Canada 483 for the 5:30 a.m. flight to Toronto. By 7:30, September 7, they were in her cousin's house on Lowther Avenue, just north of the University of Toronto. Neither of them had napped during the one-hour flight, and neither could nap now. They each had time enough for breakfast and a shower before they were out Martha's door by 9:00 a.m.

Thirty minutes and ten blocks later, they were being ushered into a conference room at the Rogers Building on Jarvis Street. There they had an hour-long chat with Ted Rogers, whose Rogers Communications Inc. had allowed him to amass a personal fortune of four-and-a-half billion dollars, making him Canada's fourth richest man. Like Paul Desmarais in Montreal, Rogers was initially amused by the presence of these two policemen, but the nature of their business soon had him recognizing both the gravity of the situation and Hudson, disguise notwithstanding.

"I *do* keep an eye on the news, you know," quipped the media mogul with a twinkle in his eye.

Irina and Hudson left with a generous offer of help in their investigations, as well as his year's itinerary and some pertinent financial data.

"Now, David Thomson," said Hudson as they clambered into a cab. "Have I told you how humiliating it was when I called up Thomson Corp., only to be told that Ken Thomson had died in June? Have I?"

"Yes, Hudson, you have. Several times. And do try to remember that I'm an officer of the law, not a therapist. Repeated accounts of that particular humiliation will not exorcise it, but merely remind me of how you fell down in your research. And, in turn, I will remind you of that fact. So you can see that telling me the same thing over and over again is counterproductive, possibly even damaging to your mental health."

"It was a Forbes list. Who knew it was out of date?"

Irina called to the taxi driver, "I sincerely hope you're travelling in a straight line, driver, because we certainly aren't back here."

"You bet, Miss. Have you there in five minutes."

Irina was buoyed immensely by having been called "Miss."

"There" turned out to be the TD Bank Tower on Wellington, in the heart of Toronto's financial district. Although the global information technology, financial services, and media conglomerate's international headquarters were in Stamford, Connecticut, here were Thomson Corporation's Canadian headquarters. And here awaited David Thomson, chairman of Thomson Corporation, co-chairman of the privately owned Woodbridge Company — which owns seventy percent of Thomson Corp. — and scion of the world's tenth richest family. As had Desmarais, Conrad, and Rogers, the fifty-year-old Thomson greeted the two policemen with unfailing good manners and more than a little curiosity. And in the end, as had the other men before him, he offered his full co-operation. At the conclusion of their interview, he even offered that they lunch with him in the executive dining room. They gratefully accepted, and dined in a manner to which they were unaccustomed, but to which they quickly adapted. Hudson became quite loquacious, especially when Thomson let on that he recognized him from the news reports, and the two men fell into an impassioned discussion about Canadian aboriginal art. For the most part, Irina was content to study Thomson, periodically offer a definitive statement on the subject at hand, nibble at her veal parmigiana, and ponder the ramifications of a dinner with Jason Conrad.

By the time they left the TD Bank Tower, it had gone one o'clock. As their appointment with Galen Weston was not until three, Hudson was adamant that they should return to Martha's to relax for an hour or so. But Irina had other ideas, and they were soon at the Royal Ontario Museum, surrounded by the splendors of ancient Egypt. Hudson had been deadened by two glasses of wine and a sleepless night, and as much as he loved antiquities, he had eyes only for the strategically placed banquettes. Irina would intermittently cruise by him, scowling. "If more people lounged about as you do, there would be no civilizations to speak of."

By three, an edified Irina and a mummified Hudson were at the head office of George Weston Ltd. and in the presence of Galen Weston, whose net worth of ten billion dollars made him Canada's third richest man. The tall, dapper, silver-haired man of sixty-six years, who controlled a food and retail empire that included Weston Bakeries, Holt Renfrew, Canada's largest grocery chain (Loblaw), and England's Selfridges, was at first a bit more circumspect than had been the other billionaires, no doubt because of a violent kidnapping attempt at his Irish country estate some twenty years earlier. But as soon as he recognized Hudson — and that was very soon, much to the latter's delight — he became entranced by the immensity and complexity of the problem and posed far more questions than Irina was at liberty to answer.

At 3:30, when Irina announced that she and Hudson had to rush off to catch the 6:10 p.m. flight to London, Weston insisted they use his limousine and chauffeur. As a consequence, the two detectives made the trip from St. Clair Avenue East to Pearson International Airport in leather-bound, climate-controlled luxury. That they'd previously arranged to have their baggage checked in at 3:30 p.m. sharp by airport security personnel made their stately procession through the rapidly clogging arteries of Canada's largest city that much more carefree. Hudson fell asleep and dreamed of still greater glory while Irina, between crossword puzzles, mulled over ways to improve Hudson's disguise. Shaving clean the head that yearned for a crown of laurel leaves was becoming a distinct possibility.

Air Canada Flight 856 touched down at Heathrow Airport on September 8 at 6:25 a.m., London time. Because both Irina and Hudson had been up the entire night before, then slept soundly through the seven hour flight, their adjustment to the new time zone would be an easy one. England's morning was their morning.

Their adjustment to the Glynne Court Hotel — a converted Georgian row house on Great Cumberland Place, just two blocks from Marble Arch and that great shopping Mecca, Oxford Street — would be quite another matter. Or, rather, Irina's adjustment to the Glynne Court would be another matter, for Hudson, being male, was less inclined to make a fuss about such matters.

As Irina gazed corrosively around the cramped and dingy lobby, Hudson said, "Did you notice, by the way, that even though they drive on the left hand side of the street here, the pedestrians pass each other on the right? Interesting, eh? Shows how counterintuitive driving on the left is."

"I wonder if the fleas in this hotel pass each other on the right, too?"

Hudson felt badly for Mohammed the receptionist, who shifted uncomfortably behind his counter. "Ah, you are two very fortunate people," Mohammed said gamely. "Each has a double bed with an ensuite."

"With running water?"

"The same water they have at the Dorchester Hotel, Madam."

Irina allowed a small smile. "I'm sorry, Mohammed. I didn't mean to be rude. This is none of your fault. Why, you're probably shackled at the ankles." Irina took up the pen and signed the registry. "No ... there's a particular Stanley J. Robertson I am seething over. When I next see him, I believe I shall blink so much that I'll induce an epileptic seizure in him."

"As you are blinking now, Madam?"

"No. Like this!"

Mohammed staggered back a pace. Irina gathered up her change and her suitcase and stomped up the stairs to her room.

Hudson laid his eighty-pounds sterling on the counter. "That's Hyde Park Corner down by Marble Arch?"

"Yes, Sir."

"And Piccadilly Circus? How do I get there?"

"Ah, yes. You are most fortunate to be staying at such a central hotel. You have only to walk down to Oxford Street, turn left, and go along for fifteen blocks until Regent Street, where you will turn right and go down it for thirteen blocks. A forty-five minute walk, no more, with much to see and purchase in between. But, Sir —"

"Yes, Mohammed?"

"The lady. If you were to continue down Regent Street, then past Trafalgar Square, and down Whitehall as far as the Houses of Parliament, there is something at the foot of Westminster Bridge which she would appreciate."

"Oh? And what's that?"

"Why, the statue of Boadicea. The warrior queen."

CHAPTER TWENTY-SIX

The Doomsday Complex. September 7, 2006. From Dryden, Jason Conrad and Chinua Amadi had taken off from the one-strip airport in a Cessna 208 Caravan outfitted with floats. Although it was 1:00 a.m., and both were jet-lagged from a three-day period that had found them in Beijing, then Montreal, then Toronto, Conrad was at the controls of the single turboprop airplane while his pilot played chess with Chinua in the spacious cabin. Canadian to the core, Conrad revelled in being both master and slave to the black, avaricious wilderness five-thousand feet below him.

Cruising at one-hundred-fifty miles per hour, they made the trip to Misquamaebin Lake in just under three hours. There they were met by an armed detail of five men and chauffeured by Range Rover along a paved, private road to the Doomsday Complex.

"Sir?"

"Yes, Chinua?"

"That you are more capable than the vast majority of humanity goes without saying, but how is it that a being who must eat, dress, and defecate as anyone else can hold the fate of millions, perhaps billions, in his hands?"

"How come I'm a colossus and you're a worm. Is that it?"

"Just so," Chinua snickered. "I grovel in curiosity and wonder."

"We are all of us created equal, Chinua. Despite what you say, there isn't much in the way of ability or talent that distinguishes one person from another. Even if you're a genius, there are still plenty of other geniuses about, and there will always be someone who can either match or surpass you."

"That is well and good, Sir, but I am interested in what makes a person such as yourself uniquely you, with all considerations of genetics and breeding set aside."

"Surely you're aware that providence is all that's left?"

"Yes, and I wish to know whether you consider your estate to be the result of either chance or the workings of God."

"If there is a God, then he's busy elsewhere. He has other projects which he finds more interesting than mankind. So he's abandoned us. But it is his legacy that every man and woman is capable of generating ideas, sometimes great ones. Whether the person chooses to implement those ideas, or to ignore them, or to subvert them to satisfy personal ambition is a matter of choice."

"And you have chosen to implement them? You are, in effect, doing God's work?"

"Correction: I am not doing God's work. I am doing God's work *for* him. I am picking up the slack."

"This is most illuminating. I have heard people say there is no God, or that he is uncaring, but I don't believe I've ever heard someone describe him as basically lazy or distracted."

"If he weren't, Chinua, there probably wouldn't be people like me. Which, I believe, is the answer to your original question."

"Not quite, Sir. You haven't addressed the question of why you choose to implement those great ideas, and others do not."

"You're the one who wanted to exclude considerations of genetics and breeding, Chinua. But I put this to you: why do you think I'm busy collecting only the finest specimens of each species?"

Chinua was stymied. He couldn't help but feel that Conrad's reasoning was facile, but the force of the man's personality was such that he could only mumble his gratitude for the revelations. And in doing so, he saw Conrad's point. The world, and everything and everyone in it, belonged to those who believed they existed for a special purpose. That was the wellspring of power and charisma.

Some twenty minutes after gliding down onto the surface of Lake Misquamaebin, Chinua and Conrad were being whisked down the entrance ramp of the facility and directly to Governor Raphael Sparata's office in Block A. While comfortably appointed, the white office nonetheless looked like the control room of a nuclear facility. Sparata, who feared Conrad at the best of times, was the colour of rotting vegetation.

"I am so sorry about the horse, Sir! Sorry, sorry, sorry! Nature is so very, very cruel!"

Conrad stared out over the facility through a panoramic window. "You preside over the most technologically advanced city in the history of the universe. You have scientists who eat enriched uranium for breakfast. You have a small army with enough mobility and firepower to successfully storm the Kremlin. But you manage to lose a bloody horse in your own backyard. So, now ... where's the fucking kitty cat?"

Sparata fell to his knees and began sobbing. Disgusted by this pathetic display, Conrad hooked the toe of his shoe under Sparata's chin and lifted the man's face toward him. "Yes?"

"We have been plagued by bad luck, Sir —"

"There is no such thing as bad luck, Sparata. Only bad decisions. Now, did you implement my suggestions?"

"Most certainly, Mr. Conrad. Most certainly. But it now appears that the personnel who were installed on the lion's most probable trajectory have disappeared. Or, at the very least, they have not once responded to our radio calls. AWOL, as it were."

"Because you don't run a tight enough ship. So what are you doing about it?"

"Even as we speak, a helicopter is speeding toward their drop-off point."

Conrad grabbed Sparata under the arms and hoisted him to his feet. "A helicopter? Singular?"

"The helicopter is carrying not one but two tracker teams, Sir!"

"But both teams will be in the same place! What's the use of that?"

"This kind of thing is not my specialty," Sparata wailed. "I am an administrator, Mr. Conrad, not a hunter. That lion killed my chief of security!"

"What about that jackbooted Franz Hauptmann, the self-styled commandant? Where in hell is he?"

"He is out there somewhere, Mr. Conrad, shooting our personnel."

"Well, at least *he's* efficient." Conrad turned away from Sparata and faced Chinua, smiling ruefully. "It's been rather a long day, hasn't it?"

"It has, Sir."

"What do you suggest?"

"About thirty-six hours of sleep, Sir."

"I don't need sleep, Chinua. I need some good news. And if nobody's going to bring me any, I'll have to make it myself. Sparata! Are there any choppers left here?"

"One, Sir."

"And *that* is the helicopter the second tracker team should have been in, you knucklehead, but ready it for me because I'm taking it out."

Sparata, though down on his heels, wasn't completely spineless. He thought he might venture a subtle counteroffensive. A fender-bender. "We saw the news, Mr. Conrad. We saw that cop spouting off about our activities."

"Who's *we?*"

"All of us, Sir — excluding those out on the trail. Word spread like wildfire."

Conrad loomed over his henchman, forcing him to lean backward at the waist. "And then you got on the intercom and reminded everybody that I'd warned them this day would come. Right?"

"Right, Sir."

Conrad stared at him for a few moments, then growled, "No you didn't. But you will, just as soon as you deal with the chopper. And when I get back, we'll discuss your future. As for you, Chinua, you're coming with me."

Chinua did not like that one bit. He considered himself physically decrepit and faint-hearted in the extreme, and he had the rapidly moistening undergarments to confirm it. Conrad immediately sensed Amadi's trepidation and slapped him on the back. "Relax, Chinua. You'll be with me.

What safer place in the world can there be? Sparata, load it up with firearms, tranquilizer guns, Tasers, and enough food and drink for a couple of days."

Chinua was horrified. "Tasers, Sir? They have, at most, a range of twenty-five feet. We'll be that close?"

"Closer, if necessary. Sparata! What make is that chopper?"

Raphael Sparata cupped the receiver of the phone. "A Bell 210, Mr. Conrad. Brand new, Mr. Conrad."

"Good. The civilian version of the Huey. A top speed of one-twenty miles per hour, a range of two hundred and fifty."

"Correction, Sir," simpered Sparata. "It's been fitted with auxiliary fuel tanks. Make that a top speed of one ten and a range of four-hundred miles."

As he hustled Chinua out the door Conrad said, "Oh, and tell them to throw in a bottle of champagne. Krug, Clos du Mesnil. Then pray for your ass that we have good reason to pop the cork."

Within twenty-five minutes, Conrad and Chinua were airborne. Under a full moon, bobbing in an ocean of stars, they flew full throttle at three-thousand feet. For the first hour, the stark silence of the dense forest below seeped into the cabin and isolated each man in his own thoughts.

Chinua gazed out the window and marvelled at the multitude of lakes that shimmered like pearls in the moonlight. If only his native country had been blessed with such riches, it wouldn't have languished in the backwaters of history. If only his country had had leaders with the heavy mettle of Jason Conrad, it might have sailed to greatness.

For his part, Conrad thought of Irina Drach, as he frequently had since their meeting some twelve hours earlier. She was tall and perfectly formed. Her features were glacial in cut and clarity. She was tough without having forfeited the female graces. And those preternatural grey eyes were full of mystery and promise. A man could lose his heart in those eyes, yet find his soul. In short, she was thoroughly seductive. Was she past the childbearing years, though? If not, then he'd finally found a worthy mate. What progeny they would produce.

"Chinua, tell me again how she reacted when you gave her the flowers."

Having been lulled into a semi-hypnotic state by the whump-whump-whump of the helicopter blades, Chinua almost jumped out of his seat at the sound of Conrad's voice. It took him a few moments to compose himself, and when he did, he was decidedly grouchy. The thought of Irina Drach made him feel defensive and insecure. "This story will not get better in the retelling, Sir. She was most unreceptive. She turned up that large proboscis of hers. The bags under her eyes pulsated in disapproval. She pursed her puffy lips. I might as well have presented her with an armful of beet greens."

"You forgot to mention her blinking, Chinua."

"I do not discuss other peoples' afflictions or disfigurements."

Conrad laughed. "How long do you think she's been a widow?"

"Not very long, Sir. She is plainly ravaged by grief. Indeed, I suspect that her soul is even more distorted than her appearance. Heaven help the next man who becomes her consort. He will be merely a stand-in for her husband."

Conrad suddenly put the helicopter into a steep dive, taking it from three-thousand feet to five hundred in a matter of seconds. Chinua, who was a poor flier at the best of times, moaned aloud and grasped at the arms of his chair as a drowning man would grasp at a life preserver. This occasioned a great deal of merriment on Conrad's part. "Hell, Chinua, if you weren't black as night, you'd be as white as Irish linen."

"I am presently white on the inside, Mr. Conrad," Chinua said tartly, "and I don't like the sensation one bit. I feel divorced from Mother Earth."

Conrad howled with laughter. "Well maybe you won't have to feel that way for long. I want you to grab those infrared binoculars back there by the weapons, open the side door, and start scanning the woods for the cat. We've just flown over the lake where I-árishóni killed that grizzly, and we're coming up to where Zarathustra bit the dust. I figure that in about half an hour we should reach the spot where Vincent de Groot and Charmaine Washington were dropped, but I won't assume the lion kept heading southeast. He might have doubled back if he got spooked by the dogs. Ergo, you shall be on the lookout for a big, golden beastie."

Not much of what Conrad had said to Chinua after his mention of the binoculars sank in. Chinua Amadi was still trying to grasp the concept of leaning out of an aircraft speeding along at an altitude of five-hundred feet. "Sir, are you suggesting that I should be leaning out of an aircraft speeding along at an altitude of five-hundred feet?"

Conrad jovially slapped Chinua on the back. "I am, Chinua, I am! Why do you think I brought you along?"

"I had rather suspected it was for moral support. Or paperwork. Oh, and perhaps laying out your clothes for you —"

The smile had vanished from Conrad's face. In a hard, authoritarian voice he said, "I didn't bring a change of clothes, did I? Now get back there and do your duty."

Chinua skulked toward the midsection of the helicopter and proceeded to flatten himself on his stomach. With great difficulty he got the door open and inched his nose out over the void. With considerably less difficulty he vomited into that very void.

Even over the sound of the engine and the blades, Conrad could hear the retching. "Enough of the hijinks, Chinua! Get to work!"

More retching.

"So you're no longer white on the inside," Conrad chortled. "You're a vivid green. Not so divorced from Mother Earth, after all."

The desperate Chinua found a safety harness, strapped it on, and secured it to the bulkhead. As he took up the binoculars and began searching the hinterland below, he cursed Conrad and all his works. Why hadn't the great man suggested such a precaution in the first place? Was he not a friend as well as a master?

He knew he would never ask those questions aloud, because he feared the truth. And Jason Conrad could afford to tell the truth as easily as he bought and sold people's souls.

"He must have been quite a man," Conrad shouted over his shoulder.

"Who, Sir?"

"Why, Irina Drach's husband, of course. He must have been a man of considerable integrity and strength to attract and hold Irina's affections."

"At the very least, he must have had a strong stomach."

Conrad coaxed a lateral swaying motion out of the helicopter. If Chinua hadn't been secured by the harness, he might have slid straight out of the aircraft. "I won't have it, Chinua. You can venture the opinion that my interest in Irina is ill-considered, but you will stop making these snide remarks about her. Immediately."

Chinua had withdrawn into the chopper like a turtle into his shell and was holding onto the legs of a seat for dear life. He vomited again. This was, of course, more problematic than vomiting into empty space, so he detached the harness and rummaged around in the cabin for something to mop up the mess.

"Never mind that," Conrad bellowed. "Pick up those thermal imaging things and get back to your post. We're coming up to Washington's and de Groot's last known position."

Chinua slipped on the harness once more and obediently prostrated himself on the floor of the aircraft. With the pool of vomit only inches from his chin, he peered into the darkness below. Of all the things Conrad had ever demanded of him, this was by far the most demeaning. It was not a sickly green he saw as he looked through the binoculars, but red. A boiling blood red.

After two days and nights of eventful flight, I-árishóni was weary. And cold. The near-freezing temperature of the night air was something completely beyond his experience. As he plowed through the underbrush, he kept an eye open for a shelter that was both protective and warm.

Shortly after he'd been awakened to this need, he stumbled across something that would suit him. It was a cave in the side of a rocky hillock, with its entrance half hidden by brambles. As he approached it, it became obvious to him that the cave was occupied, for he could hear heavy breathing and snuffling sounds. The pitch of these sounds told him that it was a large animal, but the events of the last few days had revealed to him that there was nothing in this strange, tangled landscape about which he need be concerned. There were no elephants, nor rhinos, nor hippopotami.

As he advanced into the blackness, the four-hundred-pound black bear blew heavily, clacked his teeth, and swiped at the intruder with his tightly curved claws. The lion, who'd not advanced blindly, easily averted the blow and set upon the bear with the fury of a monarch whose authority has been questioned. Howling in pain from multiple lacerations, the bear bolted from the den.

I-árishóni didn't pursue him. He let loose a warning roar, then settled onto the bed of warmed leaves. The whump-whump-whump of the helicopter's blades five-hundred feet overhead provoked a few twitches and some blinking, but he soon fell asleep.

Being but a dumb brute and therefore lacking the more privileged humans' capacity for self-consciousness, his dreams could not feature an image of himself loping freely through the African savanna. Rather, he dreamt that he *was* the savanna.

Within fifteen minutes of Chinua's unceremonious purging, the helicopter was flying over the tracking team of Reg McDuff and Victor Tarasenko. McDuff reported to Conrad that the lion's spoor was becoming fresher with each passing hour. Conrad reminded them that should de Groot's and Washington's trail diverge at any time from that of the cat, they should not be so stupid as to stay together.

Within another fifteen minutes, Conrad and Amadi were hovering over the remains of de Groot's and Washington's dogs. Their bodies were still warm enough for Chinua's binoculars to have picked them up.

"The lion," Conrad flatly stated.

"No doubt about it. One of the hounds is in two pieces."

"We're only about half a mile from where de Groot and Washington were dropped. I think we'll fly to that spot then go due east."

"East, Sir? Isn't I-árishóni's trajectory southeast?"

"It is, but at this point I'm more concerned with de Groot and Washington. However eloquent the lion's presence might be on the streets of some little town, those two would be a little more specific."

"And you think they would have gone east?"

"They would reckon that the lion would continue southeast. So, first, they wouldn't want to be sharing a trail with him. Second, they would assume McDuff's dogs have nostrils only for the lion."

"Why wouldn't they go west?"

"Westward, there's no civilization for three-hundred miles."

Chinua returned to his post at the open door. He took a few moments to furtively sweep the puddle of vomit from the aircraft then dry things up a bit before resuming his lookout position. They'd travelled about fifty miles when Chinua began shouting like a novice fly fisherman with his first nibble. "Halt, Sir, halt! There is a large animal down there!"

"The lion?"

"I don't know! Is is possible to hover at a lower altitude?"

Conrad descended to within a few feet of the treetops. "There. Can you make him out, now?"

"One moment, please. Yes ... yes ... oh ... it is a black bear."

"A black bear? That's odd. Black bears sleep from a few hours after sunset until just before sunrise. The only time they're nocturnal is when people encroach on their territory. Take the controls, Chinua. I want to have a look."

Chinua did as he was bidden and Conrad took charge of the binoculars. "He's on the move, Chinua. Go up fifty feet then steer northeast," Conrad yelled, taking his position from the stars.

Conrad tracked the panicked bear for about a thousand feet. "That bugger is wounded. He's got a flap of hide dangling from his shoulder, and he's limping. Look for a place to put down, Chinua."

"There is nowhere, Sir. Treetops for miles and miles around. There is a small lake some two miles to the east, one a half mile to the west, and another one-mile north, but of what use would they be? By the time you got back to this spot, the bear could be a hundred miles away through thick bush. And we don't even know for certain that the lion is in this vicinity. Oh, one more thing, Sir. If by some miracle you should track the lion, it will be because he has tracked you. A lion under cover of night is deadly and stealthy beyond all imagination."

"I'll use the goddamn infrared goggles," Conrad muttered impatiently. "Now, this rig should have a rope ladder. Where in hell is it?"

The helicopter was equipped with the Captron HeliCommand System. Chinua set the autopilot for attitude stabilization and positioning, and went aft, where Conrad was rummaging through each bin. He opened up a large aluminum case and tossed its contents overboard. Conrad straightened up and glared at Chinua. "That better not have been what I was looking for."

"It was, Master, and I disposed of it for your own good."

In a fury, Conrad grabbed Chinua by the lapels of his jacket and propelled him toward the open door. As Conrad shook Chinua, the latter's heels were planted firmly on thin air. This fact provoked vomiting on Chinua's part. He soiled the front of his jacket and pants. He soiled his shoes. He soiled Conrad's shoes, too.

"Regrets, Sir. I am not very good with heights."

Conrad yanked Chinua back into the fuselage, pushed him into a seat, then took off his shoes and handed them over. "I want these things as immaculate as your intentions. Got that? But do it fast, because I need you to be my eyes in the sky."

As Chinua set about cleaning up the shoes — he always travelled with leather conditioner and shoe polish for his master's shoes — Conrad returned to the cockpit and resumed their eastward journey. That Conrad howled with laughter as he yanked the throttle did little for Chinua Amadi's self-esteem. The rotund little Nigerian resolved to redeem himself by finding a needle — any needle — in the surreal haystack beneath him.

They'd been cruising at a speed of forty knots for ten minutes when Chinua spotted something moving in the forest below. Two somethings, actually. A white man and a black woman. They were being evasive. They would run for a bit, then duck under a thick clump of trees or an outcropping of rock, and then they would run again. Chinua alerted Conrad, and Conrad immediately put the helicopter on automatic pilot. With the aircraft stabilized on all three axes and hovering autonomously, he marched into the rear cabin and picked up his Armalite AR-30 sniper's rifle. He fed three-hundred grain .338 magnum bullets into the magazine, then set up the long-range gun on a tripod in the open door of the helicopter. While Chinua watched in shock, he spread himself out on the floor of the fuselage and adjusted the infrared scope. He then waited patiently for Charmaine Washington and Vincent de Groot to reappear.

"Master, Sir, Mr. Conrad, no —"

From their hiding place in a small cave, Washington and de Groot suddenly emerged into view. They first waved at the helicopter, then held up their hands in surrender. As if from another room, another universe,

Chinua heard two shots in quick succession. Through his binoculars he watched their heads explode.

"Well," said Conrad as he got to his feet and brushed himself off, "that's that. I suppose we should get back to the facility forthwith before we run out of fuel."

"Sir ... I never imagined —"

Conrad had rooted out the bottle of Krug champagne and popped the cork. "Of course you didn't. Otherwise you wouldn't have ditched the rope ladder. If you hadn't done that, I'd have had a chance to reason with them, or at least discuss some suitable form of punishment for their desertion. But you did, so ... *c'est la vie*, as they say in gay Paree. Now, before we celebrate, how about those shoes of mine? Let's have a look at them."

One hour after that noisy machine had stopped drumming at his hidey-hole, I-árishóni emerged into the crisp night air and set off eastward at a quick trot. Half an hour later, he came upon the warm bodies of two humans. He sniffed at their remains, but only out of curiosity. He was, after all, still full from his feast of moose meat.

However, as he resumed his journey he felt inexplicably lighter and more powerful. He broke into a canter. He was beginning to associate dead humans with freedom.

CHAPTER TWENTY-SEVEN

London, England. September 8, 2006. At precisely the same moment that Jason Conrad was visiting rough justice upon Charmaine Washington and Vincent de Groot, Irina Drach and Athol Hudson were each in their own rooms at the Glynne Court Hotel, unpacking their suitcases. While Hudson was phlegmatic about the quality of his lodgings, and was, in fact, quite pleased that his mattress was slightly less yielding than a wet sponge, Irina stormed about her room hanging up her clothing in the way a butcherbird impales its prey on tree thorns. She wished she could be more serene about her situation, and often stopped to close her eyes and take a deep breath. But whenever she did, the gaunt grey face of Lieutenant Stanley Robertson appeared to her. "Leave it to me," the death's head smirked. "I know of a nice hotel located in the heart of Westminster. Location, location, location … plus, it'll look pretty good on the balance sheet."

Irina got on her new BlackBerry, which was registered to a dummy account, and called Robertson at his home. That it happened to be 4:00 a.m. in Montreal did not engender any great degree of consternation on Irina's part. She offered him a piece of her mind. In fact, she offered several pieces. To the hapless Robertson, they were chunks of shrapnel.

Having unburdened herself, she contacted Inspector Leopold Duggan of New Scotland Yard and informed him that she'd arrived on schedule and would not be needing any "guidance" for the foreseeable future.

"Well then, I needn't remind you that this is not your jurisdiction, Sergeant-Detective. I therefore trust you will not attempt to secure any handguns whilst in our country? The law, you know. Very stringent. Not even U.K. police are armed, regardless of rank, unless they belong to a special unit. As a matter of fact, it might interest you to know that the British Olympic shooters have to practise outside our great country."

The gust over the phone could have turned the Inspector's earlobe blue. "In *our* great country, an officer is only as good as her word. Good day, Inspector."

As Duggan replaced the receiver, he wondered how it was that he felt like a meddlesome old fool.

Finally, Irina called Heather Liang, estranged wife of cop-killer and dognapper Liang Xueqin, and the very reason for their trip to London. Mrs. Liang had arranged to leave her job in a gift shop at the Tower of London early, and would be awaiting them at her home by three o'clock that afternoon.

As had been agreed upon, Irina met Hudson in the lobby. "She has two young children to care for," she told her partner. "I couldn't very well ask her to take the whole day off."

"Am I complaining? We'll have five hours, four anyway, in which to poke around town a bit. It just so happens that we're only a stone's throw from all kinds of famous attractions. Marble Arch, Hyde Park, Regent's Park, Madame Tussauds, the Sherlock Holmes museum, Piccadilly Circus, Trafalgar Square, Big Ben —"

"I need a drink."

Hudson's jaw dropped. "It's ten in the morning, Irina."

"I need a drink, Athol."

Athol. She meant business. He held the door open for her (there was no doorman) and they emerged onto Great Cumberland Place under a cloudless sky. Already, the weather had failed to live down to expectations.

At the corner of Great Cumberland and Oxford Street, kitty-corner from Marble Arch and Hyde Park, sat the Cumberland Hotel. A four-star hotel, Irina observed dolefully. Integrated into its ground floor was a cavernous, berserkly shiny and modern establishment called the Rhodes W1 Brasserie. As they took their seats at a small table, upon swaddling leather bar stools that looked like beige orchids, Irina ordered without looking at the menu. "Eggs Benedict and a Glenfarclas fifteen, please."

Hudson, still feeling like a child passing through the gates of Disneyland for the first time, asked for the same. The young waiter was so efficient that he was out of earshot by the time Irina and Hudson had opened up their menus and begun gagging at the prices.

"Lesson number one, Hudson. We are strangers in a strange land. We must therefore exercise caution or we'll bankrupt the Montreal Police Department before nightfall."

Having said that, Irina ate and drank without remorse. With a second Scotch, her mood changed dramatically, and she expressed interest in seeing every landmark Hudson could think of. "But I want, first of all, to see Madame Tussauds. I've heard that viewing those figures is just like meeting people without souls. I've seen enough of those in my time and it might serve to keep my cop's instincts sharp."

Hudson knew full well that Irina was dying to meet Winston Churchill, George Washington, and, most of all, Princess Diana. How anyone who considered Winston Churchill to be the greatest man of his century could also be a Dianophile was beyond Hudson, but he was immensely relieved that Irina was smiling again. When she smiled, contradictions dissolved like salt in warm honey.

Irina's BlackBerry whined. It was an email from Inspector Raja Chadwani of the Kullu Police in India.

"Hm. The mystery Israeli hasn't yet emerged from his coma. Still a heartbeat away from death, it seems. But our Inspector Chadwani is optimistic. And ambitious. He writes, pointedly, that he hasn't left the subject's bedside since he was hospitalized, and has no intention of doing so until the man can talk."

"One can only hope that the guy's speech centre wasn't blown to smithereens."

"Even if that were the case, I'm confident our Mr. Chadwani would find a way to get information out of him," stated Irina as she emailed a response to Chadwani. "He'll have him communicating with his toes if need be."

She then read aloud her email response to Chadwani. It was warm and supportive in the extreme.

"Does that mean we won't be jetting off to India as soon as the Israeli comes around? You said outright we would, yesterday. Flogging Robertson's furniture for passage, remember?"

"You're sounding a bit peevish, Hudson," said Irina as she rose from her stool. "Not at all professional."

They made their way to Madame Tussauds in silence. As usual, Irina tripped along as if she had a date with destiny. Hudson skulked at her side. As the museum and the hordes of people waiting to be admitted hove into view, it occurred to her that Hudson's pique was not about a trip to India at all. He was jealous of Raja Chadwani because of the confidence she'd placed in him.

Irina briefly considered a propitiating remark. In even less time, she dismissed the idea. Being her partner did not necessarily mean that he was blessed, and he would just have to get on with it.

Hudson knew Irina well enough to know where her thought processes were taking her, and by the time he was communing with Elizabeth I, he was again the pliable, debonaire Hudson she'd come to cherish.

They next did the Sherlock Holmes Museum and Piccadilly Circus, then ambled toward Hyde Park, where a spindly and crazed old man stood on a milk crate at Speaker's Corner, loudly proclaiming to a sparse audience that someone was abducting the animals of the world and that the mangy corgi at his feet, Prince Phillip, was most certain to be next.

Hudson lapped contentedly at an ice cream at they sat in slingback chairs under the stately plane trees in the northwest corner of the park. "I studied the tourist map when I finished unpacking. There's a number six bus that leaves from just around the corner on Oxford Street and passes right by the foot of Heather Liang's street. What do you say?"

"You're that desperate to ride a double-decker?"

"Up top. At the front."

Irina was as eager as Hudson to ride a London bus. "Well … I suppose we can do without the car. Mrs. Liang has one, and she's willing to chauffeur us back and forth between her husband's old haunts. All right, then."

They then both fell asleep under the warming sun until two o'clock, when the alarm in Hudson's gleaming, knobby wristwatch sounded. The two detectives sauntered over to the corner of Oxford Street and Park Lane, just across the street from the Cumberland Hotel. There weren't too many passengers on the bus, so a joyous Hudson got to sit up top, at the front.

When, after forty minutes, they disembarked on Chamberlayne Road in Kensal Rise, Irina was quite exhausted by Hudson's enthusiastic appraisal of the sites, and fervently hoped that Heather Liang's first act upon their arrival would be an offer of tea or coffee.

Mrs. Liang did not disappoint. Barely had the door of the narrow, two-storey brick house on Leighton Gardens swung open when a small, pretty young Asian woman with glossy black hair down to her waist pertly announced she'd just put on the tea and that they should step into the parlour and watch the telly while it steeped. She set a tray before them, laden with enough biscuits to have seen Napoleon's army through the Russian Campaign, before disappearing into the small kitchen at the back of the house and banging and clattering her way through her china.

Not having eaten anything but an ice cream since ten o'clock that morning, Hudson had eyes only for the biscuits. Irina, who'd resolved to cut back on sweets immediately after the ice cream — and not a second sooner — had eyes for anything but. As Hudson gorged himself on the Jammie Dodgers, uniquely pernicious aggregates of shortbread and raspberry-flavoured plum jam, her eyes roamed the parlour and the adjacent dining room, and noticed something anomalous: the walls needed refinishing and the furniture was well past its prime, but the rooms were nevertheless crammed with highly desirable, dauntingly expensive artifacts. Here a Rosenthal vase, there a sizable collection of Swarovski crystal figurines, here a set of twelve Riedel whisky glasses, there a Pioneer Elite sound system, and so on, and so on. The large and glossy Qum silk rug upon which she rested her feet would have financed a major makeover of the house.

Heather Liang entered the sitting room bearing a vintage Wedgwood tea service on a Raj teak tray. "Prince of Wales tea," she said as she cavalierly slammed the priceless china down onto the scarred old coffee table. "Bought it especially for you. Thought you might like something royal-sounding, you just arriving in England, and all."

Irina liked Heather Liang. Here was an utterly guileless person, as eager to be read as a newly published book. She showed Heather a still taken from the security film at Montreal's Trudeau Airport. It was a rather poor shot of Liang, but Heather had no problem. "Aye, it's him. I'd know him anywhere. Always looks like he's left the coat hanger in his jacket. Are you done with the telly, then?"

Neither Irina nor Hudson felt compelled to utter the obvious. Both murmured in the affirmative, but in such a way as to give the impression that only devotion to duty could tear them away from a cartoon called *The Cramp Twins*. After spending two minutes searching for the remote rather than making the two second walk to the spanking new fifty-two-inch, high-definition Panasonic television, Heather Liang turned the appliance off, sat facing Irina and Hudson, and beamed beatifically. "Now. Let's really get started on nailing my stinking bugger of a husband."

Irina laughed. "I can see he hasn't been able to buy back your affections."

"What do you mean ... ah, all this junk. My, you Canadian inspectors are clever. I had no idea. Yes, I expect that's precisely what he's tried to do. But it won't work, will it? Do you know I've even had the police around to take this stuff away? It must be filched, I tell them. But there's nothing they can do, they tell me, so long as these things are not on their lists of stolen goods."

"You told us on the phone the other day that you hadn't seen or heard from him in three years."

"That is so. It's always some stranger who comes to the door — hardly ever the same one, actually — and hands me some unmarked package. Sometimes the man might say, 'From Xueqin,' sometimes he says nothing."

"You've never gotten a licence plate number from any of their cars?"

"Sorry, no. In any event, I think they're minicabs the man comes in. I can tell because the drivers are usually all the colours of the rainbow."

"Minicabs?"

"Anything with four wheels and four doors. You have to book them. They can't be hailed in the street like our famous big black hackney carriages. You couldn't even if you wanted to, because they don't have those light thingies on the roof. And their drivers certainly don't have The Knowledge."

"The Knowledge?" smiled Hudson, who'd been contentedly dunking biscuits into his tea.

"Oh yes, The Knowledge. They study for years, those ones who drive the black taxis, until they know every street in London and the quickest way from point A to point B, and then they have to pass a very difficult test. They'll never get muddled like some yob in a minicab."

Heather Liang studied Hudson for a few moments. "Cor, I thought you looked familiar, 'Sergeant Curzon.' Now you sound familiar. Could you take off those naff glasses for a second?"

Hudson automatically looked to Irina. Irina nodded, and Hudson removed them.

"Yes! You're that policeman who was on the telly this morning, aren't you? And your picture was on the front page of the *Sun*, too. The animals, and all. At work, we all talked about how cute you were. But oh my, what have they done to you? A bloody shame! And does this mean that Xueqin is in even bigger trouble than usual?"

Mrs. Liang had unconsciously poured Irina more tea. Irina chose to study the exquisite detail of her blue and white Jasper cup and saucer rather than dwell on Hudson's reddening face. "Let's return to your husband, Heather. He sends you all these fabulous gifts in order to win you back, yet he never contacts you to see if he's making any progress?"

Heather furrowed her brow and looked off into space, as if the thought had never occurred to her. "Hm. I suppose it would seem strange to someone who'd never met him. But that would be Xueqin. And as I mentioned to you the other day, he was even stranger the last few times I saw him. Except for the beatings, he was quite withdrawn. Almost mystical. On the few occasions that he spoke, he would say that I was just a silly, insular, bourgeois child and that I lacked a global perspective. His words exactly."

"Heather, would you mind showing us everything he's sent to you since you last saw him?"

"Hm. It's lucky the police didn't take away any of the things, then, innit? I hope you have more than a few minutes to spare."

"We have as much time as it takes, Heather."

And so Heather Liang gave them a tour of the house, both upstairs and down. There were close to forty different items, ranging from the Panasonic television to a deluxe set of German carving knives, from the cordless phone to a set of bejewelled Hungarian hair brushes. Irina methodically examined each item and Hudson added it to his written inventory.

There was nothing that particularly inspired Irina. Excepting the antique Wedgwood tea service, everything was mass produced and widely available. "So maybe the china is our best bet," Hudson said to her. "At least it's unique, sort of."

"But antique shops are not. There must be thousands of them in London alone. We'd be better off with things like the television. At least we could trace what store it was bought in by going to the manufacturers with the serial number. No, what I'm looking for is something quirky, folksy, and intrinsic to some region. Like those, for instance."

She pointed to a pair of bookends that held up Heather's economics books. They were rough circles made of tin, and had similar celtic-looking mazes stamped onto them. "What, these rubbishy things?" exclaimed the young woman. "They came yesterday morning. If they weren't of some practical use, I'd have pitched them into the waste straightway. I certainly didn't think they were worth mentioning."

Irina inhaled sharply and held her breath. Hudson thought he should explain something to Mrs. Liang. "You must never try to second-guess the police, Heather. Irina Drach, in particular."

"May we use your computer?" Irina asked of Heather.

"Yes, of course," answered the mortified Mrs. Liang.

"Do you have Internet?"

The obtuseness of the question enabled Heather to rebound quickly. "I'd sooner have that than a loo," she snickered.

Having thus been exposed as a dinosaur, Irina snapped at Hudson. "Your key words are 'tin' and 'maze.' Get busy. And as for you," she said to Heather, "we'll take another tour of your house in case there's anything else you forgot to point out."

Heather Liang protested that there wasn't, but Irina nonetheless insisted upon their retracing their steps. As they did so, Heather couldn't help but feel she was in the company of a cranky schoolmistress, and wouldn't have been in the least surprised if Irina had held onto her earlobe the whole time.

Irina and Heather Liang were back in the sitting room, and Irina was taking great pains to disclose her more youthful affiliations, when Hudson appeared in the doorway. "I've got it. It's the Tintagel Maze, from Cornwall. Tintagel is the coastal town that legend has as the home of King Mark, of *Tristan and Isolde* fame, and also as the place where King Arthur was conceived. The ruins of Tintagel castle date back to 500 A.D. In the town of Tintagel, just east of a ruined mill, lies Rocky Valley, where the Tintagel Mazes are found. It's estimated they date from about 4000 B.C. These mazes are on a good number of the trinkets and souvenirs that are sold in the area."

"Why are they of tin?" asked Irina. "That must be significant."

"Cornwall is famous for more than smuggling, Poldark, and the Pirates of Penzance. For centuries, tin was its primary commodity."

Irina clenched her fists until her knuckles turned white. "Damn, I should have known that. Heather, did your husband ever mention Cornwall to you?"

"Never, Ma'am."

"Never 'Mum,' Heather. Either Irina or Sergeant, okay?"

Heather nodded obediently.

"Right," said Irina, leaping to her feet. "That tour of your husband's hangouts. Are you ready?"

The three of them piled into Heather Liang's car, which must have been the last Lada left in London. There were no personal friends of Liang Xueqin to call upon, for Heather didn't know of any. They spent the next ninety minutes visiting assorted restaurants and pubs. Armed with Heather's most recent photograph of the fugitive, they approached countless publicans, pub crawlers, and maitre d's, inquiring whether he'd been seen lately, or whether he'd ever mentioned some cherished locale. They came away as empty-handed as a pickpocket in a nudist colony.

"I'm starving. We should have eaten at one of those pubs," grumbled Hudson as the Lada lurched its way up Chamberlayne. "Bangers and mash and a pint of bitters. The total English experience."

"Irina and I already discussed that, Inspector," said Heather. "I'll drop you two at the Chamberlayne Pub, just across from a number six bus stop. That's the last place I can think of that Zook favoured, and also the pub he most often frequented, it being the closest to home, and all."

Heather Liang left Irina and Hudson in front of the dark, boxy building and disappeared in a cloud of blue smoke. She was off to pick up her children from their daycare, and then, after supper, to her courses at the local red-brick university.

The two policemen first approached the dozen or so people who were seated under the awning attached to the side of the pub. An afterwork crowd of mostly young adults, they lolled about smoking, drinking, and chatting in the slithering rays of the early evening sun. Although polite and receptive in the extreme, not one of them had ever seen the man in the photograph.

"They were most likely still in diapers the last time Liang was here," quipped Irina as she and Hudson entered the establishment.

The pub was a major disappointment to Hudson. He'd been expecting a cozy little haven with plush booth seating, a low beamed ceiling, polished oak, gleaming brass fitments, and a large stone fireplace. Instead, the Chamberlayne was a dark, drafty, and cavernous place with all the charm of a filling station. He stood in the doorway, his eyes dubiously flitting between the giant chalkboard menu on the back wall and the cafeteria-styled food station just to the other side of the thruway to the washrooms.

"Cheer up, Hudson," laughed Irina as she bustled off toward the stark bar. "This is not some clip joint all got up for tourists or young broker types. This is 'the total English experience.' Now go have your bangers and mash."

While Hudson sidled up to the food counter as a small child sidles up to a big, hairy dog, Irina slapped Xueqin Liang's photograph onto the bar. "I beg your pardon. Do you know this man?"

"Are you the police, then?" responded the blowsy, middle-aged woman as she topped up an oversized glass with brown ale.

"Yes. The Canadian police."

"Then you have no authority here, do you? And I don't have to answer your question."

Irina knew instantly that the woman could be of assistance. "You're quite correct. You don't. On the other hand, if you do, then you'll play a small but vital part in a matter of international intrigue."

The barmaid smoothed her shocking red hair and squinted suspiciously. She thought for a few moments about how boring her life was. "Oh, yah? Will I get me name in the papers?"

"I'm afraid not. You'll be one of the unsung heroines."

The woman smiled broadly, brilliantly illustrating the gaps in the National Health dental services. "Ooh, that has rather a nice ring to it. Beryl Matheson, unsung heroine. But can I at least tell my friends and family?"

"We'd rather you didn't. It might compromise the investigation."

Beryl Matheson thought long and hard enough to multiply her frown lines. She finally fingered the photograph of Xueqin Liang. "I don't know his name, but he used to come round here on a regular basis. Squinny chap. Quiet and secretive, like, except when he was complaining. Haven't seen him for a few years, though."

Beryl suddenly put down the picture. "Oi, how do I know you're not just a bill collector?"

Calculating that Beryl knew more, Irina produced her badge.

"Right, love. But international intrigue, eh? How do I know he isn't just another dodgy little immigrant?"

"Why would a Canadian officer be concerned about Britain's immigration problem?"

Just then, Hudson walked to a table with his plate. On the plate next to his mashed potatoes and sausages was a pile of green mush. "That young man just sitting down," said Beryl ruminatively. "He came in with you, didn't he?"

"Yes. What of it?"

Beryl stared at Hudson. Then her eyes turned to a copy of the *Daily Mirror* lying flat on the bar. There on the front page was Hudson, flanked by photographs of Amy Winehouse and David Beckham. Beryl's eyes flitted between Hudson and the tabloid several times. "No ... never. Not in my place. Blimey ... it *is* him, innit? And he's in colour, while Becks is just in black and white."

Beryl was profoundly impressed. She pointed to a grizzled man in his late forties, seated alone by the door. "That boffin over there. This is his second home. When he's in the mood he makes a point of chatting up everybody, even if they don't appreciate it." She bawled across the room. "Leon! This here's a copper, and she wants to know all about that stroppy little Chinaman!"

Nobody else in the sparsely populated pub so much as looked up upon Beryl's outburst, but Leon's reaction was swift. He looked Irina over, grinned salaciously, and patted his lap with both hands.

"There are a few things I didn't tell you about Leon. Best of British to you."

On her way over to Leon's table, Irina passed by Hudson, who was eating with good appetite. "What's the green stuff? It looks like a pile of phlegm."

"Squishy peas. And not to be confused with mushy peas. The chef said one doesn't have squishy peas with bangers and mash, but I insisted. They're quite tasty, really. Mashed with salt, pepper, butter, and enough of the pea juice to make them runny. Look how they swirl in the onion gravy."

"Fancy that. I would never have imagined that our trip to England would turn you into a hedonist."

"Looks like your friend Leon is quite the hedonist, too," snickered Hudson as he jammed a large chunk of the fatty sausage into his mouth. "Better not keep him waiting."

Irina was not about to let Hudson have the last laugh. "Two people in the space of a few hours have recognized you. We'll have to do something about that later."

"What? You've already got me looking like a bottle brush."

Irina tromped over to Leon's table and sat down opposite him. He was not a pretty sight. His chin had three day's worth of stubble on it, his long, white hair was greasy and unkempt, and the trench coat he wore looked like it cloaked every vice known to man.

"How do you do, pretty lady? I am Leon James, a barrister on a long stretch between briefs."

Irina rather suspected that, but she held her tongue.

"Therefore, do not be alarmed or deceived by appearances. I am a man of considerable means. And you are?"

"Irina Drach," she replied cautiously. "Pleased to meet you."

"Ahhh, you're a Canadian. I love Canadians. They're among the few people left who, when they visit us, still make us feel as if we're the centre of the universe. And what can I do for you … Inspector?"

"Sergeant-Detective, actually." Irina thumped the photograph onto the table. "What do you know of this man?"

"Ooh, Liang. Just let me order another another Newcastle. It helps with the memories, you see." He rummaged through his pockets for a few milliseconds. "Ah … I don't seem to have any loose change. Would you consider —"

Irina swung around to the ever-observant Beryl and called for two Newcastles. Once delivered, Irina got down to business as brusquely as possible. But Leon James would not be denied. "You're a real beauty, you know that? With a woman such as you, one could have days so perfect that the sun rains honey on one's wounds, the scent of flowers offers a breath of wisdom, and the evening sky became an indigo river that carried one's hopes far beyond every horizon."

Irina thawed. She thought she could now see the acute intelligence in his eyes. "Thank you, Leon. That was … well, sweet. But we must press on with more mundane matters. I'm trying to find Mr. Liang. Is there anything you can tell me?"

Leon downed his beer and ordered another. "Oh. Do you mind?"

"Not at all, Leon. Just help me out with this fellow."

"For the most part, I'd always found him to be a perturbed, restless soul. His situation was unsatisfactory, his surroundings were depressing, there didn't seem to be a point to anything. I say for the most part, because he'd changed dramatically the last few times I spoke to him. That would have been … oh … about three years ago. One would almost think a cult had got hold of him. He actually spoke about saving the world. But do you know what was funny? When I asked for details, he clammed right up. Isn't that odd? Avatars and acolytes just don't do that. They talk, and they talk and they talk. The nearest he ever got to telling me about heaven was some little spot he'd found in Cornwall. Heaven on Earth, he called it."

"Cornwall? Really? Where in Cornwall, Leon?"

Leon tipped his head back, and the ale disappeared so quickly down his gullet that Irina could see the beginnings of a vortex. "Ah … do you recall what I said about the effects this stuff has on my memory?"

Irina ordered another Newcastle. Beryl lingered for a few moments longer than was necessary. In fact, she hovered like a brooding hen. Noticing that her presence brought a certain degree of pleasure to Leon, Irina invited Beryl to sit with them. There was nothing Leon had to tell her that he wouldn't tell Beryl later, anyway.

"So," said Leon, "Liang is mixed up in this animal abduction thing?"

"What makes you think that?"

"Oh come now, Sergeant Drach," replied Leon as he waved to Hudson. "I'd recognize glamor-puss over there if he were in blackface and had a ring in his nose."

A confused Athol Hudson, who was now sloshing his way through a pudding, waved back at Leon.

"He's dreamy," sighed Beryl. "A right lady-killer."

"We're getting off topic, you two. Leon, you were going to wrack your brain as soon as you'd racked up another beer. Now start wracking."

"Buddha comes to mind. That wasn't it, of course, but it was something like that. Buddha, Buddha. I remember thinking how appropriate it was, him having found *the way,* and all."

Irina swung around in her chair. "Athol? Do you have your map of England with you? All of England?"

"Athol," moaned Beryl. "Oh! Such a quality name!"

Hudson dug into his bag, retrieved a map, and rose from his table.

"Oh shite, he's coming over here," Beryl squealed. "And me looking an absolute fright!"

Leon said, "Just thank God he's not seeing you on one of your bad days, Beryl. It's you who put the knack in knackered."

"Oh shush, you," Beryl whispered hoarsely, slapping his forearm. "Here he is!"

And there Hudson was, standing over the three of them while he unfurled a map. "Okay, Irina. What is it you're after?"

"Cornwall, Athol. And please sit down so we can all see."

Hudson sat between Irina and Beryl. Irina did the introductions while he spread the map across the table. Beryl closed her eyes and breathed deeply, as if to inhale his very essence.

"Here's Cornwall," said Hudson. "What town?"

"Not quite sure, old man," said Leon. "Rhymes with Buddha, or starts with Buddha. Not sure which. And if you don't mind my saying, whoever did your hair must really hate you."

"You might have a point, there," Hudson said plaintively.

"Let's start in the Tintagel area and fan out from there," said Irina. "Where's Tintagel?"

Hudson pointed to a spot on the northwest coast of Cornwall. "That much I know. Found it at Heather Liang's house."

"Hm. He never mentioned a sister," offered Leon.

"His wife," said Irina. "And the mother of his children."

Beryl raised her eyebrows. "That right? That makes him an even bigger wanker than you thought, eh Leon? Oi! Cop a load of this," exclaimed Beryl. "Bude! Not fifteen miles from Tintagel as the crow flies! Bude!"

Irina turned to Leon. "Is that it?"

"Bude … Bude … do you know, I might need another Newcastle to jog the old memory."

Irina signalled that that would be fine. Beryl sighed heavily as she rose. "You are such a bleedin' piss artist, Leon! Oh, and you, Athol," she simpered. "Something? On the house?"

Hudson thanked her but declined. She clattered across the pub to the bar.

"Don't you know it," belched Leon. "Such is the hops' power over me that the mere prospect of a drink gets the neurons buzzing. Bude it is. Definitely Bude."

By the time Beryl returned to the table bearing a beer, Irina and Hudson were rising to leave. "Goodbye, unsung heroine," said Irina shaking Beryl's hand. "Thanks for everything. And remember: mum's the word."

Beryl swooned as she shook Hudson's hand. It was only after that momentous occasion that she noticed Leon James was doubled over in pain, with his forehead flat on the table. "Leon! You look as if someone smacked you in the goolies!"

"He tried to work his way toward forbidden fruit — or fuctose, as he calls it — with a clammy, open hand and I quite naturally responded with a closed one," Irina said, bending over Leon and offering him her hand. He took it. "No hard feelings, Leon?"

"Actually, no feeling at all, Sergeant Drach. Ah … wait. Now a warm, tingly feeling. It must be love. Goodbye, Irina. We'll always have the Chamberlayne, won't we?"

"We will, Leon."

Leon finally looked up. His eyes were watery. "And goodbye, Sergeant Athol Hudson. But beware, you may suffer a follicular setback as suddenly as I suffered a testicular one."

As Irina and Hudson boarded the inbound bus, Hudson said, "I wonder what he meant by that follicular crack?"

"I've no idea, Hudson."

It was plain to Irina that Hudson's disguise was ineffective. It was less plain how she was going to separate him from every last hair on his head without bullying him. Sometimes she tired of being a bully.

CHAPTER TWENTY-EIGHT

Montreal. September 8, 2006. Lieutenant-Detective Stanley Robertson fiddled with his print of Van Gogh's *Starry Night* while FBI Special Agents David Moore and Ashantee Powell burned with curiosity as to how this pale, gaunt, and patently neurotic policemen could be the nerve centre of what was arguably one of the most pressing issues in law enforcement history.

"Listen guys," nattered Robertson, "not only do I have to contend with the Ministry of the Environment, the Armed Forces, the Canadian Security Intelligence Service, and the Royal Canadian Mounted Police here at home, but I've got agencies like the CIA, Russia's Federal Security Service, Germany's BKA, and Europol and Interpol breathing down my neck. That's about sixty organizations, total. How can I possibly tell all of them — or any of them, including you — where Drach and Hudson are? As you well know, an investigation is a delicate thing. A butterfly collector doesn't use a sledgehammer to gather specimens, after all."

"We'll find them," said Agent Powell, an extremely fit black woman whom Robertson speculated could crack walnuts doing Kegel exercises. "We already know they're in London and what rental car they're driving. Why not make it easy on yourself? Tell us where they're staying."

"Make it easy on myself? That sounds like a threat."

"You wouldn't want to be known as the cop whose obstructionism blocked the resolution of this mess, would you?"

"There is no better detective on this planet than Sergeant-Detective Irina Drach. There is no better team than Irina Drach and Athol Hudson. If any two people can resolve this mess, it is them. And besides," Robertson lied with confidence, since he'd taken the precaution of having a friend book the Glynne Court Hotel, "I don't know where they're staying. I couldn't even be sure of what city they're in, at present."

"You know, Ashantee," said David Moore, a casehardened veteran of the wars on organized crime, "it's almost two o'clock. I'll bet one of those credit card companies has flagged what hotel they're staying at, by now."

Robertson suddenly felt prescient. It was nice not having to be overshadowed by Irina all the time. "I told them to pay cash," he crowed.

Moore grinned affably. "Very well, then. We'll get in touch with Scotland Yard. Those two would have had to check in with them, if only out of courtesy. They'll have a record of Drach and Hudson's incoming calls. And I think it's a fair bet your people would've called from their hotel."

Robertson popped a fistful of jelly beans into his mouth and proceeded to water the spindly, yellowing ivy on his filing cabinet. "That's not the Irina Drach I know. She wouldn't even use her cell, but rather a distant pay phone. Help yourselves to the jelly beans, by the way. I buy them fresh twice a year."

Methodically, and with considerable equanimity, Moore began to pick out the black ones. Unsurprisingly, Ashantee Powell took a rather dim view of sweeteners of any kind. "Lieutenant Robertson, we did not come here to eat jelly beans. We came here to A, get information, and B, act on that information and be of service. The Bureau does, after all, have tremendous resources and expertise."

"Oh, I'll bet you say that to everyone."

Robertson's phone rang. He held up his hand as if to signal that she should hang onto any helpful thoughts she might have, and picked up the receiver. "Robertson, here. Ah, good day, Sir. An honour. Yes, he was rather spectacular, wasn't he? No, they're not here, presently. Yes, they're out of the country. No, I'm afraid I cannot, Sir. Yes, there is something you can do, and that is to ensure that Sergeant Drach's previous instructions to your agency are followed to the letter. Information, that's what we need. Thank you, Sir, and good day. Auf Wiedersehen." Robertson hung up and addressed Agent Powell. "The Federal Minister of the Interior of Austria, offering the services of the Bundeskriminalamt. BK for short, thank God. And what I just said to him is what I want to say to you. Use your resources to hunt up more leads, but don't think you'll be of any assistance by horning in on the lead that Irina's already got. You'll be worse than redundant, you'll blow the investigation out of the water. Surely you can understand my position. After all, the FBI itself has never been too good at sharing information, has it?"

The FBI special agents got up to leave. David Moore bent over Robertson's desk to shake the latter's hand. Agent Ashantee Powell stormed out of the office, muttering over her shoulder that Robertson's chief — no, the prime minister himself! — would very shortly be hearing from FBI director Robert Mueller.

Robertson was just in the process of chasing a jelly bean with a clonazepam when David Moore popped his head into Robertson's office. "Agent Powell's remarks were a bit ill-considered and a lot unauthorized. No hard feelings?"

"None at all."

"It's just that … well, it's this horse, Zarathustra. Of course, the whole country is up in arms about all missing animals in general, but there's just something about a champion thoroughbred that really excites people. Know what I mean?"

"I'll have to admit that Zarathustra is a lot more galvanizing than a newt."

Agent David Moore exhaled heavily. "You know, it just occurs to me that barely a word had been said or written about the people who died when he was taken. Go figure, eh?"

Robertson's phone was ringing again, but he ignored it. "Sergeant-Detective Irina Drach hasn't forgotten about them, anymore than she's forgotten about our Sergeant Perron."

"Ah, yes. The K-9 squad. That's the shits." Moore edged toward Robertson's desk. "Do you think she'll pull it off?"

Lieutenant-Detective Stanley Robertson straightened himself up to his full height. The way he felt, though, was actually a few inches taller than that. "I most certainly do."

CHAPTER TWENTY-NINE

The boreal forest. September 7, 2006. Chinua Amadi was very nearly in a state of shock. He'd always been aware that Jason Conrad's species-gathering could no more avoid bringing the occasional individual to grief than a steamroller could avoid crushing ants. This, however, was different. The man next to him in the helicopter's cockpit, nonchalantly listening to "Rama Lama Ding Dong" while he guided the aircraft back to the complex, had just executed two people whose humanity was as ineluctable as his own struggling heart. And Jason Conrad looked no more repentant than a farmer who'd just dispatched a pair of gophers.

"Radio one of the choppers and have it move a tracker team up to where we spotted that wounded black bear, Chinua. Here are the coordinates. Pity we can't take the lion ourselves, but as it is, we'll be flying on fumes by the time we make it back to the facility."

Chinua did as he was bidden, but there was a new lethargy in his movements, and his voice was leaden.

"So," remarked Conrad as he switched off the blaring Doo Wop, "you have a problem with my actions back there?"

"You are the boss, Sir," Chinua mumbled. "It is not for me to criticize."

"You think my hands would be any cleaner if I'd left it to someone else? While my back was turned?"

Chinua picked at his fingernails.

"Don't look so sanctimonious, Mr. Amadi. You, too, have blood on your hands."

This did little to improve Chinua's mood. There was a dark, heavy silence, unleavened by the rising sun. He was quiet all the way back to the facility, manifestly avoiding looking at Conrad. He never even flinched when Conrad turned his music back on and listened to the Shangri-Las moaning "The Leader of the Pack."

"Hey, Chinua, isn't this the best? She's singing about the big, bad leader of a motorcycle gang, yet she met him in a candy store. A candy store!"

Chinua passed on this jocular invitation to ridicule Conrad's music of choice. "I met *you* at a Save the Seals fundraiser."

Governor Raphael Sparata was anxiously awaiting their return. Anxiously, rather than happily. He was, of course, relieved that the deserters had been dealt with, and that Conrad had a strong clue as to where the lion could be found, but he'd been hoping for a few days to recover from his last encounter with the almighty leader. A man who accomplishes, alone and during a few hours in the middle of the night, what eighteen hundred had failed to do over the course of two days, does nothing for one's self-esteem.

As luck would have it, Conrad was exhausted and retired immediately to the stateroom in Block C. It was for his use only, and would not have been out of place on the *Queen Mary II*. An unusually subdued Chinua Amadi stayed in the small bedroom off Conrad's suite. Even more unusually, especially as he was enduring an exceedingly fitful sleep, Chinua failed to look in on Conrad even once.

September 8, 2006. When Chinua awoke, it was 7:00 a.m. of the next day. He and Conrad had slept round the clock. The first thing he did was turn on his phone and take a barrage of calls. Of particular interest was the one from England. "Hi, Chinua," said the agent. "Bernie Gold here. I've got news."

Good. Bernie Gold. A thoroughly lovable monster from New York's lower east side. "Ah. The Montreal policemen?"

"Well, as per your orders, we've been shadowing them. They're in London, and we know where they're staying. As a matter of fact — ta da! — we've got the room right next to Irina Drach's. Our listening devices are in place. The wall looks like it's on life support. If she so much as farts, we'll know about it, though I gotta tell you it would be awful disillusioning if a babe like that actually did such a thing. As we speak, Lars and Jean-Louis are camped outside the Sherlock Holmes Museum while our detectives play tourist. How perfect is that? I wonder if they'll buy magnifying glasses and deerstalker hats while they're at it."

"Do you know who they're after?"

"A few hours ago she called a Heather Liang. It's her ex-husband, a Xueqin Liang, they want."

"Ah, so Mr. Conrad was right."

"Me, I've never heard of the guy. He one of ours?"

"A rogue collector. A danger to us all. Now here's what I — or rather, Mr. Conrad — wants you to do. When they track down this Liang — and they will, as sure as day follows night — Mr. Conrad wants you to liquidate them."

"Them? Which ones?"

"All three. The two policemen and their target. And Mr. Conrad wants you to make it look as if they killed each other. Can you do that?"

"A real waste of fine woman flesh if you ask me, but it shouldn't be a problem. Been there, done that."

"Oh, one more thing. Mr. Conrad's conscience is troubling him these days. He doesn't want to know the gory details. So be absolutely sure to inform me only when your mission is completed. At an opportune moment, I will broach the subject with him. Understood?"

"Huh? Mr. Conrad wants them dead, but he doesn't want to know when they've been erased?"

Chinua feigned righteous indignation. "The less Mr. Conrad knows about such grubby details, the more unassailable his position will be. So you will report directly to me and not indulge in ignorant speculations!"

"Sure, sure, but I'd be reporting to you anyway, wouldn't I?"

"Yes, yes, of course. So sorry I lost my temper. It's just that Mr. Conrad is under a lot of strain these days. Saving the world can be such a trial."

"Gotcha. We'll call as soon as we have results. You have a nice day —"

Bernie Gold was left talking to the ethers while Chinua raced across the room. The little man slid to a halt at the door to Conrad's room, then slowly opened it. Good. Conrad was fast asleep. He was also completely uncovered. The naked figure, blanched and gaunt, reminded him of the Christ figure in Michelangelo's *Piéta*. But he was not filled with reverence and affection, as he would have been only a day earlier. He felt revulsion. Nevertheless, he pulled the covers up over Conrad.

"What time is it, Chinua?"

"It's seven o'clock, Sir. But Friday, not Thursday."

"Christ, what'd you do? Drug me? Um. Have to get up soon. Nine o'clock, the latest. Heavy day ahead. Your phone's been busy, eh? Couldn't help hearing it going off every now and then."

Chinua's blood froze in his veins. "Reports from various field commanders, Sir. Of particular interest was the call from Australia. The successful capture of a magnificent male kangaroo. A kickboxing champion, no less."

Conrad laughed, rolled over, and went back to sleep. Chinua closed the door behind him and sat down at the small mahogany desk with the banker's lamp on it. He switched it on so resolutely that he might have been hoping it would cast a dazzling light on his situation.

He was sure Conrad had not overheard his conversation with Bernie Gold. Otherwise, the man would have immediately called him on it. Jason Conrad was not one to shrink in the face of insubordination or confrontation.

But now he had to evaluate what he'd just done in light of his beliefs. He had to rationalize his actions. He looked at the banker's lamp, which cast a dim light. He shook his head woefully. This was not going to be easy.

He began by admitting to himself that ordering the deaths of Irina Drach and Athol Hudson was as much an act of personal antipathy as it was an act for the salvation of a great idea. That put him on an equal footing with Conrad, if one were to assume that the latter's actions were motivated as much by the quest for personal glory as by altruism. As for commanding the extermination of Xueqin Liang, was that not a simple act of expediency, of the sort in which Jason Conrad engaged daily?

So far, the moral calculus favoured neither him nor Conrad ... but wait! He'd never actually killed anyone with his own hands. Surely that made Conrad much more the thug?

Alas, Chinua Amadi was not a stupid man. Try as he might, he could not persuade himself that there was a moral difference between pulling the trigger and shouting "fire!" He despaired. Even if he were to rescind his orders to Bernie Gold, he'd still have blood on his hands. Jason Conrad had been correct, and he was right back at the point from which he'd started.

Chinua sank into a deep gloom. He'd so wanted to do the right thing. Then, a thought. What if he were to cancel his orders to Bernie, expose Conrad publicly, and bring down the entire operation? Would that not be atonement? No, it wouldn't. Conrad's project could not be other than it was in order to benefit mankind.

He suddenly detected a whiff of fresh air rising from the sinkhole of moral degradation. He saw a shaft of light piercing the cloud banks of self-loathing. In his very maleficence lay his salvation. He would sacrifice his own soul in order for mankind to survive, and other souls to thrive.

He poured himself a double rum and drained it in one gulp. The reasoning was flimsy, but it would do. It would have to.

Some consolation lay in his having had ideas of his own, rather than just second-guessing Jason Conrad. But where would he find consolation in betraying the first white man who'd ever lent him a respectful ear? His heart cried out for both himself and Jason Conrad.

The boreal forest. September 7, 2006. Reg McDuff and Victor Tarasenko were set down exactly where Conrad and Chinua had spied the wounded black bear. Given that the spot was densely forested, the helicopter had to hover just above the treetops while everything, including the two men, their dogs, and their gear, was lowered by rope.

"I feel like a goddamn worm on a fishing line," grumbled McDuff. "At least we're getting daylight now. That'll take away much of the lion's advantage."

"Tell me something else along those lines, and maybe I'll stop shitting my pants."

"It's been two days since he fed on that moose. Lions really only need a big meal once a week."

"And tell me that lions aren't man-eaters."

"Sorry, no can do. Especially lions from the Tsavo, like this one. When the Kenyans were building their rail line, a pair of them were tossing back Indian migrant workers like they were Cheetos."

Victor Tarasenko laughed nervously. McDuff laughed raucously, for he'd never encountered a gruesome tale he didn't like.

"Shhh! He might be close by."

"Stupid," grunted the burly redhead, whacking the younger man on the back of the head with his cap. "The bear was moving north, and for God knows how long. So what we gotta do is head south to pick up Simba's trail."

"So how do we know the lion isn't heading north, straight toward us?"

"Then we'll have found him, won't we? Mission accomplished. But everything we know about him says he'll be headed south or southeast. Hmm, that's pretty much the direction of Africa, isn't it?"

After consulting his GPS unit, McDuff found a bloody smear on a tree trunk, pressed his dogs' noses to it, persuaded them by whipping that it was in their interest to follow the bear's trail even though it grew progressively fainter rather than stronger, and set off after them at a quick march. "Okay, Victor, look lively! Lions like to pick off the stragglers!"

It wasn't long before they came upon the bear's cave. McDuff immediately divined what had transpired, and he produced the wood shavings from I-árishóni's pen at the facility. The dogs went wild with excitement and set off in an easterly direction. After an hour of struggling to keep up with the dogs in the dense underbrush, they came upon the clearing where the remains of Vincent de Groot and Charmaine Washington lay. While Victor Tarasenko was vomiting in the bushes, McDuff studied the corpses admiringly. They'd each taken a single shot bang-on between the eyes. Somebody firing at point-blank rage couldn't have done better. It had not been made clear to him who was responsible for this carnage, but he had a good idea. There was only one man he knew of who was capable of such perfection.

He released the dogs and they followed them eastward, at a safe distance. "Tell me, Victor. I've only known you a little while but I've already figured you as a complete weenie. And not much of a tracker, either. I'll bet you didn't even notice the cat's paw prints in the dust by de Groot and Washington. So how in hell did you ever become part of this organization?"

"I can shoot pretty good," replied Victor Tarasenko, patting the semi-automatic Barrett M107 sniper rifle that caused his left shoulder to sag.

McDuff laughed. "Fuck, that thing's not a rifle. It's a bloody cannon. Fifty calibre armour-piercing ammo, right? It'll punch a hole the size of a fist in a man's chest. Makes you look like a five-year-old hoisting his old man's twelve-gauge shotgun."

They walked a few paces, then McDuff stopped in his tracks. He rubbed at his big, bristly chin. "So how did you do on the five hundred metre range?"

"Zeros."

The brawny man's jaw went slack. "With the L96? No deviations from the bull's eye?"

Victor Tarasenko blushed. "At first they thought I'd missed the sheet altogether. Then they started digging."

McDuff shook his head, then moved ahead in silence. They'd gone about a mile before he spoke again. They were in a meadow with a sightline of approximately seven hundred metres. "See that birch tree at the far end?"

"The one between the jack pines?"

"The one with the cedar waxwing on that lower branch."

Tarasenko was afraid that was the tree McDuff had meant. He knew what was coming, and McDuff did not disappoint. "Punch the bird."

"I ... I'd rather not."

"Punch the bird!"

"Couldn't I just do the branch he's sitting on?"

"Listen, you. If you can't shoot a little bitty bird, how in hell are you going to plug the frigging Lion King? Punch the bloody bird!"

"No! The branch!"

And Victor Tarasenko fired, but from the shoulder and not from the prone sniper's position. The birch branch, three inches thick, was sheared cleanly away not more than an inch from where the waxwing sat. It took the bird more than a few fractions of a second to realize that his perch was dropping to the ground like a stone. Laughing, McDuff pulled down the collar of his turtleneck and scratched at his grizzled Adam's apple. "Shee-it!" He then raised his own rifle skyward and shot at a red-tailed hawk that was circling overhead. "Quick," he said as the bird spiralled downward. "That bird is officially dead, so punch him!"

Tarasenko complied. He fired a single shot and the hawk disappeared into the thin morning air. It had been vapourized by a bullet the size of a penlight.

"Well, you've got the chops, that's for sure. Just make sure you don't let me down when we catch up to the cat, or I'll shove one of those bullets up your wazoo."

The dogs had backtracked and were awaiting the two men at the far end of the clearing. McDuff barked at them to get going, and he and Tarasenko resumed their trek in silence.

I-árishóni, some five miles east of Reg McDuff and Victor Tarasenko, had heard the shots. He'd also caught the men's scent on the light breeze. Almost as if he were mulling over his next move, he slowed his pace. Then he stopped, as if he'd reached a decision. Finally, he climbed up onto a rocky outcropping and flattened himself in the scrub — as if he were lying in wait for the hunting party.

Of course, it's presumptuous to ascribe motives to the great beast, but it's worth recalling that the last four humans he'd encountered had been dead — one of them by his own claws.

The Doomsday Complex. September 8, 2006. "It is nine o'clock, Sire."

Conrad opened one eye and peered suspiciously at Chinua Amadi. "*Sire?* Do I detect a note of sarcasm?"

"No, Sir ... certainly not, Sir," blustered Chinua. "It is merely that in my reading I stumbled upon the word and found that it perfectly expresses your ascendancy over me."

"Show me the book."

"Ah ... I cannot, Your Majesty. It was not a book I was reading, but a most interesting article on the Internet —"

Conrad leapt out of bed and into his housecoat. He'd heard enough. The subject was closed. "We've got a busy day, Chinua. Got to get back to Toronto and the workaday world. Pay the bills for our little adventure here, eh? But the first order of business involves dealing with the gubernatorial aspect of the facility. Tell Raphael Sparata I want to see him in his office at ten, get Franz Hauptmann back here for noon, and call a general assembly for two. That means everyone. I want to see eighteen hundred reverent and obedient faces in that auditorium."

"Am I to understand that you will be replacing Sparata with Franz Hauptmann, Sir?"

Conrad looked disinterested, his way of indicating that the answer was obvious.

"But you as much as suggested that Hauptmann was little more than a Nazi earlier this morning."

"And he is. He has a good background in oppression and cruelty. Just the man for the job.

"He killed an Indian in cold blood, Master. Thirty-five percent of our people here are aboriginal. He will be less than adored."

Conrad headed for the shower and stripped off his housecoat. "You know, Chinua, if I didn't love and esteem you as much as I do, I would tell you to mind your business. But since I do, and your business is me anyway, I will elaborate. We cannot run this place as if it were a day camp. Half the staff are screwing up, and the other half are running about indulging in mutinous acts. Don't you think that the guy who runs this place should be as pragmatic as the people who run my businesses?"

Conrad hopped into the shower and turned on the faucet. As banks of steam rolled out, Chinua set to laying out Conrad's clothing. So, Conrad loved and esteemed him. He felt decidedly guilty and treacherous. For all the moisture that was permeating his undergarments, he might as well have been in the shower too. But that did not prevent him from returning to his own room and dialing up Atilla Lakatos, Hauptmann's adjunct. "Mr. Conrad has special orders for you, Lakatos, so listen to me very carefully. We have irrefutable proof that Franz Hauptmann is the leader of a cadre that aims to harm Mr. Conrad."

"Harm? As in … kill?"

"I'm afraid so."

"But to what purpose?"

"It's a long story, Lakatos, and we're just now piecing it together from intercepted messages, tapped lines, and the like, but it seems Hauptmann has become infected by outside ideas and wants to bring down the whole enterprise. Now, Mr. Conrad has very cleverly called for Hauptmann's presence at the facility for noon, thus affording you an opportunity to dispose of him. Do you know how that might be accomplished?"

Lakatos took a few seconds to mull it over. "Yes, I believe I do. Hauptmann likes to ride the Huey with the cargo doors open. It makes him feel like a GI in Vietnam."

"Yes, I've heard that."

"And whenever he has to relieve himself, he pisses overboard and all over the countryside. 'Canada, I piss on you,' he always says."

"There. More proof of his discontent. Now, how to dispose of him?"

"It's obvious. One would only need give him a little push and he would plummet two-thousand feet. But I don't understand. What of justice? Why is he not arrested and tortured? Why do we not make an example of him?"

"Fool! Do you think Mr. Conrad wants it known that someone even dares contemplate such an outrageous act? Wicked ideas can spread like the most virulent of diseases, infecting even the innocent. Do you not see?"

"Yes … yes … I suppose so."

"You *suppose* so?"

"Upon reflection, Mr. Amadi, I would have to agree with you. One hundred percent. Uh … what of his coconspirators?"

"They are unknown to you, Lakatos, as they work here in administration. But they will be dealt with quietly, rest assured." Through his closed door, Chinua could hear that Conrad was out of the shower and listening to CNN. He cupped the receiver. "So, then, Mr. Conrad may count on you?"

"Of course."

"Oh ... just one more thing, Lakatos. *Mr.* Lakatos. You must never breathe a word of this enterprise to anyone, Mr. Conrad included, just as no one will ever speak of it to you. You will know that your efforts are recognized by the fact that you will immediately be promoted to Hauptmann's position. Is that understood, *Commandant* Lakatos?"

"Completely, Sir! And please, Sir, relay my heartfelt thanks to Mr. Conrad for this wonderful opportunity. I will not fail. Franz Hauptmann will soon be impaled on the sharp end of a spruce tree, and it is his life's blood he will be pissing all over the countryside."

The sounds of CNN suddenly grew louder. Conrad was standing at Chinua's open door.

"Then, Mr. Lakatos, you will see to it that Franz Hauptmann is put on a helicopter right away?"

Lakatos laughed. "What comes down must first go up, Mr. Amadi."

Chinua said his goodbyes then turned to Conrad. "A most capable man, this Atilla Lakatos, Sir. Might I suggest he replace Franz Hauptmann?"

"Who is he?"

"His adjunct, Sir. He already has a deep understanding of Hauptmann's position."

"I'll leave it up to you, Chinua," said Conrad as he towel-dried his hair. "And Sparata and the assembly? Are they set up?"

"Just getting to them, Sir."

"Hm. You seem to have spent quite some time with this Lakatos. A more suspicious man might think a conspiracy was afoot."

Chinua's mouth became exceedingly dry, and his hand shook as he reached for his bottled water. Conrad laughed as he turned back into his suite. "Relax, Chinua. You'll always be above suspicion. But I have to tell you this: apart from these little glitches like the lion and that pair of truants, things have gone almost too easily. It's well-nigh spooky. I think I'd almost welcome a conspiracy against me. Liven things up a bit."

The boreal forest. September 7, 2006. After having hacked their way through the dense underbrush for almost two hours, McDuff and Tarasenko were tiring. Tarasenko was all for pausing to eat and drink for a few minutes, especially since it was well past midmorning. McDuff was adamant. "We keep moving. We're so close to him now that if we stop for a weenie roast, he'll double his lead on us."

Victor Tarasenko settled on chewing at a stick of beef jerky.

"That stuff," offered McDuff. "Its name comes from a tribe who were descendants of the Incas. They had something like it and they called it *charqui*."

Tarasenko was aghast. "Reg ... I had no idea you were a scholar."

"I'm a woodsman, sonny boy. I make it my business to know that kind of thing ... what the fuck is that?"

The two dogs, a quarter of a mile ahead, were crying in distress. One of them made a sound like that of a speeding car squealing to a panic stop, then all was silent.

"I'll track down the dogs, or what's left of them," whispered McDuff. "You'd best put away that snack of yours and get that cannon in firing position or it'll be you who ends up as a snack."

Not expecting to have much time or space to set up for a shot, McDuff grasped the AK-47 in lieu of his Mark V hunting rifle. He ordered Tarasenko to follow fifty feet behind him with his Barrett at the ready. "But for God's sake, *don't* keep your finger on the trigger. If you do and you stumble, I could end up with an anus the size of the Holland Tunnel."

They moved slowly, sometimes no more than a few feet at a time. The woods were deadly silent, as if nature were already in mourning. After navigating a sweaty quarter mile in just under an hour, with every hillock and clump of dense undergrowth representing a mortal threat, they came upon their dogs. McDuff's basset was in two pieces while Tarasenko's Plott hound was completely eviscerated.

Distraught, Tarasenko rushed forward to examine his dog. "You fool!" snarled McDuff, pushing Tarasenko away from his dog. "Stop your mewling and get back there! Don't you know how vulnerable we are standing this close together —"

Too late. From a lichen-covered promontory, the massive predator launched himself some twenty feet and brought down both men at once.

McDuff was instantly flattened on his stomach, his back broken by the momentum of six-hundred pounds flying at twenty-feet per second, and his AK-47 bounced pathetically several yards before coming to rest under a bramble bush.

With a swipe of an immense forepaw and its unsheathed claws, Tarasenko's rifle was separated from his arm as easily as that arm was separated from his torso.

According to the Geneva Convention, I-árishóni should have resisted further offensive action, taken the two men as prisoners, and provided immediate medical attention. Unfortunately for McDuff and Tarasenko, the denizens of the wild take no prisoners. Both men suffered excruciatingly loathsome and painful deaths. Their cries of agony resounded even after they'd perished, becoming part of that macabre chorus that can often be heard when the wind creeps through the dark and impenetrable forests of the north.

I-árishóni raised his bloodied snout, roared in defiance, and struck off in a northeasterly direction. Not south, or southeasterly, but northeasterly. He was about to describe a clockwise, near-circular route of some one-hundred miles in twenty-four hours. This ruse, from an animal whose species well understands ambushes and feints, would baffle his pursuers and make a mockery of their talk about trajectories.

CHAPTER THIRTY

Philadelphia. September 8, 2006. It was two minutes before six in the morning, and all was quiet at the forty-two acre Philadelphia Zoo, America's oldest such institution. Nearing the end of its long shift, the beefed-up security force was sleepy and subdued. With the exception of a few animal handlers, the employees had not yet shown up for work. The Shelley Administration Building was empty. There would be no visitors for another three-and-a-half hours.

Paying visitors, that is.

An unmarked cargo van and a flatbed truck with a crane slowly crept northward along Zoological Drive, the arcing road that defines the western border of the heavily wooded, semicircular zoo. Simultaneously another unmarked van, at the northern tip of the zoo, on the one-way public connector road between Girard Street and North Thirty-Fourth Street, slowed to a stop just in front of the main entrance.

At precisely six o'clock the gate nearest the Pachyderm House in the zoo's barrier on Zoological Drive was breached, and the cargo van and the flatbed truck drove into the service area behind the display buildings. The van on the short connector road sped across the main entrance plaza, disgorged four men at the two matching sentinel/membership cottages, then hurtled past the ticket booth and along the pedestrian walkway to the Dodge Rare Animal Conservation Center.

At the same moment, the zoo's closed circuit camera system went dead, but this didn't worry the security personnel who were not already bound and gagged. It had happened before, and it would happen again. In fact, several of the guards — those who'd been added to the zoo's security force only the day before, following that Canadian policemen's heavily publicized warning about the global conspiracy — took it rather well. Rather too well, in fact. They made their way to where the two groups of intruders were conducting their operations — some to the Pachyderm House and others to the Dodge Center — and deflected any untoward interest in the proceedings on the part of the zoo's employees.

That the alarm systems had been compromised would have been the last thing on these few employees' minds as they unconcernedly sauntered back to their respective posts.

Once the coast was clear, both assault teams got to work. Using shaped charges, the two men at the Dodge Rare Animal Conservation Center blasted their way in and went directly to the eastern wing, where the Rodrigues fruit bats were housed. The odd, flat-faced little creatures, weighing no more than ten ounces but with a wing span of nearly two feet, were quite the prize. They differ from most bats in that they are strictly herbivorous, making sonar capabilities unnecessary. They were of such special interest because they can be found only on tiny Rodrigues Island in the Indian Ocean, and the International Union for the Conservation of Nature and Natural Resources (IUCN) had placed them on its critically endangered list. The harvesters bagged the two largest males, along with several females from each of their harems, and were out of the building in less than seven minutes. One minute later, they'd collected their associates at the front gate and had turned south on Thirty-Fourth Street. They drove half a mile to Haverford Street in the suburb of Mantua, where they switched vans with one that was parked at the curb, then took Spring Garden over to the Schuylkill Expressway and followed it down until they hit the New Jersey Turnpike. Once on the turnpike, they broke out the spliffs.

The team at the Pachyderm House had a considerably more awkward task, but things went as well as could be expected. Both the male and female Asian rhinoceroses, singular examples of a species whose numbers were reduced to less than twenty-five hundred in their native lands of northern India and southern Nepal, were plodding contentedly about their outdoor compound. The five-thousand-pound beasts were enticed by handfuls of apples and other assorted goodies to come to the wall, where they were felled by powerful tranquilizer guns and then carefully winched onto the back of the flatbed truck before being concealed with canvas drop cloths. This delicate operation took a full half hour and eight strong men equipped with levers and two tarps tough enough to sling an orca. The more orthodox approach might have been to awaken them by degrees with an antidote, then frogmarch the groggy and now pliable beasts into a waiting mobile paddock, but that would have been too exacting a procedure under the circumstances. The security guards, meanwhile, did a good job of keeping the area free of rubberneckers. The truck left the grounds the way it came, the van gathered up the fake security guards and followed, and both vehicles traced the same route that the fruit bat express had taken. In Mantua, both vehicles entered a large garage. The rhinoceroses were transferred to two Ford F-350 pickup trucks, the occupants of the van split up into two cars and, one by one, the four vehicles made for the New Jersey Turnpike.

This was but one of forty operations that were successfully carried out around the globe on September 8, 2006. There were few casualties on either side. In all, sixty species were collected, notwithstanding the general state of alert that had been occasioned by Sergeant-Detective Athol Hudson's star turn. As Julius Caesar had demonstrated at Alesia, audacity needs neither numbers nor the high ground.

CHAPTER THIRTY-ONE

London. September 8, 2006. Seated once again up top at the front of a double-decker bus, Sergeant-Detective Irina Drach was doing the *Guardian*'s cryptic crossword while Hudson gawked at the sights as if he hadn't seen them just three hours earlier.

"Geez, but I love this town. So vast, so cosmopolitan."

As if to underline his pensées, a massive young black man slid into the seat across the aisle at the next stop. But for his dyed blond hair, which was piled on his head in a topknot, the young man looked like a Zulu warrior in full battle dress. His muscles didn't just ripple. They were tsunamis.

"See what I mean?" Hudson whispered.

The young man's cellphone rang. He swiftly answered it in what, to Hudson's ears, sounded like a perfect Etonian accent. "Listen to me, Gustav. Women like surprises, I'll grant you, but a house? One doesn't just buy a bloody house then expect the little lady to be thrilled. You might as well be telling her what kind of tampon to use. No, Gustav, don't use your reason on her. That's what landed you in this mess in the first place. Just act wounded and apologetic, and I'll be there in fifteen minutes to tell her what a well-intentioned boob you are."

The young man folded up his phone and glanced at Hudson, who'd been unconsciously leaning in his direction. "Germans," he sighed in exasperation. "All the sensitivity of rutting warthogs."

Hudson feigned surprise. "Are you talking to me?"

"Of course I'm talking to you. I already have your attention, don't I?"

Hudson reddened. "Well … ah … I may have heard something about a house —"

The young man smiled broadly. "Save it. Not your fault, anyway. I talk too loudly. And since I definitely have your attention now, I might as well mention that you, too, have someone's attention."

"Oh?" said Irina, setting aside her newspaper. "Whose?"

"Two chaps in the car following this bus. I was at the back of the line, just level with them, and I heard them discussing you."

"How do you know they were discussing us?"

"The two Canadian coppers on the bus, they said. A man and a woman."

"But we don't look like police," blustered Hudson.

"No, no, of course not," he clucked. "Just a lucky guess, then."

"And how'd you know we're Canadian? Canadians don't have accents!"

This was too much for the young man. He tugged at his topnot as if trying to pull out his hair. A smile cracked like the dawn. "Right you are!"

"What, precisely, did they say?" Irina demanded firmly.

"Not for polite company, but here goes. 'What a waste, her travelling with that poufter. I sure wouldn't mind taking her for a ride.'"

"That's it?"

"Then they both grunted. Salaciously, I'm afraid."

"What did they look like?"

"Can't help you too much there, unfortunately. One was blond, and huge. The car was a few sizes too small for him. Oh, and he was pink, very pink, with a big, ugly scar on his left cheek. Fresh, like. Big, booming voice, but high. Scandinavian, I believe. Spoke like he was being buggered by a troll. Didn't see so much of the driver. Medium build, long, dark hair. A Frog, most likely. Sounded like Charles Aznavour. Oops, here's my stop," he exclaimed as he leapt to his feet and careened down the stairs. "Cheerio, and good luck to you!"

Irina had just taken out her BlackBerry and was beginning to work it furiously when there was a sound behind them. It was the Zulu warrior. "They're still back there. Driving a green, late-model Focus sedan, they are. No mistaking their intentions."

"You missed your stop," said Irina.

"I can walk. The question is, can you run?"

"What's your name?"

"Shaka."

Irina raised her eyebrows. "Why doesn't that surprise me? Thank you, Shaka."

And then he was gone. Irina went back to her BlackBerry.

"What are you doing, Irina?"

"Paddington. That's the main train station?"

"I believe so."

"Ah, here we go. Trains, Cornwall ... First Great Western. God bless Google. Quick, Hudson. Take out your map and give me a major destination in Cornwall. The closer to Bude, the better."

Hudson rattled his map, smoothed it, then wrinkled his brow. "Plymouth. About forty miles."

By seven o'clock, they'd arrived back at Oxford Street. Irina was famished but loath to spend much money on dinner as she'd already thought up dozens of other ways to dispense with the force's funds. Therefore, she and a horrified Hudson ended up in the McDonald's facing Marble Arch. While she wolfed down a Big Mac, he picked at a salad.

"Oh, come now, Hudson. Don't look so sanctimonious. You've already had your dinner. I haven't. And I would remind you that big, fat sausages have no fewer calories than this thing."

"I would argue that my bangers and mash at least qualify as a national experience. What do you call this?"

"An international experience. Also, sustenance, Hudson. Protein. We have a six-hour ride ahead of us and I don't fancy gnawing away at shoe leather."

Hudson muttered to himself, for there was no arguing with the fact that Irina actually loved Big Macs. He took some consolation from her having largely eschewed junk food during the last few days. "The train you want leaves at eleven forty-five. What do we do until then?"

"Since we're being followed, I'd say we go back to our hotel and give every indication that we've settled in for the night."

"These guys will be pros, Irina. They'll wait us out."

"Do you have any better suggestions?"

"I think it would be best if we took the rental car to the station. You know my driving. I could lose them, I'm sure."

"You don't know the city. Therefore, I'm sure you couldn't lose them. No, we'll play the shell game with a couple of minicabs. Hand me your city map."

Hudson pushed the map toward her with the Marble Arch panel showing.

"Right," muttered Irina. "Here's the Glynne Court, and here's Paddington. If we were to take a minicab from the hotel at 10:30 and reward the driver handsomely for driving like a lunatic through this maze of one-way streets to, say, the corner of Edgeware and Penfold Place, where another minicab would be waiting for us at 10:45, we just might pull it off."

"Very exciting, Irina. Might even work. At the risk of sounding prosaic, though, why don't we just call on the London cops to help us out? They could shake these guys down, maybe find out who they are. At the very least they could run interference for us."

"The idea, Hudson, is to avoid having anyone know where we are or where we're going. That includes other forces as well as the bad guys."

"Oh, right.. Stupid of me." Hudson pulled the map toward him and pretended to study it. "Ah ... are you worried about our friends at that pub? Beryl and Leon? And Heather Liang, too?"

"It's a good sign that the two mystery men were on our tails the instant we left the pub, just as they had to have been after Heather Liang dropped us."

"They might have left behind accomplices to look after that end of things."

"I didn't notice two men sitting together while we were in the pub, did you? So if they don't know about Beryl and Leon, neither will their confederates."

"It would only have taken one of them. And there were a few singles seated around the place, weren't there?"

"I concede the point, but what's to be done? Must everything grind to a halt because Beryl, Leon, or Heather might be indisposed?"

Hudson was aghast. This was the first time he'd ever heard Irina express disregard for the safety of innocents. He pushed aside the map and his salad, then leaned across the table and whispered hoarsely, "Surely to God we can offer them some protection? Have the Metro Police keep an eye on them?"

"First off, Hudson, I doubt the bobbies can spare the personnel to babysit everyone with whom we've had a conversation. Second, if the London Police are made aware of Beryl and Heather and Leon and they *can* spare the personnel, then they'll most likely become aware of where we're going and who we're after, won't they?"

Hudson leapt from his chair, balled up the map, and angrily bounced it off the table. It barely missed Irina's face. "Heaven help that anything should compromise our investigation. Expediency, eh? In my book that makes us as culpable as those nutbars who go around killing anyone stupid enough to try preventing them from abducting animals and saving the world!"

Hudson stormed out of the restaurant.

For the whole time that the other diners stared at her, Irina was as still and solid as a Henry Moore sculpture. When the ordeal was over she slowly rose, blinking wildly, and went to the counter. She ordered another Big Mac. As she bit into it, however, she realized that her appetite was gone. More shockingly, the hamburger just didn't seem to be the comfort food it had consistently been since Walter's death. It mocked her. A greasy sludge coursed through her veins, infiltrating every cell of her body and turning her into a grey, bloated caricature of herself. Something like a human hippopotamus.

Irina fled the restaurant in a panic. As she made her way north on Great Cumberland Place, her mind cleared enough for her to hope that the two men following her didn't notice how much she waddled.

Ninety minutes later, as she methodically packed her bags, there was a knock at the door.

"Enter."

Hudson stood just inside the doorway, with his hands in his pockets. "Lucky we're paid up for last night and tonight. We won't be skipping out on the rent."

"Yes, lucky," she whispered urgently. "And we'll let Mohammed know first thing in the morning that we're gone. Now come in and close the door. Quickly!"

Hudson jumped and landed in an old, overstuffed club chair. "I've been thinking."

"Oh?" replied Irina without missing a trip to the closet. "Anything to do with your rash behaviour?"

"You know me well enough to know that I know I should be really sorry about that."

"Manners are not about knowing the right thing. That's ethics. Manners are about doing the right thing."

"All right, I was a clod. And a lousy cop to boot. I'm sorry."

"Apology accepted. Now, what were you thinking?"

Hudson pushed the heavy, horn-rimmed glasses back into place. He then pulled at tufts of his upswept orange hair. "Apart from Heather Liang, Beryl, and Leon coming right out and blabbing that they knew who I was, and those Toronto billionaires smirking knowingly, there have been these funny looks all day. Not the usual admiring looks but ... you know ... funny. And not simply the sort of thing you get for looking like a used Q-Tip either. In short, we have to do something about my disguise."

"Oh? And what do you suggest?"

From his pocket Hudson removed something black and fuzzy and threw it onto the dresser. "This, for one. After I left you, I went for a walk and found a theatrical supplies shop near Duke Street."

Irina scrutinized the object. "Huh. It looks something like a Hobbit might wear in the dead of winter."

Leaping from his chair, Hudson peered into the mirror and crowed, as if Irina had no idea what the object was, "It's a mustache! A horseshoe mustache like Hulk Hogan's!" He held it up to his face and spun toward her. "What do you think?"

If she hadn't been touched by his willingness to look like a perfect nincompoop, Irina would have laughed. "Now, you said the mustache, for *one*. Was there something else?"

Hudson got a towel and draped it over his shoulders. As he dropped back into the chair, he rubbed at his head.

"I should cut off your hair?"

"All of it. My lips will seem thicker, my eyebrows bushier, and my eyes and nose bigger."

"What makes you think I have a razor with me? Or scissors, for that matter?"

"In the squad room, I've seen you come back from the pharmacy with shaving cream. Ergo, you shave your legs. As for scissors … well, if you don't have any, then I'll check with the desk. They probably have a pair. And if not, I'll just go down to Oxford Street and buy some. It's Friday night. The stores are open until 9:30, or so I read in the guide."

In fact, Hudson had seen Irina surreptitiously tuck the scissors into her luggage after she'd remodelled his hair back in her Montreal home. However, he did not want her to know that he was merely hastening the inevitable. It was important that she credit him with believing it was his idea to get scalped.

Irina knew that he'd noticed her packing the scissors, but she said nothing as she withdrew them from her bag and began to chop away. It was enough that Hudson had made the effort to remove the onus from her.

They both hummed contentedly as Irina chopped away at his hair then deftly shaved away the stubble. The whole time, Hudson thrilled to the touch of her fingertips. It seemed to him as if a thousand tiny electrodes had been affixed to his scalp. Irina was acutely aware of her effect on him and held her breath. As she was wiping the shaving cream from his glistening head, he said earnestly, "Irina, there's something we have to discuss, and it won't wait."

Sinking to the bed and facing him, she folded her hands in her lap and braced herself.

"It's about Heather, Leon, and Beryl. We've hung them out to dry and I don't like it one bit. Isn't there *something* we can do?"

Jubilantly, Irina leapt to her feet and planted a big, wet kiss on the bald pate. Hudson smiled broadly. "Gee, I didn't expect that reaction. You were pretty surly the last time I brought it up."

"Your compassion, Hudson. That's one of the things I like best about you. Now paste on that caterpillar and let's see how awful you can look."

Hudson leaned into the mirror and did just that. The transformation was complete. "Wonderful!" Irina exclaimed as she clapped her hands gleefully. "You're an absolute fright! Now shave your chin. The blond stubble is a dead giveaway."

Hudson dutifully attacked his neck and chin while Irina set about cleaning up Hudson's bright orange hair clippings with a hairbrush. "To return to Heather, Leon, and Beryl," he said, "maybe you're convinced those two guys tailing us are the Mounties, or the FBI or CIA, or MI6, or something, and that our friends are therefore in no particular danger?"

Irina was on her knees and bent over. She sat up on her heels. "I don't believe so. This organization is deeper and wider than any law enforcement agency I know of. For example, I just got an email from Stan saying that so far today there have been thirty reports of animal abductions. Those are only the reported cases. Lord knows how many have really been swept up. I'm sure they have moles in many police, customs, and naturalist agencies around the world, and would therefore have gotten a heads up on us before anyone else did. So I'd expect them to be first in line behind us."

"Well, then," rejoined Hudson as he toweled off his chin and neck, "why don't we just turn the tables on these two guys and nab them instead of going after a long shot like Xueqin Liang?"

"Have you spotted a green, late-model Focus sedan with two men in it, following us?"

"No."

"Just so. These men are almost certainly specialists in covert operations. They stake out, they eliminate, et cetera, et cetera — probably on contract. It's doubtful they've ever been near an animal. Xueqin Liang has, and he'll therefore have a better knowledge of the organization. Add to that the fact that he's an accessory in the murder of a policeman, and he might be willing to enlighten us about it. Oh, one more thing. If we do anything to our tails, or even let on that we know about them, all kinds of bells will start ringing, and then we're certainly done for."

On the other side of the wall, Bernie Gold muffled a laugh and whispered to Jamal Jefferson, "They touch Lars and Jean-Louis and *they might get hurt!* Isn't that the best?"

"On the reezie, my man," said Jefferson as they exchanged high fives. Then they were once more the picture of concentration.

With brow furrowed as if he were watching a puppy being beaten, Hudson crouched on one knee only inches from Irina. "I'm beginning to sound like a broken record, I know, but what do we do about Heather, Leon, and Beryl?"

Irina got to her feet and sat on the edge of the bed. Hudson did the same, staring at her expectantly. After a great deal of painful deliberation, she said, "Get the Chamberlayne Pub on the phone. Maybe Leon and Beryl will still be there. Tell them to watch their backs. Tell them, too, that the Metropolitan Police will be shadowing them. Then get hold of Heather Liang and tell her the same thing. In the meantime, I'll ring up Inspector Duggan at Scotland Yard."

Hudson leapt to his feet excitedly as he withdrew his BlackBerry from his jacket pocket. "You really think Duggan will spare the manpower for them?"

"Oh, yes," she said ruefully. "There isn't a police force on this planet that doesn't want in on this case."

The phone calls were placed. Beryl and Leon were, indeed, still at the pub. Heather Liang had just admitted the babysitter and was preparing to leave for her accounting class. All three were shocked by Hudson's news, but all three exhibited the sang-froid for which the British are so justly famous. In fact, Hudson was acutely embarrassed by their degree of gratitude for the police protection.

Detective Chief Inspector Duggan was still in his office and was plainly delighted to hear from Sergeant-Detective Irina Drach. He was even more delighted to accommodate her. "Not to worry, Sergeant," he slavered. "We'll get in touch with them immediately — merely to reassure them, of course — but after that we'll keep our distance. Your case, and all that."

Irina sighed heavily as she pushed the end button on her BlackBerry. "I wonder if we shouldn't just forget about the train and hitch a ride to Bude with Duggan's men, or MI5 or MI6, or whomever happens to be stampeding in that direction."

"Don't be so cynical," replied an elated Athol Hudson. "They wouldn't do anything to jeopardize our investigation. They're British!"

"That may be, but they're still cops."

For the next while, Irina was back at her *Guardian* crossword puzzle while Hudson alternately studied his maps and watched television. At 10:29 he peeked out the window and spied a minicab at the curb. "It's here. Let's go!"

They flung themselves out the hotel door and through the heavy rain, flung their bags onto the back seat, then flung themselves into the minicab. "Go," Hudson barked at the driver. "Go, go, go! And take the most winding way you can get there, so long as we arrive by eleven sharp! Go fast. Pretend you're being followed!"

The cabbie, a shaggy and behemothic Afghani with a cellphone glued to his ear, said, "The price I quoted you was for the shortest route, mate. It's all about the gas, y'see? Cor, it don't come half cheap around here. Cost you another twenty quid, what you ask."

Irina agreed.

"And then," he said, as he sped down toward Oxford Street, "there'll be another twenty quid for the play-acting, if you catch my drift. Sir Larry didn't work cheap. Why should I? One more thing, eh? No minicabs allowed on Oxford Street. Such risk I take."

"All right, then," snapped Irina. "Twenty pounds! Now how about putting away the phone and getting both hands on the wheel!"

"Alligator, Shirley-Girley" the driver breathed into his phone. "Puss'n'boots are about to discover rushhour Kabul."

True to his word, the Afghani drove like a perfect madman. On Oxford Street, he sliced and diced through the heavy bus traffic with all the finesse of a meat cleaver descending on a side of beef. Men howled in outrage, woman pressed their children to their bossoms, the buses tucked in their skirts like shy debutantes.

"There are five million video surveillance cameras in this country," the Afghani shrieked as he spun his wheel like a top. "Atiq is earning his miserable fee!"

Bracing herself against the dashboard, and with her feet frequently slamming down on a chimerical brake pedal, Irina was agog. Hudson, on the other hand, was whooping like a cowboy on a runaway brahmin bull.

And so it went, with the Afghani's passengers being tossed about the inside of his car like dice in a tin cup as he wove and dodged his way through Westminster. The only infraction he didn't commit was that of going against the traffic on a one way street.

"Are they behind us, Hudson?" asked Irina through clenched teeth.

"Can't tell. Rain's too heavy. All I can make out are headlights."

It was precisely 10:42 when they arrived at the corner of Edgeware Road and Penfold Place. As Hudson and Irina wobbled their way over to the second minicab, Atiq was already back on the phone with his Shirley-Girley. Knowing that people who've just come face to face with their own mortality tend not to be chintzy, he didn't bother checking his fare. He did, however, take some moments from his telephone conversation to draw alongside the second driver and offer some pithy advice before roaring off down Edgeware.

The switch from one minicab to the other, including the transfer of suitcases, had taken all of forty seconds. Secure in the knowledge that they'd shaken their tail, Irina and Hudson sat back in their seats, breathed a sigh of relief, and gave to an exceedingly small and gaunt Ethiopian the same instructions they'd given Atiq.

After the courtly little man had introduced himself, Haddis Bekere stomped on the accelerator and proceeded to demonstrate that the perpetration of vehicular terror might be inversely proportional to the size of the driver.

Lars Madsen, who was seated in a green Ford Focus some five-hundred feet behind the Ethiopian's minicab, laughed as he focused his binoculars. "All their nonsense for nothing, eh? Speed up the wipers, Jean-Louis. I can't see them any better than they can see us."

"They depart. Do I give chase?"

"We haven't so far. Why start now?" Madsen peered through the eyepieces at the rapidly receding minicab. "Right, then. Now to phone that plate number into Smith and Hardcastle. There certainly won't be much going on at Paddington this time of night, so they'll be on our two intrepid coppers like blowflies on a turd."

"Especially as they already have photos of them."

Madsen's temper flared. "If you thought the photos were enough, then why in bloody hell did you just ask me if we should go after them?"

"Things have gone so well, I only suspected you might be bored."

Madsen got on the phone to Alex Smith and recited the minicab's plate number. "They're right on schedule," he said to Smith. "The rest is up to you. Have a nice trip. And after you've performed your duties, I suggest you go for a dip in the ocean. Very cleansing."

Then Madsen smacked Jean-Louis's head with the butt of his pistol. "*Et voilà*. You keep me from boredom, I do the same for you. Teamwork, Jean-Louis. Teamwork! That's what will keep our organization great."

Once they'd arrived at Paddington Station, after a suitably circuitous and hair-raising ride, Irina and Hudson immediately secured their tickets then devoted some time to exploring the vast glass, brick, and cast-iron structure before boarding the 11:45 to Plymouth. The shops on the concourse were closed — Hudson was distraught that the Paddington Bear stand was locked up, as he'd have liked to buy an item for his niece — but they descended on the Mad Bishop and Bear a few minutes after eleven, just as it was closing, and Hudson was able to cadge some Chiswick draft beers from a barmaid who had a weakness for young men resembling Genghis Khan.

The pair then dawdled for a while on the main concourse of the neoclassical building, window shopping and taking in the sculptures of Paddington Bear and Isambard Kingdom Brunel, the architect who built the station in 1854. They gaped at the soaring arched ceilings, each famously embedded with twelve rows of windows for its entire length. "They make me think of giant centipedes," Hudson waxed about the spans. Finally, they stopped at a newsstand, where Irina bought *The Times* for its crossword and Hudson bought a tourist's guide to Cornwall. Then it was time to board the train for Plymouth.

As the train pulled out of the station, Irina and Hudson busied themselves with their acquisitions. Neither realized that they themselves had been acquired by the man and woman just six rows behind them.

CHAPTER THIRTY-TWO

The Doomsday Complex. September 8, 2006. At eleven o'clock, Jason Conrad and Chinua Amadi were in the governor's dining room, finishing up breakfast. The governor himself was nowhere to be seen. Conrad had already informed Raphael Sparata that he was to be replaced by Franz Hauptmann, and that he ought to begin familiarizing himself with his new duties as a facilities manager. He was, of course, not doing that. He'd had a complete breakdown and was at the medical clinic begging for anxiolytics.

Chinua was ordering a third coffee when his cellphone buzzed. It was Franz Hauptmann's adjunct, Atilla Lakatos. "It is done, Sir. The estimable Herr Hauptmann went overboard at three thousand feet, just as he was pissing out of the chopper. I will say, Sir, that he went bravely, and with a formidable fastidiousness. He did not relinquish hold of his penis until he came apart on a jagged outcropping. Who says Germans are not different from you and me, eh?"

"Thank you, Mr. Lakatos. Make arrangements to have the body brought here as soon as possible."

"All of it?"

"All of it."

"I will do my best, Sir."

"What body?" asked Conrad hopefully as he wiped marmalade from his upper lip. "The lion's?"

"That was Franz Hauptmann's adjunct, Sir. A most unfortunate incident. Hauptmann was relieving himself out of the helicopter door when the machine ran into some turbulence. The poor man fell to his death."

"Bloody hell. Can't people even piss straight around here?" Conrad threw down his linen napkin in disgust. "Who was in the chopper with him?"

"There was of course the pilot, and then there was Atilla Lakatos."

"Anybody else?"

"There shouldn't have been, Sir, if my orders were followed. This was to be a very special mission."

"*Cui bono,* eh?"

"I beg your pardon, Sir?"

"*Cui bono.* Latin. Who benefits?"

Chinua did his best to look astonished and scandalized. "Sir! Atilla Lakatos is one of our most respected and loyal hands. And if memory serves me right, he was Franz Hauptmann's brother-in-law."

"He was also the man you had pegged to take over Hauptmann's old position."

"But he didn't know that, Master."

"Did he have to?"

"Believe me, Mr. Conrad. If we cannot trust Atilla Lakatos, then we can trust no one."

Conrad studied Chinua for a few moments. "Very well, I'll take your word for it. You're closer to the situation and the personnel than I am. So give him Hauptmann's old job. Now, with whom do we replace Raphael Sparata?"

"There is Sparata's assistant, Sir. The lieutenant-governor, Alfred Shakespeare."

"There's a good reason he's not having breakfast with us, Chinua. I don't like him a bit. He can't think for himself and he's too obsequious. I always get the feeling he's licked clean the red rug he rolls out for me. Anyone else, or should I go outside the facility for someone?"

"Call me crazy, but what about Atilla Lakatos?"

"Oh? And has he performed so admirably in Franz Hauptmann's old position thus far?"

"Seriously, Sir. This man is well-liked, highly respected and learns very quickly. He is most impressive. Do you know he has a Ph.D. in economics from Stanford?"

"What the hell was he doing as Hauptmann's adjunct, then?"

"At his insistence, Sir. He wanted to learn the operation from the ground up."

"You're pretty chummy with the staff, Chinua. Seem to know an awful lot about them."

"It's my job and my mission, Sir. I must attend to the quotidian details in order that you are free to think great thoughts."

"What would I do without you?" Conrad reached across the table and pushed at Chinua's shoulder affectionately. "Right. So we've got ourselves a new governor. He's having himself quite a day, isn't he?"

And so, at two o'clock that afternoon, a flabbergasted Atilla Lakatos was anointed governor before an assembly of eighteen-hundred true believers. As befitting his education, he gave a rousing and well-reasoned speech, eloquently hymned Jason Conrad's vision and, with a nod and a telling look, let Chinua Amadi know that he was profoundly beholden to him.

After the hour-long proceeding, Conrad, Chinua, and the new governor were given a lengthy and detailed tour of the burgeoning facility by a somewhat disgruntled lieutenant-governor. To be sure, Alfred Shakespeare behaved with compelling servility toward Conrad and Amadi, but if looks could kill, the usurper's mummified corpse would have brought up the rear in a wheelbarrow.

After a five-course dinner in the stateroom, in the company of select managers, supervisors, squadron leaders, and chief scientists, Conrad and Chinua were chauffeured back to Misquamaebin Lake and their awaiting Cessna. As Conrad settled into the pilot's seat he said to Chinua, "Alfred Shakespeare is not a happy camper. Are you sure Atilla Lakatos will be able to handle him?"

"Without a doubt, Sir. Our new governor is a ruthless and very ambitious man. That is how he came to my attention in the first place."

"I'm starting to get a funny feeling about the facility, Chinua," Conrad said as he started up the single turboprop engine. "Something like when a rock-solid deal turns to sand and starts to slip through your fingers."

"Not something you've experienced very often, Mr. Conrad."

"Often enough to keep me alert. We'll have to watch over our Mr. Lakatos pretty closely for a while."

Chinua's stomach was just beginning to cramp up when his phone rang. It was Bernie Gold in London, and he provided some relief. "It seems our man Liang is in a small Cornish town called Bude. Irina Drach and her partner are on their way there even as we speak. They're taking the train to Plymouth and from there they'll rent a car. And guess what? We've got Smith and Hardcastle sitting six rows behind them in the coach. Plus, we've got two relay cars parked at the train station in Plymouth, one of them Smith's own. A high-powered Bimmer. You know, you were dead right about this Irina Drach, eh? She's going to find Liang, no question about it."

"I'm glad you appreciate her intelligence. It won't take much for her to realize she's being followed."

"You know, I almost get the feeling she knows. She pulled the old taxi shuffle on her way to Paddington. If we hadn't been listening at her hotel room wall, she just mighta got away."

"Well, you just make sure she doesn't. And remember what I told you this morning."

"Jason Conrad gets it from you, not us, when the three of them go down. I got it, I got it. But y'know, Chinua, I don't know what you're getting so excited about. We don't even have Conrad's number. Say, we've been tossing ideas back and forth about how to set up the kill. You wanna hear some of them?"

"Not now! Just don't lose her!"

Conrad was levelling off the Cessna at six-thousand feet. "So. The troops are keeping up with her, eh?"

"Yes, Sir," replied Chinua, pocketing his phone. "She's worked out that Liang is in Bude, Cornwall."

"Good. That should be enough for our people to go on. I want him dead by the time she gets there. He's not only bad for us, but he could be bad for her, too."

"We're doing our best, Sir."

"Our people are staying close?"

"Six rows behind her on the train, Mr. Conrad."

"Good. Good, good, good. Comforting to know that someone's keeping an eye on her. She must never find out about this, eh Chinua? She'd have my head if she knew I was babysitting her."

"I reminded Gold of that, Sir. Perhaps you overheard me?"

"Yes, I did, actually. Thanks, Chinua."

"My pleasure, Sir."

"Something's up, Chinua."

Chinua Amadi's heart stopped. "Sir?"

"When you were talking to that character just now, you sounded more assertive than I've yet hear you sound. Aggressive, come to think of it. Could that be residual dismay over my plugging those two runaways?"

"No, Sir. It's been a long few days, that's all. I would never presume to judge any action you might take."

"But you were shocked. Admit it."

"I have since come to the conclusion that great deeds require great sacrifices, Sir."

Caribou Lake lies some twenty miles northwest of Lake Nipigon, Ontario's largest body of fresh water after the Great Lakes. One can almost walk its waters on the backs of lake trout, walleye, and northern pike, while moose and black bears practically trip over each other in the boreal forest surrounding it. It was to this wilderness paradise that Marvin and June Hamilton came on the occasion of their fiftieth wedding anniversary. While staying at the Aurora Lodge on the north shore of Caribou Lake, Marvin would finally have his chance to catch the forty-pound pike he'd been chasing all his life, and June would catch up on her reading, maybe even do a bit of bird watching.

The Wisconsin natives spent the day getting settled into their cabin, canoeing, exploring nearby nature trails, and chumming it up with a small party of Czech big-game hunters and their Cree guides while getting slowly inebriated on daiquiris and cosmos at the birch-clad bar.

Evening found them down on the beach, under a stand of stately old pines, barbecuing inches-thick Chianina porterhouse steaks. Or, rather, it found Marvin doing the barbecuing. June ran back and forth to the cabin fetching a salad, the 2000 Latour Pauillac Bordeaux, the cutlery and dinnerware, and a white linen cloth for the wooden table at the water's edge. To Marvin's delight, she even produced a pair of large sterling silver candelabras with citronella candles.

"Now how in Heaven's name did you find room for those in the luggage?" asked Marvin, swatting gently at her behind as she made once more for the cabin.

"Oh," she said coyly, "I stuffed them into your pants, where you normally keep ... you know. Oh, Marvin! This has got to be one of the most important days of my life."

"Mine too, Honey. Mine too."

"Now you make sure you don't overdo my meat, Marvin Hamilton," chimed the pretty, petite woman as she let the screen door swing closed behind her. "You always overdo my meat."

"Gotcha, Honey," said Marvin as he rescued the smaller steak from the flames. Marvin rather suspected it was already overcooked, but he knew she would forgive him, as she always did. His heart swelled and he blew a kiss in the direction of the cabin even though she wouldn't be able to see it.

After dinner they sat in the Adirondack chairs sipping at the remainder of their wine, watching the sunset, and listening to the gentle lapping of the waves at their feet. Every so often their fingertips would touch, and their spirits would commingle, and that was enough to banish any thought that they might not have very many summers left together.

The sun dipped below the treeline on the far shore and it quickly became chilly. As one, they rose from their chairs and surveyed the picnic table littered with dirty dishes, leftover salad, and half of the chocolate cake she'd baked while he'd been poring over his new fishing flies. "If it's all the same to you, Marvin, I'd just as soon leave this mess until morning. I'm feeling kind of ... you know."

June wrinkled her nose in that pixyish way she always did when she wanted something special from him.

The big man smiled and pinched her bottom. "So am I, Honey, but it's the bears, y'see. They will come, and they'll come every night after this."

She scooped up the cake. "Good point. But I'm not letting you off the hook, Marvin Hamilton — oh, dear God. Look up. Quickly. Just by the door."

"Mother of God … I didn't know they came in that size. He's as big as a bull."

"He's magnificent. The glory of nature," June said as she held onto her husband's arm. "Funny. I didn't know they had lions in Canada."

"I'm a lawyer, Honey, not a naturalist, but I don't believe they do."

"But if he'd escaped from a zoo, wouldn't we have been warned?"

I-árishóni was reclining on the lawn. But for the fact that his back was arched rather than concave, he could have been a model for Landseer's giant and regal bronze lions in Trafalgar Square. Occasionally he would yawn widely, but apart from that, and a tail that slowly flicked from side to side, he was perfectly immobile and stared fixedly at the couple.

"What do we do, Marvin?"

"He looks relaxed, Honey. I think we must be doing something right."

Indeed they were. Whether it was because they were shrouded by an alcoholic fog, or because they were at peace with themselves, each other, and the world, they showed no signs of fear.

"I wonder if he'd like this cake."

"You must be kidding. He's the king of beasts, the top of the food chain. He gets all he needs to eat."

"But how often does he get dessert?"

June walked slowly toward the lion, about halfway, then laid the cake tray on the grass. I-árishóni watched her with great curiosity and as she retreated he got up and advanced toward the chocolate confection. He sniffed at the tray, then licked it clean in seconds. He was now only about twenty feet from Marvin and June.

"Well, that was brilliant. Now he's practically on top of us. What do we do next?"

"I suggest we start cleaning up the table. If we don't, then the bears will come, as you so cogently pointed out, and there will be an awful ruckus. Our friend looks like a loner. I don't think he'd appreciate the company."

Dishes were stacked and loaded onto a tray, the barbecue was put to bed, and the tablecloth was shaken out and folded. This was accomplished in about five minutes and they were then ready for the march to the cabin. Marvin said, "I think it might be smart if we gave him a pretty wide berth, don't you?"

"Yes ... oh, my cake tray! One moment." And June walked slowly toward I-árishóni. The closer she got to him, the lower she crouched. When she was within two feet of the beast, she got to her knees. "Excuse me, big fella, but I'll be needing this now."

She reached out toward the cake plate. I-árishóni's chest rumbled briefly as she grasped it, but then he looked away as she pulled it toward her. It was now that Marvin Hamilton could really gauge the enormity of the lion, and he sucked in his breath. "June, Honey —"

Emboldened and charmed by the cat's passivity, June extended her arm and began to stroke his luxuriant, dark mane. "My, but you're a lovely fellow."

And then her hand slid downward, toward his throat. That was a serious mistake. I-árishóni immediately rose to his feet and struck at her head with a paw the size of a cantaloupe. June's detached head rolled fifty feet across the lawn. Shrieking hysterically, Marvin dropped the tray and ran toward his wife's body. Within seconds, I-árishóni had cut Marvin to ribbons with his claws and had the man's neck in his jaws. The lion shook his enormous head back and forth violently, then discarded the broken body as a man might discard a soggy, unreadable newspaper.

Night broke quickly. The shadows leapt from the woods and the gentle waves subsided, no longer eliciting light laughter as they tickled the shoreline. All was still and silent as I-árishóni floated across the lawn and sank into the bushes without causing so much as a ripple.

CHAPTER THIRTY-THREE

Bude, Cornwall. September 9, 2006. As the train rumbled through the night, Hudson grumbled. "Hedgerows. I can't make out the hedgerows."

Irina had nodded off over her crossword. She looked at Hudson with an entirely unsympathetic expression. "What time is it?"

"Two o'clock."

"Two o'clock. At two in the morning you're fretting about hedgerows? We've almost four hours to go, Hudson. Do you intend to fret about bloody hedgerows all the way to Plymouth?"

Hudson rattled his maps. "They're part of the British experience."

"We'll soon be driving in the bright morning light through the heart of Cornwall. Has it not occurred to you that you'll be seeing enough hedgerows to make sheep claustrophobic?"

"But we'll be on the A388 and A39 for the most part. Highways, not byways."

"But they're not 'M' roads, are they?"

"No, no, they're not." He rattled his maps some more. "Well, we'll see."

"And if they're not, then we'll take some byways. All right?"

Hudson grunted his satisfaction and returned to scrutinizing the blackness outside the coach. Irina closed her eyes again. In its time, darkness had given up enough of its secrets to her.

Twenty minutes later she was awakened by a light tap on her knee. A note lay in her lap. *There's a couple some six rows behind you*, it read. *A man and a woman. He in his forties, she early twenties. They nap in shifts.*

Irina turned over the paper and wrote: *He, short, with a beard? She, a tall blond?*

Hudson read it and nodded. He then looked at her quizzically.

She wrote: *They were behind us at the ticket booth. No luggage.*

Duly impressed with her sagacity, Hudson thought he might counter with boldness. He wrote: *Let me have my head and I'll lose them on the highways (and byways).*

Irina scribbled something quickly, passed it to Hudson, then closed her eyes. It read: *You're on, Fangio. Now let me sleep.*

Upon arrival at the Plymouth railway station at 5:45, some six hours after they'd left Paddington, Irina and Hudson made straight for the Intercity House wing where they rented a Vauxhall Vectra from Carhire 3000. Irina rationalized the additional expense of taking a mid-sized car rather than a mini. "We sat up all night in coach rather than taking sleepers, didn't we? Besides, we'll need a stronger car with good road manners if we're to shake our friends."

Their "friends" were right behind them at the Carhire 3000 kiosk, but seemed unperturbed by the fact that Irina's and Hudson's transaction took a good fifteen minutes, and that their own transaction would therefore take them a similar amount of time. This got Irina thinking. "They won't be following us themselves," she whispered to Hudson as they quickmarched toward the car park. "They just wanted information about the car we've taken. Someone else will be waiting to pick us up as we drive away."

Hudson's first act upon leaving North Road East, the one-way access road to the train station, was to scream around the immense North Cross Roundabout three times before exiting at Cobourg Street. It was a canny move: any car that stayed within their sight all the way had to have had more than a landscaper's interest in the sunken park that lay at the centre of the roundabout.

"It's a Mercedes," said Irina, staring into her pocket mirror. "A big black Mercedes."

"And now they have to know that we know we're being followed. What do you think their next move will be?"

"They must know we know they know we know. Do the same thing at the next big roundabout. See if we can't flush out a second car."

At Drake circle, which would access Mannamead Road and, ultimately, the A38, Hudson took the roundabout twice.

"Hm. Still the Mercedes. They're not ready to risk another vehicle just yet. Okay, Hudson. Show them one doesn't need a powerful car to shake off the devil."

And Hudson did just that. He stepped hard on the gas and propelled them through a largely residential area up Drake Circus, which became North Hill, which became Mutley Plain. At the intersection of Mutley Plain, Hyde Park Road, and Mannamead, Hudson took advantage of the fact that the roundabout there had a multistorey building at its centre. He negotiated the roundabout twice and, with the Mercedes nowhere in sight, struck off onto a quiet side street fittingly named Wilderness Road. "These roundabouts are brilliant," he exclaimed, pounding the steering wheel. "No stop signs, no lights, just merge and go, go, go! Brilliant!"

"Might I remind you that in Britain, they drive on the left side of the road?"

"There were a few moments back there, eh?"

"And I think we're lost," said Irina as she pored over the map.

"Good. That means they're lost too, doesn't it?"

Irina rattled the map.

With a bit of adroit weaving through a vast development of terraced cottages, Hudson leaked out onto Weston Park Road and made his way up to the A386. There, he turned northeast and, by good fortune as much as by instinct, shortly found himself on the A38 and speeding along in a nice straight line toward Bude. By now, the colour had returned to Irina's face. Within minutes they'd crossed the bridge over the Tamar River, whose estuary comprised Plymouth's port, and were leaving the city. Like Captain James Cook, Sir Francis Drake, and the Pilgrim Fathers before them, they were setting out from Plymouth in search of justice, high adventure, and new worlds. Not to mention hedgerows.

About one mile outside the Plymouth city limits, just as they passed the small exurb of Hatt and plunged into the Cornish countryside, Hudson plugged his iPod into the Vectra's sound system and cued up Ralph Vaughan Williams's Third Symphony. The lush and lilting music lent one grace note after another to the undulating, patchwork green quilt through which they sped. Though not quite the romantic that Hudson was, Irina succumbed entirely to the pastoral tranquility. She rolled down her window and leaned her face into rushing air that felt as cool, sweet, and fresh as spring water. Had she ever had such a moment? She thought of Walter, but without the customary agony. He'd always wished that his high-strung wife could empty her mind and fill her senses. Now, he would smile with relief.

"Whoa, check this out," chuckled Hudson as they caught up to a white vehicle. "That's got to be the dinkiest panel truck I've ever seen."

It was a Peugeot Bipper, with ATKINS ELECTRICAL, BUDE, emblazoned in red lettering on the sides and the back.

Irina, who had absolutely no interest in cars or trucks, and whose mind turned to shoes when the subject of transportation came up, ignored the vehicle but looked with interest at the driver as they passed it. He was a heavyset man with a bushy mustache and wild black hair. Irina laughed, for the effect produced was not unlike that of a walrus stuffed into a goldfish bowl.

Seeing he was the object of some merriment, the driver scowled, gave them the two-fingered V-salute, with the back of his hand facing outward, and abruptly sped up.

"What in hell's with him?" asked Hudson.

"I'm afraid I've cast aspersions on his manhood," Irina burbled. "He will now, in all probability, try to prove that he can go as fast as we can."

And that is precisely what happened. He tailgated them for half a mile then passed them going into a curve, again giving them the V-sign.

"What a bloody idiot. He came within inches of my fender. Think I should run him off the road?"

"You'll do no such thing. Ignore him and he'll fade away."

But the Peugeot Bipper did not fade away. Mile after mile it either loomed large in Hudson's rearview mirror or sat on his front bumper.

After ten miles of this, and constant cursing that the Bipper was ruining his "British experience," Hudson roared past him at well over ninety miles per hour.

"Feel better?"

"Much," replied Hudson.

"So now slow down. We don't want to be caught speeding. It could be rather embarrassing."

"I distinctly remember you saying 'You're on, Fangio.' What's changed?"

"What's changed is that there's no evidence we're being followed."

"Oh, no? What about this guy?"

"The Bipper?"

"Yes, the Bipper. As in 'hiding in plain sight.'"

"Hm. There's a thought. Sloppy of me." Irina reached for her BlackBerry and began dialing.

"Do you want me to drop back so you can pick the number off the truck?"

"Better this way. Good to find out if Atkins Electrical actually exists."

Through information, Irina got the number for Atkins Electrical. She dialed that number and was informed by a precious young woman that the driver of the Bipper would be none other than Bev Thorpe, who lived in the hamlet of Botus Fleming, near Plymouth. The woman added, confidentially, that he was a vicious brute when he got behind the wheel of a vehicle and that they'd do well to steer clear of him. Irina looked out the rear window of the Vectra and saw that the Bipper was now just a dot on the horizon. She called the operator again, this time asking for the number of a Bev Thorpe in Botus Fleming. She dialed that number and was greeted, in a manner of speaking, by a steely female voice. "Sod off, you fucknugget! I flob on you! And when I go around to me mum's and she has a squiz at the bloody great welt you left on me arm, she'll have the coppers crawling up your shite pipe."

"Good day. Would Bev Thorpe be there?"

"You sound wet. Who's this, then? One of his whiffy whores, or that carpet muncher at Atkins?"

"Am I to assume that he's left for work?"

"Yes, you may *assume* the wank biscuit's left for work. A half-hour ago. Unless he's hopped the wag, he'll soon have his ugly worker's bum in somebody's mug."

"I thank you for your help."

"Well, you're a right proper twonk, aren't you? Piss off!"

And then there was nothing.

"So," said Hudson, "what's the verdict?"

Irina pointed at her map. "Well ... here's Botus Fleming, and his charming wife said he left for work half an hour ago, so he's basically where he ought to be. Of course, there's nothing to say he isn't following us, but I rather doubt it. We can't suspect everyone going our way — especially someone who's got Bude scrawled all over his van. Look behind you. There are two or three other cars who've been with us for as long as we've been on the A388. So let's sit back, enjoy the ride, and if our friend doesn't soon let us out of his sight, *then* we'll know something's up and we'll take evasive action."

"This is the best way to Bude, Irina. He can afford to drop out of view every now and then."

"But there plenty of other towns along this route, aren't there? If he is, in fact, tracking us, he can't afford to lose sight of us."

Hudson had become nervous and fidgety. He killed Vaughan Williams's symphony halfway through the third movement and switched over to the radio. The British experience ended abruptly. On one station after another, there were endless reports and commentary about the worldwide wildlife conspiracy. The latest known animal abductions were noted with increasing alarm. There were replays, in part or in whole, of the speech he'd given at McGill University two nights earlier. Religious leaders wailed, police and military chieftains railed, and political poobahs from around the globe swore to mobilize every resource available.

And still the little white Bipper was behind them.

"Okay, Hudson," said Irina, peering at the map, "step on it. And just before Launceston turn left onto the A30. We'll detour by way of the coastal roads."

Instantly, Hudson soared to speeds in excess of one-hundred miles an hour. Scenes that had earlier given Irina a sense of tranquillity now became a psychotic blur. No curves in the road, however tight, impeded his progress. In fact, he accelerated through them. Though white with fright, Irina had to admit that Hudson displayed prodigious driving skill.

By the time they were taking the A30 ramp, the little white Bipper had been out of sight for some time.

Fifteen seconds later, as Alex Smith followed Hudson and Irina onto the A30 in the dark grey BMW, he decided he could stand the itching no longer and ripped off the full beard and mustache in one swift, painful movement. He then told Rowena Hardcastle to dial up Bernie Gold for him. "Bernie? Alex. Funniest damn thing. Some oversized numpty in this mangy little truck gives us the V-salute because we pass him at ninety, and guess what Rowena does? She pops him right between the eyes. At ninety! Corking! And then that piss-arse truck rolls through a field like a cotton ball in a hurricane." Smith leaned over and kissed the beaming Rowena on the cheek. "I told you she was right for the job, didn't I?"

Bernie Gold took issue with that sentiment. His shrieking compelled Smith to hold the phone a good foot from his ear. Rowena Hardcastle could now be treated to his every word. "Right for the job? Right? She's a stupid cunt! People will find that body, and before long the media will get hold of the story about how some guy was shot in the face as he rolled down the highway, and not long after that Drach and Hudson will pick up on that story! Now what do you suppose they'll make of it?"

"They probably didn't even notice him," said Rowena Hardcastle in a tremulous voice.

"*You* noticed him, you twat! Why wouldn't they? And even if they didn't, there's still a mysterious highway murder that occurred just behind them, and that would strike them as pretty fuckin' fishy. And what then? They speed up or weave and they lose you and you have to scour the whole goddamn city for them and you lose time! Precious time! Maybe all the time it takes for them to find Liang!"

"Bude is a town, not a city," said Hardcastle, tugging nervously at her long, blond wig.

"Listen, Bernie," said Smith. "I knew what the first leg of their route would be. Caught up to them in twenty minutes, didn't I? So I'll find them in Bude, real quick like, if they shake us off — which I doubt because I just know they're going to continue on the A30, then the A395 east, then turn north onto the A39."

"You hope you know."

"You'll see, Bernie. You will."

"If I don't, then *you* will. Mark my words."

"Take off that frigging wig," Alex Smith barked as he set down his cell. "You've done enough damage for the time being."

"I like it. It makes me feel glamorous. Like Nicole Kidman, or Cate Blanchett, or someone. Anyone. I'll just keep it on until we're in sight of them."

Smith gripped the wheel tightly and tromped on the accelerator, wishing it were Rowena's neck under his foot. As the burgundy Vectra hove into view, the pale, thin neck rotated her face toward him. "So tell me again why it's us doing the hit?"

Alex Smith sucked it in then spat it out. "Because we're the best at close quarters. And because we know as well as anyone what they look like,"

"That's fucked. They know what we look like, too."

"And what about our disguises?"

"Come on, Alex. We don't live in a comic book world where Superman puts on a pair of glasses and Lois sees only Clark Kent. I mean, look at that bloke's disguise. Doesn't fool me."

"Disguise? What do you mean?"

"No, never," Rowena laughed. "You don't know who he is?"

"Just stop braying like a bloody donkey and tell me!"

"He's only about the most famous bleeder on the planet right now! That's Athol Hudson, the animal copper!"

"Get away!"

"Agh, you men. Gits, all of you. It's a wonder you recognize anyone who doesn't have a big, squared number on his back."

Alex Smith's left arm shot out and yanked the wig from Rowena's head, revealing hair that was short, choppy, and dyed jet black. "This is big, Hardcastle. Real big. We've been given a bash at moving up, and there'll be no be titting around. This one will be my masterpiece!"

The picturesque resort town of Bude lies on the northern coast of Cornwall, with its cliffs and beaches facing directly west into the Atlantic

Ocean. The official population is about ten thousand, but between the months of May and September its ranks are swollen by several thousand hyperactive souls. The tourists come to fish, swim at the sandy beaches, surf the Atlantic swells, and take invigorating, windswept walks along the high oceanside bluffs. But for a little less than a handful of smaller industries producing such things as tools and pharmaceuticals, the main employer of Bude is service to the inland farmers and the hospitality industry: restaurants, hotels, and water-sport shops. As one might expect of a locale with a history rich in smuggling and shipwrecks, Bude is as far from being a port town as Las Vegas is.

But it would be a mistake to conclude that these stratified cliffs of Bude have always been a liability. From time immemorial, they have been exploited for their qualities as fertilizer. Bude is the only spot in south-western England with cliffs composed of carboniferous sandstone. In fact, the Bude Canal, which has lately become the grand civic restoration project, was built expressly for the transport of the mineral-rich sand of the beaches and cliffs to the inland fields by small boats.

But Bude's history is a bit more romantic than the quarrying of fertilizer. Many locals maintain that the name Bude is an attenuated version of Bude Haven, which in turn was a bastardization of Bede Haven, which means "Harbour of The Holy Men," implying that early Christians chose Bude as a landing site. To that end, there is a new residential road named Bede Haven Close, just off the equally numinous Berries Avenue.

"I like this town," exclaimed Hudson as he steered the Vectra up Belle Vue, the steeply inclined main shopping drag. "I can practically smell the fish and chips."

"Hotel first, then lunch."

"But we never had breakfast!"

"All right then, I'm flexible. Hotel first, then breakfast."

Without warning, and without running down any of the pedestrians that clogged the street, Hudson made a sharp left onto Hartland Terrace just before the crest of the hill. He drove to the end of the short street and there stood the Hartland Hotel, a multistorey building that looked as if two identical old homes with mansard roofs and dormer windows had been stitched together.

"So, what do you think?"

"Did you get this place from your guidebook, or was it just dumb luck?"

"In a town like Bude, you expect a hotel at every turn. So I turned."

"Park."

Hudson slotted the car into one of the spaces across the street, perpendicular to the hotel. They got out of the car, stretched, and breathed the ocean air, gazing down upon a beach, its parking lot, and the roiling sea beyond.

"There seems to be some kind of a hotel or whatnot down there," said Alex Smith as he slid the grey BMW into a space on Hartland Terrace just at the corner of Belle Vue. "Time for you to take a walk, see what's the crack."

"I'd have to be totally hatstand to do that! She'll recognize me."

"First off, love, they've only seen you standing still or sitting. Second, you're a lot uglier without the wig. Third, you're going to smear your lips real heavy-like with that blood-red goop of yours and look like a proper trollop. And fourthly," he said, as he removed his Ray-Bans, "you will put these on. Now get going and there's a good girl."

As Irina and Hudson entered the hotel, Rowena Hardcastle skulked down the street. The tall, rawboned young woman stationed herself in the spot just vacated by the two police officers and shivered in the breeze blowing in from the North Atlantic. She was still there, but sitting cross-legged and smoking a cigarette, when a bickering Irina and Hudson emerged a few minutes later.

"Really, Irina. So it isn't the Plaza, but surely to God you can suffer through it for a few nights!"

"I did my penance at the Glynne Court."

"We didn't even turn down our sheets there!"

"Ugh! I wouldn't have touched those sheets even if Pierce Brosnan were under them."

"Huh. I would have figured you went for the burlier type. Someone like Walter. Or Sean Connery or that new guy, if we're talking James Bond. Pierce Brosnan, eh? So, basically, what turns you on is ... uh, someone not unlike me?"

Rowena Hardcastle was thoroughly fascinated by this conversation, not only because it was the first time in her experience that police officers had actually sounded like regular human twits but also because, to her great amusement, there'd been a palpable upsurge of wistfulness in Hudson's last remark. She cranked up the volume of the directional listening device at her belt, the one disguised as an iPod, then adjusted her earphones and stopped breathing. Liquidating eight people before the age of twenty-three had not extinguished the romantic in her. In fact, she still cried like a lovelorn ingénue when she watched *Coronation Street* or *EastEnders* on the telly.

"Don't talk nonsense, Hudson. I'm old enough to be your ... well, a younger aunt, at the least. Now let's unload our baggage, shall we? We might as well stay since we're here. Can't argue with the location. We can get started on Belle Vue right away."

Rowena cackled to herself. If old toffee-nose was a day under forty, then the dreamboat was barely past puberty.

As he opened the trunk, Hudson said, "It's a hot day, Irina. They've got a pool. Right behind that wall, I would imagine. And pounding the pavement is going to be hell, so what do you say we take a quick dip right after breakfast? Come on, it'll loosen you up."

After some hemming and hawing Irina agreed. She and Hudson disappeared into the hotel, leaving Rowena Hardcastle alone with her thoughts. Though still chilled by the stiff sea breeze, she did not move. She was in no hurry to get back to the bullying, unattractive Alex Smith and the pressure of his priorities. A little quiet time to herself, especially when confronted with a natural vista, always opened up her mind, much as the sun opens up a flower.

Rowena gazed out over the beaches and the reefs, and then over the steel-blue ocean to the pale and blurry region where it merged with the sky. And then her thoughts reached out to the stars and the galaxies and the distant worlds beyond that horizon. The immensity and drama of it all overwhelmed her. How was so very, very much possible? And why was there all of this, rather than nothing? Her thoughts turned to a supreme being. But then, why would there be a God rather than nothing? Questions, questions. Maybe that was the key. Maybe the questions were dimensions greater than the answers, and man's consciousness was the most singular feature of the universe.

A car honked impatiently from down the street. She got to her feet, grumbling about the belligerent arsemonger waiting for her. So the great leader, the great protagonist — whoever he was — was no doubt right. Man *was* the measure of all things.

"They'll be staying at that hotel, and it sounds like they're going to do a door-to-door," she said as she slumped into the seat. "Now, you'll have to take care of pretty boy because I sort of like him. A regular bloke. But *I'm* going to do the old witch, no matter what. And she will suffer, mark my words. She will suffer horribly."

Having decided to freshen up before breakfast, entirely at Irina's insistence, the two officers were frolicking in the large, rectangular outdoor pool behind the wall that Hudson had pointed out to her. They'd found a beach ball floating on the water and were playing water polo. It was the first time they'd ever actually played at anything together, and they were having the times of their lives. They laughed, they screeched, they bellowed, and they inevitably made physical contact. As mindful as he was of his fake mustache, Hudson was even more mindful of what a ravishing figure Irina cut in her two-piece bathing suit, and conclusively decided that he was in love with her. For her part, Irina was not immune to the charms of this lean, well-muscled, and thoroughly gallant young man. And she wondered, and then she wondered some more.

Then Jason Conrad entered her thoughts. She really didn't know how she felt about him, or what to make of him. What would have been Walter's take on this man?

Quite suddenly, her puritanical tendencies compelled her to feel ashamed for allowing three men to occupy the same thought bubble.

Worse still, she suddenly realized that the day before had been the eighth of the month. It was on the eighth of the month that her precious Walter had been killed. She'd missed commemorating it.

As she desultorily unpacked then changed out of her wet bathing suit, Irina kept an eye on the BBC News Channel. A panel discussion concerning the plundering of the planet's animals was in progress. The learned guests speculated that either Russia, China, or North Korea was behind these abominations, although the possibility that private interests were at work was not entirely discounted. Excerpts from Athol Hudson's press conference were shown, and everyone wondered where on God's good Earth he could be. They ran a clip of Montreal's Lieutenant-Detective Stanley Robertson, in which he stonewalled as effectively as he had when his division was accused of police brutality. Irina smiled in admiration. The pressure on him from every level of numerous governments and police agencies around the world would have been enough to bow Atlas himself.

Next up was a small, heavily lacquered woman from Beverly Hills who complained bitterly that her champion shitzus had not been dognapped. They'd been left behind by Noah's Ark! Irina was just about to turn it off and go collect Hudson for breakfast when a news bulletin poked its ugly little head through the dense green verbiage. A thirty-two-year-old man, Beverly Thorpe of Botus Fleming, near Plymouth, had been found dead in his truck near Launceston in North Cornwall. Early indications were that he'd been shot in the head before his micro truck, a Bipper, rolled off the highway and plowed through a herd of grazing sheep. Arnold Woolcott, whose field had thus been sullied, solemnly declared that he'd "loved them four beasties" and, after lamenting their passing, wondered aloud whence would arrive compensation for their loss.

Irina meditatively looked out her window at the North Atlantic for a few moments. And she twice looked over her shoulder as she took the stairs down to Hudson's room.

CHAPTER THIRTY-FOUR

Paris, France. September 9, 2006. For the price of a single night in the Louis XV Suite, on the top floor of the Hôtel de Crillon, one can buy a well-equipped Hyundai Accent or Pontiac Wave, or some other mini car. For the expense of two nights in the Louis XV Suite at the Hôtel de Crillon, one may purchase a mid-sized car like the Chevrolet Impala or the Vauxhall Vectra. And for the cost of three nights in the Louis XV Suite at the Hôtel de Crillon, one could be the proud owner of an entry level BMW or Mercedes-Benz.

Jason Conrad, however, had all the cars he needed. What he required was a place to lay his weary head. After supper at the facility, he'd flown the Cessna to Dryden himself, and from there had personally piloted his Challenger jet to Charles de Gaulle Airport. Thus, as he stood on the suite's terrace smoking his Cohiba Pyramid, sipping at his decades-old Macallan Whisky, and looking down over Place de la Concorde, Paris's largest square, he rued the fact that in just a few minutes he would have to sew up the tattered nerves of his board members.

His eyes flitted over the two spuming fountains just below, the eight Chevaux de Marly statues at the corners of the square and, at eye level,

Ramses II's pink granite obelisk, whose base was planted exactly where the guillotine had sat during the French Revolution. His eyes then roamed farther afield and took in what he considered to be one of the grandest views on Earth. Straight ahead, past the seventy-five-foot Egyptian column, was the Parthenon-styled National Assembly Building, the domed Hôtel des Invalides, and the Tour Montparnasse, Paris's most infamous skyscraper and, at sixty storeys, second only to the Eiffel Tower in height. To his right were the lush, shady Champs-Élysées gardens, the Eiffel tower, and the Grand Palais, the world's largest glass and ironwork structure. On his left were the Louvre, that marvelous glass pyramid, and the sublimely regular Tuileries gardens.

"There's no doubt about it," said Conrad as Chinua refilled his glass for him. "As beautiful and orderly as nature might be, humankind is capable of surpassing it. Nature does not know itself, but through consciousness man knows both nature and himself, and therefore has the means to refashion both."

"Could it not be said, Sir, that man's consciousness is merely an act of self-revelation on nature's part?"

"No. Nature is not self-destructive, and therefore it cannot possess consciousness. The very definition of consciousness is that of a separation from nature. We humans posses consciousness, and therefore have within us the power to destroy nature and ourselves. Or, alternately, to enhance them."

"Can we not say, Mr. Conrad, that the universe is vast beyond imagination, and that our actions, destructive or otherwise, are puny and insignificant by comparison?"

"Your argument is self-contradictory, Chinua. The universe may be vast beyond imagination, but the imagination is ours. And as our imagination blooms, so does the universe."

It struck Chinua that there might be a flaw in Conrad's reasoning, that a step might be missing. But as usual he was in no mood for philosophical drivel, so he let it pass. "Most ambitious, Sir."

"Isn't it, though? We sure are a great species."

"It's almost four, Sir. They'll be waiting."

Conrad took a deep puff of his Cohiba then swirled his glass. "You go on ahead, Chinua. Loosen them up with some brandy. I'll be down shortly. Oh ... wait."

"Sir?"

"I just had an idea. Do you know that the dirtiest object in any reasonable home or hotel is the TV remote? More bacteria — E. coli and such — than even the toilet seat. They can't really be cleaned, you see. What's needed is a disposable, clear latex condom for the things. Contact whomever at Regency Hospital Supplies, the German division, and tell them I want them in production within four months. In whatever package they deem suitable, although I'd recommend boxes of fifty and a hundred. Got that?"

"Right after the conference, Sir. And the German division of Regency is called Hanover Steril, Sir."

"I know what it's called, Chinua. I know what I own almost as well as I know what I don't. Now go set the stage for me."

Chinua took his leave and Conrad's eyes once more caressed the skyline he knew so well. He'd been a regular at this hotel going on thirty-seven years, from just about the time they were beginning construction of the Tour Montparnasse. He chuckled to himself. When the tower was completed in 1972, the wags began to say that the best view in Paris could be had from its observation deck — because it was the only place in Paris from which it couldn't be seen. But he'd always rather liked it because he'd been on this very terrace, on the day the Tour opened its doors, when his lawyer informed him he'd just become a billionaire. And he'd reached that mark through property development, by putting up buildings just like the Tour Montparnasse, to boot. He laughed aloud and was untroubled that he laughed alone, or that his grandest moments inevitably occurred in either an office or a hotel room.

He butted out his cigar, drained his glass, then drifted into the sitting room of the opulent suite and sat in a red-upholstered Grand Siècle chair. No doubt about it. This two-bedroom apartment, with its silk furnishings and painted wood panels, perfectly exemplified the baroque glories that Louis XV had insisted upon when it was built in 1758. But for the usual array of discreetly disposed electronic gadgets, such as the two giant plasma televisions and the deluxe audio system, and amenities such as the cigar cabinet, the bar, the wireless Internet, and the safe, he was in a time capsule. And was that not the story of his life? Bouncing from one time capsule to another, or moving from one cultural bubble to the next? Oh, he had a home, to be sure. An imposing Georgian brick pile on the slopes of Westmount in Montreal, where he'd grown up. If he were to walk through its front door, however, the nice Filipino couple who lived there and kept it up would probably have him arrested as a house invader. Even when at his Montreal offices, his preferred digs were the Ritz-Carlton Hotel. His house had no personal mementos. Only trophies.

A millionaire at nineteen. At twenty-three, a billionaire. A multi-billionaire at twenty-three years and nine months. Canada's richest man at fifty. The world's richest man at fifty-five. And one of the world's lonely men at fifty-seven. If it weren't for Chinua, he'd be mumbling to himself like some psychotic derelict.

He poured himself another shot of Macallan and drank deep. He was becoming maudlin, and he knew it. And only five minutes earlier he'd been laughing over his splendid isolation. What had changed? He was overtired, that was it. Jet-lagged. Knackered, as they said in England. Ah yes, England. Where Irina Drach was to be found at this very moment … now, how had that happened? How had she stolen into his thoughts just at the very moment when he was feeling low and isolated? He cackled aloud and startled himself. How far gone did you have to be to practice irony in a vacuum?

He would be bold. When she was done with her little British adventure he would pursue her relentlessly. She would see that he was not merely a great and powerful man. She would see that his heart beat like any other, and that it beat for her.

Jason Conrad got up and walked into a bathroom that looked as if it had been carved out of a single, massive block of Carrara marble. He gargled with Listerine, straightened his tie, tucked his long black hair behind his ears, then rushed out of the suite, into the elevator, and down to the first floor.

He'd not chosen the Marie-Antoinette reception room because it was an example of exquisitely appointed classicism, nor because of the Gobelins tapestry or the eighteen-foot ceilings with gilt moldings and sculpted eagles. Nor even because of the terrace that offered the same view of Place de la Concorde that his own suite afforded. No, he'd chosen it because it was a certified historical site. Marie-Antoinette had taken music lessons in this room. He'd foresworn the available U-shaped conference table so that his board members would be dispersed throughout the room, perched high on ornate and dainty chairs and settees, and sunk deep into history. Like all influential and dominant men, he put great store in history: not only because he was more likely to find his peers among illustrious historical figures than among his contemporaries, but also because an immersion in history opened one's eyes to the real possibility of great deeds. And this lot would need bucking up.

Oh, and with the eleven board members scattered all about the salon, they'd be less likely to coalesce as a cabal. He'd deal with each of them on a one-on-one basis, and mollify them. Or calm them. Or crush them.

All that were not standing about the room or out on the terrace rose to attention as he entered the room. Chinua herded everyone into seats and topped up their glasses with the Courvoisier XO Imperial. There was now a great hush in the room. All eyes were on Conrad as he padded noiselessly to the French terrace doors, closed them, and stood before them. "So, Ladies and Gentlemen, we're in the news. I hope this doesn't come as a shock to you, because I warned you it would happen eventually, didn't I?"

Heads nodded uncertainly.

"You all clamoured for this meeting. Let's get started with your comments, then."

But for the sounds of eyeballs clicking in their sockets and necks creaking as they swivelled worried heads, there was dead silence.

"Well, come on, you lot. I busted my chops to get here. Speak up."

There was enough sweat in the room to float a battleship. Conrad gave them a few moments to squirm, then pounced on the florid BBC doyenne. "Miss Livingston, you're usually pretty outspoken, and I know — coming as you do from a news background — that you like to canvass people's opinions. Perhaps you'll be kind enough to give me the pulse of this timorous beast?"

Penelope Livingston took a deep, fortifying sip of her cognac then dabbed at her lips for some time, as if she'd been lapping up a thick creamed soup. "Well, well ... it will indeed be the pulse of this group," she stammered, stroking her snow-white hair with a puffy hand. "I know I speak for others when I say I speak for others —"

"Get to it, Miss Livingston," Conrad said impatiently.

"For my part, as deputy chairperson, deputy director-general, and director of the journalism group, it has been a most difficult time, these last few days. As much as I would like my people to sweep this story under the rug, I cannot but direct them to play it up as the story of the day, perhaps of the year. This story has wings, and there is nothing I can do to clip them."

"Yes? And?"

"Merely this: We believe we should cease all operations immediately. We simply cannot continue the collection of species for the time being."

Conrad looked around the room and studied the eleven bowed heads much as a pool shark studies the disposition of billiard balls. He found the head he was looking for and set up for the shot. "Mr. Liadov, I believe you've lost weight," he said to the bearded, heavyset young Russian.

Yevgeny Liadov was of two minds about being the subject of the great man's attention. On the one hand, he was immensely flattered that Conrad had noticed something — anything — about him. On the other hand — Yikes! "Ah ... yes, Sir," he stammered, pulling on his beard. "Much running and dieting. Twenty pounds, I have shed."

"I like that. Shed weight, twenty pounds lighter. Shows we're on the same wavelength. Shed light, eh?"

"Sir?"

"Oh come now, Yevgeny. You may be a thick man but you're not a stupid one. Otherwise, you wouldn't be here. You're the director of our tactical force. You know what I'm interested in hearing."

"A report, Sir?"

"No, Mr. Liadov. Not a report. That, I can get from Miss Livingston. It's your judgment I want."

Liadov rose from the dainty blue velvet chair he'd been crushing into the floor and looked around at his colleagues, almost apologetically. He then cleared his throat, managing to sound like a pug with asthma as he did so. "There have admittedly been inconveniences during the last few days, Sir. There is a lion roaming the forests of Canada, we have lost one of our best operatives in India, and another was shot dead by the owner of an award-winning chihuahua in New York City. And, as Miss Livingston has indicated in not so many words, the story of our activities not only has legs but many furry feet. There have, however, been some triumphs. Yesterday's daylight raid at the Philadelphia Zoo is only one of the most prominent among them. In the time since our operations first achieved notoriety, we have successfully completed ninety-five missions. In short, our pace has not slackened. The authorities are in the position of the fabled farmer who is too busy chasing his cows to build a fence."

"But that's just the point," exclaimed William McTavish, the grizzled director of nuclear engineering. "It's us cows and not their bloody fences we should be worrying about!"

"I want Mr. Liadov's judgment before I get yours, Mr. McTavish," Conrad said coolly. "That's his area of expertise. Carry on, Mr. Liadov."

"My final judgment, then?"

Conrad sighed and signalled to Chinua that his glass needed refilling. Then he sipped at his drink and waited for Liadov to lift his eyes from the dark, glowing wood floor and meet his own. When the young Russian finally did so, Conrad reached inside Liadov and wrung out his soul for the answer he wanted. "I believe we must be careful — even more so than usual — but I also am convinced that there is no need to suspend operations. We are so much more clever and organized than they are."

William McTavish sprang from his chair. "They? *They?* We're not just talking about the bobbies who look in on the local pub from time to time. We're talking about the FBI, the CIA, M15, MI6, Mossad, the Russian FSB, and the French DST, just to name a few! And let's not even think about the military intelligence of every civilized nation on this planet!"

Conrad thumped his glass down onto a table. "I believe Mr. Liadov is done expressing his view, Mr. McTavish. You may now express yours."

McTavish began to sputter angrily. "It's obvious we must have a vote on this matter! Else what's the point of this meeting?"

"And we shall have one, Mr. McTavish. But first, why don't you update us on what lies within your area of expertise?"

After a stubborn silence that lasted more than a few seconds, McTavish grumped, "Your Nucleonics Corporation has done a creditable job on the centrifuges. We'll be moving three thousand of them into the facility once the back end is dug out. Luckily, Canada is the uranium capital of the world, and that northern Saskatchewan mine of yours provides us with all the high-grade ore we need. Manufacturing the graphite-uranium balls on a large scale is going to be tricky, but we're getting there. We already have several hundred satisfactory prototypes using uranium dioxide kernels, and thanks to your people at Uraco the requisite twenty-seven thousand of the things should be ready by year's end. The question is, will the reactor be ready?"

"Even as we speak, the world's largest container ship is steaming its way north through the Sea of Japan with our precious cargo aboard. None but a few highly-placed Chinese officials know what the *Xin Los Angeles* is carrying. Even the ship's captain is in the dark."

"Excellent. Now may we return to the main order of business?"

"Why not, Mr. McTavish?" Conrad gestured grandly over McTavish's head and in the direction of the ten other directors. "All right, people. By a show of hands, who agrees with Mr. McTavish and is in favour of shutting down field operations for a while?"

"Uh ... Mr. Conrad?"

It was Chinua Amadi.

"Just a moment, dear people. Yes, Chinua?"

"Do I vote also?"

Conrad laughed lightly and shook Chinua by the shoulders. "But of course not, Chinua. You're not a director, are you? Now, why don't you top-up everybody's glass so we can toast the result of the vote?"

There was a brittle silence in the salon as Chinua did as he was bidden. Everyone in the room — but for Conrad himself — was acutely conscious of Chinua's humiliation, just as everyone in the room — but for Conrad himself — was acutely conscious of the major administrative role Chinua played in the organization.

"Okay, everybody. Hands up for shutting down."

Ten hands were raised. Yevgeny Liadov's remained in his lap, twisting about each other like mating squirrels.

"Hm. And those in favour of continuing operations?"

Liadov slowly raised his hand.

"Well," said Conrad icily. "I guess it's up to me to cast the tiebreaker, isn't it?" Conrad raised his hand. "There. Motion carried, we carry on."

The conference room was instantly filled with animated mumbling. It was like a monastery during vespers. Only one person, William McTavish, dared protest aloud, and even then it was more of a hiss than a howl "Mr. Conrad," he said, scrambling to his feet once more, "what's the point of having a board if you're going to ignore its recommendations?"

"First off, I would remind you that for obvious reasons this is not a legally constituted board. It is an advisory board, at best. But second, I'll point out that I don't ignore its recommendations. How could I? Each of you is at the top of his or her field, a font of wisdom and experience. You, for example, Mr. McTavish, are a highly pedigreed nuclear engineer without whom we'd be struggling to differentiate between a proton and a crouton. Are you not the man in charge of our nuclear program? A tremendous responsibility and a vital, vital role. There isn't another man on this benighted planet who could replace you. And the same goes for the rest of you. Each one irreplaceable, each fundamental to our great project. So, no, I don't ignore your recommendations. I weigh them carefully and moderate my actions accordingly. But in the end, it is I who must take ultimate responsibility for our actions, and it is I who must decide which actions to take. History teaches us that it is individuals, not committees, who shape events —"

Oftentimes the reverse is true, and events shape individuals. This was suddenly the case. Ted Seacrest, the marine biologist, had been seated alone in a far corner of the salon, and had quietly and unobtrusively been losing his grip on himself. Now bellowing at the top of his lungs ("Aiieeee, aiieeee!" were his exact words), he grabbed a cheese knife from the nearby spread, charged through the assembly, and lunged at Conrad. He was felled by two blurred karate chops from Chinua Amadi, but not before he'd plunged the knife a good inch into the side of Conrad's neck.

Conrad did not flinch nor buckle. Nor did he even instinctively remove the knife from his neck. "Dr. Habib," he said to the man rushing toward him, "I appear to be all right. Would you please see to Mr. Seacrest first?"

Dr. Jerry Habib, a communicable disease specialist who also happened to be the president of the American Medical Association, fell to his knees and examined Chinua's prostrate victim. "This man is dead."

There were gasps and moans. Chinua said nothing and looked straight ahead.

"Now, may I examine your wound?"

"If it were serious, Doctor — if it had punctured my windpipe, or either the carotid artery or the jugular vein — I'd be down on the floor with the tempestuous Mr. Seacrest. However, I'm not. Therefore, let's wind up the proceedings so I can then deal with this rather sticky new circumstance."

But the ten remaining directors, and Chinua as well, stared at him in mute horror. With considerable aplomb, Conrad directed his attentions toward Renata Fraticelli, a much-published, much-publicized economist. She was particularly aghast. "What's the matter?" asked Conrad. "Have you never seen anybody with a cheese knife stuck in his neck, before?"

She tittered nervously. So did William McTavish. And then, so did the renowned social philosopher, Henri Duguay. Soon, everyone was tittering, and then laughing aloud. It got so noisy that Conrad had to wave them into attentive silence.

Thus, with a sterling silver utensil protruding from his neck, and a dead man at his feet, he called the meeting to order and ordered a re-vote. This time — for reasons clear only to a Svengali — it was unanimously resolved that the organization should continue its species collecting, although with heightened discretion. A few other issues were dealt with, reports were given, and then Conrad adjourned the meeting. They would all regroup at Maxim's, just around the corner on Rue Royale, in two hours. The food, Conrad said, was excellent. The authentic and sumptuous Art Nouveau décor was even better. But the cigars, he declared with juvenile delight, were what he was especially eager to sample. In particular, the Impériale Double Corona. They were hand rolled in Santo Domingo — not Cuba — but on the other hand, they were aged three years.

As the directors either staggered or fell out of the Salon Marie-Antoinette, Jason Conrad allowed Dr. Habib to examine his wound. He was seated at last, while the doctor was bent over him. "You are a very lucky man, Mr. Conrad," he blurted frenziedly. "The blade entered your neck on a vertical plane. If it had been horizontal, at the very least the strap muscles would have been severely damaged. Now, I don't want to remove the knife here, but taking you to a hospital is out of the question. The media would be all over this story. We need a clinic. You might bleed copiously, so stitches are a must, and, in any event, an antibiotic is an absolute necessity. At the very least, you'll have cheese in your wound."

"Ah, what would life be without a little cheese, eh?"

The good doctor was not amused.

"Oh, and one more thing, Doc. You'll just have to take the knife out now and bandage it up. I can't very well walk through the hotel lobby looking like this, can I?"

Chinua, who'd been on his phone in a far corner of the salon, strode over to Conrad as a very nervous Dr. Habib was extracting the knife. "I've been in contact with some of our Paris people, Sir. There's a surgery in the *deuxieme arrondissement,* not far from here. Rue Montmartre. They're coming to pick us up in about ten minutes. Plus, they'll dispose of Mr. Seacrest's body in half an hour. Given that we're in the habit of having our guests register with phony passports, nobody will ever trace him to this hotel. The trail from New Zealand will go cold at Charles de Gaulle Airport."

Conrad laid his hand on Dr. Habib's forearm and gently pushed him away. "Excuse me, Doctor. I need a quiet word with Chinua."

Habib slumped over to the cheese and fruit while Chinua drew closer to Conrad and stood at attention.

"Very efficient of you, Chinua."

"Thank you, Sir."

"It's a pity you weren't nearly as efficient when Seacrest was attacking me."

"Sir?"

"It seems to me you were a little slow in responding."

"Surely you are mistaken, Sir. I did my best."

Conrad watched suspiciously for some moments as Chinua shifted from one foot to the other, sweated profusely, and looked alternately contrite and hurt. Eventually, with the hardness gone from his voice, Conrad said, "It was actually fortuitous that I got stabbed."

"Sir?"

"Impressed them with my balls. Made them vote with their hearts the second time."

He called the doctor over, then promptly passed out from the pain.

CHAPTER THIRTY-FIVE

Chandigarh, India. September 9–10, 2006. "What time is it?"

Inspector Raja Chadwani of the Kullu District Police incorporated the question into his dream. The tall, blond goddess was looking for an excuse to leave the Beverly Hills party in order that he might service her.

"You, over there. What time is it?"

This time Chadwani awoke, but just barely. "Time for yet more heavenly ecstasy."

"Then it's night?"

"Day, my lovely. Three-thirty in the afternoon —" Raja Chadwani suddenly leapt from his chair, flung open the drapes, then ran to the bedside. Joy, oh joy! It was the Israeli yak abductor! "You're alive! You're alive!"

"Don't touch me, you pervert. Where am I?"

Chadwani bent over the heavily bandaged head and peered intently into the dark eyes, as if the man's consciousness might be discerned glimmering like a fish in a shallow pond. "You are in the Nins Hospital. That is, the Northern Institute of Neural Sciences, in sector thirty-four of Chandigarh."

"Where's Chandigarh?"

"Two-hundred miles south of Manali, as the narcotized Tibetan snowcock flies."

"In the plains?"

"Indeed. Two-hundred miles north of Delhi."

"And just who am I?"

The baby-faced officer's joy dissipated like a rain cloud over the Sahara. He reeled about the room, both hands tugging at the tips of his oversized mustache. "For more than two days and nights I have sat by your bedside, and this is my reward? *Sic transit gloria*," he wailed.

"Ah, so you're a cop. And you think you're onto the case of a lifetime."

Chadwani's agony redoubled. "Do not torture me with displays of deductive reasoning! What value is all the knowledge and cleverness in the world if a man does not know himself?"

"That's very good. Did you just make that up?"

Chadwani ran back to the bedside and shook Jonathan Diamond by both shoulders. "Think, man, think! In the course of stealing his yak, your confederate slit Bhagwati Prasad's throat, but not before Prasad shot you in the head!"

"If I was shot in the head, don't you think you should stop shaking me like that?"

Inspector Chadwani desisted immediately.

"Thank you. And for your information, Derek slit that filthy swine's throat before he shot me."

"Ah yes, we Indians are sturdy. Most sturdy. But you remember the sequence of events? And you remember your confederate's name? But you do not remember who you are?"

"Full disclosure, heh-heh. I was just teasing you. My name is Jonathan Diamond. Now, as I've been out for two days and nights, you tell me — in a coma, I guess you'd call it — shouldn't you be alerting the medical personnel that I'm conscious before shaking me up in order to shake me down?"

"It will be our little secret."

Diamond laughed. "You're lucky I'm glad to be alive or I'd take a very dim view of your methods." He reached for the the buzzer at his shoulder. "Is this how I call them?"

Raja Chadwani quickly whisked the apparatus out of Diamond's reach. "No! We must talk. This matter is far greater than both of us. You must consider that you might still die, even as the doctors are interfering with you. So, tell me, who are you working for?"

"What's in it for me?"

"Your soul. Next time, you will not come back as a Jew. It might be as a snake. Perhaps even a dog."

Diamond laughed. "How about a tiger?"

"Ah, earthly pleasures are earthly pleasures. A tiger, then."

"It's clear to you that I did not kill that yak-man?"

"Perfectly clear. The killer would have had Bhagwati Prasad's blood all over his hands. You had it all over your shirt and pants, but none at all on your hands. Therefore, you were standing in front of him when his throat was cut from behind.

"I didn't want him killed. That must be clear."

"The restaurateur, Munshi Prasad, would testify that you have an honourable character. If I asked him."

"Do I see the groundwork of a deal?"

"I am Inspector Raja Chadwani of the Kullu District Police. I make no deals. But I don't believe a man should be punished for a crime he did not commit. So you will be forthcoming?"

"And then you will give me back the buzzer?"

"But then I will give you back the buzzer."

"Come to think of it, I don't really need the buzzer. I could just shout out loud."

"It would probably give you a headache. Or, I might hit you on the head and that would give you a very, very bad headache and you would die, and no one would be the wiser for you are already badly bruised."

And so an amicable agreement was reached. Jonathan Diamond did not have all that much information to pass along, as it turned out. He told Chadwani as much as he could about Derek Hull and the truck they'd hired for the yaknapping, and that there had been a rendezvous scheduled in Delhi for the day after said event, but he did not know who his superiors were — nor even who his immediate superiors were. He did, however, know one seemingly inconsequential fact about the highest echelon of his organization, something that had been passed along to him by Hull: in June of that year, the movers and shakers had met in Rio de Janeiro. "You know how human exchanges are. Tidbits attach themselves to even the most elemental lines of communication, like rust to undersea cables."

"Give me nine hundred and ninety-nine more tidbits like that and I will have a fact."

"In actual fact, I have no more tidbits. Sorry."

"Hm. You may call the doctor now. I must go and think."

Raja Chadwani went off for a tea and thought long and hard. Eventually, however, he caught himself thinking about Munshi Prasad's daughter, weighing her rather plain appearance against a decidedly charming nature. It was when he began to wonder what sort of father-in-law the little café keeper would make that he decided he'd had enough of cerebrating. The prospect of immersion in a case of brutal murder was infinitely more congenial. He returned to Jonathan Diamond's room, swore to the doctor that he would not badger the patient, then launched into a protracted inquiry that touched on the many animal abductions Diamond had taken part in during his three years with the shadowy organization. It was fortunate that Diamond's memory was prodigious, for there were close to a thousand operations, ranging from raids on insectariums to the heist of a pair of breeding hippos from the Cologne Zoo. "Did you know," grinned Diamond, "that hippopotami fling their feces with their tails when they are either agitated or being territorial?"

"No, I did not."

"You're a lucky man. There can't be a more fetid substance than hippo shit."

By ten o'clock that evening, Jonathan Diamond was too weary to talk anymore. During the five hours available to him, Inspector Chadwani had learned a great deal about field operations, but still knew nothing of the ringleaders other than that they'd met in Rio de Janeiro in June. The young detective told Diamond he'd see him in court in Shimla and drove the one hundred-twenty-five miles home to Mandi, a hill station in the direction of Manali. As soon as he arrived at his modest apartment, not far from the five-hundred-year-old Triloknath Temple of Shiva, he heated up a frozen pizza and settled in front of his computer. So, he reasoned, this was a vast organization. And judging from the nature of the enterprise, there would be no revenues, only expenditures. That called for an enormous fortune. After further cogitation, he concluded that one person was the linchpin of the organization, for such sweeping, grandiose ideas are seldom the hallmark of committees. It was reasonable to assume that the person with the vision was also the person with the funds, for few would invest their fortunes in someone else's crackpot concept. As for the meeting in Rio de Janeiro, it was not unreasonable to assume that the principals had put up in a hotel in that city and had their meeting there, for they would most likely be an international group. Furthermore, there was no reason to assume that it wouldn't have been a premier hotel: the colossally rich tend not to favour motels and flophouses.

He turned to Google for a short list of the most luxurious hotels in Rio. What he got, without much effort, were the Sofitel Rio de Janeiro, the J.W. Marriott Hotel, the Copacabana Palace Hotel, the Hotel Caesar Parque Ipanema, the Marina Palace, the Iberostar Copacabana, La Suite, the Pestana Rio Atlantica, the Fasano, the Intercontinental Hotel Rio, and La Maison Rio de Janeiro. A good start. Most fronted on either the Copacabana or Ipanema beaches.

It was now half-past midnight, September tenth. It would be four in the afternoon of September ninth in Rio. A good time to call some of those hotels, since the managers would likely still be in their offices.

Within a painfully short time, Chadwani found out that posh hotels do not disclose their guest lists over the phone, even to a policeman. And especially, he suspected indignantly, to a policeman from the Indian subcontinent. He would have to go to Rio de Janeiro. He would have to charm the managers. It occurred to him that despite his youth he was utterly devoid of charm. Never mind. He would think of something. At least he was clever.

He stayed awake most of the night, scheming. It would take all of his guile to persuade Chief Amit Chatterjee to send him to Rio, but he had several factors working for him. He toiled in a small jurisdiction in a backwater state in what the world perceived to be a third-world country. He would play on *esprit de corps,* local chauvinism, and national pride. By the time morning arrived, his bags were packed.

"You what??"

"I must go to Rio de Janeiro."

"Why do you not work by phone or email, in conjunction with the Brazilian authorities? More proper, no costs."

"I will, of course, travel fifth class, stay in a disreputable hotel, and eat Western food, but it will be a good investment on the part of the Kullu force. If I succeed — and I will succeed, for you have taught me well, Chief Chatterjee — then you and the department will be showered with lotus petals and India will henceforth be known for more than sacred cows and telemarketing."

Chief Chatterjee was a big fan of Bollywood, but he still remained convinced that Hollywood was the gold standard of the motion picture industry. In particular, he favoured old musicals. "*If* you go, I must insist that you begin with the Copacabana Palace Hotel. It is world famous. It is the most sumptuous hotel in that city. And do you know that Fred Astaire and Ginger Rogers made their debut as a dance team there, in the Copacabana Palace ballroom? And that that film, *Flying Down to Rio*, with its see-through blouses and skirts, was one of the last made before the code took effect in 1934?"

"No, Chief Chatterjee, but I am willing to learn."

"But you have just learnt it!"

"You have whetted my appetite for more movie trivia, Sir. What did they dance in that movie, for example?"

Chief Chatterjee frowned. "But the 'Carioca,' of course!"

"Ah yes, the 'Carioca.' You know, Chief, I will come back with many more facts about that great, romantic era."

"Perhaps you will also learn that a native of Rio de Janeiro is called a Carioca. Now, *if* you should go, I wish you to come back with souvenirs, also."

"But I will be on a small budget, Sir."

"*If* you go, the things I would like from the Copacabana Palace cannot be ... ah ... purchased in a souvenir shop."

"Ah, I see. A lamp, or a hall mirror, or some such."

Chief Chatterjee, a small man with oily hair and a large mustache that was the model for Raja Chadwani's own, leaned across the desk while nervously twiddling his thumbs. "We are not having this conversation, Inspector Chadwani."

"I am going, then?"

"*If* you should go, how do you intend to get there?"

"I have done some painstaking research. I will fly Air India to Nairobi, from Nairobi I will fly by KLM to São Päulo, and then I will take TAM Airlines to Rio de Janeiro."

Chief Chatterjee cackled like a hyena, baring grey, rounded teeth that looked like weathered tombstones. It was rumored in the department that his teeth got that way by his smoking great quantities of *charas*. "And how long will this take you?"

"Four days, Sir," sighed Chadwani.

"Ah, Chadwani, Chadwani. How do you expect to get anywhere in life if it takes you forever just to get merely from point A to point B? Listen carefully. My brother-in-law has a cousin who is a bigshot. A man of great wealth, a businessman in Mumbai who owns his own corporation and, therefore, his own jet. Now, my brother-in-law's cousin has a best friend whose son is in a grievous legal position for causing extensive bodily harm to an Israeli tourist at a trance party in the woods near Old Manali two weeks ago. Would you know of my brother-in-law's cousin's best friend's son?"

"I think I might, Sir. It sounds like Amit Tharoor, whom I arrested on the basis of an eyewitness account by Shashi Sharma."

"And if it could be shown that Shashi Sharma was of dubious moral character, that he sold *charas* regularly to the Israelis, would you reconsider calling him forth as a witness?"

"I might, but the prosecutor might not."

"It may interest you to know that my brother-in-law has another cousin, one who is an uncle to the prosecutor, the pulchritudinous Meena Mukherjee. As it happens, her husband works for my brother-in-law's cousin at one of his hotels in Chandigarh as an assistant manager. She would no doubt be most pleased if he were promoted to the position of manager of another of his hotels, the prestigious Chandigarh Heavenly Haven. She might, under certain conditions, re-evaluate Shashi Sharma's fitness as a witness. She might even, with your co-operation, consider charges against Shashi Sharma."

Raja Chadwani relaxed completely. If Chief Chatterjee was willing to sacrifice his own purveyor of hashish, then he was as good as on that private jet, flying down to Rio for the sake of glory and purloined trinkets from the Copacabana Palace Hotel.

"But Sir, Shashi Sharma might, in a fit of spite, reveal the names of certain distinguished clients."

"I am not worried — or, rather, I should say, it is unfortunate that he will not do so to any great extent, for my brother-in-law has yet another cousin, one whose son — a most violent and evil-tempered youth — counts several of his friends and relatives among Shashi Sharma's clients. He would, sadly, see to it that Shashi Sharma's confession is highly selective."

"Ah, I see."

Amit Chatterjee hunched conspiratorially over his desk and bathed Chadwani in bad breath. "There is something else you must be seeing. It is very important for a man to marry into a good family. Few things matter as much. Now, Munshi Prasad is, despite all appearances, a man of considerable means. And with the tragic demise of his cousin Bhagwati, he inherits a fortune beyond all expectation. As such, Munshi's daughter, Gita, is quite a prize. You would do well to consider her as a prospective wife. You would do even better to take her as a wife."

Raja Chadwani was confounded. "So you know of Munshi Prasad's overtures to me?"

"But of course! Munshi is my wife's third cousin. If you were to marry that splendid Gita, we would be related, after a fashion. Think of the possibilities."

And so it came to pass that six hours later, Inspector Raja Chadwani reclined in a luxurious leather seat aboard a completely refurbished, privately owned McDonnell Douglas MD-11. He sucked on a Johnnie Walker Blue Label and contemplated Gita Prasad's innumerable charms. There was a refuelling stop at Jomo Kenyatta Airport in Nairobi, and in just over ten hours of sybaritic delights — including the favours of the "hostess" — he was disembarking at Rio's Galeão International Airport on Governador Island, twelve miles from the city centre. By four o'clock on the afternoon of September tenth, Rio time, after having been picked up by a black Lincoln Town Car, he was standing on the terrace of a sixth-floor penthouse suite of the Copacabana Palace Hotel, looking out over Copacabana Beach and the shimmering aquamarine waters of the Atlantic Ocean. He'd died and been reborn as a maharaja, and he owed it all to Chief Chatterjee's brother-in-law's cousin. He snatched a few chocolate truffles from the proffered tray, raised his complimentary glass of champagne to Chief Chatterjee's relations, then dismissed the butler.

Raja rambled over the one-thousand square feet of white marble tiles and oriental rugs for close to half an hour. Everything about the suite — from the French fabrics and dainty moldings on the pastel walls to the neoclassical furniture — astounded him. And immaculate! He'd never been in a place that glowed quite like this. He grabbed a tissue from the marble bathroom and wiped it across the floor behind the toilet. Nothing. He got down on his knees in the living room and ran the tissue over the floor under the desk. Perfection! He looked at his shoes for a few seconds, then quickly removed them and stowed them out of sight. Clearly, they were neither salubrious nor tony enough for these surroundings. And these were not just any shoes. They were Bally shoes. Back in Himachal Pradesh, they had distinguished him.

Little by little the room worked its empowering magic on him. His five-feet-six-inches grew to an imposing six feet, his one-hundred-forty-five pounds were transformed into a powerful and trim one-ninety. He put his wonderful Bally shoes back on and swaggered down the hallway to the pool that was exclusive to the occupants of the penthouse suites. He ordered a martini (shaken, not stirred) at the restricted bar and watched as a pair of Hong Kong beauties did fairly strenuous laps in the pool. Did the rich and glamorous never rest, he wondered? Taking note of his rather drab garb, they inquired whether he was a famous writer. Yes, he answered, although he preferred anonymity. Then, calculating that it was best to stretch out from a platform of truth, he added that he was at the Copacabana for the purposes of research. The two lovelies shyly and discreetly splashed away.

Somewhat tipsy, he made his way back to his suite and turned on his computer. Irina Drach and Athol Hudson beckoned. His email to them was short and cryptic, for by now he was feeling quite omnipotent. *The Israeli revived. Am in Rio pursuant to certain information I extracted from him.*

d leonard freeston

He then went to the bedroom and laid down on a king-size bed with wide, wide pillows wrapped in cool, crisp linen of the finest quality. But he awoke after ten minutes with a start. What a fool I am, he thought angrily. I am rich and powerful! The hotel management will accede to my every whim! So he rushed downstairs and demanded to see the manager. Obsequious noises were made, and he was quickly ushered into the inner sanctum.

"Mr. Chadwani," said the balding little manager, scrambling to his feet, "I trust that all is well with your accommodations. I trust the Copacabana Palace is living up to your expectations?"

"Yes, yes, Senhor Rivera. Do be seated. I come on a rather delicate mission."

The manager sank into his chair expecting the worst. "Oh?"

"Yes. One of the smaller concerns I own, Monumental Industries of Southeast Asia, is these days the object of a hostile takeover bid. I have every reason to believe that a gang of hyenas assembled in this very hotel in June in order to discuss strategy. I should like to see your bookings for that month in order to confirm my suspicions."

"This is very unorthodox, Mr. Chadwani. Would it not be best if you gave me their names and then I gave you a nonverbal signal? With my little finger? Like this?"

Raja Chadwani slammed his fist into the manager's desk, causing the little man to push his commodious chair back several feet. "Discretion, Senhor Rivera. Discretion is of the utmost importance. I have no wish to involve you in this business in any way."

Senhor Rivera looked like a rabbit whose burrow entrance was blocked by the fox. Chadwani pressed home his advantage, intoxicated by his newfound wealth and power. "Do you know how far I would go in order to obtain that information? I would buy this hotel. In fact, so impatient am I for that information, I would buy Oriental Express's entire portfolio of hotels, all thirty-five of them, if I had to. Huh, why not? It's about time I owned some tourist venues. Then I wouldn't have to pay three thousand American dollars — one hundred twenty-nine thousand rupees — for a place to lay my head for just one night. And who knows what would happen to your position here, Senhor Rivera? A major shakeup, it would be."

306

With a whimper, Rivera called up the bookings on his computer then fetched a chair so that Chadwani might sit beside him. "Please, Sir, be seated. It will be my pleasure to guide you through the entire list."

Chadwani laughed uproariously as he sat. "The entire list? No, Senhor Rivera. The person I am looking for, the ringleader, would have stayed in one of the penthouse suites. He is, like me, a man of unparalleled wealth and taste. Let's begin, shall we?"

On the plane trip over to Brazil, Chadwani had done much more than daydream and indulge his various appetites. He'd familiarized himself with *Forbes*'s list of billionaires, paying special attention to the names of those who had more than ten billion dollars. It was therefore with an extremely critical eye that he scanned the June registry. Several notable names came up on the screen: Carlos Slim Helú, Prince Alwaleed Bin Talal Alsaud, Michael Dell, Christy Walton, William Gates III, Jason Conrad, and Nasser Al-Kharafi.

"Now we see which of them used the meeting or function rooms, if you don't mind."

The manager complied, and the list was shortened to Bill Gates, Carlos Slim Helú, and Jason Conrad. Gates and Helú had rented out conference rooms, but Conrad had rented the Nobre Room. Rivera brought up several pictures of it, and they revealed a three-thousand square foot colonnaded panoply of palm trees, crystal chandeliers, floor-to-ceiling windows, French drapery, a butterscotch marble floor with Romanesque border patterns, and access to the hotel balcony. Thoroughly extravagant, completely decadent. Rivera mentioned that Conrad had taken the room exactly as pictured, with the tables, flower arrangements, and lacquered black chairs and settees aesthetically dispersed.

"Now," said Chadwani, rubbing his hands together, "assuming these principals signed for their guests' rooms, let's see something about the people each of them hosted."

Gates had rented out the Red Room for fourteen Microsoft managers, all of whom stayed in the lower levels of the hotel. Helú had taken the Rio de Janeiro Room with a U-shaped conference table for a party of thirty communications industry people, only some of whom had stayed at the Copacabana Palace. Several of them were known to Chadwani. Conrad's party of twelve (his servant had stayed in with him in his suite) had all been given rooms in the hotel, had all been paid for personally through Conrad rather than a corporation, and were all completely unknown to Chadwani. There wasn't a notable figure among them.

"Print me out their guest lists. All of Bill Gates's and Jason Conrad's, and what you can of Helú's. And include the passport nationality and numbers, please."

Senhor Rivera did as bidden. "So many distinguished guests. The three richest men in the world all in one month. Imagine. And do you know Mick Jagger, Keith Richards, and Warren Buffet will be staying with us next week?"

"I'm afraid I won't be here to greet them," said Chadwani, impatiently rising from his seat. "Thank you for your time, Senhor Rivera."

"Roman Abramovich and Johnny Depp are here this week, Sir. If you do not already know them, I can perhaps arrange introductions."

"That will not be necessary, Senhor Rivera. I really prefer little people like you to the rich and famous. Good day, Sir."

Chadwani rushed back to his suite and immediately fired off an email to the Interpol bureau in New Delhi. He asked that they contact the Interpol offices of the countries whose passports appeared on the Conrad list. He insisted that even if the passports appeared valid, it should be determined whether or not those people really existed.

It would be 2:30 on the morning of September the eleventh in Delhi, but there would be agents on duty there, as there would be in the rest of the world. And although most of the populated world's governmental offices would be closed, those west of Rio de Janeiro — and that included all of those in North America — would still be open. Who knew? Before long he might hear something about Robert Langley from Los Angeles, and perhaps even Ted Serkin from Miami.

Except sporadically, Raja Chadwani had not slept since the afternoon at the hospital in Chandigarh. That was thirty-five hours of nervous activity, and he now felt as though even his feet were going to sleep. He checked for a response to his last email. Nothing yet, unsurprisingly. Then he dashed off a letter to Irina Drach and Athol Hudson. *Veni, vidi, vici,* it said. He laughed at his own o'erweening brass and plodded off to bed.

When he awoke some hours later, the shadow of the hotel reached halfway to the water's edge. Nine o'clock, and he was starving. But first the laptop. There were four messages. The first, from Chief Chatterjee, inquired whether the Kullu District Police would soon be answering questions from that famous network news anchor, Wolf Blitzkrieg. Answer: affirmative. The second was from his benefactor Ashok Gupta, the chief's brother-in-law's cousin, asking whether the journey and the hotel accommodations had been satisfactory. Answer: five-hundred words of the most obsequious drivel he could concoct — although he meant every word of it. The third message was from Irina Drach, in response to his last note to her, stating that details would be preferable to pretentious drivel. Answer, in four words: he couldn't agree more. The fourth email came from the Los Angeles Police Department, an official Interpol contact point. It not only said that the Robert Langley passport was fake, but that a certain Robert Langley — whose birth date and year matched those on the fake passport — had died some thirty-five years earlier, at the age of two. Answer: an obsequious display of gratitude and a request to prod their counterparts in Miami to work overtime on the Ted Serkin passport.

He was just about to compose an actual detailed report to Irina Drach when, embarrassingly, an email came in from the U.S. Marshals' office in Miami. The Ted Serkin passport was a fake, and Teddy Serkin was a long-deceased child.

With his stomach grumbling and his head swimming with visions of every conceivable delectation, he closed his window on the ambrosial sea breeze and settled down to write Drach and Hudson a particularized account of his findings to date.

That accomplished, he flung himself out the door in every hedonistic direction at once, not to return to his computer for a whole three hours.

CHAPTER THIRTY-SIX

Caribou Lake, Ontario. September 9, 2006. The infirm morning sun bled down on Detectives-Sergeant Bill Sturgess and Arthur Laidlaw of the Ontario Provincial Police as they stood on the dewy lawn between the shore of Lake Caribou and the log cabin. They were watching the forensic team and the paramedics work up the scene and the mutilated corpses of Marvin and June Hamilton. The owner of the Aurora Lodge, Barney Sewell, stood with them — or at least tried to stand with them. The fact that one had to occupy three different places in order to view the two bodies had sent him scurrying off into the bushes more than once.

"I've seen enough mangled carcasses in my time to fill a stadium," Sewell said sheepishly, as he wiped his chin on his plaid jacket. "But this is different, eh?"

Sturgess looked heavenward. "That's why some of God's creatures turn into carcasses and others turn into corpses, Barney."

The paramedics' helicopter was silent and still. Sergeant Sturgess had had only to suggest in the gentlest way that there was no need to rush off to the hospital. None of the paramedics had ever seen such utter and complete destruction of human life, not even at the worst of car crashes.

It was the rumpled, tobacco-chewing Sewell who'd found the bodies. When the elderly Hamiltons missed breakfast at the main lodge building, he'd become concerned and come looking for them.

When Sergeants Laidlaw and Sturgess of OPP Regional headquarters in Thunder Bay had heard that Barney Sewell had found whopping cat's paw prints in the sand at the water's edge, they'd pleaded with their detective-inspector for the assignment. They still hadn't been able to put aside their suspicion that the fatal shooting of chief hunting guide Willie Gleason by Minnesotan big-game hunter George Bjorn had indeed been precipitated by an honest-to-goodness African lion.

"You sonofabitch," Sergeant Sturgess had muttered to Bjorn before departing for Lake Caribou. "If you'd come clean, this probably wouldn't have happened. But oh, no. You and your pal decided that the fucking Lion King was more worthy of preservation than our good Canadian grizzlies."

"Uh … Officer Sturgess," said a sickly and pale Barney Sewell, looking to the far side of the lawn, "do you think it might be more respectful if we sorta reunited Mrs. Hamilton's head with her body?"

"Nobody touches anything until the experts say so."

The senior crime-scene technician had overheard Sewell. He gingerly picked up June Hamilton's head and placed it at her stretched and savaged neck. "We're pretty much done. No doubt about what happened here. Mr. Sewell has a point."

"Any idea when they died?" Sturgess asked Bart Murphy, the critical care paramedic.

"It was cold last night, and they would have cooled off pretty quickly, but their present temperature and state of rigor says twelve hours, more or less. But I'm no doctor, remember."

Sturgess glanced at the picnic table. "Uh-huh. But that squares with the state of their supper dishes."

"You know, that beast must be of the size and power of a road grader."

"I figure," said Sturgess.

"And he likes chocolate cake," chimed in Sergeant Laidlaw, holding aloft the cake tray. "This thing has been licked clean by a tongue as wide as a surf board."

"Well," said Sturgess, "that narrows things down. We're after a lion that likes chocolate cake." Sturgess squinted at Barney Sewell. "We'll need trackers, and good ones. Assuming he didn't hang around here for too long, he's got a full night's head start on us."

"Lark Alisappi and Wally Cheechoo. Cree. They'd find a peanut in a shit pit."

"Dogs?"

"Five of the best," replied Sewell, stuffing a fresh wad of tobacco into his mouth.

"The way I figure it, from this position and where Willie Gleason was shot by those American cowboys, the lion's on a southeast bearing. That means he'll go east along the shore of this lake before he heads south again. For insurance purposes, we can drop a tracker team at the eastern end of Caribou. He might run smack dab into them."

"You're talking forty miles, Sergeant. In twelve hours he'd have covered about a hundred."

"So at least that'll move us up forty miles on him."

"I'll get Wally Cheechoo and his dogs up there with the float plane. If they're within thirty miles of his spoor, they'll find it." Barney Sewell spat on the ground then stared straight into Sturgess's eyes. "Uh ... listen, Sergeant. I'm going to be paid for my time, right? I've got guests that've shelled out twenty big ones for the hunting adventure of their lives."

Sturgess spat exactly where Sewell had spat. "I'm aware of that, Barney. I'll get in touch with the Canadian Wildlife Service just as soon as we're finished this conversation, get some game and conservation types involved in this thing. This kind of situation is new to me. In the meantime, rest assured that your efforts will not be wasted. Besides, you'll want to do what you can to prevent further loss of life, am I right?"

Barney spat. "Fuckin' A."

Detective-Sergeant Sturgess spat, although it was but a drop as compared to Barney's bucketful. "I knew I could count on you."

The critical-care paramedic, wishing inclusion in the conversation, spat too. "So, Officer. Where on Earth does this beast come from?"

"Fucked if I know," answered Sturgess. "There've been absolutely no reports of any missing lion within a thousand miles of here. On the whole continent, actually. Something like that would be big news, and it would have been on the CBC. For sure CNN. I figure he must be what they call an 'exotic pet' that got away. Whatever the case, I've been thinking that just as I can project where he's headed, I can work backward from Lake Wawanesa in a northwesterly direction. I'll check the maps, see what's out there."

"There's nothing that I know of," said Sewell. "A few hunting camps, that's about it."

"There has to be something, Barney."

Detective-Sergeant Arthur Laidlaw, who'd been standing nearby and seemed more absorbed in the activities of the crime-scene technicians than the conversation, tapped Sturgess's elbow. "I've got this funny idea, Bill. Promise you won't laugh if I say it out loud?"

Though younger by several years than Laidlaw, Bill Sturgess was the dominant personality. It was he who had natural leadership abilities, it was he who would be promoted. And like most natural leaders, he didn't feel diminished by another's creativity. In fact, he welcomed it and harnessed it to a higher purpose — usually his own. "Shoot, Arthur. It can't be worse than nothing at all."

"Well, it's this story about the abducted animals —"

Sturgess clapped Laidlaw on the shoulder and immediately called HQ in Thunder Bay, telling his detective-inspector to get through to the Montreal Police Department. Homicide, in particular. He wanted a word with the world's most famous cop, Athol Hudson.

It's a given that dumb brutes are dumb and brutish. That they are not nearly as dumb as they are brutish is a fact that must be purloined. Pet owners regularly do this, as do naturalists and animal researchers, but the vast majority of people are only willing to concede that animals have, at most, a different kind of intelligence.

Detective-Sergeant Bill Sturgess, clever and managerial though he was, fell into the latter group. In short, he acted on the assumption that beasts cannot learn unless they are taught by the lords of the Earth, and even then that they can learn only the most rudimentary of tricks, based upon either direct and systematic reward, or punishment. Animals are creatures of instinct, he believed, and are therefore incapable of altering their behaviour by themselves, let alone consciously adopting new strategies.

How wrong he was.

After his savaging of Marvin and June Hamilton, I-árishóni had loped off in a northwesterly direction, backtracking over the path he'd taken in the wake of slaughtering Reg McDuff and Victor Tarasenko. For five hours he'd kept to this counterintuitive course. When he was halfway between the Aurora Lodge and the spot where he'd ambushed McDuff and Tarasenko, he took a sharp left and proceeded southwest at a quick clip, skirting the marshy northern shore of a small lake that teemed with fish, waterfowl, and otters.

He left a tracker team from the facility on a collision course with Lark Alisappi and his dogs from the Aurora Lodge.

CHAPTER THIRTY-SEVEN

Bude, Cornwall. September 11, 2006. But for Inspector Raja Chadwani's email from Rio de Janeiro at one o'clock that morning, the one in which he detailed his findings about Jason Conrad's strange meeting, the last two days had proved rather exasperating for Irina Drach and Athol Hudson. Armed with their photo of Liang Xueqin, they'd tromped the streets of Bude and its environs, looking in every shop and hotel and under every Cornish "pasty," but no one had ever seen, or heard of, the slight Chinese fugitive.

Nevertheless, things had not been completely dull. Between search expeditions under a pulsating sun plugged into an electric blue sky, they frequently availed themselves of the pool at the Hartland Hotel and, with even greater delight, the local beaches. There was Crooklets Beach, sandwiched between Bude and the Atlantic, and, less than a mile down the bluffed coastline, there was the much larger one at Widemouth Bay. Being fairly untravelled Canadians, they were both astonished and delighted at how much the Gulf Stream and the North Atlantic Drift could transform the pounding surf into a league of twenty thousand massotherapists.

Also alleviating the tedium of the door-to-door inquiries, though not in any positive way, were three issues that arose out of Chadwani's missives. The first concerned the fact that Chadwani was staying at the Copacabana Palace. Hudson knew of this particular hotel from his armchair travels, and heartily disapproved. "There's something funny about that," he groused. "They don't call it the Palace for nothing, and I can only assume that unless Indian cops get paid in rubies rather than rupees, then he's beholden to someone or something. The whole thing smells like a Calcutta ditch."

"You should get your mind out of that particular gutter, Hudson."

The second issue involved Irina's reluctance to leap to any conclusions about Jason Conrad. "On the face of it, the circumstances are rather suspicious," she retorted. "And they certainly warrant the attention of Inspector Chadwani's keen intellect. But we must keep our minds open. That meeting might actually be of more interest to someone investigating an entirely different matter. I don't harbour any illusions that he's a saint."

Hudson quipped, "Your mind is so open it could provide safe harbour for Edward Teach's ship."

"Unless I'm mistaken, Edward Teach was Blackbeard, was he not?"

"He was."

Irina bristled as she'd never bristled at him before. "You're out of your depth, Hudson. Talk to me that way again, and you'll end up in Davey Jones's locker."

Hudson was taken aback by the extent of Irina's wrath. He lapsed into a moody silence.

Which brings us to the third issue, and one that is germane to the other two. Hudson strove constantly for Irina's approval. Thus, her apparent esteem for this obsequious and self-serving Indian cop and the highhanded Jason Conrad rankled Hudson no end. He'd come to view them as contenders for Irina's regard, and believed himself to be diminished by comparison. Irina's displeasure at his commentaries did little to soothe him. That he was being unpleasant in the first instance was, in his opinion, of no consequence. He expected much of Irina, not the least being an ability to decipher the etchings on his soul.

Eventually, Irina did just that. "Jason Conrad met with people whom we'll never be able to trace," she said in a conciliatory tone. "That fact leads Conrad to loom large on our radar screen. But we still need a real, live person to link him with the animal abductions, Athol. You know that as well as I do. Therefore, we mustn't be distracted from our search for Mr. Liang."

Much mollified, Hudson pointed to the facade of the small department store near the foot of the Belle Vue hill: Wroe's. "Mind if we nip in there for a few minutes? It looks like we could be here for some time, and I could use a sport shirt for the beach."

"This strip is thick with surf shops. Why not get your shirt at one of them?"

"I'm on a strict budget. Saving up for a big plasma TV."

"On our way down the hill I saw a rather smart yellow shortsleeve in a window. It would look wonderful on you."

"Did you notice the price?"

"My treat. We'll call it an advance birthday present."

"I appreciate the offer, but I can't let you do that. My birthday was three months ago and you bought me that beautiful bronze figure, thank you very much."

Irina coquettishly draped her arms over Hudson's shoulders and drew close to him. "Please? Let me? You'd look so pretty in it."

Irina had forgotten herself. The gesture was one she'd often used, only half seriously, to wangle something out of her husband. It had always produced results because Walter had never seen the self-mockery in it. Nor did Hudson at this moment. All he could see was the woman he desired above all others. All he could feel was the yearning to crush that voluptuous body into his own and to enter her every orifice with all extremities at his disposal. Preferably all at the same time.

Hudson's hands had reflexively lifted to the small of Irina's back. Now, with a will that could have knotted a steel rod, he gently removed her arms from his shoulders. In the small eternity during which his eyes broke away from her eyes, and his hands relinquished her wrists, tears welled up in Irina's eyes. She hadn't felt this alone and adrift for well over a year. Maybe her gesture had been less playful than she'd expected it would be.

Hudson responded to Irina's moist eyes with a brief, self-conscious hug. "Whatever you want to offer me, I'll gladly accept. Let's go see that shirt."

In silence, they walked together up the hill, halfway to their hotel, and entered a boutique called WaveForm. The music was raucous, the decor was gaudy, and the screaming yellow shirt was the most subdued item on the premises. Hudson loved it.

A tall and muscular young man with shoulder-length blond hair, clad only in a T-shirt and baggy shorts, washed up behind them. "Try it on," he shouted over the high-voltage music of the Aqua Velvets, a new millennium surf band. "You'd look yummy in it."

As Hudson stripped to the waist and slid into the yellow silk confection, the barefoot salesman scrutinized Hudson in the way an art lover scrutinizes a Michelangelo marble. "Of course, you'd look good in anything, wouldn't you?" he exclaimed as he turned down the music. "I must say, you look a bit familiar, but I can't place you. I'll bet that if you grew your hair out and dyed it, you'd look like Pierce Brosnan. I'm not a salesman, by the way. I'm really an actor, which is why I'm uniquely placed to make comments like that and sound sincere about it. Buy that shirt. They'll go gaga over you down at the beach."

Hudson looked at the beach boy suspiciously. "Who is 'they?'"

"If you have to ask, then you don't want to know, do you? So? What do you think? And you, Madam. Don't you think your son looks divine?"

Irina gasped, rummaged in her purse for one hundred pounds, then pushed it at him. "Here. And keep the change. Either buy yourself a muzzle or put it toward a mouthectomy."

She fled the store.

"Oh, dear. Is it something Darren said?"

Hudson eyed the youth coldly as he removed the shirt, tied it in a tight knot around Darren's neck, and pried the money from his hands. "Has it ever been otherwise?"

Darren sank into a chair despondently, not even bothering to disentangle himself from the shirt. "I'm just not suited to this kind of work, am I? I have half a mind to quit."

"Good idea," snapped Hudson as he slipped back into the dress shirt with the rolled-up sleeves. "Go back to acting. Your half a mind should be more than adequate."

Darren was moping and Hudson was just putting on his blazer when Irina charged back into the shop. As Irina untied the shirt from Darren's neck, bagged it, and demanded the money from Hudson, Darren said, "I'm truly sorry if I offended you, Ma'am. My friends all say I'm better off speaking someone else's mind, and I know that to be true. That's why I'm an actor. But I will venture this: You might be a mature woman, but you are a right beauty. You remind me of Kathleen Turner just before she got fat and ugly."

"Flattered, I'm sure," Irina snarled as she slammed the hundred pounds down onto the counter. "What's your name, Sonny?"

"Darren, Madam. Darren Wipe. You know, I've often thought of changing my last name. Doesn't suit a handsome young actor, does it? No, it should probably be something like Hudson, or Grant. But Grant as in Cary, not Hugh. Or what about Clift? Darren Clift? Yes, that has a nice ring to it."

Irina fished an envelope from her purse. "Cleft might be more appropriate."

"Oh, so you noticed. My best feature, that. Darren Cleft, Darren Cleft … I just might have a go with that. Something's got to change my luck."

Irina opposed a photograph to the big blue eyes. "You weren't here the day before yesterday."

"No, I only do Mondays. I cover for that wanksplat, Roger Witherspoon."

"Have you ever seen this man?"

"Him? Yeah … how could I forget? Took him an hour to decide on a flipping bathing suit. Called him an Oriental, I did, to which he replied that Oriental is a rug. He's *Asian*, if you please. To which I replied that *Asian* is a *flu*, and maybe we should just settle on 'chinky' or 'slant.' Got on famously with him, as you can imagine." Darren sighed like Hamlet on a bad day. "Just as I do with all my customers, it seems."

"Was there anything about where he was staying?"

"Was there ever. A rental in Lower Upton. I should come back there with him, he says. Lots of weapons. Shotguns and knives and things. He could whittle off all my limbs if I fancied that."

"Nothing more specific?"

"He said he'd start with my wanger."

"I meant about the house."

"Well, given that Lower Upton is about ten houses, how specific does one have to be?"

Hudson withdrew his map from his jacket pocket. Darren laid his hand over it, obscuring it. "No need," he said. "Just go back down this hill and out the south end of town to the coastal road. Marine Drive, it's called. You want to go about half the way to Widemouth Bay and take a left on this poxy little lane called County Road. Lower Upton's about half a mile in."

Hudson removed Darren's hand from his map. "If you don't mind, I'd like to see exactly how to get out of town."

"Well, you got in, didn't you?"

"Yes. Using the map."

"Some people," Darren sighed heavily as he jabbed at the map for Hudson. Then he got up to make the bill. He rang up the register and handed Irina the receipt and her scant change. "Well, one can't expect everyone to live by their intuition and wits like me, can they? Life would be just too simple."

"Simple doesn't begin to describe it," chuckled Irina. "Thanks for everything, and goodbye." She pecked him on the cheek and held the door open for Hudson.

Irina was just letting the door go when Darren looked up from filing his toenail. "You really are quite a glamour puss for your age. If your friend weren't one of us, I'd suggest you have an affair with him."

The country lane Irina and Hudson were looking for was barely a mile past Bude city limits, but it was far enough that they were, once again, able to revel in the contrast between the obsessively tidy farmers' fields, with their obsessively tidy hedgerows, and the ungovernable wildness of the Cornish coastline.

"My God, but they're beautiful," rhapsodized Hudson about the fields. "I never knew there were so many shades of green. And so benign. Nothing like the fierce intransigence of the Canadian countryside."

Just at the point where they were to turn off Marine Drive onto County Road, the cliffs were but fifty feet away, so they parked the car, trod through the thickest, lushest grass they'd ever seen, and stood on the brink, looking out over the ocean at the horizon. Alone together and together alone, they allowed themselves to be transported to exotic and distant places. They soared and hovered on the updraft of their imaginations, just as the seabirds hovered and soared on the updraft at the cliff's edge. Gradually, their daydreaming turned into foreboding, and they breathed deeply the sea breeze just as one breathes deeply the fresh, ionized air that precedes a storm.

They got back into the car and inched their way along a dauntingly narrow and winding lane bounded on both sides by impenetrable ten-foot bramble hedges. While Hudson drove, Irina used her BlackBerry to google "house rentals" and "Upton." Nothing helpful came up. "We'll just have to do it the hard way," she said. "And here we are, half a mile in, at the first house. Dear Mr. Cleft was right on the money, wasn't he?"

"Kind of shakes your faith in stupidity, doesn't it?"

Since they weren't carrying firearms, it would have been pointless for one of them to remain by the car and cover the one who went to the door. They quickly determined that there was safety in numbers, and that they would therefore go to the door together. They rang the bell of the palatial tudor-style house and were soon face to face with a scrawny, pimply youth in his late teens. He had unruly green hair, a nose ring, safety pins in one eyebrow, and a silver stud in the middle of his tongue. The fact that he breathed through his mouth made that latter observation an easy one.

"Wot you want?"

"We're here about the canal restoration project," Irina announced. "Are your parents home?"

"You're not English. How can you be involved with the canal?"

"We're Canadian, and I'm afraid there's no helping that. Nevertheless, we're residents of Bude and have an abiding interest in the history of this area. Now, are your parents home?"

The youth crossed his arms and slouched against the door frame. "How do you know I'm not the man of the house?"

"Because you're not even a man, you little prick."

Hudson thought he ought to take over the questioning at this point. He jammed his arm in the swiftly closing door and forced it open. "You'll have to excuse Mrs. Drach but it's her time of the month, if you catch my drift."

"Huh. Jam week. But she's an old cow. It's a wonder she hasn't hit menopause yet."

"Oh, so you know about menopause," replied Hudson in his most mellifluous voice. "That means we're dealing with a man of the world, which in turn means you would know whether or not your parents are home. Are they, indeed, home?"

The young man broke wind as he laughed riotously. Irina and Hudson were able to ascertain that he had a second stud imbedded in his tongue, this one nearer his tonsils. "They're at a meeting in town about the bloody canal! All of which makes me wonder who you lot really are, and what you want. Lemme guess. You're B & E types checking to see if anyone's in, that it?"

Hudson was indignant beyond all measure. "I might stoop to such a thing, but never the lady. Look at her!"

The youth studied Irina from head to toe. "You're right. She looks like she has a pickle up her arse, just like me mum. So what are you about, then? And no codswallop."

"You're very astute, young man, so I won't waste my time or yours trying to deceive you. We are, as previously indicated, Canadian. As such, we're used to large properties. We're greedy for them. So we're getting a look at the properties along this strip with an eye to making a good offer on the one that strikes our fancy."

"Humph. You're going about it in an underhanded manner. Why not just go to an estate agent?"

"But an estate agent will only show us properties that are for sale."

"Well, none of the people around here are interested in selling, I can tell you that much. Everybody's busy fixing up their properties with an eye to retiring in them, like me mum and dad. The only one you have the slimmest chance of getting your hooks into is Upton House. That's a holiday let property."

"Oh? Upton House?"

"Yeah. Bloody great big place, at least an acre of land. Three houses down, with a whopping stone fence around it and a circular gravel drive.

Very posh. Just a squinny little Chinaman staying there, now. Has been for months, on and off. Must have bags of money, the antisocial little runt."

"Antisocial? No visitors?" asked Irina.

"I shouldn't talk to you, your insulting me like you did. I'm a sensitive adolescent. But I'll answer because you've got a good pair of top bollocks. So, no visitors, or none I've seen. Not even women. Must spank the monkey a lot. Now, if you'll excuse me, I need to go and squat, as you two plods probably deduced at the top of our little chin-wag."

The teenager slammed the door in their faces. They were halfway back to their car when he opened it again. "You know, a more convincing cover story would have been to pretend that you were potential lessors wanting to look over the vacation property."

"What makes you think we knew there was a rental property in the neighbourhood?"

The youth shrieked with laughter and slammed the door with enough force to suggest that it was for the last time.

"I suppose 'plods' means cops," opined Hudson, as he opened the car door for Irina.

"I suppose it does. Humbling, isn't it? As soon as we've saved the world, I think I'll turn in my badge. Or pin it to his skinny little ass."

Irina and Hudson drove through the gate and up the steep slope into the front yard of the imposing vine-covered stone cottage. They parked behind a beat-up old Honda that was stationed by the attached garage and, after taking a few moments to admire the tree-lined property and its central circular garden, they stood in the shady, capacious stone porch and waited for their man to answer the door. Having Googled Upton House on the way over from the potty-mouthed youth's home, Irina now knew the corporation to which the house belonged, and she was ready for a more convincing performance than the one they'd just given.

And so they waited. And waited. And then waited some more.

"His car's here, though," whispered Hudson as he rang the bell for the fourth time. "Maybe he went for a walk?"

"I don't believe he's the walking type."

"Why not? He's apparently the swimming type."

"Hm, so he is. I'd forgotten that."

Hudson looked at Irina with some consternation. "The steel trap is a little rusty today."

"I'm distracted, is all."

"Ah yes, and I think I understand why. I'm a little off my game as well —"

Irina stiffened and said brusquely, "You stay here, Hudson. I'm going around the back to take a look at things."

She left Hudson with his mouth gaping and made her way around the side of the house, past water gardens and a large goldfish pond, and onto a patio at the rear. Giving onto the patio was a solarium spacious enough to accommodate a large table and a complete set of heavily cushioned wicker furniture. From the angle at which she was standing, just at the locked door of the solarium, she could see into the country-style kitchen and just make out a small Asian man sitting at the long table. He had his arms crossed tightly over his chest and was staring back at her in alarm. That he neither moved nor opened his mouth told Irina that he was alone in the house and presently unarmed, so she picked up a metal patio chair and hurled it through the wall of the solarium. That there were no weapons at all in the house was less certain, especially in light of what beach boy Darren Wipe had told them, and she hoped to beat the odds by catching him before he got to his cache.

As she passed through the gaping hole in the glass and rushed into the kitchen, the man bolted down the long hallway, bare feet slapping on the cold slate floor. How perfect, she thought. He was heading for the front door and into the waiting arms of Sergeant-Detective Athol Hudson.

The slightly built Liang pulled the door open just as Irina got halfway down the hall. What she and the fugitive saw stunned them both. There stood Hudson. But he had a pistol at his head. Behind him, holding the gun, was a much shorter man with a pockmarked face. Irina recognized him from the queue at Paddington Station, even though he no longer had a beard. Behind him was a tall, thin, and exceedingly pale girl with short and choppy black hair. Irina could have sworn she was the girl lolling about the Hartland Hotel while she and Hudson were checking in.

"I'd like to introduce Alex Smith and Rowena Hardcastle," croaked Hudson. "They don't appear to have our best interests at heart, but on the other hand they claim they won't be killing us."

"Relax, little chap," said Smith to a highly agitated Xueqin Liang. "We're on your side. Now, why don't we all move inside where we'll be more comfortable?"

Liang led the other four past the staircase in the hall and into the kitchen. Irina followed him and Rowena Hardcastle brought up the rear. On the way down the hall, Smith quickly inspected the two parlours — one with a large plasma television, the other with a fireplace — and commented on the split-timbered ceilings throughout the main floor. "Quite plushy, Liang. Must be big enough for ten people. Well, we each spend our ill-gotten gains in different ways, don't we? Me, I bought a BMW. No company car for this sod. And Rowena here, she bought an interest in a beauty salon, can you imagine?"

Even though Rowena had a 9-millimetre pistol trained on Irina, she looked to her for sisterly sympathy and understanding. Irina was not forthcoming.

Alex Smith motioned for Irina and Hudson to sit together at the kitchen table. While he trained his pistol on them, Rowena patted them down. "They're clean."

"And what about our Mr. Liang?"

"Well, he has to be clean too, don't he? Otherwise he would've used it on the lady copper."

"Check him."

Liang, who in the space of two minutes had gone from extreme agitation to exultation, now became thoroughly confused. Nevertheless, he offered no resistance as the girl searched him, nor even when she concluded by tugging at his penis through his shorts. "Oy, he's a real pencil-dick, this one. Do you suppose all Orientals are like this?"

"Asian," said Liang, irritably. "Oriental is a rug."

Smith waved his sidearm at Liang. "We'll call you what we bloody well please. But if it'll soothe your sensibilities, you can call us Occidental. How's that?"

"Why are you talking to me like this, and why do you point your gun at me? We are of the same team."

Smith laugh sonorously. "It's not 'accidental', fnarr fnarr. The fact of the matter is, my little rug rat, that you have allowed yourself to be tracked down by these two coppers. Canadians, of all things. So some disciplinary action is called for. But what, eh? What?"

"Ah … we could dispose of them and I could be banished forever. I am very small. I could go back to China and become lost among one-point-three billion people. Nearly one fifth of the people in the world, it is."

"But they're all small, too," Rowena blurted.

"I could make myself even smaller. Behold."

Liang scrunched himself up and did, indeed become smaller.

"Why don't I just finish him off now," said Rowena avariciously, pointing her pistol at Liang's head. "He makes a big enough target. Pow!"

"A bit crude, my dear. And unnecessarily cruel. No, I think it behooves us to act in a civilized manner. After all, is not our organization in the business of saving civilization? Here's what we'll do. Liang will have the pleasure of executing our law-enforcement mates, and then we'll get him papers and put him on a fast boat to China. Conrad Container Lines does a shitload of runs from Felixstowe to Shanghai. Remember the plan."

"The flipping plan. Right."

"What do you think, Xueqin?"

Liang thought that was rather a good idea and nodded enthusiastically. Irina and Hudson had, in their time, heard better ideas, but they weren't so insensate with worry that they didn't wonder what the plan might be. And they were beginning to suspect that there was much more to the plan than Liang was aware of. But it was the mention of Conrad Container Lines that got them exchanging glances. This did not pass unnoticed by Alex Smith. "My, aren't we the clever clogs? Yes, indeed, I said Conrad Lines, and it meant a great deal to you, didn't it? No matter, my dear biodiversity troopers, you'll be dead in a few minutes anyway, so savour the fact that Jason Conrad is the reason you're after friend Liang, because it will be the last thing you taste before death."

"I've never killed anyone famous, before," said Rowena, staring at Hudson. "Pity, really, him being so hunky and all."

"And you won't be killing him either," snarled Smith. "Liang's doing the honours, remember?"

"Oh, right," Rowena said with discernible relief.

Said Irina, "Is this true about Jason Conrad, Mr. Liang?"

Liang shrugged. "Fucky fuck if I know. No one has told me."

"God," mourned Hudson, "there's something completely inglorious about an ironic death, don't you think?"

"Worse than being a footnote," grumbled Irina.

Smith's free arm reached out toward Rowena. He told her to remove the hardware from the bag slung over her shoulder and she obliged, after having put on latex gloves. "Now hand the Beretta to Sergeant Hudson and the Walther to Liang, and for God's sake don't mix them up."

Rowena Hardcastle responded with a swelling sigh. "I'm not some bimbo, you bloomin' bungalow. It was me who prepped the guns, remember?"

"Just do it."

Rowena did as bidden. Liang shrank as if he'd just been handed a live grenade. Hudson turned the Beretta over in his hand and showed Irina that it had no magazine.

"Yes, that's right," Smith gloated. "It's useless. If it's any consolation, though, it's the sidearm used by the U.S. Armed Forces and NATO. The Beretta M9 9-millimetre. As a rather poetic touch — I think, anyway — friend Liang is holding a Walther P-38. The one used by the Nazis. But it's still a much prettier gun, don't you think? Full of that old-world charm."

"I have some bad news for you, Mr. Liang," said Irina, sounding dispassionate even by police standards. "The reason my partner's gun is empty is as follows: You will shoot Sergeant Hudson and me with the Walther — me in the head probably, and Hudson in the heart or lung so that he lingers a bit — and when we are good and dead this gentleman here will put on latex gloves, insert a full magazine into the Beretta that resides in my deceased partner's hand, and make my partner's finger squeeze off a shot at you. Actually, two shots. The first will be a messy, nonfatal shot, and the second will be a head shot. The idea is to make it look like we all killed each other in a shootout. The sequence of events will appear to have been thus: Hudson shot first, at your heart, then you responded by wounding Hudson and then putting a bullet in my brain. Hudson, however, is not dead. He plugs you in the forehead, and then, alas, dies from his heart or lung injury."

"Well bugger this," roared Hudson at Smith as he flung the Beretta over his shoulder. "I'm not going to make things easy for you!"

Liang looked perplexed. "But why would Mr. Smith do such a thing? I do not know that Jason Conrad is our leader."

"Exactly so, Xueqin," smirked Smith. "Why, indeed? Anywise, even if you think you're in a crapshoot, you've still no choice but to throw the dice because the inimitable and effervescent Rowena will be holding a gun to your head at all times. As for you, Sergeant Hudson, you'd be well-advised to pick up the Beretta, else Mr. Liang, after having inflicted a mortal but not immediately disabling wound upon you, might just take it into his head to act out his sadistic fantasies and blow Mrs. Drach apart, piece by tasty piece. The Walther's magazine does hold eight bullets, you know. And that unfortunate turn of events would only marginally alter the little scenario that she has so artfully sketched out for us. Now, shall we begin? Prepare yourself, Mr. Liang. And Sergeant Hudson, do be kind enough to keep hold that weapon even in your moment of deepest torment. It's up to you how much or how little your partner suffers. Now do be a good chap and pick it up."

Hudson slowly retrieved the pistol and sat once more at Irina's side.

With Rowena's gun at his head, Liang looked to Smith. Smith nodded and Liang held the Walther at the end of outstretched arms. From across the table, at a distance of barely ten feet from Hudson, he pulled the trigger.

At first, Hudson felt only as if he'd been punched in the chest. But by the time the blood was staining his shirt and blazer, his whole torso felt afire, as if he were burning at the stake. Still, he grasped the useless Beretta tightly.

Hudson did not utter a sound, but Irina did. Calling the unholy trinity every name she could think of, she tore at Hudson's shirt and exposed the wound. It was an appalling sight. She'd seen gunshot wounds before, but never one so close to her heart. At the sight of the hole in his chest, which was just below the collarbone and to the left of his heart, she began to shriek. She dug out a handkerchief and tried to screw the twisted end of it into a hole that would have accommodated her little finger.

Liang was in shock, but Smith and Rowena Hardcastle were amused. "Why are you bothering?" smirked Smith. "He'll be dead in five minutes and you'll be finished off in less than one."

"You wouldn't know it, you bastard, but love and compassion don't quit just because the finish line is in sight!"

Liang crumpled into a ball on the floor. Rowena began kicking away at him, shrieking that he ought to get up and get on with it.

Suddenly, a storm lashed the kitchen. There were bawling orders to throw down arms and raise all hands, and every access point to the large kitchen was controlled by black-clad police assault officers. There were two from the solarium, two from the side door that led to the garage, there was one in the window that looked out over the back gardens, and there were two more from the hallway. Rowena was the first to react. She fired on one of the officers in the garageway door facing her, and although he didn't present much of a target, she still managed to hit him in the hand. His partner promptly shot her in the left eye and she crumpled like a rag doll. Alex Smith whirled about and discharged his entire magazine at the pair of policemen in the solarium doorway. Most of the bullets screamed ineffectually through the empty doorway, but one managed to penetrate the door jamb and shatter an officer's chin. His partner retaliated swiftly by blasting Smith twice in the chest. As Smith sank to his knees, he shot Xueqin Liang in the head. He was just aiming his handgun at Irina when the assault officer in the window pumped another bullet into Smith, and he was still.

With great deliberation, Hudson set aside the Beretta. He then promptly collapsed face first onto the table.

All was hushed for a few moments. Benumbed senses reawakened to a whitish cloud of gun smoke hovering lazily at the ceiling, and air that reeked of gunpowder and seared flesh. Alert to any further disturbance, the assault officers were frozen on the spot and looked like posed, menacing action figures. Irina, in ghostlike silence, was checking Hudson for a carotid pulse.

As abruptly as the thunder and lightning had ceased, a flood of emotion and urgency surged through the kitchen. Irina fetched a cushion from the conservatory, then slid Hudson down onto it in case he needed CPR, all the while shouting, "He's alive, he's alive, but he needs help right away!" In the meantime, the assault team had broken formation and, with a great deal of bellowing, clattering, and bolting back and forth, began to assess its prey and comfort its wounded. One officer, who Irina thought seemed barely old enough to fire a water pistol, let alone a Heckler & Koch assault rifle, stopped long enough to reassure her that salvation was at hand. "He'll be along in just a few seconds, Ma'am. Hang on."

He? Irina was neither impressed nor consoled. She would rock back and forth on her knees, take Hudson's pulse, then rock yet again, all the while holding the palm of her hand tightly against his profusely bleeding wound.

And into the midst of all this organized chaos stepped a tall, mustachioed man of middle years, whose aura of imperturbability was admirably complemented by a bespoke black suit and satiny Italian shoes. He stooped over Irina and said, in an immensely assured yet barely audible voice, "Sergeant-Detective Drach, I presume. Detective Chief Inspector Leopold Duggan, of the London Metropolitan Police, at your service. And these lads are the CO19 unit. My compliments upon the success of your mission, although I dare say I never doubted the outcome from the first moment of our earliest telephone conversation."

Irina did not look up from Hudson. "Now is not the time for niceties, Inspector. This man needs immediate attention. I would also point out that our mission would have been even more of a success if at least one of those three were still alive."

"Hm. Nasty wound Sergeant Hudson has there. In my opinion, however, it is neither a heart nor a lung injury. If he took the bullet straight on, he'll have at most a damn sore shoulder for a bit."

"Oh my God, do you really think so?"

Duggan cocked an eyebrow and smoothed the cowlick that incongruously stuck up from his thick black hair, for Irina Drach's tone suggested a relationship between these two Canadians that went far beyond the normal police partner bond. "Definitely. Seen it a few times. And by the way, I rather anticipated there would be injuries — if not to these three miscreants, then to you — and I therefore have an ambulance and paramedics from the Stratton Hospital in tow. As well, I have two whirlybirds and the CO19 unit's assigned medics sitting in the farmer's field at the end of the lane. They all await my signal, which I shall give immediately."

While he performed a quick inspection of his two wounded troopers, Duggan made a phone call. Within thirty seconds, the ambulance was screaming onto the property and the helicopters had set down on the extensive back lawn of Upton House. Within two minutes the police medics and the local paramedics had loaded the wounded onto stretchers.

"Do you mind if I come along in the bird with you?" inquired Inspector Duggan.

"No ... not at all," replied Irina distractedly as she felt for Hudson's pulse yet again.

As the chopper lifted off for the trip to Derriford Hospital in Plymouth, Duggan said to Irina in his ineffably hypnotizing voice, "Good of the assistant commissioner to let me take the CO19 crew so far afield, but I must confess he did not tax my powers of persuasion. I had only to mention your names. And I must apologize for storming your stage in the way we did, but I can tell you that it was never my intention to do anything but assure your safety. I had very little choice once we determined that you were being followed. But I suppose you knew you were being followed?"

Irina released Hudson's hand in order to rummage through her purse for a tissue. Duggan quickly handed her one from his own pocket, and she wiped away her badly smeared eye makeup. "Yes, but we had no idea we were leading a parade. How did you track us? A lot of eyeballing and a little bit of GPS on my BlackBerry?"

"Quite, although it took us a while to connect you two to those dummy BlackBerry accounts."

"Oh dear, I suppose I sound ungrateful. Well, I don't mean to. You saved our lives and, quite probably, this case."

"Yes, about this case ... Mrs. Drach, is it?" said Duggan, looking dubiously at Hudson.

"Mrs. Drach. Exactly," Irina answered with a wry smile. "The Widow Drach."

"Oh, I am sorry," said Duggan with considerable relief, for he could not countenance inappropriate relationships, in his own or any other force. "Well, then? You got what you came for, did you? A name?"

"Yes, thank you."

Duggan had hoped for a more expansive answer. He wasn't known as Digger Duggan for nothing. He would not be denied. "The name of the person behind this whole animal abduction scheme?"

"Yes."

"A man, is it?"

"A man."

"Did the name come as a surprise, or did it merely confirm your suspicions?"

"We already had our suspicions."

Duggan passed his hand over his thick black hair. "And the CO19 chaps slotted all three of that lot, any one of whom would have been a valuable witness. Pity about that. No direct link, fictitious ID, and not even a cellphone on either of the two aggressors. Can't even connect your man by phone number with this lot."

"In the assault team's defence, only one of the three would have served as a direct link, and he was the most belligerent of them. He was just begging to be taken down. The other two, as far as I could determine, knew of our man only by belated hearsay. Still, all is not lost. If you know where Godzilla is, it isn't too hard to determine where he's been."

Duggan smiled a smile that showed just a little too much tooth. "Sergeant Drach, let's stop pissing around, shall we? I've just saved your life. I've just saved *his* life. Tell me who it is. London is virtually the epicentre of the world. With the vast resources at my disposal, I can be of enormous help."

Irina stroked Hudson's forearm then leaned back against the bulkhead of the helicopter, tugging at a lock of her hair.

Inspector Duggan leaned forward, practically whispering in her ear, "Capturing this megalomaniac single-handedly would undoubtedly burnish your force's reputation, and you two would be bleeding heroes. On the other hand, if it got about that you refused a reasonable offer of assistance, that you were showboating, what kind of co-operation could you expect from forces around the world in the future? Sod *them*, they'd all say."

"Irina —"

It was Hudson.

Instantly, Irina grasped his hand in hers and pressed it to her breast. "Don't talk, Athol. Save your strength."

Duggan tilted his head back and rolled his eyes.

"No ... I have this idea about how to trap our man."

The London detective leapt to his feet, almost bonking his head on the roof of the chopper. "Unburden yourself, Inspector Hudson."

"Irina ... thank the Inspector for his assistance. Tell him I would offer up my life for him if called upon to do so. But also tell him that we cannot divulge the name of our man. I have a plan —"

Duggan was practically frothing at the mouth. "A plan? What plan?"

"I must've fainted from the pain, can you believe it? This has got to be some kind of personal worst —"

Irina was bent over Hudson, peering intently into his eyes.

They closed.

"Athol? Hudson?"

"What," Duggan brayed. "What?"

"I'm afraid he's gone again," said Irina, checking his carotid pulse. "Poor, poor thing."

"Yes, and about what that poor, poor thing said of his plan. Surely to God you're not going to let some little plan get in the way of a great, overarching one? A plan that combines the might and sagacity of British law enforcement agencies with the, uh, zeal of Canadian coppers?"

"I'm afraid I must, Inspector Duggan. Sergeant-Detective Athol Curzon Hudson doesn't often have a plan. When he does, one must respect and nurture it as one must a rose that's forced its way up through a crack in the pavement. Sorry."

And so it came to pass that for the fourth time in the space of an hour, someone who'd actually had the pleasure of meeting Athol Curzon Hudson wished him dead. This was a personal best.

CHAPTER THIRTY-EIGHT

Venice, Italy. September 11, 2006. Chinua Amadi was in the Dogaressa Suite, in the fifteenth century Vendramin annex of the Hotel Cipriani. He was seated on an Italian baroque chair at a small Italian baroque table in an authentically Italian baroque sitting room that managed to look as sleek as a Ferrari. The Cipriani Hotel was situated on La Giudecca Island, just fifteen-hundred feet across the basin from the southern mouth of the Grand Canal, and directly adjacent to the island of San Giorgio Maggiori, which was dominated by the domed, sixteenth-century Church of San Giorgio Maggiori. Chinua allowed his eyes to drift across the choppy jade water to the Piazza San Marco, the Doge's Palace, the Bell Tower, and the Byzantine-styled St. Mark's Basilica.

Thoughts of his own country, impoverished and retarded by millennia of sectarian violence, caused him to shrug in sorrow. Just three generations ago, his ancestors had been running around the south-central rain forests, hunting down bushmeat. His own father had eked out a subsistence living by raising millet and a few stringy animals on a parched acre in the north until he'd been murdered by a covetous farmer from the Lausu tribe. For a goat. His beloved Nigeria was a basketcase, and not even its oil wells would transform it into a prosperous, cohesive, and forward-looking society.

As usual, Jason Conrad was right. Complete subservience to a compelling idea and a messianic leader was the only way anything great got done.

He returned to his paperwork but couldn't concentrate. His thoughts went from bleak to black. He still hadn't heard from Alex Smith. Only fifteen minutes earlier he'd tried to call Smith, but the assassin's phone had just rung and rung insolently. Or perhaps impotently, for he feared the worst.

With his iPod feeding "Jailhouse Rock" to his eardrums, Jason Conrad bopped out of his bedroom and over to a small dining table next to the eighteenth-century Coromandel screens, where the butler had laid out a lunch for him.

"Good afternoon, Sir," said Chinua. "How is the neck today?"

"Pardon?"

Chinua put his hand to his neck.

"The bandage? It's fine," Conrad shouted over his music. "Neck still hurts like hell, though. Want some of this champagne?"

Chinua shrugged off the champagne, and Conrad as well. Bugger him, he thought. If the man couldn't be courteous enough to stop listening to those idiotic tunes of his for just a second or two, then he deserved to be ignored.

Conrad studied Chinua as he worked on his champagne and his smoked Scottish salmon. Chinua soon became aware of this, and he grew uncomfortable, but he said nothing. He bore down on his itineraries.

But Conrad, now picking at Venetian sautéed veal medallions with baby artichokes, continued to stare. Chinua began to sweat profusely. Did Conrad suspect something? The more Chinua asked the question of himself, the more nervous he became. And the more nervous he became, the more obvious it would become to Conrad that he had something to be nervous about. At last he could not stand it anymore. But as it was not his way to confront someone head-on, in particular Conrad, he got up and refilled the great man's champagne glass. An act of obeisance, not to mention a surfeit of alcohol, would perhaps blunt Conrad's percipience.

With his ears still ringing from Lonnie Mack's blistering rendition of "Memphis," Conrad removed the earpieces and furrowed his brow. "I'm thinking about Irina Drach, Chinua."

Chinua suddenly developed an interest in the Fortuny and Rubelli fabrics that covered the antique furniture. In fact, he developed an interest in all things that were not Conrad's eyes. He therefore set the champagne bottle down not on the table, but in thin air, and, as he recovered, he soaked the crotch of his slacks. As Conrad watched the wet patch spread he cooly said, "I sincerely hope you'll change before we go out. It would be unacceptable if it appeared that my man couldn't control himself."

"I will go right away, Sir," blubbered the stricken Chinua.

"You're not going all the way from the palazzo to the main building like that, Chinua. You'll put on a pair of my pants."

"Right away, Sir. Immediately."

"No, not immediately. I was in the middle of something. I was discussing Irina Drach."

This was beyond Chinua's worst nightmare. He would have to endure a galling indignity while his master broached a ghastly topic. With all the composure of a monk caught masturbating, he stood before Conrad, breathlessly waiting.

Conrad took his time. He applied himself to the artichokes and more champagne with calm deliberation. He'd not been unaware of Chinua's snippy behaviour just minutes earlier, and was thoroughly enjoying the latter's discomfort.

"By the bye, I'm thinking of saving Venice. My beautiful Venice."

"Sir?"

"The MOSE project. Or MOSES, as the Venetians so aptly call it. Modulo Sperimentale Elettromeccanico. The floodgates they're building at the three lagoon inlets of Lido, Malamocco, and Chioggia, to hold back the Adriatic when its tide swells dangerously. They'll be able to hold back a sea that rises up to nine feet above normal levels."

"Moses needed the hand of God to part the Red Sea, Sir. Without it, the result would have been very different, as King Canute so convincingly showed."

"Well, the problem of the rising sea levels is partly the fault of mankind — his contributions to global warming and the melting of the polar caps — and it's his job to repair the damage. Now, work was begun on MOSE in 2003, and I believe it's about twenty percent done. The projected budget is three billion Euros, or about four-point-five billion dollars U.S. I propose to underwrite the project. I think I can spare that much, don't you?"

"Is not the city also sinking, Sir?"

"It is. It was built on millions of alder pylons sunk only as deep as the sand and clay that underlies the marshy muck. Over those pylons were laid oak planks and, upon them, thick layers of marble. But if I underwrite MOSES, then the city will be free to spend the allocated MOSES money in shoring up the foundations of the city, raising quaysides, and buttressing the canal walls. Maybe even do something about the corrosive raw sewage that gets dumped into the canals. Capiche?"

"Capiche, Sir."

Conrad rose and sauntered over to the four picture windows. A thick bank of clouds had rolled in from the Adriatic and the vista, from sea to sky, was Titian blue. Suddenly the city no longer looked gay and bold, but fragile and melancholy. The glowing pink of the soaring Campanile was now a somber and diminishing brown and the usually gleaming white Doge's Palace looked like a small and sad café, where dreams go to wither and die. Conrad sighed. "You'll call Silvio?"

"Silvio Berlusconi? The prime minister?"

"The same. You know, the bugger's worth about ten billion. You'd think he'd kick in some of his own money. We're talking about Italy's very soul, here."

Chinua's spirit soared. His having to make that phone call meant Conrad had no nasty surprises in store for him. At least not in the immediate future.

Or so he believed.

"Now," said Conrad, "we were talking about Irina Drach before I got sidetracked."

Chinua's spirit crashed and burned.

"I'm thinking of calling her."

The charred and smoking remains of Chinua's dearly departed spirit were unceremoniously kicked into a filthy ditch. "You can't do that, Sir!"

"And why not?"

"Because ... because you're a suspect! She would immediately conclude that you're trying to schmooze her!"

"And she'd be right. I like her. I want to get to know her better."

"But you don't want *her* to get to know *you* better. That could be catastrophic!"

Having removed Irina's card from his wallet, Conrad began to dial. "I sincerely hope you're referring to my personality and not my judgment."

Chinua was frantic. He wrested the phone from Conrad's hand and threw it against the wall. It hit the floor in three pieces.

Jason Conrad did not become the world's richest man by being insensitive to the needs of others. He knew consuming self-interest when he saw it. He immediately retracted a BlackBerry from his jacket pocket and waved it tantalizingly close to Chinua, then watched as the gears in Chinua's head spun so rapidly that metal shavings almost spewed from his ears. "Very well, then. The phone is now out of order. I'll just have to use this little gadget, won't I?"

Chinua was frantic. He ran back and forth in front of Conrad like a bear with a trap clamped onto its hindquarters. There *was* a small chance that Alex Smith and Rowena Hardcastle had delayed springing their trap. In which case, he reasoned, Conrad and the Drach woman could have a normal, marginally awkward conversation. But why, then, had Smith not answered his cellphone? Also, Smith was going to ditch the thing if the operation was a go, he'd told Chinua early that morning — so as not to be identified in the event something went awry. But he was also going to call Chinua as soon as the mission was completed. There had been no phone call, and he didn't answer his phone! Unless there had been some delay, something had gone wrong, and Irina Drach would answer Conrad's call. She would tell him about the aborted murder attempt by two people whom Conrad knew to be in his employ, and whom he believed were charged with protecting her! Think, Chinua, think! Plausible deniability? The assertion that the two agents were rogues? Oh God, he needed time to think things through! Why hadn't he done that earlier? "I beg of you, Mr. Conrad! You cannot do this! You endanger all that we have worked for!"

Conrad began to push the buttons. "Nonsense. The worst she could think is that I'm presumptuous. She might even be glad to hear from me. There was a mutual attraction when we met, I'm sure of it."

Chinua's nice new Italian clothes — his white Enrico Monti dress shirt and his Armani slacks, even his Prada shoes — were soaked through, to the point where the champagne patch at his crotch became but a spitball in an ocean. He felt as though he were going to vomit. Rather than submit to such an indignity, he decided upon decisive and imaginative action. He wrenched the BlackBerry out of Conrad's hand and threw it against the wall. It hit the floor in three pieces.

For the majority of humanity, life is a messy affair. In fact, it can be said without fear of contradiction that it's the messiest thing most people will ever know. Not Jason Conrad. To him, life was a series of puzzles that were easily solved if one kept his head. And when they weren't, an iron will could always cram the pieces back into their box. Thus, he put his question to Chinua in a thoroughly restrained voice, keeping in mind that the answer would not be definitive but merely evidentiary. "Just what the fuck are you doing? You're acting like a castaway who's drunk sea water."

Chinua didn't know how to respond. He thought he'd touched all the bases, emotional and rational. Now, he was utterly bankrupt of ideas. He sputtered, he squinted, he squirmed. Chinua had never felt so alone, for the man before him, the one whose trust and friendship he'd betrayed, was the very one whose trust and friendship had sustained him for so long. That he'd done so out of conscience was no consolation at all. Weeping uncontrollably, he collapsed onto the lustrous floor and reached out with a trembling hand to touch the hem of Jason Conrad's pant leg.

There was now no need for Chinua to explain himself. Conrad had figured it out. He stiffly withdrew his leg. "Give me your phone, Chinua."

Still moaning, and still prostrate, Chinua complied. Conrad placed a call. "Hello, Irina? Irina! Jason Conrad here. God, it's good to hear your voice. Can't talk now except to say I'm glad you're alive, and to warn you there's a trap set for you at Xueqin Liang's hideout, if you haven't already found out."

Chinua could hear an angry rasp coming from the receiver. Irina stated in loud, clear terms that first, Hudson was seriously wounded and, second, she would be berating Conrad as soon as possible. Conrad calmly replied that he looked forward to seeing her again and straightening things out. He then dialed another fourteen digits. Chinua knew that he was calling London. He also knew what lay in store for him. "Hello, this is JC Alpha, JC Omega, singular."

Chinua could hear obsequious bleating at the other end.

"Never mind all that. I'm at the Hotel Cipriani in Venice, on La Giudecca Island. The Dogaressa Suite in the Palazzo Vendramin. I want a package removed. Okay, fine. Thank you." Conrad looked down at Chinua. "It seems we have a team in Venice. They'll be here in twenty minutes. If you wanted to make a run for it, I wouldn't stop you."

Chinua gathered himself up and sat opposite Conrad at the lunch table. "They would get me before long. They'll have a dog. May I drink with you? A glass of champagne?"

As there was only one glass, Conrad called for the butler to bring another posthaste. Conrad and Chinua didn't exchange a word during those ninety seconds, but neither did they take their eyes off each other. In all the years they'd been together, this was the first time Chinua had not averted his eyes while his master gazed at him. When the butler arrived with the second glass, Conrad dismissed him immediately and filled Chinua's glass himself. He then raised his glass. "You aren't going out as a slave or a servant, but as a man. I toast you."

"And I toast you for the man you might have been. Very few approach such greatness. Shall I tell why I turned against you?"

Conrad laughed ruefully. "No need. I heard something — the dry, cracking sound of a wishbone — when I blew those two away. One thing puzzles me, though. I kill two rogue employees and you get all moralistic, but then you turn around and plot the murder of Irina and Hudson. Isn't there a bit of a disconnect in all that?"

"Not at all, Sir. Washington and de Groot were ours. Drach and Hudson are policemen. A threat to our dream."

The two men sipped at their champagne in silence for a minute, then Chinua cleared his throat and drummed at the table for a few moments. Conrad did his best to check his impatience.

"There is one other thing I wish you would grant me, Sir."

"Anything but the gift of life. I'm not God."

"Last year, at the beach on Lido Island, I had one of the best times of my entire life. The swimming in the surf, our walking the length of the shore, the drinks in the Pagoda Lounge of that Belle Époque Hotel while looking out over the Adriatic Sea —"

"The Hotel des Bains, it was called."

"Yes, exactly, and on the chaise lounge in front of the hotel, you clowned for me, pretending to be Gustav von Aschenbach brought low by his obsession, by the ideal made actual. Do you suppose, Mr. Conrad, that we could go out there one more time? I know full well that I will end up in the Adriatic, and I would like to contemplate its beauty one last time, at leisure. I have always wanted to die with my eyes open and my soul at rest."

Conrad agreed. So when two large Italian men arrived, both as smooth and hard as river rocks, they went outside, boarded the mens' high-powered speedboat, and were docking at the foot of Santa Maria Elisabetta within ten minutes. It was a short stroll along that lush, tree-lined avenue replete with cafés, boutiques, grand hotels, and Edwardian mansions. Within twenty minutes, Conrad and Chinua were standing barefoot in the surf of Lido Beach. The two enforcers hung back at some distance, by the trees and the beach huts.

"Not the world's best sand," said Conrad rather awkwardly, digging his toes into the grey, gravelly concatenation.

"No, but the sun is shining again. And these waves, through this sea, and then the Mediterranean, and then the Atlantic, are one with those that beat upon the shores of my beloved Nigeria. I am in for a brilliant homecoming, of sorts ... but do not weep, Sir. We must all pay our accounts, and when I have done so, I will be free."

"You're the closest thing to a best friend I've ever had, Chinua."

"I loved you, Master. I love you still."

The two men embraced, then Conrad waded ashore. As he put on his socks and shoes, he could see Chinua still standing up to his knees in the water, staring out to sea. The two Italian men had advanced to the shoreline and were waiting patiently.

Without looking back again, Conrad crossed the seaside boulevard, Lungomare Guglielmo Marconi, then walked briskly back up Santa Maria Elisabetta as far as the café nearest the dock. There, he had a cappuccino and a Scotch, then caught the fastest boat back to Piazzetta San Marco.

He no longer felt like the world was his oyster. He no longer felt like such a pearl.

CHAPTER THIRTY-NINE

Northwestern Ontario, Canada. September 9–10, 2006. When Lark Alisappi and his two dogs had set out from Aurora Lodge on the trail of I-árishóni, within one hour of Barney Sewell's discovery of Marvin and June Hamilton's savaged bodies, he'd been loaded for bear. Unfortunately, he'd not been loaded for a facility tracking team weighed down with all manner of assault weapons. After tracing the lion for five hours he'd run into them going in the opposite direction. A few courtesies had been exchanged, Lark had naively stated his business and then been unceremoniously gunned down. The facility team subsequently picked up I-árishóni's southwesterly trail and set out at full clip, at least eighteen hours behind him.

The time since the June and Marvin Hamilton revelation had been only marginally kinder to Detectives-Sergeant Bill Sturgess and Arthur Laidlaw.

Upon being apprised of Laidlaw's idea that the lion was an important piece of the animal abduction puzzle, their commanding officer had thought to himself that it might be rather nice to see his name bruited about the media. Thus, he'd forbidden Sturgess from contacting the famous habitat destruction detective from Montreal — or anyone else, for that matter — and had instead decided that the lion hunt would be exclusively an Ontario Provincial Police operation; in particular, the Thunder Bay detachment.

"That flaming, double-barrelled asshole," Detective Sturgess had mused as he'd stared down at the bullet-riddled body of Lark Alisappi.

"Who would've thought the lion was armed," chirped Laidlaw.

"I was referring to the detective inspector ... wait, are you making a joke? Are you making a joke about the brutal murder of this man?"

Although they were of the same rank, Laidlaw was not mired in sentiments of parity. "No, Sir. I'm sorry, Sir. And you're absolutely right. The detective inspector is a complete asshole. Sir."

Sturgess had scanned Lark Alisappi's dogs, which were little more than bloody, pulpy heaps. "So, Laidlaw, a test. What do you think's our highest priority? Tracking the lion, or this man's killers?"

"Before we do either, we better call the detective inspector. But I think we can do both at the same time. I believe the killers are also on the lion's trail."

"On what evidence?"

"Just a hunch, actually," said Laidlaw as he picked up the dead tracker's rifle. "Oh, and the fact that none of Lark Alisappi's gear has been touched. Not even this sweet thing. Check it out. A pre-'64 Winchester Model 70, complete with controlled round feed. Best bolt action hunting weapon ever made. Most men would kill for one of these, but our assailant — or assailants — didn't. He was killed for something else."

"They," barked Wally Cheechoo, Lark Alisappi's fellow Cree tracker. "There was more than one of them. There was three, and they had more than one dog. Three, maybe four."

Cheechoo had been poking around in the bush farther along Lark Alisappi's trajectory. It was he who'd guided Sturgess and Laidlaw to this point after he'd furiously resisted being flown out to cool his heels at the northeastern tip of Lake Caribou. "Something else. My dogs tell me — and I can see with my own eyes — that the cat and those murderers went in that direction from here."

He pointed southwest.

"From this very point?" said Sturgess.

"From this very point."

"What are the chances of that? It's as if the lion had figured out exactly where Lark would run into his assailants."

The reasoning was circular, but it had suited the tracker just fine. "Yes. There is powerful magic at work here. That is why I must ask for a bonus of three-thousand bucks. Cash."

Sturgess had been outraged. "You're being paid for your services by Barney Sewell! And handsomely, I'll bet!"

Wally Cheechoo had shed his backpack, set aside his rifle, and sat down on the ground cross-legged. "Like the paramedic says, they're about five hours ahead of us. You sure could use my aboriginal wisdom." He'd then stared straight ahead and mumbled some incantation to himself.

Grumbling, and cursing under his breath, Sturgess had put in a call to his detective inspector. "Yes, yes, yes," the detective inspector had replied. "Pay the bloody redskin whatever he wants. This is the case of a lifetime. One of global import!"

And so it had transpired, in the late afternoon of the day after Marvin and June Hamilton's twilight of twilights, that Detectives-Sergeant Bill Sturgess and Arthur Laidlaw had set out on the southwesterly trail of the killer lion and assorted human assassins in the expert company of Wally Cheechoo.

In accordance with the Cree woodsman's instructions, the small Ontario Provincial Police helicopter carrying two snipers had flown ahead of them on a southwesterly bearing while the paramedics' chopper returned Lark Alisappi's remains to civilization.

The OPP officers had been airborne just long enough to begin worrying about their fuel supply when they'd spotted a group of three men and four dogs at a distance of a quarter of a mile, and from an altitude of two-thousand feet. As they'd flown in for a closer inspection, something completely unexpected had happened. The helicopter had exploded into flames and plunged into the dense forest below. The pilot had never even had a chance to radio in their discovery.

"Nice shot," Rhett Anthony had drawled.

Antanas Sruoga had patted his rocket launcher affectionately. "Ha! I cannot take much credit of a personal nature. With this device I am able to bring down a B-52."

The loss of the helicopter and its crew had proven to be a major distraction for Detective Inspector Booth Rawlins of the OPP, Thunder Bay Regional Headquarters. By the time a search party had been mounted, another helicopter had been secured, and the charred, diminished remains of the three constables had been recovered, Sturgess's party was even further behind I-árishóni and Lark's killers.

Detective Inspector Rawlins had seriously considered calling in outside forces, but the old frontier spirit had prevailed. Detective-Sergeant Sturgess would get the job done. "You stupid fuck," he'd said to Sturgess in a voice brimming with professional regard. "How could you not see the chopper go down? You cost the search party umpteen hours!"

Sturgess had been dumbfounded. Wally Cheechoo, who'd been standing next to him, had heard all. He was a bit more sanguine. Grabbing the radio, he'd purred into it, "How, Great White Chief. This is Wally Cheechoo, Injun tracker. You, Detective Inspector Rawlins, are a flaming asshole — that's a white man's expression. You also have smoke signals rising from your asshole that say Wally Cheechoo deserves two thousand more bucks for this dangerous trek — that's an aboriginal person's expression. Oh … one more thing. You go north from just about any point in this fine country of ours and the chances are ninety-nine out of a hundred that it'll be just you and the birds and the bees and the bears. But you or something like, say, a lion go south and … well, that's another bit of aboriginal wisdom, and I give it to you for free. But there's a good chance it's gonna be someone else who winds up paying for it, y'know?"

Detective Inspector Booth Rawlins had hung up in a snit. He didn't like recriminations, especially from some semiliterate Indian.

Sunset Country, Ontario. September 11, 2006. Sunset Country, in Northwest Ontario, is a vast tourist area bordered by the American state of Minnesota, the Canadian province of Manitoba, and an imaginary line that shoots due north from Thunder Bay, which lies on the northwest shore of Lake Superior. It's roughly sixty-thousand square miles of small, pristine lakes and dense forest, blessed with a superabundance of fish and game.

Fishermen flock there for the walleye, trout, and pickerel; the hunters arrive to bag moose, deer, and black bears; the hikers, campers, bird watchers, photographers, and aquatic types are attracted by the charms of a relatively unspoiled wilderness.

Ignace is a town of sixteen hundred in the heart of Sunset Country, at the junction of the Trans Canada Highway and Route 599, on the eastern shore of Agimac Lake. It's one of twenty or so towns in the region, all of which conspire to boost the count of campgrounds, lodges, and souvenir shops. At one such campground, Pickerel Pete's Campground and RV Dock, Pete Murdoch's twenty-six-year-old daughter, Layla, was scrubbing down one of the "Full Service Deluxe Toilets" while her spirited eight-year-old son, Robin, captured and tormented frogs in the nearby stream. As she mopped the floor, Layla kept a watchful eye on Robin. She'd heard about the slaughter of that old American couple at Caribou Lake three evenings earlier, and although the Aurora Lodge was a good one hundred and fifty miles away through some pretty dense forest, she was still skittish. There'd been no official word on what had killed them, but she'd heard through the grapevine that their bodies had been dismembered. To her and the good folks in the area, that meant an outsized black bear. And such animals could cover that distance in twenty-four hours. She did the arithmetic easily, for her talents were being wasted sloshing down washrooms: just over six miles an hour. The speed of an average man running lazily.

"Robin! What in hell are you doing!"

"I learned about it in school yesterday."

She grabbed the frog from Robin's hand, removed the lit cigarette from its gullet, and tossed the creature back into the stream. She then cuffed the back of her son's head with the palm of her hand.

"Ow!" he whined pitiably. "And it's true! Miss Miller read us a poem called 'The Smoking Frog,' and I just wanted to see if it would die the way the poem said!"

"I know that poem, you little prick. Robert Service. An old-time Canadian guy. It's all about the cruelty of fate, but you're not fate and you've no right being cruel to helpless little animals. And I'm sure Miss Miller would be really pissed if she heard about this! Which she's *going* to, by the way!"

Wailing at the top of his lungs, Robin scrabbled across the parking lot and into the office cum home, a large wooden structure shaped like a teepee. *Well, at least the little bugger's indoors*, she thought to herself. Then she wondered where Robin had gotten the cigarette and shrugged hopelessly. Kids these days.

She resumed her mopping, dreaming about getting out of Ignace and down to Toronto for a real job and a real apartment like other girls — make that women — her age. "Ignorance," she'd nicknamed her hometown, and was it ever appropriate. And her having to watch all these rich, educated people from the big city tramping around her patch like Gulliver around Lilliput, talking down to her as if she were mute and slightly retarded. Huh. Maybe she *was* retarded for staying here. But then she thought of Daddy. Who'd watch out for him, Ol' Pickerel Pete, the town lush himself, who at this very moment was five miles down the 599 and in the Ignace Tavern, over on Nash Street, pouring back Moosehead, chowing down on Buffalo wings, and regaling the hunters (the summer crowd was largely gone) with tales of such self-regard that Davy Crockett would have blushed? Ol' Pickerel Pete kilt him a b'ar when *he* was only two. Oh hell, make it *Pickled* Pete, like that smirking lummox of a fishing guide, Corey Farrow, liked to call him.

Layla stopped to mop her brow with her apron. It had been a blistering day, nearly eighty-five in the shade, and even though the sun was getting low in the sky it was still close to a hundred in the washroom. She stood there for a few moments, trying to feel some pride in the gleaming fixtures and the shiny floor, when she suddenly got a funny feeling. As if she were not alone.

"Robin, back to the house with you."

Robin did not answer.

"I'll count to three, you evil little brat, and if you're still there when I turn around, there'll be no chips with your hot dogs tonight. One ... two ... three ... oh, dear God."

The lion. After having led his pursuers along an imponderably circuitous route, he was but ten feet from her. Among other things — actually many other things, including the fact that he seemed the size of a pickup truck — she didn't like it that his tail was swishing feverishly from side to side. She lunged into the bathroom and locked the door behind her. There was a small window at eye level, but she dared not look through it. Instead, she cowered and whimpered in the shower stall, with the shower curtain wrapped tightly about her ... until she remembered Robin. Omigod. What if he'd left the door to the house open, as he so often did? She rushed to the window. Omigod! The door *was* open, and the beast was headed straight for it! "Robin! Robin! Lock the door! Quickly!"

Robin came to the door. I-árishóni was halfway across the parking lot, no more than forty feet from her son. "Lock the door, Robin! Now!"

But the boy stood in the doorway, transfixed. He couldn't even blink. Layla shrieked from the window. "Help! help!"

The only acknowledgment she got was from the lion, who looked briefly over his shoulder before continuing across the parking lot. His leisurely pace had put him within fifteen feet of her son. Bloody hell. All day long the hunters swaggered back and forth waving their high-powered artillery, but where were they when you needed them, when there was a target more worthy than their own feet? She flung open the door and raced to within three yards of the animal. "Na na na na, pooh pooh," she went, in a taunting, singsong voice.

I-árishóni stopped in his tracks and slowly swung around to face her. Layla's first thought was that she'd never seen such a magnificent animal in all her life, never been exposed to such a powerful life force. Her second thought was ... what should she do next?

There was a momentary standoff, of sorts. He contemplated her. She contemplated eternity. But then her maternal instincts gathered her up, and she gathered up her thoughts, and in a wide arc she slowly and steadily inched her way around the animal until she was only five feet from the doorway. Then she dove for it, forcefully pushing the inert Robin backward into the house. But in the instant that she'd accelerated, the great cat had leapt the fifteen feet to the doorway and clamped his massive mouth shut over her belt and the seat of her jeans. His upper fangs raked her lower back but she did not feel anything. Filled with both terror and resolve, Layla just managed to grab the handle and pull the door shut as I-árishóni backed into the parking lot with her dangling helplessly from his mouth, two feet clear of the ground. He then set her down and began to bat her back and forth, as if he were a common housecat worrying a wounded bird. She reflexively curled herself up into a ball with her hands covering her head, but that did not substantially mitigate the pounding she was taking. Although it prevented her from sustaining broken limbs, she still felt as if she were being pulverized by a rock slide.

What thinking she could manage was rather bleak. Even if the monster didn't use his talons or fangs, she knew it was only a matter of minutes before her internal organs began to fail. She recited a quick prayer aloud, asking God to watch over Robin and her father for her, then determined that she would try to crawl away. What did she have to lose?

Suddenly, the lion left her choking in the dust and gravel and whirled around. He'd detected the sound of an approaching vehicle. During the next thirty seconds he stood at alert while a bruised and battered Layla managed to crawl all of ten feet away from him and toward the house. A pickup truck roared into the parking lot and slammed to a full stop. It was Layla's father. When the cloud of dust had lifted and an inebriated Pickerel Pete had fathomed what was happening, he flung himself out of his truck with his hunting rifle in the firing position. Forty feet separated man and beast.

In a quavering voice, Murdoch asked, "Are you all right, Honey?"

Layla could not answer. Even if here ears had not been not ringing and she'd been able to hear, she could not have spoken. She was thoroughly winded and her lungs were burning.

The weapon Pete Murdoch was holding so shakily was a lever-action Marlin 336 SS, chambered for .30-30 Winchester cartridges. The Marlin, with its distinctive stainless steel barrelled action, is ideal for deep woods hunting insofar as its lever action allows the shooter to get off a quick second shot — something that's a distinct advantage when hunting at close range, which Pete desperately needed. And the .30-30 bullets, while most appropriate for deer, can stop bigger game provided the shot is well placed. Pickerel Pete knew this and played for time. He had to set up the perfect kill shot.

Unfortunately for Pickerel Pete, his 336 SS was fitted with a 1-4x scope. While of low power, it was still far too powerful for the forty feet that separated him from the lion. As a matter of fact, *any* scope would have been too powerful to track such a close and fast-moving target, just as any microscope would be too powerful to track the progress of an ant.

And a close and fast-moving target was what Pete Murdoch suddenly had on his hands. Few animals will sit still and watch stupidly as a hunter sets up for that perfect shot. Even those creatures unfamiliar with firearms generally recognize pointing as a hostile act. I-árishóni was upon Pickerel Pete while he was still peering through his scope, trying to get a fix on his heart. Murdoch was just squeezing off a shot as the lion bowled him over with the momentum of a freight train and thoroughly eviscerated him. He was still holding his Marlin 336 SS as I-árishóni's jaws clamped shut on his neck and separated his head from his body.

As the lion loped into the bush and out of sight, young Robin emerged from the teepee-shaped house and rushed to his mother's side. "I'm all right, Sweetie," she gasped. "See to Granddad."

Robin sprinted over to his grandfather's side, but it was not to see to him. He'd already seen events unfolding from the second-storey window and was done with the vomiting. Robin extricated the rifle from a hand in cadaveric spasm and defiantly emptied the magazine into the air. He then wrapped himself in his dead mother's arms and stayed there, trembling, until the first of the hunters returned from town.

Staff Sergeant Ed Whitfield had raced along the Trans Canada Highway from Dryden, some fifty miles to the west of Ignace, and was staring down at the remains of Pickerel Pete Murdoch. He'd taken a statement from the boy before handing him off to the nice, middle-aged lady from social services, Gwen Forsythe, and Layla's body had been removed to the District General Hospital in Dryden. Clem Brown, the Minnesota man who'd first stumbled upon the carnage, stood beside him.

Brown said, "You believe the boy about the lion?"

"Sure do. Look at this damage. Look at those paw prints. Plus, I've been in contact with Detective-Sergeant Bill Sturgess from Thunder Bay. He confirmed."

"What about your commanding officer?"

Staff Sergeant Whitfield snorted in contempt. "You don't need to hear my two bits about him. He's already up to his eyeballs in shit. Even as we speak, the deputy commissioner is winging his way over here from Central Headquarters in Orillia. And he's got a bigwig RCMP guy with him, too."

It is uncommon, perhaps even unheard of, for a policeman to discuss internal affairs with a member of the great unwashed public. But Staff Sergeant Ed Whitfield was miffed in the extreme. That egomaniacal prick, Detective Inspector Booth Rawlins, had cut him out of the action on his own turf. His very own turf! He'd been almost the last to find out there was a killer lion running loose around Ignace. Even this American boob had known about it before he had! "I knew ol' Pickerel Pete here pretty well," he seethed. "It was him taught me how to fish for lake trout. And the girl, I knew her pretty well, also. She wasn't too far behind me in school."

Sergeant Whitfield's anger very quickly melted into tender sadness. He brushed away a tear.

"Uh … when I think about it," said Clem Brown quietly, "a lion tromping around these woods is every bit as weird as if it was an elephant. Any idea where he came from?"

"Detective-Sergeant Sturgess has a tracking team working its way backward from Caribou Lake. Last he heard from them, they were headed deep into the bush in a northwestern direction. He's also had a team set down on this small lake a few hundred miles northeast of there, where some American hunters killed their guide over the alleged sighting of the lion. And that tracking team that just headed off northeast from here? They'll be intercepting some individuals who killed a Cree guide near Caribou Lake and then played bloody havoc with the team that was trailing them from Caribou Lake to here. Lost three officers and a chopper, there. Ah, but I shouldn't be telling you any of this."

"It's okay. I'm a retired cop. Sheriff's office in St. Louis County, out of Hibbing, Minnesota."

"Ah. I was wondering how you could stand to look at this." Ed Whitfield broke down and began to sob. "I went out with her a few times. Was planning on taking her to the movies in Dryden sometime next week. A real nice girl. Pretty, y'know?" Sergeant Whitfield was now weeping on

352

Clem Brown's shoulder, while Brown gently and unselfconsciously patted his back with both hands.

"Well, here come the parameds," said Whitfield as he disengaged from the older man. "They'll be wanting Pickerel Pete, and I reckon they can have him now. And the dog teams are straining at their leashes. Gotta go."

The paramedical van backed up to within feet of Pete Murdoch's tattered corpse. After a brief debate over whether to use one or two stretchers for Murdoch's remains, they settled on one and loaded him up.

Sergeant Whitfield said to the critical care paramedic in a beseeching voice, "I don't suppose you've heard anything about the girl?"

"Meaning did she come back to life? Afraid not."

The paramedic slammed the doors shut and off went the truck.

"You'll catch him soon," opined the American, kicking his big booted foot at the gravel. "They figure it was less than ninety minutes ago he was here, right?"

"Right."

"And then you'll feel a whole lot better, right?"

"Wrong. Male lions do pretty much only three things. They feed, they fuck, and they fight. That's what makes them the most dangerous critters of all. He was just doing what lions do, that's all. I'll feel a whole lot better when we get the people who put him here, and only then."

"He connected with all that animal stuff in the news?"

"As an ex-cop, you can keep my answer to yourself?"

"You betcha."

Sergeant Whitfield hesitated, but only for a moment. He was warming to the American despite his prejudices, and was eager to talk. "That's what I think. And that's what the brass is thinking, too. It's looking more and more like a problem that was made in Canada, and a problem that will be solved in Canada."

"Yep, I reckon so. Welcome to the bigs, Sergeant." Clem Brown kicked at the ground again as he surveyed the gallon of blood that seeped into the gravel. "Nature's a bitch, isn't it? It ain't Bambi out there. You bite it, and it'll bite you right back. With interest."

CHAPTER FORTY

Plymouth, Devon. September 11–12, 2006. It was five o'clock in the afternoon, just three-and-a-half hours after Hudson's surgery. He'd been lucky in the extreme. The bullet had gone clean through him, missing his heart, lungs, spine, and all of the great blood vessels. The CO19 medic in the helicopter had not been able to staunch the bleeding, but he'd given Hudson a blood transfusion and that had been enough to sustain him for the twenty minutes it took to get him onto the operating table at Derriford Hospital in Plymouth. He was now lying in a hospital bed while Irina sat at his side.

"One cracked rib," she said, shaking her head in wonderment. "Even then, the slug neither tumbled nor fragmented. Do you have any idea how lucky you are?"

"You'll pardon me if I don't celebrate, won't you? I feel like there's an eight-hundred-pound gorilla in the room, and that he's sitting right on my chest."

"Speaking of eight-hundred-pound gorillas, you said in the chopper that you had a plan concerning Jason Conrad. What is it?"

"I said that?"

Irina nodded solemnly.

"I must have been delirious. People in my condition get that way, you know."

"A likely explanation, but it's more probable you simply didn't want to let Inspector Duggan in on our little escapade."

"I'm a very sick man, Irina. Don't ask me to fess up."

"It shouldn't be too difficult, considering I share your sentiments."

"You do?"

"I do. But I'd like to hear that your reasons for doing so are noble."

"As noble as yours?"

"You said it. Not me."

Hudson expended considerable time and energy in propping himself up on one elbow. It was an eminently painful exercise, but it was the lesser of two agonies.

"Well?"

Hudson sighed heavily. It sounded like winter's first gasp over the tundra. "I could never be as noble as you, Irina. No one could. Uh … are you trying to make me feel shitty?"

"I believe that when people do something, they should be clear about why they're doing it. That's all."

"That's all?"

"Yes. That's all."

"Oh, all right then. I want to crack the case of the century — with you, of course. I want even more fame than I have now. I want to be covered in glory. I want men to crown me with laurel leaves and women to bestrew my path with rose petals. I want a promotion. I want more pay. I want to be made lieutenant-detective. I want Stan Robertson's job."

"Anything else?"

"Is there anything else?"

"Think."

"Ah … yes … one thing. I want to find Sergeant Jerome Perron's killer. He was a brother. And so, in his own little way, was Wonder Pooch."

Irina leaned over Hudson. She was about to kiss him approvingly on the cheek when his left hand suddenly cradled her head and guided her lips toward his. Irina balked for the count of three, as if about to step onto a bed of coals, but then yielded to the heat with a vengeance. While his tongue hungrily explored her mouth, she caressed it with her own. Then, with her eyes shut tight, her hands feverishly explored his face, slid down to his neck, and dug their nails into his shoulders. His hand slipped down toward the small of her back and drew her closer to him. As soon as he became aware that her hips were undulating, his hand was all over her haunches, alternately squeezing and stroking them. As they continued kissing deeply, each one trying to devour the other, Hudson pulled her down onto the bed so that she was lying beside him.

It was then that a hot and extremely bothered Irina rediscovered propriety. Or, rather, it rediscovered her. "Stop, Athol, this won't do."

"Oh, no? Maybe this will." He reached under her skirt, ravenously rubbed her bare thigh, then plunged his index finger into her vagina.

"No," she protested, as she extracted the intrusive finger, "this is not how I wanted it to be."

"But I love you, Irina, and I want you now. You're the most beautiful, desirable woman I've ever seen."

"I'd pictured this happening in a somewhat more romantic setting, not a hospital stinking of rubbing alcohol and you so covered in bandages you look like a mummy — Athol Hudson, what on Earth are you doing!"

While gazing into her fathomless grey eyes, he was casually licking the virtuosic index finger. "Getting to know you a little bit better, that's all. Yum. A bit like saltwater taffy."

She yanked his finger from his mouth. "How on Earth can I be expected to kiss you, knowing where that digit has been!"

"You talked about a romantic setting," he said hopefully as he drew her even closer and bathed in her breath. "So you saw this as inevitable?"

"Men are so stupid. I've been sending out enough signals to guide the space shuttle home."

"Our little adventure at Upton House has persuaded me that there's never a second to lose. Bugger the romantic setting. I want to be so deep inside you that it takes a backhoe to dig me out."

"Now, that's more like it," Irina muttered, somewhat derisively. "What could be more romantic than talking about tractors at a time like this? Here. Let me show you real romance!"

She leapt from the bed, pulled down the blinds, then turned off the rancid fluorescent overheads. And in the dim, gauzy light of the room, and the lambent light of Hudson's desire, she softly hummed Ravel's *Boléro* in a throaty voice as first her skirt and then her panties slithered to her ankles. Naked from the waist down, she slowly vamped her way over to the bedside and whispered seductively in Hudson's ear, "The rest, I leave to you. I want to be ravished."

Hudson was ready to oblige, but she forced his head down with her right hand so that he was flat on his back, then stroked his straining manhood. "But we still have to think about your condition, don't we? So leave the heavy lifting to me."

With that, she climbed back up onto the bed and lowered herself onto him. The slow, rhythmic grinding of her hips satisfied every carnal impulse Hudson had ever known, and by the time she was gasping, he was frantically fondling her large, well-formed breasts and on the brink of cataclysmic eruption. Happily for Irina, he was in enough pain and there was enough residual anesthetic in his system to prolong the inevitable. Somewhat noisily, they climaxed together. As one, they soared to unexplored heights of earthly ecstasy; as one they sank back down to a heavenly communion.

Buried under a mound of sheets, pillows, and blankets, they were still exchanging sweaty declarations of love when they heard a throat being cleared. Not just any throat, but the throat of Detective Chief Inspector Leopold Duggan of the London Metropolitan Police. He stood stock-still just inside the door, calmly twirling the tip of his mustache.

"Well, well," he said with some amusement, "they say Canadians are a bloodless lot. How wrong they are. There's obviously been enough blood pumped in here to revive a woolly mammoth."

Inspector Duggan was under the impression that he had Irina and Hudson at a psychological disadvantage. After all, humiliation leads to self-abnegation, which leads to a propitiating tongue. And for a brief moment, Irina *was* totally aghast. That soon ended, however, and so too did Duggan's windfall. While Hudson cringed in mortification under the blanket, Irina wrapped herself in a sheet, leapt from the bed, and stood toe to toe with Duggan, her free fist balled up in fury. "Just how long have you been standing here, you pervert!"

"It's your own fault," replied Duggan with great indignation. "The door wasn't locked."

"There is no bloody lock on the door! Haven't you ever heard of knocking?"

"I did knock!"

"Well, I didn't hear it, did I?"

"And I'm to blame for that?"

"You don't enter until someone says you can. Here, let me show you how it works." Irina shoved Duggan out the door and slammed it in his face. "Now knock!"

Duggan knocked.

"Fuck off! I'm busy!"

The voice from the other side of the door was surpassingly feeble. "I say ... I was rather hoping we could have a little chat."

Irina did not respond. She was flat on the floor, having fainted from embarrassment.

Hudson had gotten out of bed and helped Irina to her feet. It had been a painful exercise, for Irina was no mere slip of a girl, but it was nothing compared to his previous exertions.

There was no awkwardness between them as she now sat at his bedside. To be sure, there was a great deal of embarrassed tittering as they relived the excruciating details of the Duggan episode, but they soon got over that and settled into a tender coexistence, often punctuated by soft caresses and gentle kisses. At one point, Irina jammed the door with a chair and once again straddled the supine Hudson for a toe-curling round. There was no mention of the case. They traded autobiographical lore and probed each other for all kinds of emotions and insights, the safeguard of which is the raison d'être of love. By nine o'clock they'd fallen sleep in each others' arms, totally drained by both the soaring highs and hellish lows of the day.

At midnight, there was a sharp rapping at the door. Utterly befogged, Irina made her way to the door. It couldn't be the nurse, because she would have barged right in. "Who is it?"

"Leopold Duggan."

She opened the door a crack.

"I came straight over," said Duggan.

"Given that you probably sleep hanging upside down, I don't doubt that you have few problems negotiating the blackest night."

"I will let that pass, dear lady, because unless you've been watching the telly, gratitude will soon supersede your pique."

Irina remorsefully swung the door open wide and admitted the lanky policeman. That she and Hudson owed him their lives suddenly loomed large. "I apologize for my remark, Inspector. That was just plain bitchy. Do come in. I'll wake up Hudson. You're not the type to waste anyone's time."

Suitably mollified, Duggan took the seat next to the TV while Irina roused Hudson. "The telly is stone cold. And your BlackBerry isn't flashing. You don't know, then."

Irina turned on first the television and then her BlackBerry. "Know what?"

"In some wild little corner of your country — northwest Ontario, to be precise — an African lion has been busy killing people. At least four, so far. It just came on CNN, BBC television, and the BBC World Service. Even Al Jazeera, actually."

"Has anybody made the connection?" asked Irina.

"So far, it seems, no. Oh, with the exception of yours truly, of course. In fact, I'd be so bold as to suggest that I believe your man is a Canadian."

Hudson groggily said, "Does that follow?"

"To a detective, I would have to say it does. An operation on the scale of your suspect's would entail limitless legalities, massive infrastructure, monumental expenditures, and a comfort level one can find only in one's own backyard. So, would you care to tell me who'd be your main suspect? As I may have mentioned before, I'd be a tremendous asset."

"Not on our turf, you wouldn't," a bleary Hudson blurted out.

Irina was struck dumb, but Duggan wasn't. "So I'm right, then. Mr. X *is* a Canuck. Huh ... how many people would guess that Canadians could think on such a scale? At any rate, thank you, Sergeant Hudson."

"All right then, Inspector," Irina muttered woefully after throwing a sharp look in her partner's direction, "that person is Canadian. But the sergeant's question still stands. Of what use would you be over there?"

Detective Chief Inspector Leopold Duggan of the London Metropolitan Police rose from his chair and strode over to the window. He parted the blind and peered out, as if he could unravel the mysteries of the night. "Has it not occurred to you to wonder why it is my force, and my force alone, which has embarked upon this voyage of discovery with you? Haven't you wondered about the whereabouts of the FBI, the CIA, MI6, Mossad, and the DST, just to name a few?"

Irina smiled broadly. "No, never! You've actually been laying false trails?"

Leopold Duggan smoothed his black mustache and then the lapels of his svelte Bond Street suit as if primping for a society page photograph. "I only asked if you'd wondered, Sergeant Drach. I never promised any revelations."

Irina sat in her chair and with one eye watched the television for a few moments. In a press conference interspersed with stock footage of a male African lion sleeping, then roaring, then mounting a lioness, the deputy commissioner of the Ontario Provincial Police was holding forth with considerable brass, trying to describe the actions and motives of one Detective Inspector Booth Rawlins without actually taking responsibility for the force's grievous error in judgment.

With her other eye, Irina was scrolling through the long, long list of forwarded emails on her BlackBerry.

"Well?"

It was Duggan, flashing his death's head grin.

"One moment, Inspector. Please. This is a major decision."

As if to underline her words in the most orphic manner possible, she said to Hudson, "This might be interesting. Raja Chadwani. Came in just minutes ago."

Hudson was no longer jealous of Chadwani. In fact, he was feeling quite charitable — even pitying — toward all men who'd never had the honour of having Irina Drach. "What's our man in Rio have to say?"

Irina laughed out loud, then read, "Esteemed brothers-in-arms Drach and Hudson, one of which is in reality a sister. I am still in Rio de Janeiro, I am still at the Copacabana Palace and I am still ascertaining resourceful ways to spend the money of my estimable benefactor, Ashok Gupta. Take, for example, my meeting with a certain lady of the night whose number was given me by a certain concierge who shall go unnamed. I will not pretend that I did not avail myself of her professional services late this afternoon, for then you would have no choice but to think me desultory in my investigative responsibilities. To whit: she is by far the most expensive hookah I have sampled here, and moves in only the highest circles. Do you see my cunning? I certainly do. When I had satisfied her every desire, I made calculated conversation with her as I had with the many others. 'Who is the richest man you have ever serviced?' I asked her. 'All the richest,' she replied. 'Richer even than I?' I asked. 'Ha,' she replied saucily and indiscreetly. 'There is one so rich he makes you and all the others seem like street urchins. That one is so rich he does not even come to me himself, but sends his servant.' 'As names are not asked for nor given in your business, how do you know this man was his servant?' I cannily asked. 'He was a short black man who sweated like a pig,' she replied. 'Most boastful, too. He had only just tasted my delights when I knew him to be the assistant of the world's richest man, Jason Conrad. Surely you know of Jason Conrad?' 'Yes,' I replied with great guile. 'I have had dealings with him.'

"And then, fellow guardians of law and morality, her tongue — loosened no doubt by my prowess — wagged even more. She told me that this black man, a Nigerian, had taken a call from Jason Conrad as they were dressing. She is certain it was he because the African referred to him as 'Mr. Conrad.' 'Jason Conrad was apparently very concerned about securing the world's greatest race horse,' she tattled. 'The black man assured the person to whom he was speaking that a team had already been assembled and that they would not fail to capture Zarathustra in the following month. I remember the name of the horse well because who has not thrilled at his exploits?' she told me gleefully. 'And also, I have a client who is known to me by that very name. Mr. Zarathustra is given to peccadilloes which are beyond the imagination of ordinary mortals, and he pays very well for those pleasures.'

"Having fulfilled her obligations, and been remunerated generously, she left, but there I did not let matters rest. In the tradition of all superior detectives, I shadowed her. I now know where she lives and, from her exquisitely wrought mail box, her very name. That is all for now. Your humble colleague, Raja Chadwani. P.S. Her name is Maria Elena Battista and she lives at 12 Avenista Garcia de Avila, a fantastical condo in the Ipanema district."

"Well," murmured Leopold Duggan, smoothing down his cowlick, "Bozo the Clown has just built a particle accelerator in his backyard."

Irina said, "I'm sure he's more circumspect in his own language, Inspector."

Duggan was taken aback by Irina's brusqueness. "Yes, quite … well, at any rate, I'm honoured and grateful that you've shared all this with me. The question now is what can I do to help? I am at your service."

Hudson, who'd been lying with his face buried in his pillow, partly out of a persistent embarrassment, suddenly began to sing. "The girl from Ipanema, she just doesn't see, she looks straight ahead, not at he … nor at anyone else."

Duggan arched his patrician eyebrows. "Meaning what, old chap?"

"Meaning that girl needs protection," said Irina. "The kind that only you can provide, Inspector. The kind you extended to us."

"Yes. I, and half my squad, not to mention CO19. Oh, and a budget that should put the old kibosh on our Christmas bash."

Irina slithered over to where Duggan was seated, planted her hands on the armrests of his chair, and leaned so far forward that his cowlick became quite erect. Duggan was not oblivious to Irina's charms, and she knew it. "It seems to me that just you and a couple of others would be more than equal to the task, Inspector. And when the time is right, you will escort her out of Argentina and into Canada, where we'll be entering our case against him."

Duggan had hoped to work cheek by jowl with Irina, but just pleasing her would do in a pinch. "Well … I asked how I could help, didn't I? Right, then. I'll get back to London tonight and on to South America tomorrow. Just give me this Chadwani chap's coordinates, and I'll be off."

Hudson said to Irina, in a hopeful tone, "You said Conrad called while we were on our way over here in the chopper. Asking how we were, of all things. Doesn't that constitute an admission that the attack dogs who nearly killed us both were his?"

"It strengthens our suspicions against him," replied Duggan in his intractably dulcet voice. "But it does nothing to strengthen the case against him. He might as well have been asking about the weather."

"But the timing of the call?"

"Coincidence is just a feeble form of circumstantial evidence."

Irina's BlackBerry trilled. "Hm. Here's Chadwani again, this time by voice. Must be something big. Hello, Raja?"

Inspector Raja Chadwani of the Kullu District Police sounded terrible, as if his mother had died. Worse, actually, since his mother had been dead for some years and he'd gotten rather used to the fact. "Aiieee-yay-yay! Oy vey!" (The Jewish impact on Manali culture). "The most atrocious event imaginable! Hello? Sergeant Drach? Are you there?"

"I'm listening, Mr. Chadwani."

"*Inspector* Chadwani, please. Oy vey! Aiieee-yay-yay! A most unfortunate and devastating circumstance! Maria Elena Battista has died! Before my very eyes! Roadkill!" (The North American impact on Manali culture).

"Slow down, Raja, and tell me exactly what happened."

"Inspector Chadwani, *please*. And here are the facts: She was on her way to the Sofitel Hotel on Ipanema Beach when she was run down by a lorry as she was removing herself from the taxi. The lorry passed close to the taxi and tore off the door and dragged her body one-hundred feet in its underthings. And the driver did not stop but continued out of sight! I immediately gave chase in my own taxi but he disappeared. Poof! Just as he appeared! Oh, no! Oy vey ismir! It is my fault she is dead! They, that … that organization … that dastardly organization … they knew I was on the case of Jonathan Diamond and Dhamaki the yak, and they followed me here, and when I made contacts with Maria Elena, they just knew information had changed hands!"

"Calm down, Inspector Chadwani. Did you get the plate number?"

"Of the lorry?"

"Certainly not that of your breakfast."

"Yes, yes! Even in the evening light. Along the top, RJ Rio de Janeiro. KQS 8499 at bottom."

"Write these down, Inspector Duggan. Along the top, RJ Rio de Janeiro. KQS 8499 along the bottom. Now listen carefully, Inspector Chadwani. Where are you presently?"

"I am at the corner of Avenista Atlantica and Joaquim Nabuco, where lies her crumpled and torn body. I have retched at the sight, and now I and my taxi driver are about to give our accounts of this malodorous event!"

"Are you in the company of the constables, yet?"

"Ho! No! We have not yet stepped forward."

"Then don't. Slip away immediately and do not return to your hotel. Take a series of cabs, changing over at stoplights, and go to a congested part of town. You're next on their list, Inspector, so don't show your face to anyone but Inspector Leopold Duggan, a tall, dark, and handsome man with a mustache and a thick British accent. He'll be there in half a day and will contact you."

"Yes, yes —"

Irina heard a sound not unlike that of a five-pound steak flung hard upon the butcher's block, then a fearful clattering and rustling. "Inspector Chadwani ... Raja ... Raja?"

His phone had obviously hit the pavement. She held her breath as long as she held the line. At length someone began bellowing into Chadwani's phone. Asking questions, demanding answers.

Irina was at a loss. "Uh ... *no hablo Español* ... *Señor* —"

"*Inglês?*"

"*Ah ... por favor?*"

"Yes, Senhora. You mean to say *eu não falo o Português*. We speak Portuguese, here. This is Brazil, not the execrable Argentina, and this is Constable José da Silva of the *Polícias* Rio de Janeiro. And you are?"

"What's happened to my cousin? What's happened to my cousin?"

"Shot, Senhora. In the head. Dead. *Inoperante.*"

"Are you sure he's dead?"

"*Está inoperante!* His *cérebro* is on the street very much. Pieces here, pieces there. *Você compreende?*"

"What about the person who shot him? Is he in custody?"

"He? He? You maybe know something?"

"It's just natural to say that. You know, like saying 'you're an asshole' would be perfectly natural."

Constable da Silva laughed, after a fashion. "Ah. The Senhora *Inglesa* makes a joke. *Você é uma feminista,* ha-ha. But no one heard a gunshot. A silencer, eh? And we believe the bullet came by way of Avenista Atlantica, from the trees between the beach and the Sofitel. Now, you must come and identify this man and answer questions. *Imediatamente!*"

"I'll talk to your chief through channels. *Usted entiende?*"

"*Você compreende! Nao espanhol. Portuguese, por favor!*"

Irina hung up on Constable da Silva, then gave Duggan and Hudson a complete rundown of her phone conversations. "These days you take your bloody life in your hands on the streets of Rio, but this is a bit rich, isn't it?"

Hudson took Irina by the shoulders and mumbled consoling words, not only for her benefit but his own. He had been rapidly warming to the Indian policeman.

While Hudson was thus engaged, Irina began to feel spooked. Leopold Duggan was behind her yet she could not feel his presence. This man, who was such a vital force when face to face with her, simply dissolved into thin air when she had her back to him. There were no breathing sounds, nor small rustlings, nor air movements. Nothing. She was convinced that if she'd been facing a mirror, he'd have cast no reflection. She thought of her journey from London to Plymouth and on up to Upton House. All manner of agents, as well as an entire SWAT team and a medical team replete with ambulances and helicopters, had disappeared into the black hole that Leopold Duggan had conjured up.

"You're perfect," she said as she whirled about to face him.

"I've always rather suspected that," he chirped. "Nice that someone finally agrees with me."

"No, yes, no ... I mean you're the right person to go to Rio. You, more than any other, could track down these murderers."

"There's very little to go on, dear lady. A licence plate, probably fake or stolen, and police reports that will no doubt perfectly reflect the general disarray of the Rio force."

"You're right," she sighed. "Maybe it's hopeless."

"No, not hopeless. I was merely warning you that it may take more than a day."

"I knew I could count on you!"

"Ah ... are you sure you're just a sergeant, Mrs. Drach?"

"She's a woman," quipped Hudson. "All the dominion of a major-general combined with the guile of a Svengali."

Irina spun around to rap Hudson playfully on the head. When she turned back to Duggan, his laughter still resonated on the spot but the corporeal Duggan no longer occupied it.

"Humph! He never said goodbye."

"Maybe when you get to his age and level of experience, you get superstitious about goodbyes."

Irina sat next to Hudson once more. "Well, now. Since you're spinning out all these generalizations, you've obviously got your thinking cap on. How about suggesting our next step?"

"You're asking me?"

Irina smiled salaciously. "Why not? We are now having a relationship, and there can be no doubt you're the one wearing the pants."

Hudson smiled broadly. "Yes, we are having a relationship, aren't we? I like the sound of that. And I *love* the feeling of it. Come here."

Irina leaned forward and they kissed passionately for the better part of two minutes. While revelling in the taste of this magnificent woman, Hudson undid the two top buttons of her blouse, exposed her breasts, and rapaciously massaged them until the nipple were as red and firm as cherry gumdrops. At this point, a thoroughly flushed Irina withdrew and buttoned up her blouse. "I wish we could carry on like this forever, but we have a job to do and I aim to finish it. Work now, fuck our brains out later, okay? That's a promise."

Hudson lay back on his pillow and sighed in frustration. But his hunter's instinct was as powerful as Irina's drive to tidy up the universe, and he was soon propped back up on his elbow. "There's someone — actually several, but one in particular — who's been lusting after you almost as much as I have. You know that, eh?"

"I know that," she said primly.

"And you know who it is, don't you?"

"Of course."

"Irina, there's no way I would have suggested this before, mainly because I would have been too jealous and insecure —"

"But now that I've been bagged, so to speak —"

"Come now, Irina," Hudson said hotly. "You could see this coming because you're already there. And you told him you were going to call him back, anyway. So instead of tearing his head off, you'll be sweet. *That* should knock him off his game!"

"Oh, dear. I think we're having our first quarrel."

"Nonsense. We've had hundreds of them, before."

"*Our* first quarrel, lover. Not Athol Hudson and Irina Drach's."

"Look, Irina, you wanted to get back to work, and that's exactly what I'm doing. Must you be so … ambivalent?"

There was a long, uncomfortable silence. Neither looked at the other. But this was an intolerable situation, and two sets of eyes eventually sought each other out. With her eyes locked on Hudson's, Irina said, "I need this, Athol. I need this relationship to work. Are you following me?"

"Yes, I am. I love you, too, Irina."

Lips rapturously explored each other as if for the first time. When Irina and Hudson finally drew apart and gazed at each other in dizzying wonder, Hudson said, with great tenderness, "Promise me you won't let him get into your pants?"

Irina froze, then thawed long enough to slap him sharply across the face. She blew out of the room like an arctic storm, slamming the door behind her.

Hudson rubbed at his face in confusion. "What! Was it something I said?"

For a while after Jason Conrad returned from Lido to the main island of Venice, he forlornly wandered the narrow, winding streets, staring into the brackish waters of the canals and half expecting Chinua Amadi's bloated corpse to rise up from their depths. Haunted, and in need of the company of the multitudes, he gravitated back toward the Piazzetta and Piazza San Marco. There in the Procuraties, the low arcaded Renaissance buildings that ring the Piazza, he stopped for a coffee at the Caffè Florian, an establishment that dates back to 1720 and is perhaps the world's oldest continually operating coffee house. Unfortunately, he sat not only with the ghosts of illustrious former patrons such as Goethe, Casanova, Byron, Marcel Proust, and Charles Dickens, but that of Chinua Amadi as well. Cursing to himself, he fled the café and into the cramped and bustling commercial alleyways that radiate outward from the Procuraties. In the window of one of the many exclusive jewelry shops he spotted a diamond- and ruby-encrusted crucifix that went for sixty-thousand Euros, or roughly eighty-five-thousand American dollars. He was not unaware of the irony inherent in such an object, but he bought it anyway. The shopkeeper, recognizing him as the world's richest man, accepted a cheque, and for that Conrad was grateful. It spared him having to explain that the assistant who normally carried his cash for him had just been executed on his orders.

As he strolled by San Marco Basilica and around the Doge's Palace, he happened upon the Bridge of Sighs, the enclosed white limestone structure that spans the Palazzo canal and connects the prisons to the interrogation rooms of the Doge's Palace. Conrad thought back to the first time he'd ever seen the bridge. He'd been eleven years old and his mother was explaining that it had been so named by Lord Byron in recognition of the fact that prisoners on their way to the dungeons would stare out at the beauty of Venice, past the stone bars of the windows, and exhale remorsefully.

"It's not so big," young Conrad had complained.

His mother laughed. "Whatever made you think it would be big?"

"Why else would they call it the Bridge of Size?"

Mrs. Helena Conrad had enveloped him in her arms and the intoxicating scent of moonlit gardenias, exclaiming proudly, "My little man. Always thinking big."

Conrad chuckled to himself, then choked on the memory. One short year later, she was dead of pancreatic cancer.

He decided it was time to leave Venice. This preternaturally brooding city was no place for someone in his state of mind. Since the speedboat he'd retained was moored in the shadow of the Campanile, he was aboard within minutes and soon packing up his effects at the hotel on La Giudecca. He noted, with mixed feelings, that all traces of Chinua's existence but for his computer had already been erased.

With Conrad on board once more, the boat skirted the main island of Venice, raced and beat the vehicular traffic on the Ponte della Libertà, and deposited him at San Giuliano on the mainland. From there, a taxi sped him to Venice's Marco Polo Airport, where his Challenger 604 was ready and waiting. Within two hours, it had refuelled at Schiphol in Amsterdam, and by nine o'clock that evening, New York time, he was having dinner with Donald Trump at Le Bernardino in Manhattan.

When Conrad awoke the next morning, it was in his house on the beach in Southampton. This boxy, modular house on Meadow Lane was his place of sanctuary and contemplation. Designed in 1932 by Le Corbusier, its manageable size and purity of design made it a radical departure from the other multimillion-dollar homes along the strip. It was neither rambling nor covered in cedar shingles. Conrad loved his retreat's industrial simplicity, its eternal modernity and seamless functionality.

Nevertheless, Conrad had slept badly. To be sure, he'd been overtired from all his travelling, but his disquiet ran deeper than that. He missed the omnipresence, the infernal busyness of Chinua. While aboard his jet over the Atlantic, he'd already placed a call to his New York office, demanding they supply a secure and high-level replacement for Chinua, "who'd inexplicably decamped in Venice," but he just knew that the next assistant would not measure up. Chinua had not only relieved him of the grubby minutiae of daily business and life, but had reached a point where he could not only sense Conrad's moods but actually read his mind. That this latter talent led to Chinua's undoing did not escape Conrad, but he had to admit that the fat, sweaty little man had been perfect right up to the moment he'd developed a mind of his own.

He turned on the television. After the regularly scheduled lamentation over the whereabouts of Zarathustra, the horse of the century, and yet more clips of Sergeant Athol Hudson's pretty little mug, CNN got back to the unfolding drama of the African lion that had savaged select natives of Northern Ontario. The authorities hadn't yet caught or killed him, but the noose was tightening. It was only a matter of hours, perhaps a day at the most, before the killer cat was brought to bay. Conrad's heart sank at the thought of all those gun-toting yahoos closing in on that magnificent beast. His heart sank even further when the reporter breathlessly intoned that the party in which he was "imbedded," the one backtracking the lion's northwesterly trail, was moving along at the pace of a spooked deer. Conrad reckoned that he had two days in which to figure out a course of action.

As was his wont, he remained calm, and was settling into a rational assessment of his options when his BlackBerry sounded. His heart soared. The only people who had his cell number were the several dozen CEO's scattered around the world, and two particular individuals. As none of the CEO's would dare call him at such an hour on a Tuesday morning, and as it was too soon for the New York Office of Conrad Inc. to have found Chinua's replacement, it could only be one particular individual.

"Irina?"

"Sergeant Drach to you, Mr. Conrad. Especially after what you did to Sergeant Hudson."

"I don't know what you're talking about, Sergeant Drach, but I'd be most relieved to hear that he's recovering well."

"Well enough, thank you. I've no doubt he'll fare better than that lion of yours."

"Oh dear, you're in a bit of a snit this morning, aren't you?"

"It's no longer morning here in England. As if you didn't know where we were."

"Well, I hope you've found what you're looking for over there. Quite frankly, I've grown exceedingly bored of this animal business, and if I have to watch your partner's press conference one more time, I'll toss my shoe through the TV screen."

"Or you'll have one of your goons toss your Gucci loafer through the TV screen. Heaven forbid you should handle something that's actually touched the ground."

"Sergeant Drach — Irina, if I may be so bold — you didn't ring me up to hurl insults and slanderous accusations at me, I'm sure of that. Could it be — dare I hope — that you'd be interested in seeing me socially? For dinner, perhaps? One of my London-based concerns, Radler Brothers Financial Group, has a Boeing business jet, the BBJ1. Marble bathrooms, leather sofas, and swivel seats, master bedroom with a queen-sized bed, et cetera, et cetera, ad nauseum. It just happens to be in Plymouth today and it could have you here in time for dinner."

"Where's 'here?'"

"New York. Is there any other 'here?'"

"Maybe not, but as for *my* insignificant little 'here,' I don't remember mentioning I was in Plymouth."

"Oh, you're sharp," he said, without any hesitation. "It's one of the things I like best about you. But my phone gave me a readout of your area code, you see. 1752. And I should know it's Plymouth because I have a shipyard there that services Devon Dockyards, which just happens to be the largest naval base in Western Europe. So, you'll come?"

The suggestion was made whereby the Boeing would be ready for Irina in one hour's time. She would arrive at JFK at about five o'clock in the evening, New York time, and they'd see some sights before dining at Per Se.

"*Per Se?* I've read about that place. I certainly don't have clothes with me that would be appropriate!"

Conrad was charmed and relieved by her squeal of horror. He had begun to doubt that she could ever be a cop second and a woman first. "No problem. We'll go shopping. Saks Fifth Avenue. My treat."

"No. No charity."

"Charity? Never. It would be an investment on my part."

"An investment in my compliance?"

"An investment in my happiness, Irina. You've no idea how much I've been thinking of you."

"Won't the store be closed?"

"Not at that hour, I don't believe, but in any event I can easily arrange for the appropriate departments to stay open until you've found something that pleases you."

This was tempting. Irina pictured herself draped in a ruched satin gown by Jean Paul Gaultier, preferably in antique gold, with a nice little pair of oxblood Manolo Blahnik slingbacks and a matching Fendi bag. But no. A clear conflict of interest. And just what, by way of physical favours, would he expect in return? "Thanks, but no thanks, Mr. Conrad. Why don't we just go to Katz's Delicatessen and I can wear what I bring with me? That's where Meg Ryan did that famous fake orgasm scene in *When Harry Met Sally*, you know. Also, my New York friend Rhonda says the pastrami there beats Montreal's smoked meat. I'd like to see for myself."

Conrad chuckled to himself. How like a woman. She thought only of clothes, and — what, the ten or fifteen thousand they'd cost? — and yet it never entered her mind to consider how much it cost to operate the

Boeing. But what the hell. If she wanted a sandwich on the Lower East Side, then it was worth every penny of the eighteen thousand dollars an hour it took to get her there for it. Besides, anything that induced her to contemplate orgasm was just dandy by him. "As you wish. Katz's it is."

It was agreed that the Boeing pilot would phone her when he was leaving Heathrow, and that he would contact Conrad when he was two hours out of JFK. "I ... uh ... I won't be using the chauffeur this evening. I have two cars here in the Hamptons. A Bentley Continental GT and an Aston Martin Vanquish. Which ride would you prefer?"

"Oh dear, don't you have anything else?"

Conrad had completely missed the sarcasm in Irina's voice. "I can get whatever you fancy, Irina. A Ferrari, a Maserati, a Rolls Royce —"

"Which car is more fun to drive, Mr. Conrad? The Bentley or the Aston Martin?"

"Why, the Aston."

Irina did not want to be near a boy showing off his toy. "Fine. Then we'll take the Bentley. See you later, Mr. Conrad. I have to get ready for the trip, now."

As Irina stuffed her suitcase, Hudson said, "Good of Duggan to get our stuff down from Bude for us. Uh ... did Conrad mention what kind of Bentley and Aston Martin they were?"

"No, he did not," she replied as she stooped over and kissed him warmly. "And I don't care to know, either. I, um ... I'm afraid I have to go now, Athol."

"How about you jam the door and we have a proper farewell?"

This isn't fair, thought Irina as she lifted her skirt and knelt astride Hudson. Why must I leave the company of a man who needs me for that of someone who has everything?

Meanwhile, Jason Conrad was close to tearing his hair out in exasperation. What had he been thinking? His plate was already full. There wasn't room for yet another scrap, no matter how tasty. Since when did he let his hormones do the talking for him?

He sat motionless for a full two hours, reflecting upon his situation. Finally, he reached for his phone and dialed London. "This is JC Alpha, JC Omega, singular."

Like a sickly sweet perfume, obsequious bleating emanated from the earpiece.

"Never mind all that," snapped Conrad. "I want a package removed."

CHAPTER FORTY-ONE

Sunset Country, Ontario. September 12, 2006. At about the same time that a large hunting party set out from Ignace just ninety minutes behind I-árishóni, three more heavily armed teams were dispatched respectively from Dryden, Atikokan, and from the Rainy Lake Reserve. Dryden was northwest of Ignace, Atikokan was due south, and Rainy Lake was southwest. This comprised an area of roughly eighteen-hundred square miles. It might seem like a lot of room in which to manoeuvre, but with each mile that the hunting parties advanced in pincer-like formation, I-árishóni's range effectively shrank by sixty square miles. Worse still for him, his brisk pace of ten miles per hour put him at risk of running into one of the intercept teams within hours.

It had been almost a week since the lion had eaten the moose and he was getting hungry, but he dared not stop to hunt. For the same unmediated reason he'd not eaten any of the humans he'd killed, he was aware that he'd been something of a bad cat and had violated a law that superseded that of the jungle.

Sensing the great beast was on the run, those deer who found themselves in his path got out of the way, but without any great sense of urgency or panic.

THE SIXTH EXTINCTION

It had just gone midnight and I-árishóni had been on the move for three hours when the inexplicable happened. The great cat turned southeast. One can only speculate upon his reasons for doing so — it might, after all, have simply been that Africa beckoned in this hour of need — but in any event, it was a fortuitous choice. His new course had him flanking the northbound Atikokan mob to their east and heading through open wilderness in the direction of Thunder Bay and its population of one-hundred-fifteen thousand. By two o'clock on the morning of September the twelfth, when the tracking team from Ignace realized I-árishóni had changed course, they and the Atikokan group were practically on top of each other, but the lion was a good thirty miles outside their proposed area of encirclement. The two helicopters, each equipped with infrared devices, were immediately recalled from deep within the intended ring of entrapment, but their confidence in predicting the cat's trajectory had been shaken and they therefore dispersed over a much wider area, lessening their chances of detecting him. They'd suddenly gone from shooting fish in a barrel to shooting craps.

I-árishóni, sensing that he was drawing ever nearer to his Kenyan home, broke out into a canter. With the grizzly wound completely healed, he was now capable of a sustained fifteen miles an hour — considerably faster than his hunters could manage. By 8:30 in the morning, his lead over them had been widened by ninety miles. And, as any woodsman will testify, a mile in the bush is ten on the trail.

It had been some time since he'd detected the haphazardly distributed nature of the helicopters' droning and the faint, querulous yapping of the dogs, so I-árishóni at last yielded to his hunger. In the shallows of one of the myriad lakes he'd been skirting stood a moose feeding on pondweed. He did not wait for it to come ashore. With a leap of fifteen feet he landed on its back and, with his fangs, clung to its neck even as they were both submerged in three feet of water. When the colossal ungulate had shuddered out his final breath, I-árishóni dragged him ashore and feasted for close to an hour. He finished up with long draughts of cold, sweet water and then set off once more in search of the vast, sun-scorched savannas.

Following his call to London, Jason Conrad sat in perfect stillness for yet another two hours. The sun was nearing its zenith and its light flooded through the window, bathing him in its glory. But he could not feel the warmth. He felt only the cold and damp of shadows.

He lit a cigar in the hope that it would put some fire in his belly. Instead, he gagged. He tossed it onto a nearby scatter rug, not caring whether or not the house burned down around him. It didn't, of course. The Montecristo smoldered for a few minutes, then went out. Chinua Amadi had had every article in this and every other of his homes bathed in flame retardant.

He tried not to think of Irina and stared out to sea, but the emptiness of the horizon only mirrored the emptiness within.

At the appointed hour, to the nearest nanosecond, the doorbell chimed. Conrad peered into his handheld CCTV monitor and saw a middle-aged man who fit the description given to him by the New York office of Conrad Inc. The man was Herculean, and had the dress and demeanour of an undertaker. The stillness of the man, along with his short ponytail and bowler hat, made it appear as if someone had parked a René Magritte painting on his stoop. Cursing that he no longer had Chinua to get the door, he wearily slid into his slippers and padded across the marble tiles to admit his new assistant. "The retinal scanner is to your left," he said over the intercom. "Use it, then enter your company ID number on the keypad just under it."

The man did as instructed and he was given the green light. Conrad pulled open the door.

"Mr. Conrad," said the big man in a plummy Knightsbridge voice, "I am Lesley Perkins and I will be serving you until death do us part — most probably my own."

"Well, you're not lacking in brass, are you?"

"Nor should I be, Sir," stated Perkins flatly as he settled his bulk onto a vintage Art Deco daybed by André Arbus. "I am a most capable administrator, having served as CFO of your Golden Fleece Securities firm for four years. I also know that you don't mix checks with stripes, and I can — because of my years with the SAS — shoot your off testicles while I bang out one-hundred-and-forty words a minute on my laptop. Observe."

Perkins withdrew a computer from his case and began typing furiously with one hand while, with the other, he withdrew a Para Ordnance .38 Super from the shoulder holster under his jacket and blasted into a thousand pieces a faun figurine that was on a desk across the room.

"What the hell? That was a three-hundred-year-old Meissen!"

"Wrong on two counts, Mr. Conrad, if I may be so bold. The first Meissen porcelain was not produced until 1710. Also, the piece was fake. The colours were all wrong, you see. Too lurid."

"And what about the hole in my bloody wall? That's not fake!"

"I am also a skilled handyman, Sir. I will render it invisible while you savour the lunch I will prepare for you shortly. As you see, I brought some groceries and white wine with me. Now," he said smugly, as he directed Conrad's attention to the computer screen with his bright and disproportionately small eyes, "observe that I have typed out every word that's been said since I walked in that door, including my next two sentences. Notice that even capital letters are included, despite the fact that I used only one hand. There are many benefits to being oversized."

Conrad couldn't help but smile. "Where have you been hiding all this time?"

"In plain sight, Sir. I would also hasten to add that I was never made CEO of Golden Fleece Securities because the current CEO is second cousin to a certain J. S. Thurman, who sits on the board of Conrad Inc. You should rectify that situation, Sir."

"In due course, *you'll* do something about that, Mr. Perkins. It will be one aspect of your new job."

"Then I'm acceptable to you, Sir? Very Good. Oh ... I'd hasten to add that as you are the world's richest and most successful businessman, you're most likely either more intelligent or more ruthless than I am. Probably both. We will therefore be a good fit. I will know my place and be quite content in it."

Cackling uncontrollably, Conrad flopped down into the chair facing the television. "What's for lunch, Jeeves?"

"Thai glazed shrimp, Sir, with pomelo, ruby grapefruit, sweet chili sauce, and a Thai lime-leaf dressing. It is after a recipe from Jump, a restaurant in your hometown of Toronto. I did not think it unlikely that you'd appreciate a taste of home after galavanting all over the Europe."

"My hometown is actually Montreal, Lesley. Not Toronto."

"Very good, Sir. Montreal. Thoroughly cosmopolitan yet of a manageable size. And the French fact lends it a certain *je ne sais quoi*. Much better than Toronto, which is more like a whopping Woolworth's. But I would venture that you actually spend more time in Toronto than Montreal, do you not?"

"I do."

"There it is, then. In these peripatetic times, home is not necessarily where the heart is, but where you hang your hat."

Conrad's attention was caught by the TV news. Gwen Forsythe from social services in Dryden was recounting what young Robin Murdoch had told her about the beast that had killed his mother and grandfather. "As big as a cow, says the poor little tyke. With teeth and claws like butchers' knives. Tore up Robin's grandfather like he was a tabby with a mouse — Robin's words exactly. Now, what I want to know is, where are the experts? Seems to me he shoulda been caught by now. How many more motherless children will there be before this is over? And how many childless mothers? Oh Lordy ... I can't talk no more."

Ms Forsythe buried her face in her hands and commenced blubbering inconsolably. The pert young reporter, perfectly aware of what made for good television, allowed the camera to linger as the distraught woman wiped her runny nose on her sweater sleeve. Then, when she was certain that Ms Forsythe had thoroughly disgusted the viewers, thereby making herself appear perfectly sublime by comparison, the reporter commandeered the camera lens. "There you have it. Tragedy in a wilderness paradise. Who would have thought it possible? Back to you, Don."

Lesley Perkins had edged so close to Conrad that his long black jacket brushed against Conrad's sleeve. "That lion is yours, Sir."

Conrad did his best to appear nonchalant, and he succeeded admirably. "Whatever do you mean, Mr. Perkins?"

"What I mean, Sir, is that you're a hunter. You have that hungry look. Money, flesh, it's all the same, isn't it? In addition, you didn't flinch in the least when I pulled out my pistol. You made a fuss only when I destroyed your property."

"Did you bring enough groceries for two, Mr. Perkins?"

"Certainly, Sir. Great men have great appetites. Knowing they've done all that can be done, they know how to relax and enjoy the pleasures of life."

"Forget about the wall. I want you to have lunch with me. There are quite a few things you should know."

They shared the Thai shrimp — which was superb — and Conrad told Lesley Perkins about his grand project. For a full hour, Perkins listened without speaking a word. When at last he pushed his plate away from him and drained the last of his Lincourt Chardonnay, he said, "Hm. And here I thought it was Gerry behind it all."

"Gerry?"

"The Germans, Sir. So resolutely green. So resolutely … resolute."

"But if you'd had to think of an individual?"

"Oh, certainly not you, Sir."

Far from being relieved at this answer, Conrad was somewhat irked. He couldn't think why this should be so. "And why not?"

"Because you are known, in certain quarters, as a tightfisted megalo-maniac."

"What quarters, exactly?"

"Why, the world press, Sir. Have you not noticed?"

"No, actually."

"But then, what individual could be suspected of such breathtaking altruism? Why, you make Bill Gates and his foundation look like a church basement bake sale. Imagine. Saving all of Earth's life forms from extinction. And there's nothing in it for you, either. Or is there?"

"Oh, I've toyed with the idea of having myself and a few select individuals cryogenically preserved, but then who'd defrost us, eh? Aliens?"

"One never knows, Sir. One never knows. But it would be a worthy venture. Imagine a species with you as its fountainhead." Perkins finally removed his bowler hat and Conrad could see why it had taken him so long to do it. Not only was he as bald as a billiard ball, but there was an ugly crater in his skull, two inches above his left ear. "An old SAS wound, Sir. A terrorist's RPG. But enough about me, and to return to that lion. Given that he's yours in more ways than I could have imagined, I think it might be good for you to personally hunt him down. You are, after all, rather in a funk about Chinua Amadi and this Drach woman, and I believe some positive form of closure might do wonders for your morale. I would imagine that a generous gift to the police forces involved would not only enable them to more effectively cordon off the area in which he's moving, thereby quelling criticism of their efficiency, but it would also leave them several million dollars richer, and able to purchase all the police toys their greedy little hearts desire."

"Millions?"

"Millions, Sir. It's the only way."

"I must confess that I'm ambivalent about your suggestion. There are moments when I find myself actually rooting for the animal."

"But he's doomed anyway, Mr. Conrad. Some copper is bound to miss his own foot and accidentally shoot the beast. Why, then, shouldn't it be you who fells him? It would be pure poetry."

Conrad rose from the table and slumped into his seat in front of the television. A parents' coalition from Thunder Bay was shrieking hysterically about the prospect of I-árishóni roaming the streets of their city. "Leave me for a bit, Mr. Perkins. Clean up the dishes, or something. I have to think."

"Very good, Sir, but remember that time is short."

"Oh, and Perkins? Were you hoping to accompany me on such an expedition?"

"But of course, Sir," smiled Lesley Perkins through teeth that would have brought honour to a plow horse.

The burly Englishman, who'd only just begun to stack the dishes, suddenly interposed himself between Conrad and the TV. "Sir, as your employee — your right-hand man, as it were — am I to assume that I act with your full authority?"

"Correct. You will assume all the duties and functions of Mr. Amadi, with perhaps a little less creativity. The next person who double-crosses me will be crucified, and I'm not speaking metaphorically."

Perkins took out his cellphone and began dialing. "Very good, Sir. Well … hello, Helena. Guess who? Yes, my funny little accent's a dead giveaway, isn't it? Now, please connect me with your venerable CEO. Well, Helena, I don't give a rat's ass if he's in a meeting with the Pope, because I'm here with the only person who matters *more* than the Pope. Yes indeed, Mr. Jason Conrad himself." Perkins cupped the receiver and whispered to Conrad, "Golden Fleece Securities, Sir … Oh, hello Herbert. Hm, it's good you sound put out, because that's exactly where you're about to be. I want you to clear off your desk and be gone from the premises by four o'clock this afternoon. Just think, in the space of a few hours you'll have gone from being dead wood to a dead duck."

There was a great deal of screaming issuing from Perkins's receiver. He held the phone at arm's length for a few moments and then, when the noise had died down, he put it to his mouth. "Of course Mr. Conrad agrees with me. Here. I'll put him on." Perkins held out the phone to Conrad. "Sir?"

Conrad took the phone. Golden Fleece Securities was a piddling enterprise in comparison with most of his holdings, and he could afford to experiment with it and Lesley Perkins. "Do as you've been instructed, Mr. Barker. My office in Toronto will send you both an email and a fax confirming the directive. Good day, Sir."

Conrad turned off the phone then handed it back to Perkins. "You better fucking hope you're right about him, or that I don't find out this just just some creepy personal vendetta, Mr. Perkins. Golden Fleece is an old, sentimental favourite of mine."

"You probably know that it has a market capitalization of just over one half billion. What you probably don't realize is that if Herbert Barker weren't such a yitney, it could have been a mid cap two years ago. It had a growth rate of one percent. Grass grows faster than that. Send in some of your hotshots from Conrad & Kerner and you'll see what I mean."

"I'll do just that. Now, let's leave the world of high finance behind us and get back to the dishes, shall we? Or do you not think you can handle the transition?"

Perkins snapped to attention and saluted. "I most certainly can, Sir! Yes, Sir!" He then set upon the dishes like an assault team upon an enemy camp. While Perkins was in the kitchen, Conrad wondered how such a man — infinitely more complex than Chinua — would last as a glorified butler. Because he found Perkins curiously engaging, he hoped that it would be for a good while. Not only for his own convenience, but because nobody could be allowed to vacate that position alive. Security must always come first.

His eyes reverted to the television. Hudson's omnipresent face was just dissolving into some film of a mother polar bear and her cub seemingly stranded on an ice floe.

Conrad thought back to the week before, when he'd first laid eyes on Irina and Hudson, then chuckled at the memory of the young cop's patently jealous and protective demeanour. Hudson probably hadn't realized it about himself at the time, but he was infatuated with her and probably had been from the moment he'd become her partner. And why not? Here was a woman who came along but once or twice in a lifetime, with undiluted features, oracle eyes, thunder in her heart, and the salty, engulfing physicality of the ocean. God, but he hoped she'd have a quick and painless death.

He turned off the TV. Enough with fretting about the state of the world or other peoples' problems. A little quality time with Jason Conrad was in order. So he sat. And then he sat some more. But nothing happened. He was contemplating the void.

This was largely a function of the way in which Jason Conrad's brain worked. His mind was like a supersaturated solution in a beaker. Introduce a seed crystal into the solution, and the solution instantaneously turns into a fabulous crystalline mass. Withhold the crystal, and you have nothing but sludge. He was a builder, not a creator. In his mind, ideas did not spring spontaneously out of nothing, but the introduction of even the most meagre of notions would unleash a torrent of ancillary ideas. Thus, in passing from the kitchen to the table for the final handful of dishes, Lesley Perkins precipitated a grand adventure. "Done any thinking about the lion, Mr. Conrad?"

But of course! The lion! The beast was his! Conrad's pulse quickened. In a thrice, he'd mapped out how he would expedite negotiations with the police, the logistics of the trip, how much it would cost him, what weapon he would use, and who would accompany him. "Pack your bags, Perkins. We're off to Northern Ontario in about three hours' time."

"I would remind you, Sir, that I have not yet *un*packed them. Therefore, I'm ready to leave this very instant."

"Three hours will be fine, Perkins. I want Conrad Communications to inflame the media about this project, my lawyers to offer a package of twenty million to the police forces involved, and I still have to fire off that notification of termination to Herbert Barker. Now, who do you recommend replace Barker and yourself? Take your time with this."

Without the slightest hesitation, Perkins fired back, "Paul Cassini of Amherst Funds for CEO, Sir. I happen to know he's quite bored over there and is ripe for the picking. And for CFO, I would counsel that we stay in-house. David Gold, VP of finance, would do nicely. He's young and tough, but not rash."

Conrad eyed Perkins with a new respect. "Paul Cassini, eh? Good choice. I've wanted him under my roof for quite a while. As for this Gold fellow, I believe I'll take your word for it. So you'll put them in play?"

"Me, Sir? I certainly will, Sir," replied Perkins with considerable relish. "I'll offer Cassini Barker's old salary, but with an eye-popping bonus tied to performance."

"That's the way to go, Perkins." He gestured toward a computer case on the console. "That's Chinua's laptop. Password's JC Alpha, JC Omega, singular. Everything you need's in there. Get busy."

"Yes, Sir," said Perkins, moving toward the console.

"But finish the dishes, first."

Perkins was, among other things, an avid student of history. As he transported the few remaining dishes into the kitchen, he thought of a box. A very special box, covered in rich crimson velvet. It had a large round hole on the top and was open at the back, so that a bucket could be slid into place under the hole. This was King Henry VIII's royal stool. The attendant who controlled this royal stool, the groom of the Close Stool, was charged with inserting the bucket at the appropriate moment, withdrawing it when the king's steaming feces had piled into it (castles were draughty in those days), and wiping clean the royal behind.

The position of the groom of the Close Stool was not nearly as humble as it may sound. Apart from being the one who determined when it was appropriate for the doctors to inspect the royal slops, that man was also known as the chief gentleman of the Privy Chamber. Being on such familiar terms with the king, he wielded considerable power. For example,

Henry had used his chief gentleman of the Privy Chamber to circumvent the usual channels and dispatch both the third duke of Buckingham and Cardinal Wolsey. That gentleman could also exercise considerable influence upon patronage appointments and personal access to the king. And who knows, really, to what extent this man influenced the king's very thought processes? The definitive answer to that question ended up on the great slop heap of history.

Thus, it was with no little joy that Lesley Perkins loaded the dishwasher.

CHAPTER FORTY-TWO

White Lake Provincial Park, Ontario. September 12, 2006. At one of the trailer sanitation stations in White Lake Provincial Park, a cheery and verdant little spot about thirty miles inland from Lake Superior and midway between Thunder Bay and Sault Ste Marie, Leighton Campbell was all set to pump the black water out of his spanking new sprint class RV and into the park's sewage hold. It had been a long haul from Edmonton, and his shiny baby was bulging at the seams with ten days worth of excrement.

His daughter, Phoebe, an elfin eight-year-old with silky blond hair and coruscating blue eyes, pointed to the fifteen-foot flexible hose. "Poo will pass through there, Daddy. A river of feces, according to Mommy."

"Sometimes your Mommy gives out more information than is needed, Sweetheart," said Campbell as he glowered at his wife Loreen. The pale and lanky software engineer, who flitted phantasm-like through his workaday virtual world, had bought the RV and embarked upon this voyage to Quebec City in an attempt to prove that, yes, he could cope in the world of sun, sky, and slime. Still, some things were just a bit too earthy for him.

"I think the hose is leaking, Leighton," said a perturbed Loreen.

"Oh, poo," exclaimed Phoebe with considerable disgust, for the slow trickle of slops from the pressurized tank was turning into a gusher. Leighton Campbell, camper and adventurer extraordinaire, had not seated the bayonet coupling properly.

"Never mind, Sweethearts, don't panic," he said as his and Loreen's feet were soaked with the effluent. "I'll fix it."

"Leigh, Honey, shouldn't you just shut the system off, or maybe just let it drain —"

Too late. Leighton Campbell had bent over, grasped the coupling, and forced it back into position — this time, securely. In the process, however, the foul sludge had sprayed about in protest, and now he and his adoring wife were stained with it from head to toe.

"Oh, Daddy," clucked Phoebe, as Campbell absently ran his dripping fingers through his shoulder-length hair, "you can be such a bonehead, sometimes."

"Now, Phoebe," said Loreen with commendable forbearance, "we've made it this far almost without incident, haven't we? A record, of sorts. All your father and I need is a good shower. And the campground showers are just on the other side of that tree stand. So be a darling and fetch us some towels and a change of clothing from the RV — we daren't go into it like this — and then you can lock yourself inside while we scrub down. We won't be very long."

Her parents hadn't been gone more than two minutes when Phoebe spied something astounding from the cockpit seat. A lion, not thirty feet from the RV. The most resplendent being she'd ever beheld. Because she had no context in which to place this creature — due entirely to her father's abhorrence of television and radio — she immediately conferred a mythical, mystical status upon him.

After some deliberation, though not much, Phoebe Campbell decided it was time to present herself to the beast. With hands folded behind her back she advanced the fifty paces toward the lion. He was standing, facing her, and watching her every inch of her way.

"Look," she said, when just five feet from him, "Paddington Bear wants to meet you." She held out the stuffed animal to him.

The lion did not budge, but he rumbled loudly enough to startle her.

"Oh, don't do that. Paddington is a friend, and so am I. Phoebe Campbell is my name. And you must be Aslan. My Daddy's read all your books to me, you know. My favourite is *The Lion, the Witch and the Wardrobe*. I even saw the movie."

I-árishóni sat back on his haunches and held up a paw. The long and vicious claws were fully extended. Without fear or hesitation, Phoebe took the immense appendage in her hands and began stroking it. "Do you have something stuck in it? Hold still, I'll have a look."

As she scrutinized the paw, all the while stroking the back of it, the claws retracted. The lion did not attempt to lower it, nor did he look at her. On the alert for danger, he was busy scanning the grounds.

Phoebe patted the paw gently, then let go of it. "Nothing. Know what I think? You're just a big baby."

I-árishóni lowered his paw to the ground, then assumed a reclining position. Phoebe longed to stroke his mane, or perhaps even sit astride his back, but she thought that might be too forward. Her parents had taught her to be bold, but not pushy. Instead, she sat cross-legged on the ground, just feet from the massive head, and sang "Over the Sea to Skye" in a high, honeyed voice.

"That's one of my Daddy's favourites. It always makes him weepy. Would you like another? I know tons."

Phoebe took the animal's docility for consent and warbled two more ditties. She'd just begun another, the theme song from *The Lion King*, when the beast was suddenly on his feet with tail switching, ears twitching. Phoebe knew immediately that someone must be coming. Probably her parents, as she didn't hear an engine noise. She rose to her feet and stood awkwardly by the lion, like someone on a first date who didn't quite know how to say goodbye. I-árishóni inadvertently resolved Phoebe's dilemma for her. With a snout as great in girth as her waistline, he gently nudged her, and it happened to be in the direction of the RV.

"But maybe you should meet my parents," she said petulantly. "After all, they lead pretty boring lives."

She spun around to reason with him, but he was gone.

When the much refreshed Leighton and Loreen Campbell unlocked the RV door and let themselves in, Phoebe was curled up on the bunk, reading a book. She'd already reconsidered mentioning the lion. There was no point in flirting with danger.

As Irina stepped off the private jetliner and onto the tarmac of JFK Airport at precisely five o'clock, she was a highly compressed bundle of conflicting ideas and emotions. The flight in the sumptuous Boeing BBJ1 had, on the one hand, been exhilarating. She'd never been exposed to such luxury, and the waiter and hostess had been attentive beyond all expectation. As a policewoman, she'd been accorded a fair bit of obsequious behaviour in her time, but never before had she been treated like royalty by perfect strangers. She could get used to this, she thought to herself. On the other hand, the experience had been profoundly unnerving. Despite her considerable adaptability, this level of wealth was so far removed from all she knew that bourgeois buttresses now tumbled down around her sensible, mid-range shoes and left her feeling just a teensy bit like trailer trash. Irina was thankful she'd insisted upon Katz's Delicatessen rather than that tony restaurant and the extravagant clothes. If she hadn't, she'd most likely have turned into a pumpkin at the stroke of midnight.

As she scanned the door to the nearby Conrad International building, looking for a sign of the great man himself, her thoughts travelled reflexively to her appearance, just as her hand travelled reflexively to her hair. Then it hit her. She hadn't done that stupid blinking thing for days, nor had she craved junk food. Athol Hudson? Had he been responsible for this rehabilitation? Her hand guiltily abandoned her hair.

"Sergeant Drach."

The low voice seemed to emanate from some distant atonal region where expressiveness would likely be condemned as a capital crime. In fact, it came from a brawny young man who was standing in front of a Cadillac limousine parked only twenty feet from her. He was dressed from head to toe in loden green and wore a chauffeur's cap. He also wore a very straight, very angry scar from the corner of his eye to the corner of his curled lip.

"Yes?"

"Regretfully, the client could not be here to meet you. A business meeting broke out when he least expected it. I will take you to him. He should be done by the time we get there."

When Irina had dealt with the customs and border officials, the chauffeur held the car door open with the same flair that an undertaker lifts the lid of a casket.

"You haven't told me your name or where we're going."

"The name is Harlow, Madame. Don't ask me my first name because it has fallen into disuse. Occupational hazard. And we are going to the client's retreat in Southampton. You will enjoy it. One can still swim at this time of year. The Gulf Stream, you know."

Irina slid onto the rear grey leather seat and Harlow slammed the door shut on her. The windows were so deeply tinted that the sun was a pale disc with all the warmth of a silver dollar.

Harlow had no sooner taken the driver's seat and started up the motor when he picked up the car phone and pushed one of its buttons. "Excuse me, please, but I must tell the client that we're on our way. What the ... this doggone phone is out of commission! Uh ... you wouldn't happen to have a cellphone on you, Sergeant Drach?"

Irina handed him her BlackBerry. "No long distance calls, eh?"

"I'll just raise the barrier between us while I talk to the client, Sergeant Drach. It's embarrassing to me, frankly, how subservient I can sound."

A smoky lexan barrier shot up from behind the front seat. One second and an epiphany later, she felt like someone who'd just stepped off the edge of a cliff and was paddling in thin air. Shit, she cursed to herself! Nowhere but down from here. She tried the doors. Locked. The windows wouldn't lower, nor would they yield to the heel of her sensible, mid-range shoe. And the windows were so deeply tinted that nobody would be able to see her thrashing about. She set about trying to scratch the tint off the windows.

"That won't do you any good, either," said Harlow over the intercom. "The tint is not a film. It's right in the Lexan."

Once she'd settled down, Irina quickly realized that they were not headed toward Southampton. She'd never been to New York, but she did know, having excitedly perused a map on the Boeing, that Southampton was east of both the city and the airport. Yet here was the sun to her left. They were going north. First, on the Van Wyck Parkway, then onto the Grand Central Parkway. At a gigantic cloverleaf, they turned into the late afternoon sun on a stretch called the Long Island Expressway. She didn't need the road signs to tell her they were going into the city.

"This is ridiculous," she said in her haughtiest, bravest voice. "People know I came here to meet Jason Conrad. He won't get away with this, and you'll be going down with him."

"I can't talk to you," Harlow said in his tuneless voice, "but I will say this much. I've heard about you, and have been warned. But I'm not worried. You may have nine lives like a cat, but you're looking at your tenth go-round. Tough luck, Ma'am. And what's this stuff about Jason Conrad?"

"That's who you're working for."

"No kidding? *The* Jason Conrad?"

"I'm not in a kidding mood."

"Wow. You should feel honoured."

At the 11th Street toll booth in Queens, just before they dropped into the Queens Midtown Tunnel and under the East River, Irina tried desperately to attract attention, making as much fuss as possible. She waved frantically, she screamed until her throat ached and she pounded the doors, windows, and ceiling of the Cadillac until her knuckles bled. All to no avail. The windows were far too dark and the car was completely soundproof.

"Now don't go making a mess of yourself, Sergeant. Save that job for us. We're the pros, after all."

On the other side of the East River, Harlow followed East 37th to Lexington, then went down it to East 34th. There, he took a right and went three blocks over to 5th Avenue. Irina gawked. That short trip through the limestone and concrete canyons of New York had led her to the base of the Empire State Building.

"Is that what I think it is?"

"Yup. The tallest building in the world."

"If I'm not mistaken, there are several taller buildings in the world. There's Taipei 101, the Petronas Towers, even the Sears Tower here in the U.S."

"Correction. There are higher buildings, but the Empire State is still the tallest. There's a difference. It's like … well, a high man is someone who knocks his friggin' forehead on a door sill, but a tall man is … well, tall. Y'see?"

"I do. A tall man stoops with grace and power as he passes through a doorway. Like your Mr. Conrad does."

"That's it! Damn, you're as sharp as they said you were. And have you actually met Mr. Conrad?"

"I have."

"Wow."

"I can't see the upper part of the building from this angle, Mr. Harlow. Do you suppose you could open the window a bit?"

Harlow howled with laughter. "You'll be able to see it plenty out the back window as I go along to 8th Avenue. Then I'm gonna go up 8th and Central Park West and you'll still see it. You'll also get a great view of the west side of the park. First time here, right?"

"Righto."

"Prepare to be amazed."

"We have a park in Montreal that was designed by the same man who did Central Park, Frederick Law Olmsted. Mount Royal Park, it's called."

"We'll also pass the Dakota Apartments, where John Lennon lived and died. It faces the lake in the park. Imagine, him being shot down like a dog, and all."

"Yet you're probably going to shoot me down like a dog."

"Oh, no. Not at all. We've got more imagination than that. Anyway, John was killed by this obsessed crank, whereas I'm doing my job. My *job*. There's a difference, see? It's the American way."

Irina sank back into her seat and tried to enjoy watching some of the world's most expensive real estate whiz by. As they passed the former Beatle's faux-French Renaissance digs, she started to hum *Imagine*. Harlow joined in, but had to give up after a few bars because he was all choked up.

It occurred to Irina that Harlow was not the cold fish she'd first met on the tarmac at JFK. He still sounded as in he were speaking from inside a floor drain, but he seemed, basically, to be just another sentimental fool trying to put food on the table. She laughed aloud. A sentimental fool? He was going to kill her!

"What's so funny?" said Harlow, adjusting his rearview mirror to better study her.

"I'm about to die. This is for all the times I should have laughed, but didn't."

"Huh. A bit of a philosopher. Well, it sure makes a nice change from all the crying and moaning I usually get."

They'd travelled north about two thirds of the two-mile length of Central Park and were at about the level of the Jacqueline Onassis Reservoir when Harlow suddenly turned left on West 97th Street and scooted across Broadway and over to West End Avenue in the Upper West Side. There, in the middle of the tidy and densely populated residential neighbourhood was a building at the corner of 97th and West End. Like many of its neighbours, it was a fairly nondescript twenty-floor brown brick apartment building dating from the twenties or thirties. Harlow jerked the limousine sharply through its open garage door on 97th and sped toward the rear of the deserted facility where two men stood waiting. The tall, leonine black man sporting cornrows with cowry shells and a banker's three-piece pinstriped suit immediately closed the garage door. The other, a grotesquely overweight white man with long and greasy hair, wearing Bermuda shorts and a loud Hawaiian shirt, immediately approached the car and bade Harlow roll down the window. Harlow, obviously revolted by the man, took his time in reaching for the window controls.

Irina was similarly repulsed. The man was standing under a bright fluorescent light and she could see that his face was as pockmarked as the moon. "I'll make you a deal. Get me out of here, set me free, and I'll see you never have to work another day in your life."

The ugly man rapped at the window.

"Now where you gonna get the kind of money I need?"

"My life savings. I have just over four hundred thousand."

"Sorry, Sergeant. Not enough for the risk involved. Besides, I probably wouldn't do it even if you had more. I've got a job to do."

Harlow turned off the intercom then rolled down the window. He and the ugly man exchanged a few words, then the black man opened the back door and yanked Irina from her seat as if she were a rag doll.

"Well, well," said the fat man, "look what we have here. You're kind of a sweetheart, aren't you?"

"Go fuck yourself."

"Oh, and spunky, too. I like that. But listen, babe. I don't aim to fuck myself. I aim to fuck you. You guys wanna pin her down for me?"

The black man said, "Bobby, my man. That ain't part of the plan. We be sticking to the plan, see?"

Ugly man wrestled Irina from the black man's grasp and began to paw at her. She slapped his face. He laughed, pushed her to the dusty concrete floor, then pushed his pants and briefs down to his knees. As he flung his considerable weight on top of her, she simultaneously scratched at his cheeks and administered a sharp knee jab to his groin. This infuriated the three-hundred-pound behemoth. "Help me with her, you assholes," he bellowed as he choked Irina with one hand and lifted her skirt with the other.

With her free hand, Irina gave him a karate chop to the side of neck. His bulk protected him from everything but the pain, and in a rage he clasped her neck with both his large hands and proceeded to bang her head repeatedly on the floor. The black man grasped the fat man by the shoulders and attempted to pull him off Irina. This restrained him just enough for Irina to recover her senses and gouge at his eyes. He retaliated by delivering a stunning blow to the side of Irina's face and then rose to confront the black man. "Motherfucker! You're supposed to be on my side!"

"Easy, Bobby. Be cool. Man says her corpse is supposed to look fine, not like she was gangbanged by a herd of hippos."

The fat, ugly man's Bermudas and briefs were now down around his ankles. He was still tumescent. "Oh my God," said the supine Irina, wiping the blood from her mouth. "How are you going to violate me when you aren't well enough equipped to rape a gerbil?"

Irina had calculated that this might be a risky thing to say, but she'd further calculated that a wild card is better than no card at all. Her gamble paid off.

"Yo, Harlow," tittered the black man. "What's this dude's name, anyhow? Bobby, or bobbed?"

The fat man withdrew a gun from the holster under his loud Hawaiian shirt and shot the black man in the face.

"I think an apology is in order."

It was Harlow, and he was aiming a Ruger .44 magnum revolver directly at the fat man. Bobby was now flaccid. "No it isn't. He dissed me."

"I wasn't talking about Luther. I was talking about the fact that you're not doing your job properly."

"Well, fuck you! You're not the boss of me! Fuck you, fuck you, fuck you!"

Agitated in the extreme, Bobby was pawing at the ground like a wounded elephant — insofar as the pants around his ankles would permit. Whether he actually meant to aim his Sig Pro 9 mm at Harlow or whether it was an unintended consequence of his thrashing about will forever remain a mystery because Harlow left no time for explanations. He shot the fat man right between the eyes. The high velocity and large bore of the .44 magnum cartridge splattered the Cadillac, a full ten feet behind him, with blood and bits of brain tissue. Irina, too, was showered by human debris.

Bobby collapsed in a heap just beside Irina, who was now propped up on one elbow. His Sig Pro 9 mm, hidden behind his enormous bulk, was only inches from her free hand.

"Cute," said Harlow, visibly impressed. "One wisecrack and suddenly it's two down and one to go."

"That's the power of humour, for you," replied Irina, wiping bits of the fat man from her face and hair.

"Yes, I've often wondered: is it humour that sets us apart from the rest of the animal kingdom? After all, beasts don't laugh or tell jokes."

"I can't say I've given the matter a lot of thought, but it seems to me that humour presupposes self-consciousness. Therefore, it's self-consciousness that sets us apart."

"But chimps possess self-consciousness, don't they? I mean, they can look in a mirror and recognize themselves as themselves. I've heard they even model hats and do vain stuff like that. But I wonder if chimps are capable of laughing?"

"You know, you've raised an interesting question. I'll be sure to investigate the matter when I get out of here."

Harlow laughed. "Now there you go, again. Always joking around. I like that. But I have a job to do, you understand, and you have about as much chance of leaving this garage alive as Luther and Bobby do."

"Oh, really?" Irina hoisted the fat man's 9 mm pistol and pointed it at Harlow. They were now ten feet apart, each with a pistol aimed at the other. "Drop that gun."

"Oops. Careless of me, wasn't it? I'd clean forgotten about that thing. Now it comes down to this: whichever one of us fires first comes out of this alive."

Irina fired, penetrating Harlow's forehead. He was dead before he hit the floor. "Sorry about that," whispered Irina as she raised herself from the floor and stood over his corpse. "But you're not the only one who has a job to do."

From one of the garage walls hung a coiled hose. With it, she rinsed off her hands and face then sprayed down the Cadillac. She dug into her suitcase for a change of clothing. She cursed because her sensible, mid-range beige suede shoes, among her favourites, were now bloodstained. Ruined! Her black Aldo pumps would have to do.

Irina retrieved the car keys and her phone from Harlow's pocket, hopped into the Caddy, and after closing the garage door on her way out, roared off into the night.

It was 11:59 p.m. GMT, and Hudson was bored. He'd actually been bored from the moment Irina had left, but at least it had then been lunchtime and he'd been distracted by the special magic of tapioca pudding. All day he'd paced back and forth, occasionally stopping to glance at the television or to study the compelling view of the parking lot. Periodically, the nurse would stage a sneak attack and shoo him back into bed, but he was fully committed to his misery, and no sooner had the squeaking of her crepe soles receded down the hall than he was back on his feet. Having prowled about his room like a caged animal for almost twelve hours, he sympathized entirely with that cornered lion back in Canada.

The lion. Of course. The whole world's attention was focused on the beast. Conservancy groups were demanding that the animal be returned safely to his natural habitat while such groups as Mothers Against Children as Animal Feed were shrilly calling for his posthaste extermination. Why wouldn't Jason Conrad's attention have been similarly captured? He reached for his maps, his precious maps. No doubt about it. The lion didn't have long. But who had the most affinity with him? Who, among all others, had considered him a specimen worthy of preservation for the ages? Who, therefore, would most want to confront the animal and attain some kind of apotheosis?

He dialed Irina's number. It took a few rings, but her blessed voice finally flowed from the earpiece like honey — or so it seemed to him. "Jesus Christ, Hudson! You picked a helluva time to call!"

"What's up my little chickadee?"

"I've just taken part in the worst carnage since the siege of Leningrad. Well, make that since yesterday, anyway. And now I'm on something called the Henry Hudson Parkway headed to God knows where."

Hudson sucked in his breath. "You're all right?"

"Just fine."

"Oh … thank God. And where, exactly, would you like to be headed?"

"The airport."

"I take it your date with Mr. Conrad didn't go too well?"

"It was a setup. The bastard tried to have me killed."

"Oh, dear. So, where to from the airport? Back to my waiting arms?"

"Tempting, Hudson, but I've got this idea. Something tells me that our Mr. Conrad isn't even in New York. And the more I think about it, the more I believe he's to be found in the vicinity of that lion. The beast is an unquestionably formidable animal. The world-conquering Jason Conrad will want to subdue him personally. Besides, that lion cannot be too far from Conrad's bunker, or storage shed, or whatever the hell he's built, and that will be a major concern. So I'm off to Ignace, Ontario, by way of Toronto and Thunder Bay. What do you think?"

"Brilliant. Especially that bit about Conrad's facility. Wish I'd thought of it."

"Now, why would you wish that? We're not in competition with each other, you know."

"Hm. Wish I'd thought of that, too. Anyway, I'll see you in Ignace."

"No, you won't! You're a sick man! You've got a hole the size of a sewer main in your chest! You should be in bed!"

Hudson was in front of the television. Suddenly, he was staring at the happy visage of Jason Conrad. Conrad was standing at a podium at Ontario Provincial Police headquarters in Thunder Bay, Ontario. To his left was the force's deputy commissioner and to his right was the deputy commissioner of the RCMP. Conrad was taking questions from an army of reporters. Hudson held the phone to the TV speaker. "You should listen to this, Irina."

"Mr. Conrad," asked the reporter from NBC, "it seems to me that you're turning a crime scene into a playground. Is that ethical?"

"It's a given that the animal has to die, either by my hand or those of the police. He's killed humans and will therefore do it again. Thus, the only pertinent question is whether or not it's ethical for the two police forces involved to be enriched by ten million dollars each. Of course, I can't speak for them, but I'd venture that the money will be used to advance the cause of law enforcement. Gentlemen? Do you feel it necessary to add anything to that statement?"

Both deputy commissioners did. They each responded at great length about the equipment that would be secured, the increased services and training that would be facilitated, and the pertinent upgrades to their IT systems. The reporters, as a body, found this boring in the extreme.

"Mr. Conrad," said a sweet young thing. "Do you think it's fair that you should hunt down the lion?"

Conrad affected a profoundly quizzical expression. "Fair to the lion, or fair to other people?"

"Other people."

"Are you kidding me?"

"No, Sir. Not at all," she huffed. "I'm referring to the fact that you have billions upon billions while others don't."

"Well, now. Those that don't have billions upon billions should work harder, shouldn't they? After all, my money was not a gift."

"But the wherewithal to accumulate those billions *was*, wasn't it?"

"So you're telling me that life isn't fair. Boohoo. Is it fair that you should be so darned cute, and therefore able to secure a plum job with the BBC, while untold millions can't?"

Conrad had just committed the cardinal error of singling out a member of the press corps for scrutiny and ridicule. But as life is essentially unfair, one man's error can be another's triumph. Thus, the world's most powerful private citizen stared at the reporter and dared her to pursue the matter, secure in the knowledge that he neither risked the wrath of the voter nor even — because his interests were so preponderant and diversified — the consumer.

The reporter shrugged helplessly and sat down. There was an interval of about thirty seconds before the next question came. "The beast is enormous, Mr. Conrad, Sir," said the reporter from ESPN. "What kind of weapon will you be using?"

"First, let me say something about lions. Ask any big game hunter and he'll tell you without hesitation that the male African lion is the most dangerous animal there is. Why? Because he's all about confrontation. Apart from fighting, all he does is eat, sleep, and copulate. He doesn't even hunt unless he's too young, too old, or down on his luck and without a pride of females to do it for him. Whereas most other great animals will take evasive action, the lion will come right at you if you're perceived as a nuisance. Even the mighty tiger, because of his slinky, solitary nature, will oftentimes avoid a confrontation. The lion is truly the king of beasts. And a hunter can never be too careful with him. It's frequently been reported that a lion who's taken a bullet to the heart will still be able to charge and take down the hunter." Conrad reached for the mahogany rifle case at his side and lovingly extracted a weapon with a glossy, hardwood handle and a long, blueish barrel. "This, Ladies and Gentlemen, is the Remington 700 ABG. It's the best bolt action rifle in the world. But it's chambered for the .375 Remington Ultramag cartridge rather than the .458, which has a considerably higher muzzle velocity. Why? For the sport of it. He's a lion, not an elephant, and I want to give him a fighting chance."

"But, Mr. Conrad," queried a reporter from the CBC, "from all you've said, it would already be horribly risky to give a lion a fighting chance. Especially this one."

"I'm sorry, but I don't understand. Is that a question?"

"After a fashion, yes."

"Let me get this straight. You're asking me why I would take a risk?"

"Yes, Sir."

Conrad seemed genuinely baffled. "Wouldn't everybody?"

As he sat down the reporter meekly mumbled, "I don't think so, Sir."

"Huh. I wish someone had mentioned that to me much earlier on in my life. That way, I might have been a millionaire at twelve rather than nineteen."

There was considerable tittering among the media people but no one dared venture another question. Not one of them could be sure whether or not he was having fun at their expense. After a minute of excruciating silence, Conrad slid a bullet into the chamber, cocked the gun, and put it to his shoulder. He pointed it over their heads and toward the back of the hall. "Does everybody see the poster with the police car on it?"

Every head swivelled in the direction of the poster. It was a small one, and it was some sixty feet from him. The police car in question was at most four inches long.

"See it? Good. I will now shoot out its right front tire."

He pulled the trigger before either of the two policemen flanking him had a chance to react. No one in the audience witnessed the emphatic recoil of the rifle against his shoulder, but everyone heard the loud pop. And everyone certainly saw that the police car's right front tire become a smoking, one inch hole.

As the deputy commissioners of the OPP and the RCMP stood by immobile and impassive, all eyes returned to Conrad, who smiled. "I may not be going out there with absolutely the most powerful weapon, but I won't be helpless. Any more questions?"

Stunned silence.

"Then I thank you for coming, Ladies and Gentlemen, but I really must be going now. He who hesitates is lunch."

Hudson withdrew his BlackBerry from the TV speaker. "He's gone and I'm back, Irina. Did you get all that?"

"I take it he hit his target?"

"Scary. Not a millimetre off in any direction."

"He should have been arrested for a stunt like that."

"If Siroca and Kinsey had bit their tongues any harder, the fronts of their uniforms would have been bathed in blood."

"What do you think he was up to?"

Hudson was flabbergasted. Irina never asked his opinion on such matters. She was always so quick and true when it came to analyzing peoples' motives. "You're asking me?"

"You're a man. Maybe you can tell me why he would act like a jumped-up gonzo."

"Ah … hiding in plain sight?"

"Doesn't wash. Even if he weren't our man, the whole thing would invite unwanted speculation."

"He *is* a jumped-up gonzo?"

"No. He is no ordinary man … Omigod, I just sailed through Times Square. Times Square!"

Hudson, an adept with maps, quickly pinpointed her location. "You're on 42nd Street?"

"Going east toward the Queens Midtown Tunnel. I saw a sign. Ah, now I'm just passing a park. Bryant Park, it's called. Hey — isn't this the one that was known as 'Needle Park' in the sixties? Hookers and drugs? That Al Pacino movie?"

"Yes. *Panic in Needle Park*, and I see you're cutting through the heart of Manhattan to get from the west side to the east side. Doesn't the car you're driving have SatNav?"

"OnStar. It's a Caddy."

"So why aren't you using it? There's got to be a better route."

"Because I don't know how it works, see? You're the tech freak, not me."

"What, tech freak? You push a button and an operator comes on and talks to you."

"Well, I'm too busy going the slow way to look up a faster one. Now, let's get back to my question, shall we?"

"Sorry, but I'm bereft of ideas. Insofar as the whole business is an act of some sort, though, I do agree with you."

"So do I," said Irina, "and here's what I think: He knows he's running out of time. It's an invitation for you to go to him. He wants to finish you off personally, just as he wants to finish off the lion personally."

"Me? That's nuts. You're the real threat."

"He thinks I'm dead, remember?"

"I'll bet he already knows his guys screwed up. I'll bet he knows you're still alive."

"Okay. That would make my hunch about his invitation that much more credible, right?"

"Right. He's made a life out of closing deals. He wants to close this one, as well. Ah ... what do you think he'll do about that tracking team working its way backward from that lodge? They're bound to uncover his Noah's Ark."

"You're making me repeat myself, Hudson. That's why he wants closure with us and the lion, at the very least."

"Right. I'm outta here. I'm on my way to Ignace. See you there."

"No, you won't. You're convalescing. Stay there."

"I'm coming over and I'll take another bullet for you if I have to."

"Mm, that sounds romantic, but it's out of the question. Besides, lover boy, the hospital will never release you. Bye. I'll be in touch."

Hudson started to pack. He'd been serious about taking a bullet for Irina, if need be.

"So, Perkins," solicited a grinning Jason Conrad as he and his new aide piled into their limousine outside OPP headquarters, "how do you think that went?"

Lesley Perkins said, "A little over the top, Sir, but undeniably effective. I especially enjoyed watching the expressions on the faces of those police commissioners. They both looked as if there was more gas pressure building up in their guts than at the muzzle of your Remington. By the way, have you considered a recoil compensator for the weapon? Quite a kick it has, and you're by no means a hefty man."

Conrad said sharply, "Let's get back to answering my question, shall we?"

Perkins shrugged manfully. "It cannot but have succeeded in piquing the interest of Drach and Hudson, Sir. So successful was it, in fact, that I cannot help but feel like a Kamikaze copilot."

"Relax, Perkins. It will end well."

"What bothers me, Sir, is that I'm not quite clear about what you mean by 'well.'"

CHAPTER FORTY-THREE

Rio de Janeiro. September 12–13, 2006. Inspector Leopold Duggan of New Scotland Yard caught British Airway's daily flight 0249 out of Heathrow at two in the afternoon, about the same time that Irina had left Plymouth for New York City. He arrived in Rio de Janeiro twelve hours later, at ten in the evening, Rio time. Largely because he'd been gawking at ravishing photos of Rio on the plane, he didn't hit the ground running so much as doing the samba. From Galeão International Airport (or Antônio Carlos Jobim Airport, as the Cariocas prefer to call it) he took a lengthy taxi tour of what he considered the most breathtaking city on Earth before arriving in Leblon, a fairly affluent district in South Rio adjacent to Ipanema. For there, on Avenida Afrânio de Melo Franco and facing the Scala Theater, were the headquarters of DEAT, the branch of the Rio Civil Police that handles all crimes committed against foreigners.

At DEAT headquarters, Detective Chief Inspector Leopold Duggan of the London Metropolitan Police told Gustavo, his taxi driver, to wait for him and went straight to Lieutenant Jorge Vilele's office. Or, rather, just outside Vilele's office, for he was forced to cool his heels for a good thirty minutes.

"*Tenente* Vilele," said Duggan acidly, offering his hand as he was finally admitted. "I trust you can spare more than a moment for me?"

Vilele, a large, swarthy man with a crooked nose and long, exceedingly glossy black hair, peremptorily took Duggan's hand then flung himself into his chair without offering the Englishman a seat. "It depends what you are wanting, Senhor."

This was too rich, even for the quintessentially stoic Duggan. "I beg your pardon? We spoke not long ago and you assured me that I would be given complete access to your database. Huh. Never mind the database, then. Just tell me to whom this blinking licence plate is registered: 'RJ Rio de Janeiro' along the top, and at the bottom, 'KQS 8499.'"

"To whom. To Whom!" Vilele laughed loudly, baring smoke-stained teeth. "My *Inglês* not so good, but this I know. An educated man only uses 'whom.' Hooom! Hooooom!"

"Educate me further. Answer my question."

"Ooh, not a *pedido*, but a command. You are bigshot in England?"

"Big enough to know a pipsqueak when I see one. And you haven't seen anything, yet. Just wait until Inspector Chadwani's superiors get over here."

"Ah, yes. Chief Amit Chatterjee. A most excitable man. Not like you. But he will have the same problem as you, eh?" Vilele half raised himself out of his chair, leaned across his desk, and blew hot, stale breath into Duggan's face as he proclaimed loudly, "*Primeiramente*, I am not a pipsqueak! *Em segundo*, this pipsqueak is in charge of the Chadwani file, and I do not need help from gringos!"

"Very well, then. Have you at least looked up the person to whom that plate is registered?"

"Ah, you go again, there. To whom!" Vilele got out of his chair and prowled back and forth behind Duggan. "Many tourists come to Rio, many die. I am busy. I have eighteen dossiers that await my concentration."

Duggan didn't bother turning around to look at him. "If you're so damn swamped with cases, then why are you refusing help with one of them? Ah yes, of course. Stupid question." He reached into his inner jacket pocket and withdrew a fat, sealed envelope. Still staring straight ahead, he held it aloft and gently waved it.

Jorge Vilele greedily snatched it. "How much?"

"Two thousand."

"Yankee dollars?"

"Of course."

Vilele went round to his desk and removed a folder from the top drawer. "Everything there. The vehicle was reported stolen by the owner three days ago, but I give you anyway the registration of the vehicle, names, and *telefones* of witnesses ... *tudo*."

"My goodness, how thorough. It's almost as if you'd planned our little transaction."

"As you did, *não*? We are alike in some ways, Inspector."

Duggan bolted from his seat and dashed around to where Vilele stood. He kneed the startled Brazilian in the groin, then slapped him hard enough across the face to send him reeling backward. "We are enough alike that we must both breathe the same air, but you pollute it while I must tolerate your stench. Now, don't get any inappropriate ideas about retaliation. I'll let you keep the money because I'm in a bit of a rush, but any funny business and this sordid episode will mushroom into a diplomatic row. Good day, Sir."

Jorge Vilele did not reply. He was lying flat on his back, listening to the music of the spheres. Duggan relieved him of his .9 mm Glock.

Duggan hopped back into the taxi. The driver — with whom he'd become quite friendly during his visit to Sugarloaf, Corcovado and even a favela — took him to Praça Santos Dumont, in a respectable neighbourhood that was sandwiched between the hippodrome and the botanical gardens. Duggan's objective lay in a tall, snow-white apartment building facing the park which had bequeathed Avenida Praça Santos Dumont its name.

The driver, Gustavo, said, "Very fancy, no?"

A good thing, mused Duggan, if it could be assumed that Ellis Ripperton of apartment 1409 was, in fact, connected to the deaths of Raja Chadwani and Maria Elena Battista. An affluent killer was more liable to know whence came his marching orders.

"Shall I wait for you, Inspector?"

Duggan was leafing through the folder. "Hm? Ah ... I don't know how long I'll be, Gustavo. It could be some time."

"No problem. I'll charge you."

"Ah, yes. Of course. Wait then."

Gustavo reached into his glove compartment and pulled out a Desert Eagle .50 semi-automatic pistol. "I could wait forever if you don't have one of these. Do you?"

Duggan turned the enormous pistol over in his hand. "I have *a* gun, but nothing like this. What makes you think I'd be needing it?"

Gustavo Santarrita laughed. "Inspector! When you came out of the police station, you had a look in your eyes which would have frozen solid a glass of rum. And now, again, as you examine your papers, it is there. And why would you come halfway around the world, operating like *um lobo solitário*, if it was but for something such as a traffic violation?"

Duggan smiled grimly as he pocketed the Desert Eagle. "Thank you, Gustavo." He took out his BlackBerry and handed it to the driver. "Do me some little favours, will you? If I'm not back in half an hour, get yourself out of here with all possible speed, then use the speed dial to call this person, Sergeant Irina Drach. Tell her I have failed." He handed the folder to Gustavo. "But also tell her that it is because of this man, Ellis Ripperton, that I have indeed failed." Duggan then pulled out his wallet. "I think now would be a good time to settle with you. Here. I've included the cost of that extra half hour."

Gustavo pushed back the proffered money. "One does not often have the sense that good will triumph over evil, but I believe that now is such a time. Pay me when your work is done. God be with you, which means *O Deus seja com você.*"

Duggan thanked him then entered the building. Sitting behind the brass and marble console was a Hispanic guard who was at least twice Duggan's weight without having an ounce of fat on him. He challenged Duggan in Portuguese. Duggan shrugged, said, *"Inglês,"* then gave Ellis Ripperton's name. As the guard began to dial his phone, he asked: *"Que é seu nome?"*

Duggan's smattering of Spanish proved useful. "Jason Conrad."

The guard repeated Conrad's name into the phone. Moments passed, and he said once again, this time with a heavy frown, *"Que é seu nome!"*

"Jason Conrad."

The guard muttered Conrad's name into the phone once more. Then he shook his head in frustration and handed the receiver to Duggan. "*Conversa ao Senhor Ripperton. Conversa!*"

The policeman took the receiver and held it to his ear. "It's rather late, isn't it? Hope I didn't wake you, old bean."

"Who the fuck is this!"

"Not quite Jason Conrad, I'm afraid, but I had to get your attention. Especially since you wouldn't know me from a hole in the wall. Fact is, I just got in from London, and you know what that means, don't you?"

"No. You tell me."

"Here? Standing in a lobby? Over the phone?"

There was a long silence followed by fevered mumbling. "Put the guard back on the phone."

The guard held the phone to his ear for a few moments, shook his head as if Ellis Ripperton were standing before him, then hung up. He raised his bulk out of the comfortable, ergonomically correct leather chair and swaggered around to where Duggan stood. Grinning maliciously, he began to pat Duggan down, beginning with the armpits. He never made it as far down as Duggan's waist. With the palm of his hand, Duggan landed a ferocious blow to the side of his head, just behind the temple. The man, a full foot taller than Duggan, went down like a sack of flour from the back of a U.N. relief truck. Duggan withdrew a small white pill from his vest pocket, propped open the unconscious guard's mouth, and forced this pill down his gullet. He then dragged the guard twenty feet over to the maintenance closet and stuffed him into it. Before closing the door, he first bound the guard up in a hose, then applied liberal amounts of Krazy Glue to the latch, the lock, and the guard's ruby lips.

"Well," the policeman said to himself, rubbing his hands together with both satisfaction and anticipation, "I presume the intended search was the prelude to an invitation to go on up, so let's get on with it, shall we?"

He took the elevator up to the fourteenth floor and knocked on the door of apartment 1409. A young Brazilian beauty dressed in a silk babydoll outfit, complete with garter and buckled choker, opened the door with a giggle. Duggan could see a balding, middle-aged man sitting in a leather chair against the far wall. He was naked from the waist up.

Over by the window stood a younger man, fully clothed in a smartly tailored suit. He was brandishing a sawed-off shotgun.

"That guard downstairs. Is he one of us?"

"Sure is," said the half-naked man.

Duggan breathed a sigh of relief, muttered that the guard was a good man, then put on a forbidding frown. "You should see what you look like. A bunch of thugs. What if the police were to bust in here? What kind of impression would you make?"

The middle-aged man laughed. "They would never bust in. They come here by invitation only. Now, I'm Ripperton, as if you haven't already guessed. Who in hell are you?"

Ripperton was pasty and greasy, with a sizable paunch. He spoke in a heavy southern U.S. drawl. Duggan would have been hard pressed to decide whether he was from Louisiana, Georgia, South Carolina, or Alabama, since natives of those states all sounded alike to him. In any event, he found the man repulsive, and this fact actually abetted his pretense. He sounded disapproving in the extreme. "I am Leopold Duggan, and I come here from Ontario by way of London. You've made rather a mess of things, haven't you? The police have witnesses to the death of Maria Elena Battista, not to mention the licence plate of your lorry. And they have the bullet that killed that Indian policeman. What were you thinking?"

"Aw, relax. The rifle's been disposed of, and I reported my truck stolen three days ago. It's only reasonable for them to assume that she would have been run down by a stolen truck. After all, who would be stupid enough to use his own wheels? Fernando, here, he's the one that plugged the Indian. Not a bad shot, eh?"

"Still too messy for Jason Conrad's taste."

"You mean to tell me that Mr. Conrad actually pays attention to our activities?"

"Mr. Conrad pays personal attention to all that goes on in his realm. That's why he's the leader and you're just one of his foot soldiers."

Ripperton squirmed in his chair. To Duggan, he looked like a slug on a stovetop. "Tell Mr. Conrad I'll be more careful in the future. And tell him not to worry about this episode. By now, the truck is a burned-out heap somewhere in the Amazon jungle and Fernando's Zastava is at the bottom of Rio bay."

"Zastava? The M76?"

"Yes, that one," murmured Fernando proudly. "I hit that little snoop from a distance of five-hundred yards. Not bad, eh?"

"Not bad at all." Duggan turned to the girl, who was nestled with her knees up in the big chair beside Ripperton. He motioned to the hall behind them. "You, love. Is there anybody back there?"

"*Não*. But there is big bed. You wan' come back with me? Lil' fuck?"

Duggan had what he needed. In one smooth, swift motion he turned off the tiny digital recorder in his pocket and withdrew the .9 mm Glock. He shot Fernando right between the eyes. As the girl ran about the room aimlessly, screeching and keening, he took out Gustavo's Desert Eagle .50 semi-automatic. "Not of much use in tight situations, this thing," he said to the stupefied Ripperton. "Too big for proper concealment, too much recoil for rapid fire. But it's first rate for target practice."

"No ... no!"

Duggan took careful aim then fired, reducing Ripperton's hand to a bloody, pulpy stump. The girl fled the room, shrieking hysterically and tearing at her flesh with her fingernails. Ripperton stared at the mess at the end of his arm as if he couldn't quite comprehend that it belonged to him. Then he began to moan plaintively, "I'll never play pool again. And I'm such a fucking good pool player."

"Cheer up, sport. The prosthetics these days are bloody marvels."

"Does that mean you aren't going to kill me?"

"That's right. But it doesn't mean I won't blow off your other hand. Or your feet, for that matter."

Abasing himself completely, Ripperton crawled on his hand and knees to Duggan's ankles and sobbed violently. "We have to stop the bleeding. Look! I'll be as drained as a kosher chicken in minutes. Help me. Help me!"

"First, you must agree to help me."

"Anything," he blubbered. "I'll do anything! Just don't hurt me anymore! Please, please don't let me die!"

With Ripperton's own belt, he fashioned a tourniquet. He then reached for the phone and dialed his BlackBerry's number. It took quite a few rings but an uncertain Gustavo finally answered. *"Sim? Sim?"*

"Still downstairs, then?"

"Sim, sim!"

"Good show. Wouldn't want to try hailing a cab with what I presently have on my hands. Two things, Gustavo. First, if you have a tarp in your car, I'd recommend you spread it out over your back seat. Second, do you know a down-on-his heels doctor? Somebody who'll work without asking any questions? Perhaps in those favelas of yours?"

"Yes, yes, to both questions! *Sim, sim!* Oh, I am so glad to hear your voice! I was just about to leave!"

"Thank God you didn't," he said, glancing at his watch. "It's gone past 3:00 a.m. One can only suppose that your streets are quite dangerous this time of night."

CHAPTER FORTY-FOUR

Wawa, Ontario. September 13. Sergeant-Detective Irina Drach woke from a brief but overdue sleep in the somewhat isolated Parkway Motel on the Trans Canada Highway in Wawa, Ontario, on the northeastern shore of Lake Superior. From the moment she'd concluded the phone conversation she'd been having with Hudson as she drove east on 42nd Street, things had gotten hectic in the extreme. Realizing that she was going nowhere a little too fast, she'd pulled over to the side of the road and dialed her commanding officer's cell number.

"Irina," sputtered Lieutenant-Detective Stan Robertson, "you're late with your call. Lucky I left my cell on, considering I'm home and in the middle of my dinner. How's Hudson doing?"

"Fine. Plotting to fly the coop, if he hasn't done so already. But I'm in a jam. Are you in front of your computer?"

"I *can* be in two seconds."

"Get to it and go to Google Maps. Quickly."

Forty-five seconds passed. "Okay. Google Maps. Next?"

"Manhattan. Grand Central Station on East 42nd. Got it?"

Fifteen seconds passed. "Ah … da-dah, da-dah, da-dah … got it."

"Good. That's where I am, heading east in a car. All I know about this city is that the Queens Midtown Tunnel gets me to JFK. Question is, where do I pick up the tunnel?"

"Ah … da-dah, da-dah, da-dah … keep going east over to 2nd Avenue — that's four blocks — then take a right and go down four to East 37th. Turn left into the tunnel. It becomes the 495, the Long Island Expressway, and you'll stay on that for about ten miles till you hit the Grand Central Parkway. There'll you'll bear right, southbound, and that'll take you right to JFK. I'm now looking at the traffic flow option and it says that route is pretty fast for this time of day and this day of the week. Now, what time's your flight?"

"I don't know. Just the first one I can get to Toronto."

"Jesus, Irina! All this rushing? For all you know, there isn't a bloody flight until tomorrow morning!"

"Don't you swear at me! And you've got the bloody computer, so find me something!"

"All right … all right … stay on the line. I'll get back to you as soon as I've got it."

In the time that Robertson was doing his research, Irina had zoomed through the tunnel and covered most of the distance to the Grand Central Parkway. "I'm here," announced Robertson some ten minutes later.

"Where were you? I'm halfway back to bloody England."

"I suppose you've passed the ramp for the 278?"

"I just passed a turnoff marked Lefrak City. To my left is a forest of highly undistinguished high-rises. Apartments, I'd imagine."

"Okay, but you haven't hit the Grand Central Parkway and that's good, because you're going to be going north on it. I repeat: north, not south. You, my dear Sergeant, are off to LaGuardia where you'll catch Air Canada 727 at 8:40."

"Yikes! It's already eight o'clock. How much farther out is LaGuardia than JFK?"

"It's closer. Much closer. Two miles, as opposed to fifteen. Now, listen carefully. I made a phone call to a buddy in the NYPD, Lieutenant Giancarlo Donato. He'll be smoothing your way at the airport. Go to your gate in the central terminal and airport security will meet you there. You just show your passport and badge and they'll make a seat for you and see that your luggage gets aboard."

"What about my ticket?"

"They'll have it. Oh, and Irina? I told Giancarlo your flight was vital to resolving the animal caper. Don't make a liar out of me. By the way, where in New York were you coming from?"

"The corner of 97th and West End Avenue."

Robertson groaned loudly but was secretly delighted. The best mind in the force had just done something worthy of a bimbo, and it was so, so refreshing to feel superior to her for a change. "Oh, dear God. The Upper West Side. Tsk, tsk. You went all across town when you were just a few blocks from the Triborough Bridge and the 278, which would have put you about five minutes away from LaGuardia. What were you thinking?"

Irina had no illusions about her relationship with cars and trucks, nor the road system that validated their existence. She had even fewer illusions about Stanley Robertson, who definitely did not validate hers. "Okay, Mr. Transportation Czar," she snapped, "here's what I need you to do. By the time I reach Toronto ... which is when?"

"10:20 p.m."

"By 10:20 p.m., you should have lined up a plane that will get me at least as far as Thunder Bay. I don't care if it's private, or an airliner, or even a police contraption. Just have it waiting for me on the tarmac."

"Thunder Bay? Ah yes, the lion. I've just finished watching Jason Conrad's circus act from there on the tube. I wouldn't be in any hurry to go on a camping trip with that guy."

"I'm ready to pitch my tent. All I'm missing is one little peg, which I expect a certain steely Englishman will be sending along sometime soon. Two, actually. By the way, did you ever get anything useful from the fraud guys about Conrad's finances?"

"Not a peep from them. I suspect they're in way over their heads. It would take a rocket scientist just to figure out how much he spends on bumwad."

"Nice, Stanley."

"You mentioned 'a police contraption.' I take it you're ready to let other forces in on this case?"

"No choice, really. How else am I to get inside the police perimeter?"

Irina had touched down at Pearson International in Toronto at 10:20 p.m. on the nose. An RCMP Pilatus PC-12, a single-engine turboprop airplane with a range of more than two thousand miles, had been flown in from London, Ontario, and was waiting for her. She'd wasted no time boarding it and had, en route to Thunder Bay, immediately set about deciding exactly where she needed to go. Her first order of business had been to find out where Jason Conrad had been set down. It turned out to be just north of the tiny town of Terrace Bay, on the northernmost shore of Lake Superior. Using information from both the ground-level trackers and the helicopters, Conrad had calculated the lion's trajectory and speed. Clever Conrad. And clever lion. The beast had adjusted his course from southeastward to eastward, completely avoiding Thunder Bay and the northwestern shore of Lake Superior. It was almost as if — even at a distance of fifteen miles from its waters — he'd divined that the great lake presented an insurmountable barrier.

At a cruise speed of three-hundred miles per hour, the Pilatus would get her the six-hundred miles to Thunder Bay by 1:00 a.m. That would not do, for she'd still have had to backtrack one-hundred-and-twenty miles to Terrace Bay by helicopter, as the town's little airport had been abandoned for a year. It would be 2:30 a.m. by the time she got there, and Conrad would have been six hours and forty-two miles farther along, assuming he could grind out about seven miles per hour. The lion, pounding along at a punishing pace of fifteen miles per hour, would probably be as far along as Wawa, or possibly even Lake Superior Provincial Park.

How Conrad ever hoped to catch the lion with just boots and dogs was beyond her, but she was quite confident that he could, given the chance.

"Pilot? Sergeant? Does Wawa have an airstrip?"

"Sure does, Ma'am."

"All right, then. Forget about Thunder Bay. Put me down in Wawa."

Irina had calculated that Conrad would be about fifteen miles shy of Wawa by 8:30 in the morning, at approximately the same time she'd put together a tracking team of her own. This would do.

The RCMP Pilatus landed in Wawa at 12:30 a.m. Half-an-hour later, Irina was checking into the Parkway Motel, which was a mile south of the airport on Highway 17. By 1:05 a.m., she was lying face up and fully clothed on her bed, fast asleep.

It was now 6:30 in the morning, and she was in the homely but sparkling yellow and white tiled bathroom, brushing her teeth. Although normally averse to foul language, she thought this was a rather special occasion. She leaned into the large mirror and grimaced through the toothpaste foam. "You silly bitch. You can't go into your own backyard without getting lost, yet here in the middle of nowhere you want to track down someone who at a hundred yards can shoot the tits off a mouse?"

The phone rang, as it inevitably does when one is brushing one's teeth.

"Mmph?

"Good morning, Sergeant. Leopold Duggan, here. I trust I didn't wake you?"

Irina swallowed the toothpaste.

"Oh, dear. I'd hoped for something a bit more receptive than the gag reflex."

Irina cleared her throat. She sounded like a truck with a low battery struggling to start up. "Good morning? How do you know I'm not in England?"

"Because, dear lady, I have as much faith in you as you do in me. You'd go to where Jason Conrad is to be found on the assumption that my mission would be successful. For my part, I'd expect that you wouldn't want to waste any time."

"And I haven't wasted my time?"

"Indeed not. Even as we speak, I'm sitting in the office of the most genial Lieutenant Jorge Vilele of the Rio Police, DEAT division. We have with us one Ellis Ripperton, who has just given us a statement which explicitly connects the murders of Inspector Raja Chadwani and Maria Elena Battista to a Doo-Wop Doo-Wah Consulting, Inc. Working backward from the number in Mr. Ripperton's cellphone, I uncovered that this company is a nine-man operation based in London, England. And guess who the CEO is?"

"Is that lieutenant confident enough about all this to seek a warrant for Conrad's arrest?"

"Indeed he is. He went so far as to wake up a judge at five o'clock this morning. All the judge wants in return is that we ensure his name be spelled correctly when the story gets played by *People* magazine. That would be Joaquim Barroso. Two *r*'s, one *s*."

"Thank you, Chief Inspector."

"Can I be of further assistance? Shall I come to Thunder Bay?"

"Thanks, Inspector, but everything that's going to unfold will unfold in the next few hours, I'm sure of it."

"Oh, one more thing. Silly of me to forget. I had my people trace any and all calls placed from Doo-Wop Doo-Wah Inc. to Montreal on or about September the fourth, the day your Sergeant Perron was killed and Bismarck the wonder dog went missing. Just nine days ago, eh? Who'd believe it? At any rate, yes, such a call was indeed placed. Very early in the morning to a Motel Chablis on St. Jacques Street. I'm afraid I couldn't take things any farther, but I'd imagine your people will be interested in rushing the desk of the Motel Chablis with a photo of that dead Australian. Oliver Harvey, wasn't it?"

"Oh God, Leopold," Irina gushed. "I could just smother you with kisses."

Duggan laughed in a way Irina had never before heard him laugh. "If I thought for a moment you were serious about that, I'd *swim* to Thunder Bay!"

"God bless you, Leopold."

"And Godspeed to you, Irina."

Irina was just getting back to her tooth brushing when the phone rang again. It was Detective Inspector Booth Rawlins. Or, rather, the former Detective Inspector Booth Rawlins. In light of his vainglorious decision to rely solely on the resources of the Thunder Bay OPP in the pursuit of I-árishóni and the facility death squad, and the resultant deaths of Pickerel Pete Murdoch and his daughter Layla, he'd been summarily busted to Corporal. "Good day, Sergeant Drach. This is ... ah ... Booth Rawlins of the Ontario Provincial Police, Thunder Bay Regional Headquarters. Just to inform you that the party of hostiles responsible for the deaths of the Indian tracker Lark Alisappi, and the three constables in the search helicopter after the slaughter by the lion of the American citizens Marvin and June Hamilton, have been defeated. There was a firefight just six hours ago and we prevailed. They are all dead and we live to fight another day. Good day, Sergeant Drach."

"Hold on, there," Irina snickered. "Is this is a person or a recording?"

The crisp voice became a pitiable moan. "Recordings don't feel like shit!" Click.

Things were unravelling rather quickly for Jason Conrad, she contemplated as she dialed. And they were bound to get much worse. The party that had set out from Caribou Lake four days earlier, backtracking the southeasterly path of the lion from the point at which Lark Alisappi had been murdered, were surely close to letting the cat out of the bag. They must already have trekked a few hundred miles northwest.

"Detective Inspector Bill Sturgess, Ontario Provincial Police, Thunder Bay Regional Headquarters."

"Good morning, Inspector Sturgess. I trust I'm not calling too early."

"No, Sergeant. As a matter of fact, I was just about to call you. Within the hour your dogs, your hiking outfit, and your equipment will be delivered to you by chopper. Oh, and I hope you won't mind, but I'm assigning you a Cree guide as well. Wally Cheechoo. The best."

"Inspector —"

"Sorry, Sergeant Drach, but it has to be. Commissioner's orders. And I agree with them. Let's be realistic, here. How on Earth do you expect to handle three dogs or those woods, not to mention your kit, all by yourself? I'm already cutting you an awful lot of slack."

"I'm on a delicate mission. He'll be in my way."

"No, Ma'am. I'll be along with you to see he isn't."

At about 2:30 a.m., just as Irina had anticipated, I-árishóni had arrived in the vicinity of Wawa. Mighty though he was, he was weary. For twenty-four hours, he'd kept up a pace that would have worn down even Zarathustra.

He was on the eastern shore of Lake Superior, where the madly meandering Michipicoten River fed into the vast lake. It was just three miles from Wawa and less than half a mile from the tiny village of Michipicoten River. He'd paced up and down the shores of the waterway for about a quarter of a mile, looking for narrows. Not finding any point where the crossing was less than five-hundred feet, he ... well, here we must descend into anthropomorphization and declare that he basically said "screw it," and settled into a thick copse of trees on the northern bank for the night.

It was now 8:30 in the morning. Although the sun had been beating down on his leafy retreat for a full ninety minutes, it was not its intensifying heat that finally roused him, for he was not unaccustomed to lolling about under a scorching sun. Rather, it was two things inextricably linked in his brain: the sound of a hovering helicopter, and the yelping of a dog.

A cocker spaniel, Butterfly, was taking her master for his morning constitutional. From Nate Ferguson's modest clapboard home on Queen Street, they'd walked briskly up to Blue Avenue, then turned in the direction of the river's mouth. As they made their way along the mile-long strip of road, and Blue Avenue became Government Dock Road, Butterfly became progressively more agitated and noisy. Nate Ferguson, a wiry and heavily bearded old salt who'd years earlier retired from work as an engineer aboard the Great Lakes grain ships, trusted Butterfly's nose more than all his own senses combined, so he slowed their pace considerably. Something was up. Something of more consequence than the sound of a distant helicopter. Something of even more consequence than a wolf or a bear.

"Butterfly! Get back here, old girl."

More than willing to forego a show of bravado for the sheltering shadow of her master, Butterfly fell into growling lockstep with Nate. The old man now had to consider the possibility that something sinister was afoot. But his thoughts were rudely interrupted as the helicopter, an RCMP Squirrel, rapidly approached, hovered momentarily over the bush, then set down on the runway-straight road twenty feet ahead of them. It disgorged a heavily armed Mountie who, with his Lee Enfield rifle resting on his muscular forearm, strode quickly and deliberately toward him. "Sorry, Sir, but you'll have to turn around and go home. We'll escort you by aircraft."

"But I take this walk every morning! What's different today?"

"You don't have a TV?"

"Sure don't. Already got enough bullshit in my life. Married forty-five years."

"You haven't heard anything in town?"

"Keep to myself. The townsfolk are woodsy types. I'm merchant marine."

"I'm sure your wife isn't merchant marine. And seeing as how you've got no TV, she must gossip with the townsfolk. Didn't she bring home any news?"

"She probably did, but I didn't listen, see? Never do. How else do you think we've survived these forty-five years? So why don't *you* tell me what's up? Otherwise, I don't move. I got my civil rights."

"Move along, Sir."

"Why? Because I don't have a TV?"

"No, Sir," said the officer, his voice rising, "because of that."

The policeman abruptly raised his weapon to his shoulder and aimed it toward the treeline some thirty yards away. There stood I-árishóni, proud and defiant.

"Holy Christ," exclaimed Nate Ferguson in wonderment. "Is that what I think it is?"

"I'm afraid so, Sir," whispered the sergeant. "Now, there's been a slight change of plans effective immediately. You and your pet just follow me to the chopper, steady as she goes and no sudden movements. We'll get you home safely."

"Shoot the bugger. Shoot!"

"Sorry, Sir. Can't do that," said the officer as he backed up toward the helicopter. "Now please follow me."

"What do you mean, you can't do that? He's as big as a barn."

Sergeant Bruce had lost his patience. "That's not why I can't shoot! Now get in the goddamned helicopter, you little pecker!"

Nate was many things: he was old, he was short, he was wiry, he was fuzzy, he was cantankerous, and he may even have been a little smelly. But he was no pecker — at least not in his own mind. With a strength that caught Sergeant Eddy Bruce completely off guard, he wrested the rifle from the Mountie and took a quick shot at the lion. The bullet grazed the animal's shoulder. It didn't do any damage, but it induced a searing pain and I-árishóni charged. At a speed of fifty miles per hour, he was upon the little party of humans in mere seconds. Sergeant Bruce was eviscerated and Nate Ferguson had a multiplicity of bones and organs either broken or crushed. In an attempt to protect her master, Butterfly had thrown herself at the jaws of I-árishóni and that is exactly where she ended up. As the great beast savaged the two men with his claws and paws, she dangled lifelessly from his jaws. When he'd slaughtered Sergeant Bruce and Nate Ferguson, he bit down hard and severed her head from her body. He spat out her head as heedlessly as a teen spits out a wad of gum and turned his attention to the terrified constable in the helicopter, which was just then lifting off. I-árishóni covered the twenty feet to the aircraft in barely one second and launched himself at the open door just as it was four feet off the ground and rising rapidly. The Squirrel immediately pitched over and splintered as it cartwheeled for one-hundred feet. When the dust had settled and the smashed rotor had sputtered to a full stop, the lion emerged from the wreck unscathed. The pilot did not.

I-árishóni briefly surveyed the carnage and the twisted metal, then set off at a trot, this time with the Michipicoten River at his back. He was retracing his steps of the night before. The lion knew that he was drawing farther away from the African savanna, but he also knew, instinctively, what many humans take a lifetime to learn: that the road home cannot be measured in miles.

Lesley Perkins was a large, powerful man whose years in Britain's Special Air Services had honed his physique, his reflexes, and his hawking instincts, while his time as CFO of Golden Fleece Securities had contributed immeasurably to his patience and powers of concentration. Yet by nine-thirty on the morning of Wednesday the thirteenth of September, as he, Jason Conrad, and the aging Ojibway guide from the Michipicoten First Nation reserve closed in on Wawa, he'd had just about enough. He had spent the better part of the previous ten hours shouldering one-hundred pounds of gear at a brutal pace through pitch black, and he didn't see any reason why they couldn't stop for an hour or so. "The dogs must be exhausted, Sir," Perkins muttered to Conrad. "Perhaps we should rest them for a bit."

"Are you kidding?" replied Conrad as his phone rang. "It's all Charley can do to hold them back. Hold on a second while I get this."

That they were perched on a rocky promontory just above the treetops assured him of a fairly strong signal. Conrad put his phone to his ear and listened for a full two minutes to an extremely strong signal. Then, in a low, chilled voice, he said, "A most unfortunate event, Commissioner, but a bargain's a bargain. Besides, from what you tell me, I'm as liable to get the animal as any of your men are. Maybe even more so. Now just calm down, let me bag the beast, and we'll deal with the fallout as soon as I'm done. In the meantime, don't try anything funny — and that goes for any PR initiative — or I'll make sure you're so covered in dirt by the end of all this that people will be checking your asshole for turnips."

Conrad pocketed his phone and began polishing the barrel of his Remington 700 ABG with a small microfibre cloth.

"Anything of interest, Sir?"

"Actually, yes. The lion's doubling back from near Michipicoten River Village. Retracing his path."

"Ah ... anything else? You mentioned dirt."

"It seems our feline friend has terminated three more people. Two Mounties and a civilian. Oh, and he brought down the police helicopter while he was at it."

Perkins was incredulous. "It was in flight?"

"Had to have been. Pieces of it were scattered over a two-hundred yard radius."

Charley Bushell was alarmed. Gros Cap 49, the very land upon which they were presently standing, was his reservation, and it abutted Wawa and Michipicoten River Village. "Did the commissioner mention the name of the civilian?"

Conrad did not look up from his rifle. "Given that the Michipicoten First Nation is currently haggling over land and substantial sums of money with the Ontario government, I would hardly have referred to one of your tribesmen as a civilian. 'Combatant' would have been more appropriate."

"It is possible for an aboriginal man to be friends with a white," said Bushell hotly.

"Is it? Well ... in that case, the man's name was Nate something. Nate Ferguson. Oh, and his dog was destroyed too. Butterfly, of all things. Is it possible for an aboriginal man to be friends with a dog?"

Partly out of sorrow, partly out of fury, Charley Bushell plunged into the bush. "I must prepare the dogs," he shouted over his shoulder. "And yes, an aboriginal man can befriend any living being!"

"Then how about charming that lion out into the open," Conrad shot after him. "Right where I can plug him."

All this was somewhat distressing to Lesley Perkins. He'd known his master for less than twenty-four hours, but in that short time he'd witnessed a marked contraction in Conrad's personality. The man's focus was legendary, and, as a former SAS commando, Perkins certainly had a deep appreciation of that particular quality, but it seemed to him that even as he took the measure of the man, Conrad was measuring himself out in smaller and smaller portions. He was becoming a mere shadow of himself even as he shadowed the lion.

"Well," said Conrad to Perkins. "You've gotten your little break after all. But now it's time to move on."

"Before we do, Sir, we must discuss tactics."

"Tactics? What on Earth do you mean? We run into the lion, I shoot him."

Perkins gestured toward the heavy pack that he'd set down on the ground of the small clearing, and then, as he spoke, he knelt and absently picked at the fruit of the wild blueberry plants that occupied the interstices of a half-buried boulder. "Behold, Sir. Two perfectly serviceable hunting rifles lashed to my backpack. Of what use are they there?"

"Do I detect a lack of faith in my hunting abilities?"

"Sir, you detect a great deal of faith in the hunting abilities of that lion. He's killed God knows how many people and now it seems he's swatting helicopters out of the air like he was blooming King Kong. I just think we should be prepared for every contingency. It might be crucial to your survival as well as mine and Charley's."

"No can do. That lion is mine. I can't take the chance of you or the Indian popping off at him if the going gets rough."

Perkins obstinately stretched himself out on the ground. He was gobbling the tiny blue fruit by the dozen. "Then I don't go any farther."

Jason Conrad carefully leaned his Remington against a rock and drifted around behind Perkins. He stood motionless, two feet behind his aide. "You occupy a uniquely sensitive position. You realize what the penalty is for deserting your post?"

Perkins laughed. "You wouldn't dare. You're more civilized than that."

Conrad withdrew the razor-sharp, nine inch hunting knife from his belt and slashed Perkins's throat.

With his life's blood spurting from his both his jugular vein and his carotid artery, Perkins struggled to his feet and turned to face Conrad. He tried to speak, to express his shock, but couldn't. His larynx had also been severed.

"Sorry I didn't shoot you," said Conrad. "Quicker, and less messy. But I couldn't take a chance spooking the lion, could I?"

Perkins fell forward, dead. The whole episode had taken five seconds.

Conrad then sat where Perkins had sat, picking at the berries that Perkins had picked at. He seemed unconcerned that many of them were blood-spattered. Within a few minutes, Charley returned. He surveyed the scene, but said not a word.

"Ah, Charley. Where are the dogs?"

"Tied to a tree just a hundred yards thataway."

"Good. I'll take them and continue on. You go home. You can have the backpack too, if you like."

Charley shouldered the backpack and prepared to leave.

"So. No comment about any of this?"

"It's plenty plain what happened here," whispered Charley. "Just as it's plain what's going to happen."

"You're betting on the lion, eh?"

Charley shrugged and started walking. "I'm betting on the demons within you."

"That son of a bitch! I'm Commissioner of the RCMP. The top cop in Canada and one of the top cops in the world. The Mounties, for crying out loud! The stuff of legend. And he tells me he can arrange it so I look bad!"

Even as she held the BlackBerry to her ear, Irina signalled to Detective Inspector Bill Sturgess and their guide, Wally Cheechoo, that she was ready to move out. They'd be picking up the lion's trail where he'd killed the two RCMP officers and Nate Ferguson. "But you must know, Sir, that there is always hell to pay when you bargain with the devil."

Commissioner Bentley gagged. "What are you? A cop or a schoolmarm?"

"I will not dignify that with an answer," Irina replied frostily.

Bentley laughed ruefully. "Right you are. Who am I to pass judgment on someone else, anyway? Three men and a pooch dead. What were we thinking? I've already sacked Deputy Commissioner Siroca, and I'll be resigning, myself, in a couple of days. You'll forgive my vulgar rant?"

"I'm flattered that you saw fit to confide in me, Sir."

"Don't be flattered. Most people in the intelligence community will soon be treating me like I carry the ebola virus, and the politicos will want nothing more than to see my head on a spike outside Parliament Hill. But enough about me, Sergeant Drach. That's not why I called. I just want you to know that you'll be operating in a very secure area. All told, there'll be nearly two hundred RCMP and OPP officers working a forty mile ring around Conrad and that lion, so there's absolutely no need for you to be risking your life. If you run into problems, please, please fall back and we'll take care of things."

"I appreciate your concern, Commissioner, but I aim to do my job. I have here in my pocket a faxed copy of a warrant for the arrest of Mr. Jason Conrad, signed by His Honour Remy Fortier of the Quebec Court, in connection with the shooting death of Sergeant Jerome Perron of the Montreal Urban Police, K-9 squad. I also have a warrant issued by a Judge Barroso of Rio de Janeiro. I intend to execute those warrants personally. "

There was a long, long silence followed by a gasp of realization. "Good Lord, Sergeant Drach. Am I right in supposing that what's driven you so far has been neither the global significance of this case, nor glory, nor even the reputation of your force, but simply the death of one fellow officer?"

"But of course. I didn't know him all that well, mind you, but on the few occasions we'd worked together, I'd found him to be a rather sweet man."

"God, I wish I'd met you twenty-four hours ago. Good luck, Sergeant Drach."

Irina hopped into the back of the RCMP van and sandwiched herself between Sturgess and Wally Cheechoo. For the whole of the two mile trip to the helicopter wreckage on Government Dock Road, she petted and played with Wally's three dogs. One of them, a rumpled burgundy beauty of a bloodhound called Zsa-Zsa — so named because Wally considered her a slut — particularly delighted Irina. In contradistinction to the German shepherds, two steely creatures who bristled in anticipation, Zsa-Zsa draped her droopy self over Irina's shoes and sighed repeatedly as Irina feathered her floppy ears.

"Those ears are not just for show," volunteered Cheechoo. "When she's nosing the ground, they keep the particles she's trailing from blowing away. If single microscopic human skin cells were laid out at four-foot intervals, she could still follow that trail. And as much as four days after they were shed, too."

"Why, then, do you bother to bring the two shepherds along?"

"Like Zsa-Zsa, they don't yap when they're following a spoor. More than that, though, they look out for her. They've already saved her wrinkly little ass from a few bears and wolverines."

Bill Sturgess said, "And who's going to save their asses from the lion?"

"You know, things don't add up the way we think they're supposed to out there in the bush. Two rights can make a wrong. And two wrongs can make a right. So it could be that Jason Conrad will be the one to save them."

"You think it would be wrong for Conrad to kill the lion?"

"Maybe. And maybe it would be right for the lion to kill Jason Conrad."

For all his charm and surpassing good looks, Sergeant-Detective Athol Curzon Hudson was not a presumptuous sort. Indeed, the root of his charm lay in his being oblivious to the effect he had on others. He was rather like the princeling who, upon wandering through the palace, is unaware that all doors are being flung open exclusively for his benefit.

Being a policeman, however, he was not ignorant of the obeisance accorded wounded heroes, and he was determined to milk it for all it was worth. He'd no sooner gotten off the phone with Irina, as she hurtled through New York City, than he contacted his lieutenant and demanded he find a way to get him from Plymouth to Ignace, Ontario, within the next ten hours. "But if you happen to be talking to Irina, don't tell her about this. I want it to be a surprise."

Since Lieutenant Stan Robertson just as soon preferred to have his two detectives in the same general area — on the same continent was especially desirable — he had no qualms about acceding to this request.

It was fortuitous that Hudson had added the little caution about Irina, for just two minutes later, Robertson was guiding her through the streets of Manhattan and straightening out her security situation at LaGuardia Airport.

As a consequence, it was twenty minutes before Robertson could begin to address Hudson's request. Many calls were made. His dinner got cold. More calls were made. His wife got even colder, and eventually announced that he was on his own and she was going out to find her soulmate, "Whoever that might be."

"Aw, Sweetheart. I'm in a jam. Somehow I've got to get Hudson from England to Toronto overnight. I've tried everything. Airlines, every police force I can think of, fat cats, even the military. Nothing. It's after midnight over there and nobody's coming this way this time of night."

"Pity you couldn't just stick him in a box and FedEx him," she snapped. "That's about as much comfort and style as any cop deserves."

She slammed the door on her way out. But Lieutenant Robertson didn't slam the door on her suggestion. He may not have been one of the most brilliant and creative detectives on the Montreal force, but he'd evolved into one of its most effective commanders by virtue of his ability to build palaces using other peoples' rubble. Immediately, he got on the phone to the FedEx office in Vancouver. Why Vancouver? First, because Vancouver is a major terminal for transoceanic shipments. Second, because that city is three hours behind Montreal, and it would have only been 5:00 p.m. There was still a chance that some managers would be on the job. People who could actually make decisions.

He was in luck. It took four calls, countless holds, and innumerable transfers, but he finally found himself speaking to a bright, authoritative, and highly placed young woman who was thoroughly familiar with the animal abduction saga.

"Righto ... let me just check something here. Oh! We've got an

ATR-42 turboprop feeder plane that leaves for London in fifty minutes. Can your dishy Sergeant Hudson be at Plymouth Airport in half an hour?"

"His bags are packed."

"Good, because we've got a Toronto-bound jet leaving London at 2:00 a.m, local time. That suit you?"

"Couldn't be better."

"G-r-r-eat! Now, do you have another phone, there?"

"My cell, yes."

"Super! I'll hold this line while you call him on your cell and get him scooting over to Plymouth Airport. Then you'll come back to me and we can hash out the security and procedural details."

And so it came to pass that Hudson arrived in Toronto by 5:00 a.m., local time. Prior to landing at Pearson International, he'd established communications with the RCMP, and they'd appealed to the Canadian Forces Air Command for assistance. Thus, a VIP jet from the 412th Squadron — a white, rebadged Challenger 600 — had been flown posthaste from its Ottawa base to Toronto and was waiting for him on the tarmac. Having been brought up-to-date on Irina's movements by the Mounties, Hudson had changed his destination from Ignace to Wawa and arrived there at 7:00 a.m. By 9:30, with the help of the RCMP and the OPP, he'd been outfitted with a guide and three tracker dogs.

And Irina knew nothing about any of this.

And Commissioner Bentley knew everything about this. But he'd said nothing about it when he'd talked to Irina. As far as he was concerned, the more men there were in the field — especially the likes of that perceptive and celebrated detective, Athol Hudson — the better her chances.

"Forward, ho!" bellowed Hudson as he brought his plaid-clad arm down in a chopping motion.

Ahmet Gul, a towering and dour Turk with a waist-length ponytail, considered one of West Africa's premier hunting guides, spat contemptuously on the ground. "You may now even say 'tallyho' if you wish, but once we move, you will keep your mouth closed. And why are you even here? Who are you that you should be privileged to hunt with me?"

Hudson looked at him askance. "Don't you look at television?"

"Television is but moving shadows and light. Not real."

"Newspapers, then?"

"Newspapers are but shadows and light that do not move. Even less real. All that matters is the moment when you confront a beast and one of you must die."

Hudson coolly stared at Gul's scoped Sterling Davenport Lion Rifle, chambered for .375 H&H Magnum cartridges. "It all comes down to whichever one of you has the quickest trigger finger, Mr. Gul?"

Gul narrowed his steely little eyes, stroked the wispy mandarin beard, and spat again, this time within inches of Hudson's boot. Hudson could have sworn he heard the loamy forest floor sizzling. Yet he'd not come this far and this fast to be intimidated by anyone, not even the offspring of Godzilla. "Don't do that again, Mr. Gul. I'm in charge here. Now, forward ho!"

Gul did not budge.

"Tallyho!"

Gul spat again.

In one blurred motion, Hudson raised his Mauser M 98 and put a bullet through the brain of one of Gul's three dogs, which were tethered to a tree some twenty-five yards away.

Gul's jaw dropped. "Why do you do that?"

"Because, Mr. Gul, I'm not too sure where the heart is located in quadrupeds."

"That was my best dog!"

"If you'd been more forthcoming, I'd have known that. Right?"

Ahmet Gul shrugged and scuffed his way over to his two remaining animals. He removed them from the vicinity of the dead Redbone Coon Hound and took a few minutes to calm them. That done, he shouldered his backpack and made a gathering gesture in Hudson's direction. He was ready to go. Using the silk scarf that Irina had left in Hudson's hospital room, he gave his dogs the scent and they hastily departed from the site of the devastated RCMP Squirrel helicopter, just twenty minutes behind Irina Drach, Detective Inspector Bill Sturgess, and guide Wally Cheechoo.

Having rounded the northeastern corner of Lake Superior's Whitefish Bay, I-árishóni was headed due west, retracing his steps of the night before. One mile to his southeast, the Irina party was trailing him, while Jason Conrad was coming at him directly from one mile to the west

The lion suddenly began to grimace, but not out of any particular feelings of distress or disapproval. Rather, it was because that is what cats do when they smell something significant. In a gesture called flehmen, they widen their lips to allow air to waft over the Jacobson's organ, a highly sensitive piece of olfactory tissue located on the roofs of their mouths. What I-árishóni was responding to was the scent of Jason Conrad and his dogs, borne on the west wind.

He slowed his pace, then finally stopped and roared defiantly. Ahead of him was man and dog. To his left was a body of water as limitless as the sky. Behind him — as always when he killed, he knew — were more men and dogs. So I-árishóni went northeasterly about one-thousand yards, just far enough that all his pursuers would have to approach him from the same direction. He then slid into a thicket and waited, perfectly immobile. The lion in him said it was time to stand and fight.

Jason Conrad was making good time. In fact, he was tumbling tirelessly through the bush at about the same speed as one normally jogs on the track. The prospect of coming face to face with the lion made him feel stronger and more alive than he had in years. And why not? He was already at the top of his food chain, and he was ready to face a creature at the top of another. A battle of the Titans, he envisaged. Two great predators in a life and death struggle.

The dogs no longer tried to run ahead of their leashes. They'd learned very quickly that the man who held them was not to be trifled with. Everything about his movements and voice made it plain that he was the leader of the pack. If called upon to sacrifice themselves for his sake, they would do so without hesitation. And they knew better than the human how soon that would be.

As Irina stumbled along behind Wally Cheechoo and Bill Sturgess, she was appalled at what was going through her mind. There were no great ideas, nor complex stratagems, nor even imaginings of imminent events. No, what Irina had buzzing through her brain like an angry bee was "You deserve a break today ... at McDonald's." She didn't disagree with the sentiment expressed therein but she wondered, as she approached the confrontation of her life, whether Napoleon had been humming a jingle about croissants on the eve of the Battle of Austerlitz, or if Julius Caesar hadn't been thinking about a platter of peacock tongues prior to the Battle of Zela. One couldn't be certain, but she doubted it, and therefore made a concerted effort to refocus her thoughts. It wouldn't be seemly to perish by bullet or fang whilst contemplating an Egg McMuffin.

Thus, while Wally Cheechoo and Detective Sturgess were twenty yards ahead of her and trading woodsmen's lore, Irina changed course — without being noticed. Having focused her mind on the situation at hand, and having arrived at the conclusion that the lion could not long resist the lure of the east, she veered off in an east-northeast direction.

It was the only way. She had to deal with Jason Conrad by herself.

Sergeant-Detective Athol Curzon Hudson was astonished at how quickly Ahmet Gul and his dogs were plowing through the bush. He could barely keep his oversized woodmen's boots flopping fast enough. But he was even more astonished when Gul suddenly pulled up on the canines and scratched his enormous head. "Look there! In that direction lies the way of at least two men and several animals, including the lion."

Hudson looked, and saw only trees and brush.

"Now look here! Only one person can have passed this way. There can be no doubt that the woman has detached from the rest of her party."

"Are you sure?"

"Are you stupid? My dogs follow only her. And are you blind? Look! Look!"

Hudson looked, and again saw only trees and brush. "All right, then. Can you tell me how fast she's moving?"

Gul let out his dogs and lurched forward about fifty feet. "Here, the foliage and branches reveal little disruption. And look here, at her boot prints in that sandy soil. Not much pressure on the balls of her feet. Slowly and carefully, she moves."

"Okay," said a humbled Hudson. "Give me a few seconds to think this through."

While Hudson pondered the matter he seemed, to the impatient Gul, to be like a man waiting for a bus. When he asked Gul whether he was sure Irina was alone he seemed, to the incredulous Gul, to be like a man who'd just missed the bus. "Fucking! Have I not pointed out that there is only one set of prints this way? And have I not shown that the injury to the surroundings can only have been caused by one person?"

"Don't you talk to me in that tone of voice or I'll shoot the rest of your bloody dogs!"

Gul bowed slyly. "Then we shall not be able to track your lady friend, and she will be eaten by the lion."

"What do you mean? You just said that in *that* direction lies the path of the lion!"

"Dear Sergeant, this female is no fool. Firstly, she moves slowly but surely because she knows the Indian tracker and the RCMP officer will not double back for her. She knows they will not waste time in searching for her, in particular since their dogs have the lion's scent and not hers. She senses they will be of the opinion that the best way to protect her is to make haste and get to the lion by the surest means available. Secondly, she knows that the hypotenuse of a triangle is far shorter than the sum of its other two sides."

After having recovered from the shock of hearing this loathsome barbarian use the word *hypotenuse* in a cogent sentence, Hudson adopted a more conciliatory tone. "You're telling me that she's taking the most direct route to the lion?"

"This I believe."

"But how can she know that the lion is not straight ahead, that way?"

"Is she a good detective, Sergeant?"

"The best."

"Of course she is. So she has done the logical thing. She knows he will retreat from the water's edge and keep the forest to his back. She also knows that he will want his enemies coming at him from the front, not from behind or at his side."

"The implication there is that the lion has done the logical thing. Is that possible?"

Ahmet Gul's substantial belly wobbled with laughter. "If there were no logic in nature, there would not even be chaos! There would be nothing!"

"Um ... shouldn't we be moving while we talk?"

"Agh! For a genius, I am so stupid. Of course we should be moving. And fast! We have a good chance of overtaking her before she gets to Conrad or the lion."

"Just one more thing," huffed Hudson as they plunged through the forest. "How do we know she separated from the other two at precisely the correct angle? That she's headed straight for the lion?"

"Fucking! One who knows the logic of nature can also know its mysteries."

After Irina had dropped out of sight, Detective Inspector Bill Sturgess had not proven to be very good company for Wally Cheechoo. During the previous half hour, while chewing at the inside of his cheek until it bled, he'd nattered incessantly about the perils that awaited her. "She was my responsibility, goddamn it. I should've kept an eye on her at all times. And why doesn't she answer her radio?"

Cheechoo no longer replied. He was all talked out, and Sturgess was beyond consolation, anyway. Only when the dogs abruptly turned sharply to the right, in a path perpendicular to Whitefish Bay, did Cheechoo feel moved to open his mouth. "Gitche fucking Manitou."

Sturgess's forehead, which was already beaded with sweat from the heat of the midmorning sun, was shiny enough to have dazzled Cortés the conquistador. "What?"

Wally Cheechoo muttered, in his irreparably low voice, "Jason Conrad has passed by here." He pointed northeast. "Look. On the same path as the lion. And unless the lady cop doubled back or walked into Lake Superior, she's headed where they're headed."

"Shit. You mean she's going to have the lion *and* Conrad for company?"

"Not for sure, but there's a chance. She don't seem like the type to guess at things. And if she was guessing, I'd reckon it was a very educated guess."

"How long ago was Conrad here?"

Cheechoo stooped to the ground and ruffled the flattened grass. "Not long. The grass hasn't started to spring back yet. And the cat's prints in this here sand have been worn some by the wind off the lake, but Conrad's are still sharp as a woman's tongue."

"Answer my question. How long since Conrad was here?"

"Fifteen minutes, maybe."

Rather than causing him to completely decompensate, the gravity of the situation served to make Sturgess more focused and purposeful. "We've spent enough time here," he barked. "Time to move. And fast."

However, the gravity of the situation also made Wally Cheechoo more focused and purposeful. He sat cross-legged on the ground, arms resting on his legs with palms upward, and mumbled something quite arcane to himself.

"What the fuck are you doing?"

"You said this Jason Conrad is bad, right?

"Maybe even more so than the lion. Why?"

"Well, it seems to me my fee should be increased by a coupla thousand bucks. I signed on to track one evil spirit, not two."

Sturgess was aghast. "How can you be so mercenary at a time like this?"

"You white men always talk about how us Indians lack initiative. I'm just doing my bit to fix that."

"Would you be pulling this stunt if Irina were a native woman?"

"Maybe not."

Sturgess stroked his chin contemplatively, then stared for a few moments at Cheechoo, who seemed to be rooted in the ground. "Well … I guess this is what you'd call honest bargaining, eh?"

Cheechoo was silent for a good minute, and then he sighed. "Maybe not. I don't really believe the cat is an evil spirit. A desperate man may turn his back on his own true nature, but a desperate beast can only embrace it."

Sturgess aimed his rifle at several distant points, on more than one occasion squinting and whispering "Pow" to himself. Then he lowered the stock to the ground and leaned on the barrel. "I'll tell you what, Wally. You can have that extra two grand if we move out of here on the double. My force and the RCMP got millions out of Conrad, and hell, it would only be just if some of it was used against him."

Wally Cheechoo leapt to his feet, shook Sturgess's outstretched hand, then gathered up the leashes of the dogs. "These dogs will fly like the wind if I let them. Can you keep up?"

Sturgess bent over Zsa-Zsa the bloodhound and extended her enormous ears while the two German shepherds anxiously milled about his feet. "So, Sweetheart," he said to her in baby talk, "you gonna use these to fly, like Dumbo?"

"Don't touch those!" barked Cheechoo. "Those are my livelihood!"

Sturgess immediately dropped the ears and straightened up, but he didn't have time to mollify Cheechoo. His radio sounded. "Sturgess, here. Go ahead."

He listened intently for about forty-five seconds before signing off with curt thanks. "Huh. The team I sent out from where that old American couple, June and Marvin Hamilton, were killed is now about two-hundred-fifty miles northwest of Caribou Lake. It's at a point on an almost straight line between Lake Caribou and that small lake where the American hunters killed Willie Gleason over a lion sighting."

"That's the good news, I guess. What's the bad?"

"The team I set down at Willie's lake has been mashing around in the woods for days and can't pick up the lion's scent."

"So when did those American hunters sight the lion?"

"Uh ... eight days ago."

Cheechoo stared at Sturgess incredulously.

"Yes, I know," muttered a blushing Sturgess. "The trail goes cold after three or four days. But I had to do something, didn't I?"

"Even the trail from Caribou Lake will be getting cold any minute now."

Wally kicked the ground a few times, for he didn't like advising other people in the matter of their own affairs. On the other hand, he liked Detective Inspector Bill Sturgess enough that he didn't want to see him busted from his new rank after just two days. "If I was you, I'd forget about the dog teams and concentrate on fly-overs due northwest from Willie's lake. The place the lion came from should be pretty big, and easy to spot. So now, shouldn't we take off? I sure do want to earn those two thousand extra bucks, you know. This Injun don't want handouts."

And they thus took off as fast as Zsa-Zsa's stubby little legs would carry her. She didn't exactly fly like the wind, but Bill Sturgess was soon winded and struggling to keep up. Between gasps, he managed to order up Wally Cheechoo's recommendation.

Irina had been navigating her way through the bush with the aid of her compass, and hating every minute of it, when she came across a most unexpected sight: a man in a small clearing disassembling a blue pup tent and packing up his gear. A short, portly black man of indeterminate age who perspired profusely. She watched for a few minutes, unobserved, then advanced toward him with her rifle on her shoulder and her finger on the trigger. "Don't move, Mr. Amadi."

Chinua Amadi froze in a stooping position when he saw what Irina was holding. "Good day, Sergeant Drach. Would that be a Ruger 77 RSM Mark II?"

"I believe so, yes."

"Chambered for .458 Lott Magnums?"

"My guide told me I could bring down an elephant with this thing."

"Ah. That would be the Lott, then. Never fear, Sergeant. I'll gladly turn to stone if you assure me you won't be pulling the trigger."

Irina moved in closer to Chinua. His perspiration was puddling on the rocky outcropping just below below his inclined head. The bowled depression in it looked like a small birdbath. "Where's Conrad?"

"Actually, I was about to ask you the same thing. After I'd suggested you point that thing somewhere else, of course."

In the same moment that she lowered the rifle, she raised her police pistol to within inches of his face. "Is this better?"

"Much. At least now my mother will be able to recognize my poor, dead body."

"You can straighten up, now, and answer my question."

He stood up, and massaged his lower back. "You're not going to believe this, but I'm on a quest quite similar to yours."

"That's not credible. How can you have gotten inside the police perimeter without being accompanied by Jason Conrad?"

"The tent, Sergeant, should go some way toward substantiating my contention that I entered this zone well before the police, before Conrad, and even before you. I've actually been trudging through this Godforsaken wilderness for nearly two days. Why? Because I need a firm word or two with Mr. Conrad. As do you, apparently."

"A firm word? Oh, my. Not the usual obsequious drivel?"

"He left me for dead in Venice. Of course, I deserved such a fate because I'd betrayed him, but the mere fact of my survival does not elevate me to sainthood. I must take stern action. Uh ... perhaps we could work together? After we each lay down our weapons?"

Irina waved her sidearm. "What on Earth are you talking about?"

Amadi extended his hands. "These, of course."

Irina was convulsed with laughter. "What? Those pudgy little things? I suppose you're going to tell me they're 'lethal weapons.'"

"No, I'm going to show you." And in a shrew's heartbeat, Chinua Amadi had sent her pistol flying over her shoulder and gotten her in a choke hold. "Now that we're on more comfortable terms, would you be interested in knowing how I betrayed Mr. Conrad?"

Irina could barely breathe or swallow. As a matter of fact, she couldn't answer, either.

"Well, then," Chinua muttered into her ear, "it will be my pleasure to tell you. It was I, not Mr. Conrad, who ordered you killed in Britain. As much as I disagreed with his methods, I still believed in his original vision. And you, of course, were a significant threat. Since you've no doubt blabbed to all and sundry about Mr. Conrad and the great enterprise, I don't imagine you in particular are much of a danger anymore, but I will at least have the satisfaction of dealing with him by myself."

He strengthened his hold on Irina's neck and squeezed, and then squeezed some more. So far as Irina could still think clearly, she knew she had only a few seconds remaining, assuming he didn't just break her neck. So with all her might, she brought up her heel between his legs. If he'd been any taller, and she any shorter, the movement would have been ineffectual. They were, however, quite a good fit, and the effect on Chinua Amadi's testicles was bracing, to say the least. He immediately slackened his hold on Irina's neck and his body bent at the waist. This was all the opportunity Irina needed. Her elbow shot out and caught Chinua on the side of the head, slightly above the ear. A swinging anvil couldn't have had more effect. He sprawled sideways about six feet then collapsed in a heap, out cold.

When he regained consciousness minutes later, a still-gasping Irina was hovering over him, pistol pointed at his head. She'd searched him for a concealed weapon and found none. "I wasn't sure you'd make it. You're lucky. You might have died of severe head trauma."

"Truly, I am blessed."

Irina stooped for a closer look and peered into his eyes. "Hm, a slight concussion, but in the context of the current events, nothing about which to bother my pretty little head. Now, we have a few things to discuss, but first take these. And I'm giving them to you not because I pity you, but because I want you to think straight."

She handed him a few Tylenols.

"Can I get water? I have some in my canteen."

"See, you're not thinking straight," she replied, unsmiling. "You deserve to be left high and dry. Go on, swallow them."

The dazed Chinua promptly did as he was bidden.

"All right. So you were behind the attempt on my life in Bude. What about New York? You, again?"

"No! I swear! I would have told you when I had you in the choke hold were it so. I ... uh, felt like boasting. This is the first I'm hearing about such an attempt."

"The betrayal of Conrad you mentioned. That would have been trying to kill me?"

"Indeed."

"And it was for that very thing he sentenced you to death in Venice."

"It sounds romantic, I know, but the outcome was in actual fact quite squalid. I shot both my appointed executioners in the face with the gun they'd intended to use on me. They got in too close, you see."

"It would seem our Mr. Conrad is a bit conflicted about me, wouldn't it? He orders your death for trying to dispose of me, but then turns around and tries to kill me himself."

Chinua appreciated this turn in the conversation, this shift from the subject of his own culpability to that of Conrad's. "Yes, yes," he clucked. "That is why I was driven — yes, driven! — to have you eliminated. His infatuation with you posed a danger to the project. Now, why he should have finally turned against you would be a matter of much speculation. Did he finally see you for the threat you were, or has his obsession with the beast rendered all else irrelevant? The latter, to be charitable. He is like a man staring at the sun. The rest of his world fades into darkness."

"It goes without saying that Conrad must be brought to justice," Irina whispered, as if confiding an innermost secret. "And he will be. However, I suppose I don't wish him death under the tooth and claw of that lion, the prick. Does that make any sense?"

Chinua was thunderstruck. "Am I to understand that you're not going to kill him?"

"Of course not. I'm going to arrest him. Believe it or not, that's what police officers prefer to do."

"Well . . . this enriches my opinion of you, Sergeant Drach. Considerably."

"My, the things people say at the point of a gun —"

Suddenly, and in consequence of the throttling Chinua had given her, Irina's neck went into spasm. Her attention wavered for only a fraction of a second, but thunder struck. She was now flat on her back, pinned under her powerful adversary. With his thumb, Chinua administered such a piercing pinch to the inside of her wrist that her hand reflexively let go of the gun.

"Oh, dear God. You stink of stale sweat. If you're going to shoot me, do it soon. Please!"

But Chinua did not reach for the gun. Nor did he attempt to strangle her again. Instead, he leapt to his feet and made a V-sign with his index and forefinger. "Peace."

Irina rubbed her unbelieving eyes. "I beg your pardon?"

He stood firmly planted on the spot, still with the silly fluorescent smile and the peace sign. Irina covered her eyes and began to laugh uncontrollably. Chinua offered her a tissue to wipe away the tears, then helped her to her feet. In response to her utter confusion, he said emphatically, "I was not joking when I said I had revised my opinion of you, Sergeant. There is a nobility about you, and there is certainly a nobility about Mr. Conrad that should never be forgotten."

Irina studied him appraisingly for about two seconds, then started running. "Right! Now that we're bosom buddies, leave everything behind except your weapon and a change of underwear. Move, move, move! I'm fifteen minutes behind schedule."

Chinua hurriedly gathered up his bulging knapsack, his rifle, and Irina's pistol. "You know, my chief character defect has always been my willingness to follow anyone who knows where they're going. This time, however, I believe I've gotten it right —"

But Irina was already crashing through the bush.

Barely ten minutes had passed since Irina's and Chinua Amadi's departure when Hudson and Ahmet Gul arrived at the abandoned campsite. At the edge of the clearing, Gul barred Hudson from advancing. "Wait! There will be footprints and such. I am the expert."

While Gul stalked around the campsite studying things, Hudson lifted his eyes and gazed at the hole in the high canopy of pine, maple, and oak. It was still only midmorning, so the tufts of light didn't brush the ground, but the upper parts of the tree trunks were lit up in sharp relief and looked to him like strong, dark beams supporting an illuminated stained glass ceiling of dappled greens and celestial blue. Until Guls's gruff voice shattered the silence, he was transported to a wondrously ordered and peaceful place.

"Fucking! Are you all right over there? You have this great big red patch on your shirt. Just below your shoulder."

Hudson looked down, then raised his hand to his chest. It came away wet with blood. "Yeah, I'm fine. Just tell me what you've found."

"You sure?"

"I'm fine! Get on with it!"

Gul shook his head dubiously. "Huh, you look don't fine. Anyway, here is the scoop. They left in a big hurry. The tent is half dismantled. There is food and clothing left behind. Something else. She was taken by force."

Hudson felt as if some homunculus were working over his guts with a wire brush. "How do you know?"

"Look over here. Two sets of footprints very close together. Toes to heels, as if she were held from behind."

"Oh, but it looks like a lot of scuffling went on over *here*," said Hudson hopefully. "She might have gotten free."

Gul was indignant. "Are you not stupid? Who is to say the scuffling did not occur first? Not me, that's who! And who is the expert tracker?"

"How many of them were there?"

"One. I see only one set of prints apart from hers. Pup tent bears that out. No room to bed down with even a flea in that thing."

Hudson untied the leashes of the dogs. "It has to be a confederate of Conrad's. Let's move!"

Gul snatched the leashes from Hudson with one hand, and with the other tore open Hudson's shirt and stared at the blood-soaked bandage. "Fucking, man. You belong in a hospital."

"I belong with Irina! Move it!"

The dogs strained at their leashes. They trembled with excitement. Their quarry was near, and they knew it.

So did Jason Conrad. He didn't need the dogs to tell him that. The lion's presence was as palpable as the shadows cast by the thicket of birches one-hundred yards ahead of him.

Conrad halted, released the dogs' leashes, and waited for the inevitable. It came within ten seconds. A screeching, atonal symphony of terror and pain.

And then something occurred that he hadn't expected, but it appealed to his morbid sense of humour. The lion kicked all three limp bodies a good twenty yards out into the clearing. He grudgingly cheered the beast's sheer brass.

Conrad now knew exactly where the lion was, and he made a few quick computations. Taking into account a lion's typical charging speed of fifty miles per hour, he calculated that I-árishóni could cover the one-hundred yards separating them in just about four, maybe five, seconds. That was time enough for one single shot, given that he held a bolt action rifle. Placement of the .375 Ultramag bullet would be everything.

It never occurred to Conrad to widen the gap between himself and the lion for safety's sake. However, it did occur to him to back up twenty yards in order that he might gain enough time to unpack a bottle of vintage Scotch. As he slowly stepped backward, the lion growled menacingly, but he still did not show himself. I-árishóni had yet to smell any fear.

Having poured himself a stiff eighteen-year Talisker, Conrad advanced once more, reclaiming his position at the one-hundred yard mark. Crouching, with the rifle barrel propped on his one raised knee and the whisky resting in the dead leaves beside him, he settled in for a long wait. He did not expect to get off a shot at I-árishóni until the lion charged, nor did he want to. What normally passed for big game hunting — gunning down, from a safe distance, animals who were peacefully going about their business — did not appeal to him in the least.

A lot went through Jason Conrad's mind as he knelt there, sipping at his drink. At first he revelled in the sensation of the whisky, and analyzed the components of its flavour: the pepper and smoke of the attack, the honey on the palate, and the salty finish. But Conrad was not a sensual man, and the diversion of the liquor, while comforting, did not long occupy him. His thoughts soon turned to the days when he'd first dreamed of his grand project, of the love and concern he'd felt for the Earth and its myriad, magical life forms, from the lowliest protozoan to the most brilliant of mathematicians. This love had very quickly metamorphosed into a sense of responsibility, light at first, but becoming more burdensome when he began to implement his project. As his concept gradually became reality, and his organization grew and became more effective, a profound shift began to occur in his thoughts and feelings. The sense of responsibility transmuted into a sense of ownership, particularly as the facility neared completion. The living organisms, the precious plants and animals, became objects to be banked, and the obstacles — flesh and blood human beings

— turned into bad loans that needed to be written down. Real blood flowed as reality once again became a bloodless concept.

How could that have happened? And how ironic was it that at a moment when his humanity was at its most bankrupt, he should be confronted by the raging heart of nature?

As if to underline that thought, the beast rumbled in contempt.

Unbidden, Chinua Amadi and Irina Drach crept onto his cerebrations. He almost wept in remembrance. They'd been different from all the others. He'd loved them. Couldn't he have been stronger? Couldn't he have done better by them?

As he lifted the glass of Talisker to his lips they both appeared to him. There, in the bushes to his right. So lifelike. And they were both pointing rifles at him. Well, he had it coming. "Go on," he said to the apparitions. "Do your worst. Shoot. Of course, it would be more glorious to be torn apart by the king of beasts than gunned down by a pair of ghosts with a grudge, but this way would be more sentimental, wouldn't it?"

"We're not ghosts, Mr. Conrad," said Irina. "And you're under arrest for murder, conspiracy to murder, illegal transshipment of endangered species, graft, fraud, blackmail, and just about everything else humanity has been able to cook up since it was booted out of the Garden of Eden. Now, drop the gun and put your hands in the air."

Jason Conrad did not need a reality check. By now, he was quite aware that Irina and Chinua had survived his machinations. He was actually relieved, and glad to see them. "I should have guessed you two would make it, although how exactly you did it will be fascinating to hear."

Chinua, his trigger finger twitching, said, "Should we become raconteurs in our dotage, Sir, we'll always know exactly where to find you. Now please, drop the weapon."

"The lion is waiting for me to do just that, Chinua. He's a clever bugger."

"Drop the rifle, Sir."

"Don't say I didn't warn you." Conrad set down his rifle, then raised his glass and drained it. "*L'Chaim!* To life!"

And I-árishóni did just that. He sprang to life, and was upon Conrad within seconds, tearing at him with tooth and claw. In a cloud of dust, flesh ripped, bones cracked, and blood spewed. Blown back by the sheer mass and kinetic energy of the beast, as would one be by a typhoon, Irina and Amadi hesitated for a few precious seconds. By then Conrad looked as if a bomb had gone off in his hands. The flesh was stripped from the arms that had tried to hold back I-árishóni, revealing splintered bones. Fingers were missing. His face had been shredded and in its place was a death mask. He was eviscerated, and his intestines spilled out onto the ground.

Having calculated that the risk of hitting Conrad with a bullet was mitigated by the unspeakable carnage she was witnessing, Irina squeezed off a shot and the massive .458 Lott Magnum punctured the lion at 2,200 feet per second. He stopped dead, then bolted into the bush at the far side of the clearing, limp notwithstanding. She'd hoped for a followup shot, but the Ruger's turnbolt action was too slow. He was gone.

Chinua Amadi, who'd been watching the attack in paralyzed horror, retched violently, then slowly made his way toward the ruin that was Jason Conrad.

Conrad was still alive. As Chinua tiptoed forward, the industrialist tilted his head toward him. "I could use a laugh right about now," he gasped through rent lips. "Tell me how you got away."

"Absurdly easy, Sir. I played at being terrified, and they let down their guards. They were thugs, with thug brains. As did you, they underestimated me."

"Are you implying I'm a thug?"

"You treated me as a child, Mr. Conrad. As someone who would love you unconditionally. You abused my faith in you, just as you abused the conception that brought us together. That is thuggish, to be oblivious to the feelings of others."

"You're no saint yourself, Chinua. You tried to do away with Irina, remember?"

"At least I hated her. I saw her for the threat she was."

"Forgive me, Chinua?"

"Yes, Sir. I forgive you."

Irina materialized at Conrad's feet and stared down at him.

"That cat's a tough son of a bitch," murmured Conrad. "Did he get away?"

"For now," said Irina.

"Seeing as how it's not going to be me that kills him, I find myself hoping it's for good," Conrad managed to lift his head and view what was causing the excruciating pain in his torso. With the one arm that could still move, he tried, vainly, to stuff his intestines back into his body cavity. "There'll be no deathbed confessions from me, Irina. I've already spilled my guts about as much as need be, although I will add that I loved you both, in my own way. Now, Chinua. How about it? Finish me off, I beg of you."

In this macabre tableau, Irina was standing at Conrad's feet with her rifle barrel lowered. Chinua Amadi was positioned at Conrad's head, facing her. He raised Irina's pistol, and, kissing the barrel, said solemnly to Conrad, "For old times' sake, Sir, and for the glory that might have been."

He lowered the gun and a shot rang out.

Chinua spun one-hundred-eighty degrees, then collapsed into a heap beside Conrad. Sergeant-Detective Athol Hudson hurtled through the young cedars at the edge of the clearing, smoke still billowing from his rifle. Breathlessly, he asked, "Are you all right, Irina?"

"Never mind me," Irina replied, gaping at the spreading blood stain on Hudson's shirt. "What about *you*?"

"Nothing, really. Just a slow leak." Hudson looked down at Conrad. "Oh, my *God*. Nothing like that."

Conrad stirred, but just barely. "I'm afraid God's not here, Sergeant Hudson. Unfortunately you are here in his place, and you have just screwed up my going-away party."

"Conrad? Jason Conrad?"

"No need to be delicate, Sergeant," Conrad rasped. "I know I've looked better."

"Mr. Amadi was about to put Mr. Conrad out of his misery," Irina solemnly pronounced.

Hudson knelt by Chinua and examined him. There was a gaping hole in his chest. "You were going to let him?"

Irina pursed her lips and looked not at Hudson but at the ghastly wreck that was Jason Conrad.

"Amadi's in pretty bad shape, too. Have you called for the medics?" Hudson asked.

"No. Conrad was attacked only seconds before you arrived."

There came another gunshot, and a bullet penetrated Jason Conrad's head.

He was dead.

Amadi relinquished his hold on the sidearm and it fell to the dust. Blood was trickling down his cheek. Plainly, he was dying.

"Bloody hell, in more ways than one," Irina murmured. "Mr. Amadi was going to furnish me with volumes about Conrad's activities,"

A distraught Athol Hudson said, "I guess I fucked up, big time, didn't I?"

Irina raised Hudson to his feet and embraced him. "No no, no. You thought I needed saving. You did what any good cop would do —"

A coughing sound. Chinua lifted his head a few degrees, trying to look at Irina. "Not to worry. In my knapsack there are names ... numbers ... records of transactions ... I was going to redeem myself."

Then Chinua Amadi, too, was still.

Irina looked heavenward, sighing deeply. There were a few moments before she spoke, and then it was only in the quietest voice. "Well, time to call for help, isn't it? That lion, Athol. I've never seen anything like it —"

Ahmet Gul suddenly pushed his way through the cedars and parked himself in front of Irina and Hudson. His dogs were quite excited to have finally arrived at Irina, and jumped all over her. Gul did nothing to restrain them until Hudson pulled out his pistol. "I am Ahmet Gul, and it is I who led the sergeant to you. I have been waiting diplomatically while you have your sickening emotional reunion."

Irina thrust her face in his and poked at his barrel chest. "Listen, Buster. You can make fun of me, you can even make fun of Hudson, but you will not make fun of our relationship! Understood?"

"What of the lion. Did anyone get off a shot?"

"You're changing the subject!"

Gul spread his arms, with his palms turned skyward. "But of course. What else is one to do with a woman? Otherwise, one ends up talking of laundry and kitchen floors."

Now Irina was steaming. She would have jerked his beard if it hadn't looked so greasy. "*This* woman got off a shot, and she hit him. He ran off at full speed in that direction, limping."

Gul was incredulous. "At full speed, he ran? Limping?"

"Limping!"

"How big was the animal?"

Irina held the edge of her hand against Hudson, halfway up his chest. "The sergeant is about the same height as Conrad. This high, at the shoulders."

Gul laughed derisively. "Fucking! That high, eh? And do you know how a woman describes a mouse? As big as a dog, she will say."

"Good God, man," Irina replied hotly, pointing at Conrad. "Look at what he did to Conrad."

Gul briefly looked over Conrad's body without pity, then reverted to Irina. He was having fun goading her. So much, in fact, that he didn't notice how agitated his dogs had become. "I have seen such a thing before. Perhaps not so bad, but I have seen it. I am unmoved."

All at once Irina was rigid, as if she'd been freeze-dried, and her voice had become carefully modulated. "Perhaps if you were to turn around, Mr. Gul, you'd change your mind about unmoving."

Gul looked rather cavalierly over his shoulder. What he saw, forty yards away and poised to charge, was I-árishóni. When he'd rotated his head back to face Irina, his eyes looked like they'd suffered whiplash.

"Do not budge," mumbled Gul. "Do not be provocative. Do only as I say. I have years of experience with these beasts."

With his finger caressing the trigger of his lowered rifle, Hudson whispered, "Can I at least set up for a shot?"

"No!" And then Ahmet Gul lowered his voice to a barely audible level. "No, no, no, no, no. I dare not even turn around. We must all be perfectly still. Such a large and powerful beast could be upon us in two seconds — not enough time even to lift your weapon. And do you think a lion such as that does not know what a rifle is for?" He looked accusingly at Irina. "You have already taught him that!"

"Well excuse me," sniffed Irina. "It seemed like a just cause at the time." A heartbeat later she added, acidly, "Don't you think he'll interpret all this whispering as a plot against him?"

"I laugh! Ha-ha! The lady cop jokes in the face of death. Ha-ha! Now please do as I say."

Alas, Gul's dogs could not follow the preceding conversation. Having cowered and quietly skulked for an appropriate amount of time, they were now emboldened by the lion's seeming passivity. They curled their lips, bared their fangs, and began to growl threateningly. I-árishóni, who had a particular distaste for canines of every description, could restrain himself no longer. In just over one second, from a standing start, he'd covered thirty yards. Then he leapt and covered the remaining ten yards airborne — a feat not all that unusual even for a lion of normal proportions. He landed squarely on Gul's back and simultaneously broke the guide's neck and crushed a substantial number of his lower vertebrae. The *coup de grâce* was a quick and brutal mauling of Gul's face and neck. He then set upon the dogs with a ferocity that would have bewildered even the most seasoned of naturalists.

As for Hudson and Irina, they'd been sent sprawling by the considerable forward momentum of Gul's and the lion's bodies. This convulsion of animal aggression had also separated then from their weapons. Thus they both played possum while ten feet away the lion did something to the dogs that could only have been improved upon by liberal amounts of Hamburger Helper. A satisfied I-árishóni then loped off into the woods.

Gul was dead. His dogs were even more dead. And Irina and Hudson, each badly bruised by the impact, took a considerable amount of time to right themselves. As soon as her head had cleared, Irina scrabbled over to Hudson on her hands and knees. "Dear God," she moaned, fussing over his blood-soaked bandage. "Your wound has opened up!"

"Only on the outside, though. Otherwise I'd be dead. Look, Irina, let go of the bandages, will you, and let's both set up with our long guns? That hellcat is going to be back, and soon, I just know it. And if we move, we'll just be more vulnerable to ambush. So we'll stand or sit back to back — or bum to bum, heh-heh — and put in a call for a chopper. Got your radio on you?"

"It's here. And I'll use my BlackBerry as a GPS."

"I wouldn't bet on that working too well. The computer figures out a cell's location by its angle of approach to cell towers, the length of time it takes the signal to travel to multiple towers, and the strength of the signal when it reaches the towers. There aren't a hell of a lot of towers out here, I don't think. And even if there were, all these trees would lengthen the amount of time it takes for the signal to reach a tower. So it may be a while before the chopper finds us. But turn it on, anyway. As a matter of fact, use the cell to call Lion Command. Let's test it out."

Irina tried her cellphone, but there was no signal. "Bugger. So much for GPS. So why don't we build a fire? A big, smoky fire?"

"Brilliant," said Hudson. "I'll start collecting wood while you call them."

"No you won't. *I'll* start collecting wood after I call them. First, there's your shoulder to think about. Second, the one who's handiest with a gun should stand guard."

Irina used her radio to call for help. She told Lion Command to look out for smoke signals and gave them, as best she could, her compass bearings relative to the downed helicopter. "You know, Hudson. With all that's been going on, I plain forgot about Wally Cheechoo and Bill Sturgess. Surely to God they'll be arriving here soon."

"I heard that," bellowed an irate Bill Sturgess over the radio. "I am not quite sure why you didn't answer me before, because I called you as soon as I noticed you'd dropped out of sight —"

"Well, I turned the radio off, didn't I? I was on a secret mission."

Sturgess made a rude noise, then counted to ten. "Let it be known that the goddamn cavalry is on its way, although I can't tell you how bloody long and how bloody far away we are!"

After an abortive attempt to placate Sturgess, Irina signed off. "I have a question, Mr. Tech Whiz," Irina said to Hudson. "How come the police radio works out here while the cellphone doesn't?"

"The displacement of the nearest cell towers is just not right for this neck of the woods, I guess. As far as the radios go, they've seeded the area with repeaters, and they've even got one in a continually airborne chopper just for insurance. We've got radio signals bouncing all over this hell's half acre."

"So what about satellite phones? Now, I know everyone likes the radios because everybody is on on the conversation, whereas with the sat phones it's strictly one on one, like with cells, but at least they have reliable GPS units. Why weren't we issued those as well as the radios?"

"Because, Irina, what we have here is a joint operation of the RCMP and the OPP. I assume the best minds dove for cover when they heard what was going down. So, let's get busy with the fire, shall we? It might even keep the lion at bay."

For a few nerve-racking minutes, Irina collected as many broken branches and as much kindling as she could. It wouldn't make much of a fire, but they reckoned that when they heard the search helicopter, they could produce enough smoke by heaping on the spare clothing Chinua had in his knapsack.

"He sweats a lot. Or did, rather," quipped Irina. "I've no doubt that even after a thorough washing, his clothing will still be almost as damp as a baby's diaper. Ergo, lots of smoke."

Having gotten a small fire going, they assumed the aforementioned position of vigilance.

"Do you hear what I hear?" Irina said

"It isn't the sound of a chopper, that's for sure. I'd say it's more like the sound of a growling beast of prey."

Detective Inspector Bill Sturgess let his eyes travel down the steep slope of the ravine and bobble on the babbling brook one-hundred feet below. "Jesus fucking Christ — or should I say 'Gitche fucking Manitou.' This is the fifth gulch we've come across. I suppose you're going to tell me we have to get across it way over there?"

"The inspector is a seer."

"And then we're going to have to waste fifteen frigging minutes while the dogs find the scent again?"

"The inspector is a wise man. A veritable shaman."

"Why in fuck can't we just climb down this slope? The lion did."

"The lion is a cat. A creature of the wild. We and the dogs are not. We are at the apex of evolution. We are distant from the wild ways."

"Oh, please, spare me the aboriginal wisdom."

"All right, then. There's no way we're going to get the dogs' sorry asses down this cliff."

"Fuck, fuck, and triple fuck."

Wally Cheechoo sat down, cross-legged, with his palms turned upward. He mumbled inscrutable things.

"Uh-oh. Is this going to cost me another couple of grand?"

"Had I wings, I would soar across this canyon like an eagle. But I do not, and I must therefore endure indescribable hardship. Fifteen hundred more bucks. The Wednesday special."

Sturgess's face turned the colour of a steamed lobster. "You fucking people want to be treated like everyone else except when it suits your purposes to be different!"

Wally's eyes were closed and he had a smile on his face, as if he were on a hotline to the Great Spirit. "That makes us just like everyone else. And that searing indictment, by the way, will cost you another five-hundred smackeroos."

As they sat back-to-back in the clearing, all was silent and still, as if nature were waiting with bated breath. The sun poured down on them like boiling oil.

Hudson wiped his dripping forehead with the sleeve of his shirt and swore that if the lion didn't make his move soon, he was going for a shower, damn the consequences. Irina had other things on her mind. "We have to talk about the future, Athol Hudson."

"If there's to be one. That animal has his own plans."

"*Our* future, Athol."

"You want to talk about relationships at a time like this?"

"Look on the positive side. If our future is to be brief, then so, too, can be the conversation."

"All right then, I'll start. I love you. Is that brief enough?"

"Brief doesn't mean leaving out the essentials, Athol."

"I forgot to mention that you love me. There. The essentials."

"You're missing the point. What you've said describes the present. I want to talk about the future."

"So I'll love you, and you'll love me, and we'll make love until neither of us can see straight. Then we'll go to the optometrist and start all over again."

"Don't play the cute and clueless male, Athol. You know perfectly well where I'm headed."

They were still facing away from each other. Hudson allowed his head to rest against hers. "Yes. I'm thirty, you're forty-five."

"One and a half times your age, to put it bluntly. And I have a son who's two-thirds your age."

"I don't see what that has to do with anything. You've heard it a million times before: love conquers all."

"When you're sixty, Hudson, and still blessed with the vigor of a middle-aged man, I'll be a seventy-five-year-old hag. I'll be shrivelled, stooped, and most likely ill from something or other."

"Never! People are staying younger and healthier much longer these days. Look at you! Anybody would guess you're thirty!"

"Unless I'm standing alongside a real thirty-year-old, like you. But that's not all, Hudson. There's also the matter of our being partners. We cannot have a deep personal relationship, you know that. It not only impairs our effectiveness as a fighting unit, but puts each of us at considerable and unnecessary risk. We'd each back away from hard decisions at one time or another. We'd be led by our hearts. Look at the very situation we now find ourselves in. I've no doubt you'd risk your life to save mine. The upshot of that could be that we both lose our lives, and not just one of us."

"My life wouldn't be worth living without you, Irina."

"Just so. From a professional point of view, a good cop would have been needlessly sacrificed."

"So we won't be partners, professionally. I could live with that. But there's no reason for us not to be partners emotionally!"

"Oh ... and there's one more thing of vital importance, Athol. Children. Without them, we cannot be a link in the chain of life. And I know you. You'll want children, and you'll be a wonderful father. But I'm already past the childbearing age. I couldn't give you any."

Hudson laughed bitterly. "What do you propose? That I stop loving you, just like that? We can adopt, for Christ's sake!"

"Not good enough. So when, or if, we get out of this mess, I would recommend that we don't see each other anymore, and that we ask Lieutenant Robertson to split us up. This lunatic bonfire will sputter and die away if we don't stoke it. In time there will be only wisps of smoke, and mercifully they'll disperse even as we grasp at them."

Hudson laid down his rifle and spun around. He smiled gamely, but there was more sorrow in his smile than there might have been in an ocean of tears. Covering her face in kisses, he murmured desperately in her ear, "Jesus, Irina! It's been only about a day since we made love. How can you talk about smoke?"

"Because I've rehearsed it over and over and over again," she said in a flat voice. "Now please don't make this any harder for me. I mustn't think and I especially mustn't confront my feelings — oh, God. Athol, turn around and pick up your firearm! Now!"

Too late. There was the sound of streaming darkness and I-árishóni was at Hudson's back, pummelling and clawing at him. The young cop gave Irina a mighty shove, rolling her some six feet out of harm's way, then turned to face the lion with his hunting knife in hand. Even as the beast mauled him face on, he managed to plunge his knife into the lion's cheek. But that was all. Within seconds he was down, slashed to ribbons. The lion paused momentarily, then pounced in Irina's direction. She shot him squarely in the chest, where his heart ought to have been, but that did not slow him in the least. A millisecond later he had knocked her onto her back and was astride her, his cavernous mouth agape. As he began to tear at her, Irina pushed the barrel of her Ruger into his mouth. Just as fangs the size and colour of ivory chess bishops closed over the barrel, she yanked down as hard as she could on the stock of the rifle and pulled the trigger. The .458 Lott Magnum entered the roof of his mouth and pierced his brain.

Just ten minutes later, Detective Inspector Bill Sturgess and Wally Cheechoo burst into the clearing. And one minute after that, the OPP helicopter set down, having been guided to the site by Chinua Amadi's smoking underwear. Irina didn't acknowledge anyone's presence. She kneeled, bleeding, beside Sergeant-Detective Athol Curzon Hudson's lifeless body, stroking his face and reciting, over and over again, the poem she'd written for him during her transatlantic flight. Sturgess could not make out her mumbling, so he extricated the crumpled piece of paper from her swollen hand and read it to himself before passing it over to Wally Cheechoo.

THE SIXTH EXTINCTION

My darling Athol,

I couldn't think of a poem which adequately expressed my feelings about you, so I wrote one. Please be appropriately flattered — it's my first attempt at such a thing. Furthermore, on the wild presumption that the poem is self-explanatory, I offer no commentary other than to say that you will eventually find someone who can fly higher and farther than I.

Had I not gone blind
To all that I beheld,
Nor fretted over days
Which no one could foretell,
I might have stayed aloft,
High above the dark,
I might have flown forever,
Companion to the lark.

Had I not gone deaf
To songs beyond my sphere,
Nor recoiled at the touch
Of those who drew too near,
I might have stayed on high,
Gathering every star,
And kept in mind that freedom,
Is never very far.

Can we learn again
Or does it get too late?
The lark calls out to me
"It isn't up to fate,
Spread your wings, return aloft,
High above the dark,
One can't fly alone, forever,
Even though he be a lark."

CHAPTER FORTY-FIVE

Montreal. September 14–22, 2006. Without its dealer, Jason Conrad's house of cards soon collapsed. The fly-overs that Detective-Inspector Bill Sturgess had ordered soon located the facility, and a detachment of the Canadian Army was airlifted in to take control of it. The Doomsday Complex personnel surrendered without a fight, and the nuclear materials, as well as the biological specimens, were promptly turned over to an international cadre of scientists. Due to the concomitant confusion, Conrad's field operations continued for up to a week longer, but once they ceased, innumerable endangered species were once more shoved toward the edge of the abyss.

The ship aboard which the Chinese had dispatched the pebble-bed reactor, the colossal *Xin Los Angeles*, had been under the command of a perspicacious and high-minded captain. By the time he'd cleared the international dateline, he had divined the nature of his mystery cargo and properly concluded that his government was up to no good. After opening the sealed forty-foot containers to confirm his worst fears, he alerted the American Air Force base in Anchorage, Alaska, and put into Dutch Harbor of the Aleutians under the sheltering wings of F-15 Eagles.

The *Xin Los Angles* was subsequently sailed out into deep American waters off the state of Washington and scuttled. She took down with her the uncontaminated nuclear reactor. It having been an American invention, there was nothing about the pebble-bed that was of the slightest interest to the U.S., except perhaps its potential as a component of the world's largest artificial reef.

Due to both his notoriety and his lasting influence on global economic matters, Jason Conrad's funeral was a major social event. The captains of industry, the cream of society, and more than a few heads of state were in attendance at the ostentatious ceremony. Of all those hundreds present, however, only Irina Drach could lay claim to having known him on more than a superficial basis.

After some detective work, Irina and Lieutenant Stanley Robertson unearthed the Nigerian village where Chinua Amadi's family lived. His body was sent home, at the expense of the Montreal Police Department, with a commendation and a personal message from Irina to the effect that he'd been a force for good. At his ceremony of passage his aged mother cried tears not of sadness but of joy, for who lives forever, anyway?

Chief Amit Chatterjee saw to it that Inspector Raja Chadwani's cremation was the event of the year. As befitting the glory that Chadwani had brought upon his associates and his country, Chatterjee arranged a funeral with both police and military honours (he had a third cousin in the Indian Army). Although a Hindu funeral is not the gut-wrenching affair that its Western counterpart is, Gita Prasad shed more than a few tears. But her grief was nothing as compared to her father's. Inconsolably, Munshi Prasad wept the tears of the dispossessed.

Sergeant-Detective Athol Curzon Hudson was given a hero's funeral. Representatives of just about every police force in the world were present, politicians from the municipal to the federal level paid homage, and the event was covered by every major news outlet in the world.

Among the policemen in attendance was Inspector Leopold Duggan of New Scotland Yard. With Lieutenant Stanley Robertson at one side and he at the other, the shattered Irina Drach was able to retain her composure without forfeiting her fathomless sorrow, nor absolving herself of the crushing guilt over what she now felt was the misbegotten nature of her last words with Hudson.

During her eulogy, she took a few minutes to remember Sergeant Jerome Perron of the K-9 squad, and to affirm that he had died an honourable death.

Irina's visage soon replaced Hudson's in the popular imagination, but her studious avoidance of publicity, as well as her insistence on quickly returning to routine police work, resulted in the gradual erosion of the collective memory. Eventually, a thoroughly reformed Irina — as trim as a gazelle and no longer blinking — had a new partner and was able to go about her business in as much anonymity as a comely woman could expect.

The bodies of Charmaine Washington and Vincent de Groot were never found. Nor were those of Reg McDuff and Victor Tarasenko. In fact, none were even missed by the rest of humanity. But Mother Earth remembered. Even though they'd been at war with her, she clasped them to her loamy breast and gave them eternal peace.

And I-árishóni? Irina wanted him returned to his beloved home on the Tsavo plains for burial. She was supported by the Kenyan government, which insisted upon the repatriation of one of its native sons. His body was laid to rest where he'd lived most of his life, and a simple marble column was erected to mark the spot. Even though he'd been at war with humanity, it gave him immortality.

"But how can you think of honouring a beast who slaughtered so many people, including your partner?" asked the incredulous CBS reporter.

"He was overpowered by civilization and pushed back in the only way he knew," Irina replied curtly. "And Sergeant Hudson was not slaughtered like some lamb, by the way. He died fighting. He died saving my life."

Crowds of humans enthusiastically visited the location for quite some time, but they eventually melted away under the blistering African sun. It was left to the creatures of the Tsavo plain, the lions in particular, to tread softly by his grave and sense, however vaguely, that no life form can exist strictly on its own terms.

OF RELATED INTEREST

Ultimatum 2
Major-General Richard Rohmer
978-1-550025842
$21.99

Ultimatum 2 is an action-packed, fast-moving saga. The American president is fed up with the hundreds of millions of dollars given to Russia to clean up high-level nuclear waste. His solution is to give the Russians an ultimatum: do this my way, or else! It is delivered in person by the secretary of state during a secret rendezvous in Norway.

A second ultimatum follows from the United States, Russia, and the United Kingdom to the government of Canada, after they decide that an international nuclear waste disposal site should be created in Canada. The Canadian prime minister tells their emissary there's no way Canada will become a nuclear waste dump. The Americans threaten to invade. How the matter is resolved is ingenious.

Nightshade
A Sam Montcalm Mystery
Tom Henighan
978-1-554887149
$11.99

Deadly nightshade — the poison plant par excellence — and in historic Quebec City at an important scientific conference concerning the genetic manipulation of trees it means *murder!*

Police, RCMP, and a mysterious FBI agent from Washington converge on the scene. But the sharpest eye belongs to Sam Montcalm, a despised "bedroom snooper" from Ottawa whose primary concern is to clear a First Nations activist of the crime. Sam is middle-aged, tough, and sophisticated, yet he's also a lone wolf who feels displaced nearly everywhere, and his relations with his colleagues, the police — and with women — are always complicated. "You're a psychic wound without a health card," a friend comments.

The story moves to its surprising climax as Montcalm follows the trail of murder back to Canada's capital and into the Gatineau Hills, his deep sense of cynicism about human nature confirmed as he closes in on the killer and struggles to come to terms with himself.

Available at your favourite bookseller.

What did you think of this book? Visit *www.dundurn.com*
for reviews, videos, updates, and more!